IGOROTDŌ:
The Enlightened
Warrior Within

REXCRISANTO DELSON

This book is a work of historical fiction. In order to give a sense of the times, some names or real people or places have been included in the book. However, the events depicted in this book are imaginary, and the names of nonhistorical persons or events are the product of the author's imagination or are used fictitiously. Any resemblance of such nonhistorical persons or events to actual ones is purely coincidental.

Published in the United States by Cordi Heritage House

ISBN: 0615470017
ISBN-13: 978-0615470016

DEDICATION

This book is dedicated to my late parents Crisanto and Dolores Delson, and my late sister Dorothea Delson.

ACKNOWLEDGMENTS

I am blessed to have had three very inspirational people in my life: my late parents Crisanto and Dolores Delson, and my late sister Dorothea Delson. It took their deaths to spark the dormant creativity within me that led to my pursuit of becoming a writer. As a writer, I rely on using words to express anything real, but am unable to find the words to fully express my gratitude for being the kind of role models they have been and continue to be in my life. Thank you for instilling the values of faith, love, purpose, and heritage in my life. You have taught me that without these things, I would forever be lost in the abyss of purposelessness and emptiness. You are the main inspiration behind this book.

One can never say enough about the importance of family and friends. For this reason, I would like to thank my wife, Michelle, and children: Joshua, Mikayla, and Gabriella. You have been patient with me while I spent countless hours away from you to work on this book. You provided me the inner fuel to see this project to its completion.

To my sisters Natividad Delson, Maria Eitmann, Connie Brown, Anne Hejmanowski, and their families; your support and prayers continuously remind me of the importance of family. To my cousins Brian Bantali and Dr. Maria Luz D. Fang-Asan; for all the inspiring ideas that found their way into this book. To Auntie Virginia Wooden, for your unrelenting support in the fundraising campaign of this book. To the rest of my relatives in the Delson and Lengua clans, both of which are too enormous to mention individually; your past, present and future support is greatly appreciated!

There was a time when I was short of ideas for the book and was on the verge of giving up, until I was visited by Henry Sadcopen, an Igorot who convinced me to wear our native attire while playing our gangsa instruments during a Filipino parade in Chicago. His fervor to stay connected with his heritage inspired new ideas for the book, but most importantly, re-kindled the spark that kept me writing. He passed away shortly after that parade, but I will always be grateful to him and his family for jumpstarting the writing of this book.

I would also like to thank Ikka Nakashima and Hoichi Kurisu for steering me towards a newfound appreciation for their Japanese culture, but most importantly for teaching me that there can be nothing nobler than living a life for others. Nakashima's perspectives on *Chanoyu* and Kurisu's passion for Japanese Restorative Gardens exemplify how one's culture can make a positive difference in the world. Without their influence, I would not have been able to write this book.

As with any endeavor, there are costs involved. Certain research, editing, marketing and publishing costs were paid for through the financial support of many people. I would like to thank all those who contributed, especially: Brian Bantali, Bernadette Carling, Connie Brown, Natividad Delson, Owitte and Gary Malabato, Rosalina Cadwising, Anne and Ray Hejmanowski, Simeona Bantali, Joseph and Stella Delson, Karen and Sebastien Michallet, Teddy Delson, Anthony Wooden Sr., Lydwald Wooden, Seth Dyre Mayaen Wooden, Tante Wooden, Shemaiah Wooden, Julie Tukaki O'Conner, Leslie and Miguel Farolan, Estifania Yagao-Esparza, Marylyn Lopez, Rae Joyce Baguilat, Noemi Ruth Delamor, Marivel Damong Operana, Ruben Salazar, Pete and Lety Quijano, Edgar and Ely Pasule, Pio Salitsit Tongalog, Mike and Lalaine Isobal, Joan Duyan, Mary Alice Bernal, Rex Pe, Marlon & Marissa Jose, Aiza Abnasan, Yvonne Abnasan, Amy Abnasan, Magay Lawan, and Jiji Palangdan Lingaling.

Finally, there are those whose hands-on involvement demands my utmost appreciation. To my good friend Joe Ongtengco, who was the first to read and critique my manuscript; your encouraging feedback meant a world to me. To my editor Floyd Largent; you aligned the literary feathers of the book in a manner that allows it to sore to new heights. To Joshua Delson, who created the book's cover; your ability to conceptualize and create the ideal book cover exceeded my expectations.

"All I've got is a red guitar, three chords and the truth"
- Bono, U2

CHAPTER 1

Still upset over the outcome of the previous day's Presidential election, Alex woke up from a confusing dream that reminded him immediately of the thousands of dollars he'd contributed to Mitt Romney's failed campaign. A pain stabbed through his midsection, like an ulcer coming on. Unlike his campaign donation of four years ago, this one stung hard. He just couldn't believe that people were willing to suffer through another four years of disappointment.

Feeling the residual effects of last night's alcoholic pacifiers, he slowly rolled out of bed, goosebumps canvassing his body as he left the warmth of his blanket. When he stepped onto the marble floor, a piercing cold shot upward through the soles of his feet, dispersing whatever ill effects remained of last night's consolation drinking. *Damn, if I could bottle* that *I'd make a fortune,* he mused. Arms tightly crossed, shivers overtook his nude body as he quickly lifted his feet up and down in turn, as if he were standing on ice. Which he practically was.

He turned toward the clock to check the time, but couldn't see the LED display for some reason. *Electrical outage*, he realized suddenly.

Great, just great! He turned towards the windows and saw streaks of buttery yellow light beaming in through the tiny gaps between the slats of the wooden blinds. He fumbled around on the bed searching for his robe, and in doing so, accidentally nudged the body of his girlfriend, Heather.

"Hey," she said sleepily. "Watch who you're poking."

"Sorry, babe, gotta find my robe," he replied.

Heather poked her head outside the blanket. "I don't smell any coffee brewing, and it's freezing. What happened to your heat? I knew I should've gone home last night."

After finding his robe, Alex swathed his body and quickstepped across the cold floor towards his nightstand. He picked up his Blackberry to check the time. "Holy shit!"

"What's wrong?"

"I'm *so* frickin' late!" replied Alex, as he tossed his phone onto the bed and dashed towards the bathroom on numb feet.

Shortly after turning on the water, Alex heard the shower door slide open. He wiped the shampoo from one of his eyes and found Heather standing there in the dim light from the frosted glass window, a towel wrapped around her. She twirled her long blonde hair around one finger and winked at him. "Well, aren't you going to invite me in?" she asked, a seductive look on her face.

Alex wiped the soap from his other eye and stared longingly at her beautiful body, sorely tempted. She peered at him with her soft blue eyes and raised one of her eyebrows while seductively biting her lower lip. Then she pulled out the tucked-in corner of the towel and revealed her unnaturally large breasts, before slowly letting the entire towel fall to the floor. She looked down, and saw that he was becoming *very* excited.

"I guess that means come on in, huh?" she said.

"Babe, you really are gorgeous!" Alex replied enthusiastically.

"Thanks. Now, if you're done talking, I have something for you." She entered the shower cubicle, immediately began kissing him, and whispered, "You're already running behind. What's another half hour or so?"

Alex wanted to give in, but remembered how important it was to get to his office on time, today of all days. He somehow pulled away, albeit reluctantly. She raised a puzzled eyebrow. "I can't," he said. "I just can't. Not now, babe. Not today."

But Heather wouldn't hear of it; she pressed her body against his back and began kissing his neck and caressing his chest and abdomen. For a moment, Alex became aroused again and began succumbing to her advances....but his good sense reminded him of his tardiness. He snapped out of his daze and turned the water to the coldest possible setting. The icy blast immediately chilled her ardor, setting them both to shivering. "Goddammit, Alex!" Heather shouted. "I can't believe you're thinking about *work* at a time like this! You're always thinking about work!"

Traces of shampoo still in his hair, Alex stepped out of the shower and began drying himself. "Believe me," he said earnestly, "Last night was unbelievable, but I have some very important things I need to do at the office today. Sorry, but I really gotta go. Enjoy the shower...and lock the door behind you, will ya?"

She glared at him, slid the shower door shut, and yelled, "Fine!"

He quickly changed into an Armani suit, rushing out the door and into the elevator. Just as he entered the parking garage, he realized he'd forgotten his Blackberry. *Dammit!* Wasting no time, he tossed his laptop and other things into the backseat of his Beamer and ran up the stairwell. When he re-entered his bedroom, Heather stood there with a scowl on her face as she twirled another woman's panties around her finger.

"These aren't mine, Alex," she said in an accusatory tone. "Got something you need to tell me?"

"Those must have gotten mixed in by accident by my laundry service. Don't worry, I'll get it straightened out." He grabbed his phone and ran out the door shouting, "Have a great day, babe, I'll see you tonight!"

***

Heather stared after him, exasperated, trying to ignore the suspicions and jealousy racing through her mind. A thirty-five-year-old junior accounting exec with, admittedly, structurally enhanced breastworks, she'd met Alex three months before. Although she frequently travelled to China, Korea, and Japan for business, she had never felt attracted to an Asian man before, so she was shocked by her body's reaction to him. Until then, her dream had always been to marry a handsome WASP, so dating Asian men had never crossed her mind.

Of course, by then she'd also begun to lose hope of finding the perfect man to marry. No man she dated could remain in a monogamous relationship for longer than six months. For some reason she could never fathom, they eventually had affairs with other women or just walked out of the relationship before it became too serious. She knew she needed to start broadening her horizons...and that's when she met Alex at a nightclub.

After being introduced by a mutual friend, they engaged in friendly conversation. During their tête-à-tête, his ethnicity never came up, but Heather couldn't help but notice that he was Asian; his almond shaped eyes, jet-black hair, and rich brown skin were a dead giveaway. He didn't appear Chinese, Korean, or Japanese, so she figured he must be Malaysian, Filipino, or maybe Polynesian. Whatever the case, she was quite taken by his handsome looks. She especially loved his eyes and muscular figure. Moreover, she was relieved to hear that he spoke great English, with no trace of an accent.

The attraction was mutual, as lustful thoughts swirled in Alex's mind. He couldn't keep his eyes off her. Every time she looked away, his eyes went to her breasts. The uncontrollable bulge in his pants became a discomfort that was hard to bear. His only goal that night was to end up in bed with her, and judging by the 100-watt smiles she kept sending his way, he knew his chances were great. To accomplish it, though, he had to be on his "A" game, and brought all the charm and humor he possibly could to bear.

Three hours and many drinks later, he knew he had her falling head over heels for him. They went from sitting across from each other at their small table to sitting side-by-side and exchanging flirtatious nudges and touches that ignited their lust for each other. "I think it's time we took this party to my place," Alex whispered in her ear then.

Without saying a word, she picked up her purse, said goodbye to their friends, and walked out with Alex. While waiting for the valet to return with his BMW M6 convertible, she cornered him at the entrance and passionately kissed him. The passion continued through their drive back to his place. On several occasions, their kissing and groping almost caused him to swerve off the road. When they arrived at his condo, they wasted no time, leaving behind a trail of clothing leading to his bedroom. Two hours later, they fell asleep in each other's arms. Ever since, they'd repeated their passionate evening rendezvous as often as possible.

On his way to the office, Alex stopped at a red light and peered in the rearview mirror. After pulling off the small pieces of tissue that covered the cuts he'd acquired shaving in the near-dark of the bathroom, he glanced down at his ankles and saw two different-colored socks. "Great. That's all I need," he mumbled. If anyone noticed, he'd just have to pretend it was a new fashion, all the rage among the young and trendy.

As the light turned green, he noticed a store window displaying a large poster of President Obama emblazoned with the word *FORWARD*. Alex shook his head in disgust, muttering, "Right. Forward to oblivion."

He spent most of the morning returning emails, texts, and phone calls. After he caught up with his messages— finally—he began preparing for the dreaded meeting with his accountant and financial advisor, to continue discussing the financial status of his company, America Prime Investments. He wasn't looking forward to the meeting, as he expected nothing but bad news; he had a gut feeling that he'd probably have to lay off more employees during the oncoming weeks.

The day had barely begun, yet an enormous headache began to mount.

Alex reached into his coat pocket for some Motrin as he watched the accountant and advisor pull into the parking lot simultaneously. He popped three into his mouth as he stepped out of his office to get his fourth cup of coffee. He could feel everyone's fear congealing in the air.

After gulping down the pills, he tried to lighten the atmosphere a bit by reminding his managers to make sure everyone had the chance to watch Obama's acceptance speech later in the larger conference room.

The meeting with the bean counters confirmed their need to lay off more than half of his staff, which left Alex feeling numb and dispirited. After both men had left the office, Alex and his business partner, Norman, closeted themselves in Norm's office to discuss who would have to go. The very thought of making such drastic cuts caused Alex's throat to tighten and his heart to pound; many of the employees he'd have to cut had been with him since he'd started the company fifteen years before.

Norman, of course, was more concerned about his own future than anyone else's. Relatively new to the company, he handled the life insurance investments portion of the business that Alex had brought him in to expand. A 20-year veteran in the insurance industry, Norman had made a fortune selling consumers cash-value policies that were designed to profit insurance companies and their agents, while often leaving consumers underinsured. He knew that consumers were better off owning term insurance and investing outside of the life insurance industry, but the commissions on term insurance were miniscule compared to cash-value insurance.

Years of putting himself first had not only diminished Norm's integrity, it had also callused his heart towards the well beings of others. For the hundredth time, Alex wished he'd never allowed Norman to buy into API. On this difficult day, he was of little help in determining where the cuts should occur. After less than half an hour of discussing the life insurance segment, he wrote down a list of names, starting with the highest-paid people in his department. Little thought went into it; it was all about numbers to him. After handing it to Alex, he excused himself and rushed out to close a big sale.

Alex stared at Norman's list for ten minutes before he began compiling his own. What had taken Norm five minutes took him much longer. Each time he wrote a name down, thoughts about that person's loyalty and how the layoff would affect his or her family bothered him. He knew he needed to be more like Norm, but it just wasn't in his nature. Sometimes he wondered why he'd gotten into this business in the first place.

After an hour of going back and forth with names, he felt mentally drained. Just as he was about to take a break, his secretary gently knocked on the door and informed him that the President was about to give his speech. *Might as well take a break,* Alex thought. *Maybe Obama can shed some hope on this mess.* He slowly stood up, took a deep breath, and walked out to watch the speech.

He tried his best to hide the bad news by smiling brightly and applauding after each musician and band finished performing for the President, but those who knew him well could already sense that something was wrong. As the President finally began his speech, Alex tried to look interested, but his mind drifted off into his financial woes.

In addition to his business problems, most of his personal investments had been diminished in recent stock market disasters. He'd had to sell his luxury homes in Florida and California, and couldn't afford his two yachts anymore. The reality of losing everything he cared about the most, including some of his valued colleagues and friends, weighed heavily on his mind.

Unlike most of his acquaintances, Alex had no family or loved ones to fall back on during these tough times, except for Heather...and he'd probably ruined that already. His parents and only sister had died in a car accident while he was in college, and all the rest of his relatives still lived in the Philippines. He knew that his mother was an only child and that his father had twelve siblings, but they were basically strangers to him, and he'd only met a few. His grandfather and an uncle had visited the family once, but that had been so long ago that he remembered them only vaguely. It wasn't until the deaths of his parents and sister that he began corresponding with his relatives via phone and email. But they were no consolation to him; all they seemed to want from him was talk, talk, talk or money, money, money. Eventually, he'd buried himself so deep in his business and social life that he stopped communicating with them altogether.

Alex was well aware that he was considered quite the catch by the ladies. He tried not to let that make him feel too cocky; he knew how temporary that could be. But he was good-looking (if he did say so himself), and worked out each day to maintain his lean and muscular shape. He'd built a successful investment firm, had been featured in several trade and entrepreneurial magazines, owned property on all three coasts, and lived in a luxurious downtown condominium that overlooked a spectacular view of Lake Michigan. On top of it all, he had beautiful women constantly at his beckon and call.

His Facebook profile had the maximum 5,000 friends allowed, of which none were his relatives. The pictures he posted of himself were mostly of him at parties and social events, surrounded by people drinking alcohol and posing festively for the camera. Most of them featured gorgeous women; lately those had been all about Heather, his earlier conquests buried deep in his albums. Anyone looking at his profile would think he was a happy man with plenty of friends...but this was far from the truth. In reality, none of his "friends" knew the Alex that hid behind the façade of his success. They were more interested in bathing in the glow of his achievements and helping him spend his money than in learning a single thing about his true personality.

Well, soon there might be no glow left, no money to spend.

Although he seemed to have everything a man his age could want, the truth was that, deep down, he'd always felt that something was missing from his life. It just got worse after his family died. No matter how much financial independence and prestige he acquired, he still felt unfulfilled and insecure...but his material success made it easy for him to hide the pains of loneliness, depression and emptiness that gnawed at his soul.

He hated holidays, especially Thanksgiving and Christmas, because they forced him to face the truth: that he had no one to share them with. Being around happy people during the holidays made him feel uncomfortable at best, and more deeply disturbed. It especially bothered him to be around average people who were genuinely happy, but had much less material wealth or had achieved much less success than he had. One Christmas Eve, he'd met with a young man named Bill Lango, who came to his office seeking investment advice for his non-profit, which was already large and growing rapidly. Alex was impressed when he learned how much money Bill's company had raised, but was shocked to learn that Bill kept only a tiny percentage for all the hard work he did. He couldn't fathom doing so much work and pocketing so little. Yet, there was something about Bill that Alex envied. He smiled constantly, his eyes gleaming with an almost joyful sincerity. His personality was genuine, and he radiated a sense of confidence that only a person of great character and high self-esteem could possess. Alex found him so intriguing that he wasted no time on agreeing to take him on as a new client.

Bill seemed equally intrigued by Alex. He once told Alex he looked at least ten years younger than he actually was, and that he was impressed that someone so young knew so much about the financial world. It didn't take long for him to realize that Alex was the right person to manage his company's portfolio.

Alex met Bill regularly thereafter, and during one of their visits, he began mentally comparing his life to Bill's. They were both single, the same age, had started their own successful companies, buried themselves in their work, and had accomplished a great deal—but something about Bill made him completely different from Alex. One day, Bill caught Alex off-guard with a particular comment: "You're so fortunate to be so successful so young."

Alex smiled sardonically and replied, "Wanna switch places?"

"Are you kidding? I wouldn't give this up for anything!" Bill said enthusiastically.

His reply surprised Alex. Most people would have taken him up on his offer—at least jokingly—but Bill displayed a sense of contentment and happiness that eluded Alex. He felt envious, because Bill had found something Alex still yearned for, and it was obvious to him that Bill viewed his work in a much different way than he did. For Alex, work was a coping mechanism. It allowed him to avoid dealing with his inner struggles by keeping him so busy that he didn't have time to think about anything else—with the occasional time-out for partying and skirt-chasing.

This strategy had worked pretty damned well for years, but ever since the stock market had started circling the drain and the economy fell into recession, he'd been losing control of that coping mechanism, bits at a time, until there was very little of it left. He began to wonder how much longer he had before he went off the deep end.

As the financial stability of his company worsened, so did his personal finances. None of his banks would extend his credit, and letters from debt collectors began appearing, along with their annoying phone calls. As a result, his worries and associated stress levels escalated to a point where his physical well being began to be affected.

He began experiencing sudden feelings of dizziness. Sometimes he felt as if he were walking on a boat, the floor rocking up and down to the rhythm of some strange sea. At first, he convinced himself that he just needed more sleep, but that was hard to get—and one day, for the first time in his life, he experienced severe chest pains. Sharp and sporadic, at times they were isolated to his chest, where he also experienced a sudden tightening. At other times, the pain radiated to either his left or right shoulder. As much as he worried about having a heart attack, Alex kept the pains to himself, refusing to seek medical attention.

One evening, a stranger approached him in the parking lot of his condominium complex, and served him with papers to appear in court. One of his creditors was taking him to court to collect a past-due balance of $20,000—a sum that had once seemed paltry to Alex, but now threatened his financial well-being. The stress was so great that Alex needed something to take his mind off things, so he called Heather and took her out to dinner. She knew he was under a lot of stress, so she put on her sexiest lingerie and covered it with her newest dress, which revealed a great deal of cleavage and thigh.

After a quick dinner at his favorite sushi restaurant, Alex brought Heather back to his place, where they engaged in an evening of erotic pleasures. Afterwards, she fell asleep in his arms. Alex tried to sleep, but couldn't stop thinking about his financial woes.

He didn't nod off until almost sunrise.

CHAPTER 2

Four weeks had passed since the layoffs in November—or "the Bloodbath," as the remaining staff called it when they thought Alex wasn't listening—and there was every indication that the coming year would prove to be an even greater challenge than expected. Work had taken on new meaning for everyone at America Prime Investments. In the past, everyone had bought into Alex's optimistic mantra: "If you love what you're doing, you'll never work a day in your life." This notion seemed absurdly optimistic now, given the terrible economy, and Alex found himself running a company staffed by employees who no longer loved and could not love what they did. Even Alex lost his passion, and found himself "working" seventeen hours every day, including Sundays.

His problems finally caught up to him one morning when he collapsed on the floor of his own kitchen. After several hours of lying there unconscious, he slowly opened his eyes to the blurry sight of the legs of a kitchen chair, wondering what the hell had happened. He felt lightheaded, disconnected from the world, and for a moment, he wasn't sure where he was. Surely he hadn't gotten falling-down drunk...?

Too weak to get up, he rolled onto his back and stared at the ceiling fan as it slowly revolved. He dragged his eyes over far enough to look at the clock, and saw that it was almost noon. That's when he realized in a flash that he was in his kitchen, and that he must have been lying on the floor for over four hours.

He sat up slowly, and leaned back against the dishwasher as his strength failed him. A sudden cough shot up through his lungs, accompanied with a sharp pain and followed by a glob of thick mucus. He rolled his eyes upward and felt a fever settling in.

Fuck, what now?

The floor vibrated under him, and he felt a frisson of fear until he realized that it was just his phone. He reached out somehow, picked it up, and saw that he had ten missed calls and seven unopened texts from Norman. The first text read, "Where are you? Accountants are here." The last one read, "Did what I could, but you need to sign some papers. Call me ASAP."

Still sitting on the floor, Alex called Norman and explained what happened. He told him that he would try to make it into the office in a few hours, but his partner urged him to go see his doctor. Alex was reluctant, but eventually agreed, and told Norman to just fax the papers for him to sign.

Fortunately, his doctor was just a block away, and he was able to work Alex in immediately. After a short visit, the doctor diagnosed Alex as having severe flu complicated by bronchitis. He attributed his fainting spell to stress and lack of sleep. The doctor gave him a prescription for sleeping pills, and instructed him not to do any work for a week so he could recover at home—but Alex fought him on not working. Eventually, the doctor convinced him to at least take three days off.

For the next two days, Alex was so sick that he spent all day and night in bed, while Heather visited twice a day to care for him. On the third day, his fever broke and he felt stronger, able to move around much better. The following day, he wanted to go in to his office, but Heather wouldn't hear of it. Her firm and seductive ways convinced him to stay home with her that day.

After spending most of the morning in bed together, Alex showered while Heather went to a nearby deli to buy food for their brunch. Still wearing his robe, Alex turned on his 103-inch plasma television and began brewing coffee for both of them. When Heather returned with the food, something on the television caught her attention. "Hey, come quick!" she shouted from the entertainment room.

"What's wrong?" Alex replied.

"Check out what's on CNN," she said loudly.

Alex picked up his coffee and quickly walked to the entertainment room to see what she was talking about. They both sat down and listened to the news reporter talk about how a $198 million provision of a proposed Senate stimulus bill would authorize single payments of $15,000 to surviving Filipino veterans of World War II. The reporter went on to describe how Filipino veterans had been fighting for decades against the American government's refusal to grant them the veterans benefits FDR had promised them in 1941, but that Congress reneged on in 1946. Their interest grew as they watched scenes from past protest demonstrations by Filipino veterans.

"Wow," said Heather. "I never knew about this. Do you have any relatives who could receive any of this money?"

Alex shook his head and continued to watch. When a scene was shown of a man chaining himself to the White House fence in 1977 in protest against this long-standing injustice, Alex continued shaking his head in disapproval. Then he put down his coffee in disgust. "I can't believe those idiot politicians!" he snarled. "Our country's in a major financial crisis, and they're wasting our stimulus money on *this* bullshit?"

She looked at him in shock. "You can't be serious, Alex. These are Filipinos who fought for our country. *You're* Filipino!"

"No," replied Alex in a firm voice. "I'm an American, just like you. It doesn't matter that you're Swedish by blood; nor does it matter what blood runs through *my* veins. What matters is that we're both Americans, and I'm telling you—all those millions of dollars should be going toward upgrading the infrastructure of this country. It's the right thing to do. These politicians just don't get it. They're not the ones who have to send people to the unemployment lines. Where are the tax cuts we need?"

Just then the phone rang, and Alex stood up to answer it, but was pulled back down to the couch by Heather. He tried standing again, but she pulled him down again. Thinking it could be an important call, he started to try again, but the look in Heather's eyes convinced him to stay seated. "You promised no work today," she reminded him.

Alex kissed her on the cheek and continued watching the news. The ringing of the phone stopped; then the answering machine beeped, and a woman with a strong Filipino accent began speaking: "Alex. This is your Auntie Toring in the Philippines. I need you to call me as soon as possible. It is very important, so please call."

"Who was that?" asked Heather.

"It's one of my aunts," he replied. "She's been asking me to send them more money to help one of my cousins. I can't deal with this now. They have no clue what's going on here. I should never have sent them money in the first place. They keep sending me letters about how my cousins are struggling and how I need to help them financially. They think I'm a billionaire or something. Did you know I found out that my so-called 'struggling' relatives have maids? How could anyone struggle and still afford maids?"

"So why did you send them money before?" Heather replied.

"It's complicated," said Alex, bowing his head. "Ever since I was a kid, I remember my Mom and Dad arguing about how my Dad would send money to our cousins in the Philippines to help them. Now that my parents are dead, I get periodic requests for financial aid from relatives I don't even know. This is just another one of those requests, that's all. They think life here in America is easy. They've got no clue how hard I've worked to achieve what I have."

Heather apparently didn't know how to react, and just sat there in silence. Several moments later, Alex's Blackberry began ringing. He looked at the caller ID and saw that it was an international call. "It's her again," he said, as he pressed the ignore button.

Then a text alert sounded on his phone. Alex ignored it and walked toward the kitchen. Almost soon as his back was turned, Heather said, "Babe, you better read this."

Alex stopped in his tracks, turned around, and gave her a look of frustration. She held out the phone. "I know," she said. "But it says 'Emergency.' Shouldn't you read it?"

Alex reluctantly took the phone from her hand and read the message. It read, "Tito Alex. Pls call txt or email my mom @ rosalta@emailpi.com. Lolo Santo is vry sik, dyng & askng 4 u."

Alex stood there in silence, staring at his Blackberry. Sensing this was serious, Heather turned off the television, walked to him, and embraced him from behind. "Who's Lolo Santo?" she asked, reading the screen.

"My grandfather," replied Alex numbly. "Lolo is Filipino for grandfather."

"Oh my God! I'm so sorry. What are you going to do?" Heather asked.

"I don't know," he said, shaking his head. "I really don't even know him. He visited us once when I was a kid, but I don't remember much about that visit. I thought he'd come for my family's funeral, but he was hospitalized at the time. For all I know, this is just another way of getting me there so they can beg for more money." He shrugged. "Anyway, I can't afford to go anywhere when my business is on the verge of folding."

"But Alex—"

"I don't want to talk about it anymore." Looking lost, he wondered off into the den and shut the door.

* * *

Heather knew he needed to be alone, so she didn't pursue him. But she picked up his Blackberry, copied down his aunt's email on a Post-It note, and quietly went into the kitchen to use her laptop. She immediately logged into her Facebook account, and began searching to see if his aunt also had a Facebook account of her own.

She found his aunt's Facebook page, and started browsing through her friends list to see if Alex was there. His aunt had 150 friends, and every one appeared to be Filipino or Asian. After searching through the entire list Heather, was unable to find Alex, so she went back to her own profile to open Alex's. Surprisingly, his large friend list included very few people who looked Filipino or Asian. After skimming through it, she was able to count the total number of Asians, including Indians, on both hands. None of them looked remotely like Alex, and their last names were different from his.

* * *

While Heather snooped through Alex's Facebook profile, he poured a glass of brandy from a crystal decanter and sat behind his desk. He drank a few gulps, stared at a picture of him and his father, and reminisced about working alongside him as an intern at his father's firm. It was there that he'd realized he could do well in the world of securities and investments, but more importantly, it was there that he spent some of the most precious times with his father. As long as Alex could recall, his father had been too busy to spend quality time with him. For Alex, it seemed that the only thing that really mattered to his father was his work. The only time he remembered having good one-on-one time with his father outside the office was when he was in fifth grade. Alex had been fascinated with fishing then, but his father never had the time or interest to take him. One day, though, his father gave in to his begging and took him to Lake Michigan. He remembered sitting on the edge of a pier, fishing with his little kid's rod-and-reel combo, while his father sat there empty-handed, constantly looking at his watch.

After an hour of silence, Alex finally caught a fish—but to his dismay, it was only a tiny bluegill. He was disappointed that it wasn't a big bass, walleye or salmon, but his Dad seemed very relieved that he'd finally caught a fish, as if that were enough to get it out of his system. Immediately after Alex removed the hook from the fish's mouth, his father told him he was late for a meeting and made him pack up his things and leave. They never went fishing again.

Alex never forgot that day, and how he'd felt like a burden to his father.

After drinking the last of his brandy, his thoughts went first to the disturbing text from his cousin, then to the last time his parents had visited the Philippines. They had returned very upset, because some of his relatives had accused his father of being selfish for not supporting them financially. His mother was also hurt, because they implied that it was her fault. Alex remembered his mother saying to him, "The only good thing about the trip was being able to see your grandmother again. Everything else was a nightmare."

Alex had once entertained thoughts of visiting the Philippines, but after his parents' bad experience, had no real interest in visiting his homeland. Instead, he remained in America, where he assimilated completely into its melting-pot society and eventually identified himself as American, not Filipino.

* * *

Two days after receiving his cousin's disturbing text, Alex received a strange call from a man who refused to identify himself. He told Alex that he was a good friend of his grandfather's, and had been instructed to deliver a message to him in person. Alex wanted to meet him the next day, but the stranger said it couldn't wait, and was very insistent on meeting that very evening. Alex was hesitant to reply immediately, because there was something about the man's tone of voice that made him suspicious and uncomfortable. But after a brief pause, his curiosity got the best of him, and he agreed to meet the stranger at a nearby coffee shop.

Alex arrived 15 minutes early and looked around for anyone who appeared to be waiting for someone, but the few people there were already with others and showed no signs of waiting for additional visitors. He walked around the corner of the room and didn't see anyone there except a pale college student tapping on a laptop. Shrugging, he decided to wait a bit longer and stepped into the line to buy a cup of coffee.

In front of him were two young men in their late twenties who appeared to be slightly drunk. After placing their order, the girl asked them if they had meant to say "Venti" instead of "Large." They seemed offended by her question, and began making fun of her and the store's fancy coffee terms. "What the hell is the difference?" one guy groused. "Large is large. It's plain English."

"Or do you not understand plain English?" said the other. "Do I need to spell it out for you? L-a-r-g-e C-o-f-f-e-e."

The girl tried ignoring their comments and just poured their coffee, but Alex could tell that she was holding back tears. He wasn't sure if they were picking on her because she wore a modern Islamic *hijab* over her head or if they were simply assholes by nature. He felt bad for her, and wanted to say something to the two, but kept quiet because he didn't want to get into a confrontation with them. He knew he needed to say or do something, but he just couldn't.

After paying for his coffee, he put a five dollar bill in the tip jar, hoping that it would bring her some sort of joy. She just wiped the tears from her eyes and rushed into the back room after handing him his coffee. Again, he wished he'd said something, but as usual, it was too late.

Ever since he was a child, he'd found it easier to avoid confrontation than to stand up for what he believed in—even if it meant conforming to or accepting things he knew were wrong. Being accepted by others, being part of the norm, was always more important than doing or saying something that could jeopardize his social acceptance. He hated this part of himself, and was quietly upset for not having the courage to say something to the idiots in line ahead of him.

He walked away from the bar and quickly took his mind off what had just happened by checking the stock market on his Blackberry. Not so great. After sitting down at a table, he began thinking about the man he was meeting. He looked at the time on his phone, and realized he was already a few minutes late. *I'll give him five more minutes,* he told himself.

After ten more minutes of waiting, the man still hadn't shown. By then, Alex had become very suspicious about the whole situation; everything about it felt strange to him. He kept asking himself *why* he was meeting some stranger at a coffee shop, and what was so important that it couldn't wait until the next day.

Suddenly, a man who seemed to appear out of nowhere startled Alex by sitting down directly across from him. He was dressed in corporate business attire, wore dark-tinted glasses, and carried a briefcase. His skin was brown and he spoke with an accent that suggested he was Filipino, but Alex wasn't sure if he was or not.

Alex was about to introduce himself and ask him who he was and what this was all about, but the man stopped him with a lifted hand before he could open his mouth. "I don't have much time," said the stranger, as he placed his briefcase on the table and opened it.

"Much time for what?" asked Alex.

The stranger ignored his question, slid an envelope toward Alex, and said, "This is the package. Do not show this to anyone, and I mean anyone—especially any of your relatives. Wait until you're alone to open it. Your grandfather wants only you to read it."

Alex replied, "Wait—why isn't my grandfather giving this to me himself?"

The man quickly stood up, took his sunglasses off, looked Alex in the eye, and said harshly, "I'm sorry, but Santo is dead."

Before Alex could react to the news, the man picked up his briefcase and walked briskly toward the exit. "Wait!" Alex called out, but the man just kept walking, and disappeared into the crowd as soon as he stepped outside.

Alex sat there numbly, a lump in his throat. He couldn't believe that his lolo was truly dead. A feeling of guilt washed over him, given that he had interpreted the news from his aunt and cousin as nothing more than a plot to get him to send them more money. Then the guilt immediately changed to confusion, as nothing that had just happened seemed to make any sense.

Alex picked up the envelope and rushed out to his car. Once inside the Beamer, he held the envelope up to the dome light, trying to examine the contents. It appeared to contain paper and something flat and hard. He decided to wait until he arrived at home to open the envelope, and began driving. After a few miles, though, he couldn't wait any longer, so he pulled into an empty parking lot to open the envelope.

Inside was an airplane ticket to the Philippines, a handwritten note, and a small key taped to a piece of paper. The note read, in English written in a shaky hand:

"Dear Alex: I am leaving you a special inheritance. It will be waiting for you at my funeral. I know you have worked hard to earn what you have now, but what I have to give you is worth more than everything you have achieved. I have arranged it so that it can only be claimed if you come to my funeral. If you decide not to come, you will forfeit any share that is yours. I have chosen you for this inheritance for special reasons. Guard the enclosed key, because you will need it to open its matching locker at the airport in Manila. Do not tell anyone of this. It is vital that none of your relatives knows about this. It's best not to tell anyone at all that you are going to the Philippines. Let's keep it only between you and me. I still remember visiting you in America when you were a small boy. I wish we could have spent more time together as you grew up, but I assure you: we will eventually meet in spirit. I know I can trust you to keep this a secret. Love, Lolo Santo."

Alex looked at the plane ticket, and saw that the departure was scheduled for the following morning at 6 AM; and that made the cloak-and-dagger nature of what had happened that evening all the more real. No wonder he couldn't wait until tomorrow to meet the courier...

At first, his mind was clouded with reasons why he couldn't go at such short notice. But then he suddenly recalled a story that his father had once told him, about some kind of treasure his lolo had found during World War II. According to his father, Lolo Santo had helped a dying

Japanese officer, and had been given something in return for his kindness. Those who heard his Lolo's story, including his own father, didn't believe it, because they couldn't believe any Japanese capable of such a thing. Their hatred toward the Japanese, which stemmed from World War II, was so great that the notion of a good Japanese soldier was beyond comprehension. In addition, nobody ever saw such a treasure, because his lolo refused to show it as evidence.

As a child, he remembered his Mom telling him that their homeland in the Philippines was loaded with gold and that the Spaniards, Japanese, and Americans had all wanted to get as much of it for themselves as they could. This recollection compelled him to read the letter again. The words *What I have to give you is worth more than everything you have ever achieved* especially caught his attention.

This could be worth millions, he thought. *I know he must have known how much I was worth before all this...crap happened. Yeah, this has to be worth a lot.*

The thought of the family legend being true, and the possibility that he might inherit a treasure from his grandfather, sent a rush of excitement through his body. It was the bright light at the end of the tunnel for him.

Alex put the car into drive, and sped home to pack for the trip.

CHAPTER 3

Alex arrived at the airport a bit later than he liked, worried that he might miss his flight. Once inside the terminal, he rushed to the airline ticket counter. The lady at the counter must have recognized him as Filipino, for she greeted him in Tagalog: "*Magandang gabi*, sir. *Pwede ko ba kayong tulungan*?"

Alex didn't understand a word she said, and just looked at her with a blank expression. "I'm Mexican," he replied.

The lady smiled and said, *"Lo siento, señor.* Do you have any bags to check?"

He replied, "No, just these two carry-on bags."

Then he noticed that the ticket was for a coach seat, and asked if he could upgrade it to first class—but she regretfully informed him that all the first class seats were already taken. She could see that this didn't make him any happier and apologized, finished processing his ticket, and wished him a happy trip.

Alex didn't respond; he just took his boarding pass and began walking quickly toward the departure gate. As he walked, an uncomfortable feeling began settling in as he thought about the language barrier that awaited him in the Philippines. He'd never learned Tagalog, because his parents never spoke it inside the house and among close friends. In fact, he never heard any Tagalog until sixth grade, when his father left his engineering career to sell real estate properties in Florida to a predominantly Filipino market. It was only then that he realized that most Filipinos spoke Tagalog.

The language his parents spoke was called Kankanaey; it was one of the several native languages spoken by the indigenous peoples who lived in the Cordillera Mountains of Luzon, the people collectively known as Igorots. When Alex immigrated to America with his parents, he only spoke Kankanaey. Prior to sixth grade, he thought *every* Filipino spoke Kankanaey. He even thought all Filipinos were the same, and didn't know about the differences between Igorots and other Filipinos.

By that point, Alex was so concerned about fitting into his new, predominantly white world that he didn't care to know anymore more about his Igorot heritage. He wanted to fit in with his American friends so much, in fact, that he quickly forgot how to speak Kankanaey. By the time he was in high school, the only languages he understood were English and some Spanish.

When he arrived at the departure gate, he was relieved to see that nobody was boarding the plane yet. The waiting area was crowded, but Alex was lucky enough to find an available seat. Once he sat down, another uncomfortable feeling set in when he realized that almost everyone there was Asian. He wasn't certain, but everyone seemed to be speaking to each other in Tagalog.

Adding to his discomfort was the smell of garlic mixed with soy and dried fish-like odors that filled the room. It was the same smell he remembered as a child each time his mother cooked. The smell of Filipino food had lingered on his clothing, and he was always embarrassed by how he smelled in school. By the time he reached middle school, he'd begun wearing long coats or robes in the morning to keep his clothes from smelling. He also began wearing cologne so he could smell like the more popular boys in school.

Shortly after sitting down, the lady next to him began speaking to him in Tagalog. Again, Alex said he was Mexican; and, like the lady at the ticket counter, she apologized and spoke in English. She asked him if he had ever been to the Philippines, and he responded by telling her it was his first time, and that he was going to visit a friend who was there with the Peace Corps. "Where in the Philippines is your friend?" she asked, curious.

"Some place called Bontoc."

She looked puzzled and asked, "Where is that?"

"I'm not exactly sure," replied Alex. "I just know it's way up in the mountains north of Baguio City, on the island of Luzon."

With a look of surprise, she responded, "Oh yes, I know this place! All the people who live there are called Ifugao. Yes, that is the proper term. So your friend is with the Ifugao people. Wow, you must like adventures!"

"Why do you say that?" Alex asked.

She paused for a second and said, "Because it's so far up in the mountains, where people still live primitive lives. You know, people there still wear g-strings. Did your friend tell you this? They're still somewhat backwards. You know, they have very dark skin with very crinkly hair like the blacks here. Some even have extra growths on their rears that look like tails."

This was the first time Alex had ever heard such things. He was about to question her claims when a voice from the airport speakers announced the boarding of his flight. Alex quickly stood up, even though he knew the handicapped and those alphabetically ahead of him were boarding first. He picked his bags up and immediately started walking toward the gate, without even saying goodbye to the woman.

When everyone finished boarding, Alex was glad to see he that had an empty seat next to him. As the plane started down the runway, he became nervous and jittery. Flying was one of his least favorite things.

Well, not flying so much as the possibility of plummeting thousands of feet to his death if something happened to go wrong. As much as he was looking forward to his inheritance, he dreaded the next 22 hours on the plane.

Shortly after Alex finished the refreshments he was served, the plane encountered some turbulence. He felt his heart beat faster and his hands began to sweat profusely. He pulled a magazine out of the seatback and began reading it to get his mind off the turbulence. After reading several articles, the turbulence subsided and he was able to relax a bit. Just when his nerves settled, a short burst of turbulence spiked his nerves again. This time he put on a pair of headphones and began watching the featured movies to get his mind off his fear of crashing.

It worked for a while, but as the second movie ended, the plane encountered severe turbulence again. The plane momentarily plunged, and to his shock, the oxygen masks dropped from the overhead compartment, just like they described in the preflight safety drill. The abrupt bumping and shaking also caused several overhead compartment doors to pop open. People all around him panicked. A lady seated in front of him screamed while another lady directly behind him shouted, "Oh my God!" With one fist tightly clutching an arm support and the other holding the oxygen mask over his mouth, Alex closed his eyes and braced himself for the last moments of his life.

The turbulence lasted about fifteen seconds, but it felt like eternity to Alex and the other passengers. Finally, the plane leveled off and smoothed out. Even though the turbulence had ended, Alex's heart kept pounding like crazy, and he was sweating profusely. Not wanting to experience any more turbulence, Alex reached into his pocket for the travel-sized pack of Tylenol PM he'd purchased earlier, but couldn't find it.

Wonderful.

He grew increasingly nervous without his sleeping pills. He glanced at his watch and realized he still had approximately eleven more hours before reaching Seoul, South Korea, where he would take a connecting flight to Manila. After a series of minor bumps, he couldn't take it any longer and started ordering miniature bottles of vodka from the attendant. Several drinks later, his nerves were calm enough for him to sleep a while.

Once inside the Inchon airport in Seoul, he rushed to the nearest concessions store, hoping to find some Tylenol PM or anything similar. He was in luck: There was one last bottle on the shelf.

He still had two and a half hours before his connecting flight began boarding passengers, so he decided to find a decent place to eat and drink. The vodka high remained, so he decided to take the conveyer belt instead of walking. As he passed store after store, the airport began to feel like a shopping mall.

At the end of one of the conveyor belts, he saw a sign for Korean restaurants on the upper level. The thought of Korean food immediately caused his stomach to sit up and beg for its sweet spiciness. Without hesitation, he walked up the escalator to get his share of *ohjinguh bokkeum* and *kalbi.*

The spicy stir-fried squid and sweet, barbecued short ribs were the best he'd ever had. After his meal, he took out his lolo's letter and slowly read it again. Thoughts of his inheritance led to the strange encounter with the man who had delivered the letter...and suddenly, a strange feeling swept over him. He felt as if someone were watching him; for no reason at all, the feeling quickly segued into fear. He turned his head in all directions, but saw nothing and no-one out of the ordinary. *It must be that strange man's behavior back at the coffee shop that's got me feeling this way,* he reasoned.

On his way toward his departing gate, Alex stopped at an electronics store to browse. The first things he noticed were the wall-mounted flat screen televisions broadcasting a Korean weather channel. A slight sense of motion sickness developed as he looked at the storms hovering over the Pacific Ocean between Korea and Japan. Quickly, he checked his pant pocket to make sure the bottle of Tylenol PM was there. He clutched it tightly, and slowly made his way to his gate.

As he boarded the plane, the sight of so many empty seats had him wondering if people weren't flying because of the storms. As soon as the captain announced there would be some slight bumps on the way due to the weather, he opened his bottle of Tylenol PM and swallowed two pills.

Shortly after they began their ascent, they encountered significant turbulence. By then he was a ball of nerves, so he took another two pills. He pulled down the window shutter and closed his eyes, hoping to sleep through the rest of the flight. The Tylenol PM worked, and he quickly fell into a deep sleep.

As they neared the Philippines, he experienced a disturbing dream. A mysterious person kept walking up and down the center aisle of the plane, a person who wore a red coat with a hood that covered their head. The hood protruded several inches in front of the face, casting a dark shadow that hid the person's identity. He couldn't tell if the person was a man or a woman, because the coat was obscuring. The mysterious stranger finally sat down next to Alex and stared straight ahead. Alex slowly turned his head, trying to see the face underneath the hood; but each time he tried, the person slowly turned his (or her?) head the opposite direction. Alex noticed how dark and wrinkly the person's hand was; and for some reason, that sent shivers up and down his spine.

The plane suddenly touched down on the runway in Manila, waking Alex from his odd dream. He opened his eyes and quickly checked to see if the person in the red coat was sitting next to him, but the seat was empty. He scanned the plane to see if that person was anywhere in sight, but saw no such person.

The voice of the pilot sounded over the speaker system as he welcomed everyone to Manila in both Tagalog and English. After wiping the drool from his mouth and chin, Alex opened the shutter on his window, and saw palm trees along the runway. Feeling very groggy from the long sleep, he opened his eyes wide and shook his head, trying to banish the cobwebs.

Once inside the airport, Alex anxiously proceeded to the section where the lockers were located, the locker key tightly clutched in his hand. The first wall of lockers he saw was numbered differently than the key in his hand, so he walked from section to section, but still couldn't find the locker.

After nearly half an hour, he finally found the right section of lockers at the far end of the airport. Within seconds, he found the locker that matched his key and inserted it, jittery with anticipation. As soon as he opened the locker, a strange feeling came over him—that same eerie feeling from Seoul, the sensation that someone was watching him. He quickly closed the locker and looked around to see if there was anyone paying him any particular attention, but there was nobody nearby.

He opened the locker again, but was disappointed to see only a small envelope inside. He'd been hoping for a large sum of cash or gold. When he picked up the envelope, that eerie feeling of someone watching came over him again; so rather than open it right there, he shoved it in his hip pocket and went to the nearest restroom.

After locking himself inside a stall, he opened the envelope to find a bus ticket and another hand-written note from his lolo. He felt a stab of disappointment, but at the same time, was pleased to see the note in his lolo's wavering but careful handwriting; obviously he was still on the right trail. The note instructed him to call his Uncle Pael to inform him of his arrival, and to ask him to pick him up from the bus station in Baguio City, where his uncle lived. It also reminded him to keep everything confidential, and that he was to give everyone the impression that he was only there for the funeral. Lastly, it informed him that a man would approach him during the funeral to deliver further instructions, and that he needed to listen to whatever that man said.

Alex wasted no time, going to the nearest phone to call the number included in the letter. Pael was his father's next youngest brother, but Alex didn't know much about him except that he was a colonel or similar high-ranking officer in the Philippine military or police. He recalled the letter of condolence from his Uncle Pael at the time of his parents' funeral. It was the one letter that stuck out from the rest, because of the many good things Pael mentioned about his father. Apparently, if it weren't for his father's encouragement and advice, his uncle wouldn't have become the man he was.

His uncle was pleasantly surprised to hear from him, and excited to learn that he'd arrived in the Philippines to attend his Lolo Santo's funeral. Pael tried to insist on picking him up directly from the Manila airport, but Alex explained that he'd already purchased a bus ticket to Baguio City, and didn't want to inconvenience anyone. It wasn't easy, but his uncle gave in and said he would be waiting at the bus station when he arrived.

Relieved, Alex left the airport for the bus station. The heat and humidity was so intense that his shirt was drenched with perspiration after only a few minutes. Once at the bus station, he glanced at his watch and saw that he had thirty minutes before it was time to board the bus. A churning in his stomach told him to use the restroom before boarding, so he turned to a person next to him and asked him where the bathrooms were; but the man only spoke Tagalog. He walked over to a lady who looked like she worked there, and she politely pointed in the direction of a small building with the letters "C/R" painted above the door. "Comfort room," she said as she pointed.

Alex quickly walked to the building, and was very disappointed to discover that the so-called "comfort room" was anything but. Inside were four stalls without doors. The toilets weren't toilets, but wooden boxes with holes cut on the top to sit on. Rather than sit on the filthy wood, Alex stood on the wood platform and squatted. But when he finished, he noticed there were no toilet paper rolls! He spoke through the divider that separated his stall from the adjoining one, but that person didn't reply. With no other choice, Alex reluctantly reached into his pocket, removed some receipts, and used them as toilet paper. He made sure to wash his hands thoroughly afterward.

On his way out, he saw that people were paying a man at the entrance for pieces of toilet paper. What a scam. He wanted to complain, but noticed from the corner of his eye that his bus was leaving without him. He looked at his watch and saw that he still had at least ten minutes before the bus was supposed to leave. "What the hell!" he shouted. He ran toward the bus, shouting and waving his hands, but to no avail: the bus went on without him. "Bastards," he muttered as he jogged to a halt.

On his way back to the ticket counter, a small rattletrap vehicle with the hand-painted words "Pinoy Turist Coche" on its door pulled up next to him and drove very slowly alongside. Alex was startled when a young Filipino man in his early twenties stuck his head out the window and began speaking to him in Tagalog. "I don't speak Tagalog," Alex said grumpily as he kept walking. "I'm an American, dammit."

"No problem," the man said in a thick yet understandable accent. "I speak English. Mister, you need a driver? I drive for you."

Alex kept silent for a moment, then replied, "That depends on how much you're charging and how much English you know. Is your English good?"

"But of course. I speak good English. I love American television!"

"Okay, let's talk," replied Alex.

The young man pulled over, stepped out of his vehicle, and approached Alex. He was barely five feet tall, very dark-skinned, and wore a black tank-top emblazoned with the picture of a boxer labeled *Manny Pacquiao.* Not having a clue who the boxer was, Alex noticed that the young man's hair, mustache and little beard resembled that of the boxer on his shirt. "Is that you?" he asked.

"Oh no sir," the young man replied with a big smile. "I am fast, but I don't have the power. Only Manny has that kind of power. You like Pacquiao?"

"Sorry, I don't follow boxing much," replied Alex.

"How about basketball?" said the man. "Michael Jordan, Shaq, Kobe, Lebron?"

"I'm impressed," replied Alex. "You know your basketball, and your English is pretty good. Let's talk money now."

Alex told him he needed a driver and translator for the next couple of weeks. At first, the young man looked disinterested; but when Alex told him he would pay top American dollar, the young man's eyes lit up and he became very attentive. After negotiating an agreement to become Alex's personal chauffeur and translator for the next two weeks, he loaded Alex's bags into the trunk and opened the back door for him. After Alex entered, the man closed the doors and jumped into the driver's seat. He reached into a small cooler for a bottle of Coca-Cola, popped off the cap, placed a straw in the bottle, and handed it back to Alex.

"We need to stop at my house for a moment, sir, so I can gather some of my things for the trip," the young man announced with a big smile.

"You like to smile a lot," Alex said as he gladly accepted the bottle of Coke.

"But of course, sir," he happily replied. "It is easier to smile than not."

Alex reached forward and said, "I'm Alex."

"Nice to meet you, sir," replied the young man, as he firmly shook Alex's hand. "My name is Bong Bong."

Alex raised an eyebrow and said, "I've never met a Bong Bong before."

Bong Bong replied, "Actually, it's Bonifacio, but everyone calls me Bong Bong, and you can too. Is this your first time to the Philippines?"

"Yup. My first time."

"This must have been a last-minute trip for you, sir."

"Yes it was. How did you know?"

"Well, you didn't bring a *balikbayan* box, sir."

"You don't have to keep calling me sir," said Alex. "I prefer Alex— and what in the world is a bakaba box?"

Bong Bong smiled again and answered, "No problem, sir. I mean Alex, sir. The ba-lik-ba-yan is the big box that Filipinos from America bring when they come back home to visit. It usually contains Spam, chocolates, Levi jeans, and anything American. The word "balik" means going back, and "bayan" means hometown."

"Interesting," said Alex. "I didn't know that, Bongabong. Well, home for me is America, so I guess I don't need a bakabayan box."

"It's Bong Bong, sir," laughed Bong Bong.

Pretending to have said it correctly, Alex replied, "Well, of course it is, but can I call you Bong instead? Bong Bong sounds like 'dumb dumb' to me."

Bong Bong laughed again and replied, "Sure! I like Bong. It sounds American."

Alex chuckled and murmured under his breath, "Yeah, that's good, just don't smoke it too much."

Bong didn't get the joke, so he ignored it and kept driving. When they arrived at Bong's house, Alex remained inside the car while Bong ran inside to fetch his things.

At first, Alex wanted to lean his head back and nap while he waited, but the shouts of a young boy selling cigarettes nearby caught his attention. The kid looked about eight years old and wore dirty clothes too big for him. His bare feet didn't seem to mind the intense heat that saturated the severely cracked concrete. As Alex watched the boy peddling cigarettes to passersby, he noticed how filthy the streets were, and how threadbare the people's clothing seemed. All sorts of trash littered the streets, and the smell of raw sewage filled the humid interior of the car. He wanted to roll up the window, but it was too hot. By then, several minutes had passed and Alex couldn't stand the stench inside the car any longer, so he opened the door and stepped out of the car.

He released a huge sigh of relief as a breeze momentarily dissipated the stagnant air, and continued looking around. He was amazed at how many people there were all around him, most just sitting around on their haunches next to their ramshackle houses, doing nothing but watch the world go by.

He glanced at his watch several times over the next few minutes, growing increasingly impatient. Just as he was about to walk up to Bong's house and see what the hell was taking so long, Bong slammed through the door clutching a medium-sized duffel bag and hustled toward the "Turist Coche." Alex smiled with relief and got back inside the car. Bong threw his bag into the trunk, hopped into the driver's seat, and drove off at a rate that had the car shaking as they rattled through the potholed streets.

"That's all you have for the next two weeks?" asked Alex, his voice jittery with their passage.

"Oh, I only need a few clothes and other items," replied Bong.

"Okay then. I sure hope Baguio City isn't as dirty as this," said Alex, and immediately cursed himself for not being more tactful.

"Oh, no sir," replied Bong, not offended. "It's much more beautiful, and it's not as hot because it's way up in the mountains. We call it the Summer Capital, because so many people go up there to get away from the heat. You'll like it much better there."

"Good to know."

A few miles outside the city, Alex began feeling the jet lag and became drowsy. He tried keeping his eyes open, but the heat was too much. Before he knew it, his head drooped and he fell asleep. He dreamt of a dark silhouette following him down some poorly lit street. After hearing footsteps for what seemed the entire length of a block, Alex quickly turned around, only to see the silhouette duck around a corner. He sensed danger, and his heart began pounding so loud he couldn't hear anything else until he stopped in his tracks to collect himself. Just as his heart began to calm down, the sounds of footsteps resumed from around the corner. They sounded like they were drawing closer, and for a long moment he just stood there, waiting for the silhouette to appear.

Suddenly he couldn't stand it any longer, and began running.

In the way of dreams, the pavement suddenly turned to dirt and he found himself pushing through the thick brush of what appeared to be a jungle or forest. The sound of footsteps pounding on pavement turned into the cracking of twigs and leaves underfoot. He stopped, spun around, and saw that the silhouette was actually that of someone in a long, red, hooded coat—the same person who had invaded his dream on the plane into Luzon. The person kept coming straight toward him, making no attempt to hide now.

Alex froze, just waiting for something bad to happen.

The sound of a slamming car door and the shaking of the vehicle suddenly woke him. He straightened, wondering where he was; he opened his eyes wide as he wiped the crust from their corners. "You're awake," said Bong as he settled into place. Apparently he'd just gotten back in the car. "You were sound asleep for the last four hours, and I didn't want to wake you since I knew you must be very tired. Did you have a nice rest?"

Alex wiped his mouth and chin before replying, "Yeah, but where are we?"

"We're at the bus stop in Baguio," Bong replied proudly. "We actually beat your bus here, hah, so I went inside to see if your uncle or anyone was there waiting for you, but only a few people were there, and none of them were waiting for anyone."

"Are you sure we're at the right bus station?" Alex replied, still shaking the sleep from his head.

"Yessir, Alex. This is the only bus station in town."

Just then, the bus Alex was supposed to be on entered the parking lot. Alex and Bong got out of the car to see if they find anyone looking for Alex, and immediately saw two men who appeared to be surveying the crowd exiting the bus. One was an older man in his seventies; the other looked to be in his thirties.

Alex approached the older man and asked, "Uncle Pael?"

The man turned, peered at Alex, and said something Alex couldn't understand.

Alex immediately knew it wasn't his uncle, because he didn't reply in English. Still curious, he looked at Bong for the translation, but Bong looked confused. He spoke to the man, but it was clear they didn't understand each other. Just then the younger man stepped in and said in Tagalog, "I am sorry, but my father only speaks Ibaloi."

"What did he say?" Alex asked Bong.

"The old man only speaks his native Igorot dialect, so I will talk to his son."

After a series of questions and answers with the son, Bong turned to Alex and told him that the older man was not his uncle, and that they don't know anyone with his uncle's name. They continued looking for Uncle Pael until the bus was empty and everybody had left the area. It was clear that Pael wasn't there, and Alex began to wonder if he might have misunderstood what his uncle had told him on the phone.

A man dressed as a bus station attendant called out to Alex in English, "Excuse me, sir. Is your name Alex?"

"Yes, that's me," replied Alex.

"Your uncle Raphael was here thirty minutes ago," the man said. "He was in a hurry, though, and had to leave. He said there was some sort of family emergency, and instructed me to give you this." He handed Alex a large manila envelope. Inside were some Filipino currency and a piece of notepaper, which bore Uncle Pael's full name and an address written on it. He looked to the man and asked him what else his uncle said.

"The address on the paper is where he said to tell a taxi to take you. I think he said it was his house. Those pesos are more than enough to pay the fare."

Alex thanked the man, and handed the note to Bong. Bong looked at the address and began asking the man directions in Tagalog. After he finished scribbling them down , they both got into Bong's "Coche" and drove away. As he drove, Bong pointed out that the street name of his uncle's address was the same as his uncle's last name.

"My last name, too," Alex said absently. "My father was his brother."

"Your uncle must be an important person," said Bong.

"Either that, or it's sheer coincidence he lives on that street," replied Alex. He doubted the latter, but it wasn't that uncommon a name, really. Not in the Philippines.

When they arrived at the address, Bong drove slowly up a long driveway that led to a small courtyard parking area at the back of the house. The outdoor lights flicked on, and an attractive older lady stuck her head out the door to see who had arrived. She looked unsure, but as soon as Alex stepped out of the vehicle, she rushed out the door with both hands on her cheeks. "Alex?" she called out.

"Yes ma'am," he replied.

"*Ay Dios ko!*" she said as she approached him. A skinny Filipina who looked to be in her mid-fifties, she was a little taller than Bong and wore a simple purple sundress. When she smiled, her large teeth and small gums became plainly visible. Alex stayed where he was and smiled as she approached. He wasn't sure who she was, but pretended to be happy to see her by holding out his arms to greet her. When she reached him, she gave him a big hug, placed both her hands on his cheeks, and looked at him with a big smile. She rattled off a few sentences in her native dialect, but he just looked at her blankly. "Oh, sorry," she apologized in English. "I forgot you don't speak Kankanaey anymore. I'm your Uncle Pael's sister, Auntie Virgie."

"Oh yes," Alex said. "I remember Uncle Marcelino showing me your picture at my parents' funeral. I'm sorry I didn't recognize you right away."

"No, no, that's okay," she replied. "I'm so happy you're here, Alex, and so sorry we could not make it to the funeral. Your other uncles and aunties and I were all so upset when our visas were denied. It can be so difficult at times, getting a visa to America, but luckily Marcelino's was approved. Anyway, thank God you were able to come! Do you have many things? Let me help you."

Alex told her it wasn't necessary, and then introduced Bong to her. Bong greeted her in Tagalog, and she responded in the same language. After they exchanged some pleasantries, Alex and Bong followed her into the house. Once inside, Alex asked where his Uncle Pael was. Virgie's pleasant demeanor quickly turned into a very concerned and worried one. "I'm afraid something terrible has happened to your lolo," she said softly.

Alex nodded, then replied, "Oh, I know about his death. That's why I'm here—to attend his funeral."

"No, it's worse than that. How do I say this...? Someone has stolen father's body from the hospital, and Pael went up to Bontoc with some others to find it."

Neither Alex nor Bong could believe what they were hearing; both just sat there at the kitchen table with stunned looks on their faces. "Who would *do* such a thing?" Alex asked after a long moment.

"And why?" added Bong.

Auntie Virgie wasn't sure herself, she said, and seemed just as confused. She told them that Pael had heard that the people responsible for taking the body were relatives who had never converted to Christianity. He and others believed that the body had been taken back up to his lolo's hometown of Bontoc; they suspected that the non-Christian relatives didn't want him to have a Christian burial.

Bong began shaking his head in disbelief. She saw this and began talking to him rapidly in Kankanaey, but Bong immediately reminded her that he didn't understand Kankanaey. She apologized and continued conversing in English, so that Alex also understood what she was saying. Bemused, Alex pretended to listen, but his mind drifted. He wondered if this had anything to do with the inheritance he'd come to collect. Why the secrecy? How much was the inheritance actually worth—enough to hold a body hostage for? Who else knew about it? Would they come after me, too?

The thoughts generated the same kind of fear he'd experienced in his dreams with the red-coated person. It felt so surreal that goose bumps rose all over his body. He didn't understand why he was scared, but he knew something terribly strange was going on—

"Well, what do you think, Alex sir?" asked Bong, breaking him out of his reverie.

"About what?" Alex replied, returning his attention to the conversation.

Bong replied, "Since my shocks need to be replaced, I will not be able to take you all the way up the mountains. It seems I cannot take you any farther. I suggest you do as your auntie recommends, and go with one of your cousins to this place called Bontoc."

"Yes," Virgie interjected. "Your *manong* will be arriving in a few hours to accompany you in the morning."

"Who is Manong?" asked Alex.

Auntie Virgie smiled. "I'm sorry, I keep forgetting that you were raised in America. *Manong* is what you call a relative older than you. It is a way of showing respect. Your cousin Brian is coming in a few hours; in our tradition, you would address him as *manong* Brian."

"I get it," Alex replied. "Does he speak English?"

"Unfortunately, his English is very poor," she replied. "It has always been difficult for him to learn, and he hates the fact that the lowland schools are taught in English. He hated school so much, in fact, that he kept running away every time your auntie and uncle sent him away to the city to learn. He never got along with the city kids. By the way—try not to say anything about the scar on his face. He doesn't like talking about the day when a bunch of lowland kids cornered him after school and teased him. That was when he was cut in the face by an evil boy. It was an awful experience for him."

"Does he still get into a lot of trouble?" asked Alex.

"No, that was a long time ago," she replied. "Now he just works in the mines all day and gets drunk every night." She sighed. "He used to have a lot of anger toward lowlanders, but nowadays he's learned to control it, especially since many of the stores where he buys his liquor are owned by them. Sadly, he doesn't speak much English. He understands some words, but hates it for some reason. When he's not with Kankanaey speaking Igorots, he prefers to speak Ilocano, but he does speak some Tagalog."

When his auntie stood up to leave the room momentarily, Alex glanced at Bong, concerned, and asked, "Could you still come along to Bontoc as my translator?"

"Ah, but I do not speak Kankanaey," Bong reminded Alex. He went on to explain that a number of different languages were spoken in the Cordilleras, and that he himself would be just as much of a tourist as

Alex—not only their language differed, but their customs as well. He made it sound as if Bontoc lay in a totally different country. "Besides," he told Alex, "This is the farthest I've ever travelled from Manila. This is only my third time here, and I have never been beyond Baguio."

Alex didn't understand how the mountain region could be so different from the lowland, and just sat in silence for a moment. Was it just a kind of hillbilly thing, or was it like the North /South difference in America? Either way, Alex wanted Bong to accompany him, because he already felt comfortable having him around. "I'd still feel more comfortable if you could at least accompany me until I catch up with my uncle," Alex said to Bong.

He wasn't sure why Bong didn't reply right away; then he thought it might be a renegotiation tactic, so he offered Bong more money than they had originally agreed upon. After a few moments of consideration, Bong accepted his offer. "I admit I could use the money," he said, flashing startlingly white teeth, "and besides, I love the idea of having an American friend around!"

Brian arrived shortly thereafter. He was taller than Alex by at least five inches, a lot skinnier, and somewhat dirty. His jeans were soiled, and his T-shirt looked like it hadn't been washed in quite some time. His bowl-shaped mop of oily hair looked overdue for a cut; his bangs hung over his eyelids, almost hiding his eyes. Alex immediately noticed the wide scar that ran from his left ear to about an inch from his mouth.

When Auntie Virgie introduced him to Alex and mentioned that he was American and only spoke English, Brian noticed Alex looking at his scar, and just timidly smiled and nodded his head. On the other hand, when she introduced Bong to him and told him that Bong was from Manila, he gave a big smile and made a point of greeting Bong in Tagalog, as if to show off the little he knew. After a few pleasant exchanges between Bong and Brian, they all made their way to the kitchen for dinner.

Everyone ate with their hands except for Alex, who tried but couldn't manage without most of the rice falling to the table and onto his clothes. Bong noticed how difficult it was for him, and taught him how to eat the Filipino way by using the fork to push food into the spoon—but Alex also found that difficult. After several failed attempts to shovel food into his mouth, he realized he'd become a one-man comedy show for the three. He played along, and kept amusing them with his feeble attempts to eat their way.

Once he began getting a hang of it, he found the food to be very tasty. His favorite dish was meat cooked in a thick brown soup. At first, Auntie Virgie called it "chocolate meat," but when Bong saw how much he enjoyed it, he told him impishly that he was eating pork blood. Alex paused with a mouthful of chocolate meat, looked at the three as if he might vomit, then smiled and kept eating. They all laughed.

At first, Brian seemed intimidated by Alex, and kept his conversations directed toward Bong and Virgie. It didn't help that Alex kept staring at Brian's scar; he didn't mean to, but couldn't help himself. Most Americans would have had something like that removed by the time they were Brian's age. Bong noticed his fascination, and softly nudged Alex's leg with his foot. Alex looked at Bong, and saw him making eye and hand gestures suggesting he stop looking at Brian's scar. Until then, Alex hadn't realized that he was staring so much, and gave Bong a look of thanks for bringing it to his attention.

Eventually, Bong began including Alex in the conversation with Brian by asking his opinion of some of the things they were discussing. Soon, Bong began asking Brian how to say certain words in Ilocano. Brian smiled, seeming more than happy to teach him. When Alex noticed how empowering it was for Brian to teach Bong, he began asking how to say some words in both Tagalog and Ilocano. First he asked Bong for a Tagalog translation, and then Bong would ask Brian for the Ilocano translation. The first word he asked to translate was the name of the chocolate meat he so loved.

"*Diniguan,*" replied Bong, as he then looked over to Brian.

"*Dinardaran,*" Brian added with a big smile.

"Delicious?" continued Alex.

"Masarap," Bong replied.

"Naimas," Brian followed.

This went on for another fifteen minutes, as Auntie Virgie watched joyfully, happy to see that they were having a good time. Despite the language barriers between the three men, they got along very well.

CHAPTER 4

The mysterious red-coated man followed Alex as he stumbled through the moonlit thicket, desperately trying to find his way, his arms held out in front of him to fend off branches. Suddenly, he stumbled over something—a tree root?— and fell noisily to the ground. The footsteps were still some distance away, but approaching rapidly.

Short of breath and too tired to go any farther, Alex crawled under a nearby clumping shrub, sat, and balled up as tightly as possible to keep his body hidden under the leaves and branches. He listened for the footsteps even as he desperately tried to control his heavy breathing, for fear that he would be heard—but that and the sound of his pulse beating in his ears was too loud for him to hear anything else.

As his breath came under control and the volume of his heartbeat lessened, he noticed that the wind had ceased, along with the sigh of leaves and swaying branches. In the eerie calm that settled in, the sound of footsteps was nowhere to be heard, though he strained his ears as he peered into the darkness.

Soon, the wind began to pick up again; but instead of the sounds of ruffling leaves and swaying branches that had accompanied it before, a clacking noise filled the air, like large hollow poles hitting each other. The shrub he was tucked under mysteriously disappeared, and he found himself leaning against a thick bamboo trunk. Even the smell of pines had changed to the astringent, clean smell of live bamboo. The clouds above gave way to more moonlight, and he found himself crouching in a bamboo forest. When another gentle breeze swayed the bamboo, he realized that the curious clacking noise came from the bamboo stalks striking each other as they swayed in the wind.

Alex had no idea what was happening, so he picked a direction and began walking through the forest. After going no more than fifty feet or so, he thought he heard a whispering in the wind. He stopped dead; the whispers stopped. His goose bumps returned and the hairs on his head tingled. Then he heard a soft voice, chanting his name.

The clouds opened up further, allowing more moonlight to glow through. He could see more, but couldn't see who was calling his name. Then he glimpsed a moving figure from the corner of his eye: the red-coated person again. When the figure began walking toward him, Alex turned to run—and ran straight into a bamboo trunk, hitting his head and knocking himself senseless in a performance worthy of the Three Stooges.

He woke up to find himself in Auntie Virgie's guest bedroom. He sighed in relief; it was only a dream. That established, he lay back on the bed with his eyes open, staring at the ceiling. "Why am I having these dreams?" he wondered. "Who's in the red coat? Could it be Lolo Santo?" He supposed it *could* be, but that didn't seem correct somehow.

He didn't want to go back to sleep and risk another such dream, so he fought to stay awake; but his physical need for sleep soon got the better of him, and his eyes slowly closed. Just as he was about to fall into a deeper sleep, he was awakened by the sound of a rooster crowing. The sunlight began to creep into the nearby window as he dozed, and before he knew it, it stared him in the face. Still tired, Alex pulled the pillow over his eyes, but the sound of a car door slamming shut caught his attention.

He stood up, walked to the window, and saw Brian and Bong loading things into an SUV. They glanced up and saw Alex in the window, and gestured. Their meaning was clear: it was time to get ready for their trip further up the mountains. Nodding, Alex immediately went about gathering his things to get them out to the truck.

After a heavy breakfast of rice and leftovers, the three drove off toward Helsema Highway, which took them further into the Cordilleras. As Brian drove them out of Baguio City and through La Trinidad, Alex and Bong took in as much of the scenery possible. Alongside the roads were cultivated fields of vegetables and patches of wild lilies. The countryside, with the distant mountains beyond, looked pristine and beautiful at this hour.

Half an hour into the trip, Alex began thinking about his dreams again. He knew they had something to do with his inheritance, but he wasn't sure how. *Could my lolo be trying to tell me something? If so, I'm not picking up on what it is.*

"Wow," said Bong suddenly, breaking Alex out of his reverie. "Look at all those strawberries! I love strawberries!"

"Me too." Alex peered out into the strawberry fields of La Trinidad. "You really haven't seen this before?"

"No, this really is my first time up the Mountain Trail," replied Bong.

"The roads are nicely paved," Alex noted. "It's not nearly as bad as Auntie Virgie made it out to be."

Bong asked Brian about the road, and whether it would be this smooth all the way to the Mountain Province. Brian just laughed, then told him that the roads wouldn't get bumpy until after they reached the province of Benguet, which was still a few hours ahead. He went on to explain that the vegetable fields that carpeted the mountainsides had once been forested with towering pines. Bong found it fascinating and relayed the information to Alex, who kept staring out the window at the fields. He took notice of how homes were scattered throughout the fields, and how they were grouped by the roadside. It seemed that each field had its own house built right next to it. He was impressed to see that the farmers were out tending their fields so early in the morning. When he asked about it, Brian said through Bong, "Oh, they're up before the roosters."

After a while, Alex's eyes grew heavy again, and his head began nodding. He wanted to sleep, but didn't want to miss any more scenery; but try as he might, he soon found himself resting his head against the window, and eventually dozed off. An occasional bump in the road woke him, and each time he re-adjusted himself in the seat and went back to sleep. Just as he was about to fall into that deep stage of sleep the rooster crow had prevented earlier, his body lunged forward and the truck's window banged against his head. Needless to say, that woke him immediately, and he quickly sat up straight to see if everything was all right.

Everything was fine; or "co-pah-say-tic," as Brian put it, proving he knew *some* English. He was just pulling off to the side of the road to stop. Bong pointed to a sign at the side of the road that read, "Highest Point" in several languages, and told Alex he wanted to take a picture next to the sign. Alex rubbed his eyes and slowly got out of the truck. He was able to read the rest of the sign as he approached it: "Highest Point Philippines Highway System Elevation 7400 feet." Bong set the timer on his camera and took several pictures of them standing next to the sign.

Afterward, Alex stepped closer to the edge of the road to urinate. As he stood there doing so, he became captivated with the mountain scenery around them. The mountains were bearded with trees, and seemed to caress the clouds above them. The sense of mixed splendor and awe that ran through him was something he'd never felt before; and he decided that even if nothing came of his expedition, this experience was worth the price of admission.

Bong approached Alex with a look of amazement in his eyes and said, "I've seen pictures of these mountains in magazines and books, but it's totally different to see them with my own eyes! You know, I learned something new while you were sleeping. "I always thought everyone up here was called Ifugao—but your *manong* corrected me. There are actually many different tribes or clans up here, all with their own names and languages. He told me that your relatives are mostly Kankanaey and Bontoc, It just goes to show how little we lowlanders know about life up here."

"Aha! That would explain why a Filipina lady at the airport referred to the people who lived in Bontoc as Ifugao," said Alex.

After a 30-minute break, they proceeded up the road. Brian drove more slowly now, because the road's surface was wet from the many small waterfalls that cascaded down the face of the mountain immediately adjacent to the road. Eventually, the road developed more noticeable curves and bends as it steadily narrowed and roughened. The concrete soon gave way to dirt, gravel and stones. As bumps and eroded holes in the road increased, the road became narrower and increasingly dangerous. At one point, Brian had to back up a hundred feet to allow a bus to pass, since the road was only wide enough for one vehicle. As it passed, Alex couldn't believe how crowded it was; there were at least a dozen people on the roof, hanging on without benefit of any type of safety harness.

"That would never be allowed in America," Alex said, shaking his head. "Are they crazy? Don't they know they could fall off and die, just like that?"

Brian smiled as he looked at Alex in the rearview mirror. He glanced at Bong and said a few words. Bong then told Alex that as dangerous as it looked, Brian rarely heard about people falling off. Alex responded by shaking his head again in disbelief.

As the tires splashed through water-filled craters in the road and bounced off large bumps and rocks, Alex became more and more nervous. At one point, the road barely extended a foot beyond the side of the truck's tires on the passenger side, with no wall, fence, or railing to keep vehicles from falling off the precipice. The bumpiness doubled; and soon, he felt like he was riding a bull up the mountain. A mad bull.

Alex's nerves balled up as he stared down the precipice, which gave way to a splendorous view of lush green mountains both up close and at a distance. Glancing at his watch, he saw that they'd been driving on the graveled highway almost two hours now. He asked Bong, "How far have we gone since we left the pavement?"

"Looks like about 35 kilometers," Bong said cheerfully. After doing the math, Alex was astonished to realize that they'd taken so long to drive just 21 miles. Bong saw Alex's reaction and said, "In Manila, we have traffic congestion to blame. Here, it is just the mountains that are to blame."

"Yeah—it would have taken me only about half an hour, at the most, to drive this far back home," replied Alex.

A few minutes later, they came to a complete halt, because several vehicles and a bus were stopped in the middle of the road. Brian got out of the truck and joined a group of people standing and sitting along the roadside. After speaking with several of them, he returned to their truck and told Bong that the road was closed due to a landslide caused by heavy rain a few days before. He told Bong that they would follow the group up an alternate road, and then pantomimed that they should eat first. Alex understood Brian's hand gestures, and immediately grabbed the food Auntie Virgie had prepared; then they joined the rest of the group of waiting people, who were also eating. When they reached the group, Brian introduced Alex to them in Ilocano. Except for the words, "Igorot," "America," and "English," Alex didn't understand a thing he said. He just smiled, shook the hands of three of the men, and nodded to the women in the group.

Alex sat on a flat boulder and dug through the bag, looking for utensils to eat his food with, but couldn't find any. Bong saw him looking and looked like he wanted to say something, but before he could say anything, Brian caught Alex's attention and gestured to him to use his hands to eat. After Alex noticed everyone eating with their hands, he sighed and clumsily attempted to put a handful of rice in his mouth—but he was as unsuccessful at it as before, because most of it fell to the ground before reaching his mouth. "Not *again*," he murmured.

The women giggled amongst themselves; then one of them demonstrated how to eat with her hands. Alex noticed how she used her thumb to push the food along her fingers. With a big smile, Alex carefully followed her example. The next two attempts failed, as everyone watched and laughed. Like his Auntie Virgie and Brian, they found it enormously amusing. Soon everyone was demonstrating the proper way to eat with their hands. On the fourth attempt, Alex managed to get a whole fingertip full of food in his mouth without dropping anything. Everyone cheered as Alex gleefully chewed.

As they ate, Alex listened to their conversations, trying to pick up on their inflections, tones, and words. Every time someone looked at him while saying something, Alex knew they were talking about him, but didn't have a clue what they'd said. When this happened, Alex looked to Bong for translation, but Bong would have to ask Brian for the meaning in Tagalog. Sometimes, it took Brian several attempts before Bong understood enough to tell Alex what had been said.

The women were very generous, and kept offering Alex different kinds of food and desserts. The men were also quite friendly toward him. Alex had never met these people before, yet he felt very much at ease with them. Unlike in America, where he was accustomed to keeping his distance with strangers, he felt as if he were part of a family.

After a while, Alex saw a man walk to the side of the road to urinate. His bladder was full, so he joined the man. As he stood there urinating with his back toward the rest, enjoying his view of the mountain, an older lady from the group came up a few arm lengths away from him, squatted, lifted her red-and-black hand-quilted skirt, and also began urinating . Alex quickly looked the other way, and turned his body slightly away from her, feeling very embarrassed..

After lunch, they proceeded to follow the small caravan up the mountain. No matter how much Alex tried to calm his nerves, he remained on the edge of his seat as they continued up the very bumpy, very narrow roads. Farther up the mountain, they came to a sharp turn in the road that looked too narrow to pass because a large boulder had fallen from above and wedged itself against the mountainside, partially blocking the way. The smaller truck in front of them stopped, and the driver left the vehicle to see if there was enough space to pass. He turned and gave Brian the thumbs-up before proceeding around the bend. Alex watched as the smaller truck negotiated the curve successfully, but he couldn't help but notice that its tires were barely a foot away from the edge of the precipice. "What do you think?" Alex asked Bong.

Bong relayed the message to Brian in Tagalog; Alex's *manong* just smiled from ear to ear and nodded. With a sigh of relief, Bong turned to Alex and said, "No problem. He's a pro at this."

They proceeded at a walking speed around the sharp bend. Both Alex and Bong sat at the edge of their seats as the road beneath them seemed to disappear from their side of the SUV. Alex's knuckles turned white as he clutched the headrest in front of him while looking down a 500-foot drop. After Brian had made his way around the bend successfully, Alex let out a big sigh of relief, then turned around to watch the bus behind them maneuver around the same boulder...but the bus didn't seem to want to move.

Brian and the driver from the lead truck stopped and jumped out to see why the bus wasn't moving. After talking with the bus driver, they returned and told Bong that the bus and other trucks had to back up and turn around, because they were too big to make the turn. The caravan was now reduced to only two trucks.

As they left Benguet Province and entered Bontoc, the road began to descend slightly, though it remained as bumpy and narrow as ever. Just when the winding curves seemed to straighten out, the leading truck sharply swerved to avoid something in the road: another large boulder. Brian immediately swerved as well to avoid it. Then the leading truck swerved again to avoid *another* boulder in the road. Again, Brian swerved—but this time he overcompensated and began fishtailing. "*Ukinam!*" he cursed, trying desperately to regain control.

"Oh my God!" cried Alex. He clutched the headrest in front of him and froze. He couldn't say or do a thing. His eyes were locked on to the edge of the road and the precipice that taunted them. Brian lost all control, and the truck began to spin. The spinning broke Alex's visual lock on the steep precipice, so he just closed his eyes, expecting to fall to his death at any moment. Suddenly the truck hit another boulder, bounced off it, and came to a complete stop. The rear driver's side tire hung off the cliff as the truck slowly rocked back and forth. Still clutching the headrest, Alex slowly opened his left eye to see where they were.

"Adi Kaman kut kuti!" yelled Brian.

"Nobody move!" repeated Bong.

Alex began to lean to his left to see if he could tell how far off the road they were, but Bong shouted, "No! You might make us fall!"

"What do we do, then?" shouted Alex.

Brian looked at Alex and gestured at him not to move, then told him to wait for help, saying, *"Aguray. Aguray para iti tulong."* Alex understood his hand and eye gestures, and assumed that Brian had told him to stay very still, which he did.

"Look, here he comes!" exclaimed Bong, as he pointed to the lead truck, which was slowly backing up towards them.

The driver jumped out and ran toward them with his hands on his head. Then he looked down the road and saw a small bus approaching. He frantically waved his hands, trying to catch their attention so that it would not swerve into them. The bus driver saw them, luckily, and turned his lights on and off to signal his awareness of the accident.

Luckily, the lead truck had a chain long enough to reach the SUV. After several men from the bus helped the driver attach it to the front axle of Brian's truck, the lead truck slowly backed up, pulling Brian's truck forward until all its tires were back on the road. After thanking the men who had helped them, Brian carefully backed up the road to a point where it was wide enough for him to turn around and let the oncoming bus pass.

"Thank *God,*" said Bong as they moved forward.

"Is the truck okay? Can we keep going?" Alex asked, his guts feeling like one big knot. Bong turned to Brian and relayed the question; Brian shifted the gears and nodded his head in relief. Once there was enough space for the bus to pass, Brian said something to Bong, put the truck into park, and stepped out to catch his breath.

"I think he said he's driven down this road many times, and this was his first time to have a near-death accident," Bong said to Alex.

As the bus crept past them, Alex and Bong waved their hands to thank the men who had helped. All the passengers were standing and staring at them as they passed...and unexpectedly, Alex noticed the red-coated mystery person standing among them. As usual, Alex couldn't make out a face, because the hood shadowed everything underneath it. He could feel the person's eyes looking at him, though, and a shiver ran up his spine. It felt as if the watcher was looking straight into his soul. He pointed at the bus and asked Bong, "Do you see that person in the red hoodie?"

"Who?"

"That person there, with the red hood."

"Sorry," said Bong. "Too many people standing."

Alex could still see the stranger staring at him as the bus disappeared around the bend.

CHAPTER 5

It was dark by the time they neared their destination; the truck lights could barely reach the road's surface, because of a low-lying fog that had suddenly appeared. As they approached what seemed to be a house, more and more people began appearing along the sides of the road. Everyone was heading toward the same destination. Most were dressed in jeans and casual attire, and many were barefoot. Some carried bushels of flowers, while others carried food and porcelain jars.

Alex looked out the window as they drove slowly past the front entrance of the house to park the truck. Many people were gathered outside the front door talking to each other. Some were crying, while others seemed to be carrying on pleasant conversations, smiling and laughing. The front door was wide open, revealing a room crowded with people. A man saw them park, and approached them with curiosity. He looked closer until he finally recognized Brian behind the wheel, whereupon, with a big smile, he greeted Alex's *manong* in a fluid string of words.

"That's definitely not Ilocano," Bong said to Alex.

Alex said, "It might be Kankanaey." The words seemed vaguely familiar, like he could almost understand them.

After exchanging a few joyful words with Brian, the man smilingly ran toward the house to announce their arrival by shouting, *"Nakadanon da ed sina!"*

"What's he yelling?" asked Alex.

Bong shrugged. "I don't know a single word he said, but I'm pretty sure he's telling everyone that we're finally here."

The three exited the truck and began walking towards the house. Moments later, several men stepped outside, caught sight of them, and began moving towards them. As they approached, Alex realized that the tall man leading them looked very much like his father; he had to be one of Alex's uncles, and by his upright military bearing, he suspected he knew which. The man peered right back at Alex and called out, "Alex?"

"Uncle Pael?"

"Yes," replied the older man, as he reached out to embrace Alex.

Alex wasn't sure how to react, but something within him told him to go ahead and pretend that he was happy to see his uncle. He put on a smile and returned his uncle's hug. Just as he was about to release him, his uncle took another good look at him and gave him another big hug.

Pael looked much younger than Alex had expected, but his smile was almost identical to Alex's father's. He even had the same deep horizontal lines on his forehead. Immediately, Alex knew Pael was much like his father—another hard thinker. The name Pael was short for Raphael. From the things his father and Auntie Virgie had told him, Pael was the third of his brothers and sisters to leave the Mountain Province to earn a better living in Baguio, where he was respected by both Igorots and lowlanders alike.

After embracing Pael, something came over Alex. Even though he didn't know his uncle at all, he felt an immense sense of true happiness just knowing that he was back home with his relatives. The feeling didn't last more than a few seconds, though; the happiness faded into a vague apprehension when flashbacks of the agony his relatives had imposed upon his parents resurfaced. He recalled the many arguments between his father and mother regarding his father sending money to his siblings in the Philippines. It had always seemed that money was the direct cause of the discomfort between his parents and his relatives. For reasons unknown to him, their Filipino relatives never appreciated the hardships his parents had undergone in trying to raise a family in America.

Alex remembered vividly how difficult it had been for his parents to support the family, and all the sacrifices they'd made to put them through good schools. When he was in fourth grade, his father's business had been doing so badly that he'd had to file for bankruptcy; but even then, he managed to send small amounts of money to his relatives. Eventually, his parents just couldn't afford to send them any money at all. One day, his mother had cried because of something his relatives had told her; apparently, they were upset that his parents had sent them a box of hand-me-down clothes instead of *new* clothes. Ever since, Alex had thought of his relatives as selfish and mean.

"Welcome back home!" Uncle Pael said in the here-and-now.

It was the first time Alex had heard the Philippines referred to as his home. It sounded strange at first, but something in him liked how it sounded. Still, it was strange enough for him not know how to respond, so he just smiled.

Alex introduced Bong to his uncle, and then his uncle began introducing four of his cousins to them both. They all had Americanized names and spoke excellent English. After the introductions, Alex could see that there were many people in and around the house who looked eager to meet him, so he asked his uncle to introduce him to them.

"I will be more than happy to do so," replied Pael, "but first I need to say something to you in private." Alex nodded, so Pael pulled him aside for a moment. "I'm sure your Auntie Virgie told you what had happened to your lolo's body, correct?" asked his uncle.

"Yes sir. I still can't believe it," replied Alex.

"Well, it's true. I don't want you to be blindsided by this, but just be aware—there are those who do not want a Christian burial for your lolo, even though it was his wish."

"Who are these people you're referring to?"

"Let's just say that they're a branch of the family who still reject Christianity. Well, it doesn't matter now, because we found his body. Unfortunately, we found it almost three days after he passed on, so it was impossible to properly embalm him. We did what we could, but the decay had already set in. We brought him back here to your Uncle Wawak's house. His coffin is in the *sala* and people have been coming and going all day and night to pay their respects and pray over him. You will be staying here until the actual funeral, if that's acceptable to you?"

Alex was surprised to hear that the body was actually inside the house—he couldn't believe it wasn't at a funeral home. Maybe they didn't have one in Bontoc. He had strong reservations about sharing the same house with a corpse, but he didn't want to offend anyone, so he said, "Of course, no problem."

He followed his uncle and cousins inside the house, not knowing what to expect. As he entered the *sala*—the parlor—people immediately approached him. Pael began introducing him to relatives and friends. They greeted him with smiles, laughter, hugs, and kisses, as if he were a prodigal son finally returned home after a lifetime away.

He supposed he was, at that.

Alex couldn't keep up with all the names and how everyone was related to him, because they said so many things at once. While most of them spoke to him in English, their thick accents made it difficult for him to understand them. He tried his best to listen to each one of them, but the stink of embalming fluid overlying decaying flesh was too much of a distraction.

After meeting several dozen of his relatives, Alex excused himself and made his way quickly toward his lolo's coffin. Pael followed right behind him, quietly handing him a handkerchief as they approached. Grateful, Alex used the handkerchief to cover his mouth and nose and made sure to breathe through it as the smell quickly became almost too much for him to bear.

The coffin lay open, but a clear plastic sheet covered it to help minimize the smell. His lolo was dressed in a white *Barong Tagalog* shirt, which was the formal shirt of the lowlanders, while a red Igorot woven cloth covered him from the waist down. His complexion was so dark that his wrinkled skin looked black instead of its natural brown. A picture of him dressed in his native g-string, called a *wanes*, had been placed above him on the lid of the coffin. The picture showed him bearing a big smile on his face as he struck a native gong, or *gangsa*, while dancing.

Pael saw him looking at the picture and said, "That was taken 30 years ago, just after he returned from his last trip to America. You were still very young then."

"Oh, but I remember," replied Alex. "I never saw him dressed like this, but I certainly remember how he always smiled at me. He was a very happy man, and he made me laugh during that visit. Wow, I can't believe it's been more than 30 years since he visited us—and I still remember his face like it was yesterday." He looked down again at his lolo and thought, *It's hard to believe the man in this coffin is the same man. He looks nothing like his picture.* Life had clearly been hard on Santo in the past three decades, and the three days his body had spent unburied had been even harder.

Uncle Pael made the sign of the cross, and told Alex he would be towards the back of the room if he needed him. He then walked away, leaving Alex by himself at the coffin. Alex took another step closer and whispered, "Why am I here, lolo? What is it you wanted to give me?"

Just then, a cool breeze passed through the room, and Alex felt the presence of someone right behind him. He turned quickly, but saw nobody nearby. Chills ran up his spine, and the hairs on the back of his neck rose. He looked back down at his lolo suspiciously—and only then noticed a slight grin on the old man's leathery face. He felt the presence behind him again; and again, when he turned, he saw only his relatives and their neighbors across the room, sitting and quietly talking amongst themselves. He turned again to look at his lolo, and his eyes widened when he saw that the grin on the corpse's face had disappeared. Had it ever really been there?

Time to move on.

After a couple of hours spent talking with relatives and friends of relatives, Alex let out a big yawn. A moment later, Uncle Pael appeared before Alex with his bags, which he'd left by the door while socializing. "I think it's time you got some rest, nephew," Pael said, interrupting a conversation between Alex and one of his cousins. "Come on, I'll show you to your room." Alex smiled, made his goodbyes, and followed Pael up the stairs. Bong followed right behind, carrying his own bag.

As they entered a small room with two twin beds, Alex immediately noticed the miniature wooden shields and hand-carved replicas of battle axes mounted on the walls. The bed covers were made of red hand-woven native cloth, the same material he'd frequently seen people use as clothing and bags since leaving Baguio. After looking around the room, he immediately began opening the windows. "Ahh, that's better," said Bong. "I'm glad I'm not the only one who is bothered by the smell."

"I'm glad I don't have a full stomach," replied Alex. "Otherwise I'm sure I would have thrown up earlier."

One of Alex's aunts entered the room a moment later with fresh towels and sheets. She told Alex that people would be coming and going out all night and into the morning, and suggested they keep the door closed to minimize the noise so they could sleep better. Alex had already forgotten her name, to his chagrin, so he just called her "Auntie." Then he turned to Pael and asked him where the bathroom was located.

"You're lucky," said his uncle. "Here in Bauko, plumbing is a luxury that most people cannot afford, but your Uncle Wawak is one of the few who has an indoor toilet." He then smiled and laughingly said, "You're staying at a five-star luxury home tonight."

His auntie said primly, "If it is being used, you can use the outside C/R on the other side of where you parked, but take a flashlight with you, because the ground is very uneven. Okay?"

Alex thanked his auntie and uncle, and both he and Bong proceeded to the bathroom. When they got to the hallway, they found five people in line waiting to use the toilet. Upon seeing Alex and Bong walking toward them, those waiting offered to let them go ahead of them. Alex insisted that they stay in line, told them he could wait until later, and turned around to use the outside C/R.

They stepped out into the dark, and Bong turned on a small handheld flashlight he dug from a deep pocket of his cargo pants. Alex's auntie hadn't exaggerated in calling the ground uneven; they would surely have stumbled and fallen without the light's guidance.

Halfway to the C/R, an old man carrying a long machete appeared from nowhere and startled both of them. Bong's eyes fixated on the knife while Alex stared at the man's angry face. His eyes raged as he stared into Alex's and growled, *"Dakayo ay duwa egay kayo kuma ud immali! Adi kayo maibilang isna no iyali yo nan ugali din Amelika ya taga baba. Si alapo yo et kalebbengan na ay masulot nan kaugalian di Igorot isnan nay timpo na ay natey! No man nilayad na nan Amelika ya nan kaugalian na, naneng ay Igorot pay laeng siya. Sino kayo man ay umali isnan ili mi ta itdu yo din ugali yo?"*

Alex and Bong stepped back as the man stepped forward and unleashed his verbal assault. Unable to understand a word he said, Alex froze with fear and confusion as the old man sputtered unwelcoming words through his decaying teeth. When the old man finished, he spat on the ground and walked away, muttering sounds of disgust. "I...have no idea what that was about," Bong said, as he and Alex turned to each other in bewilderment. "But I think it is safe to say that not everyone around here is happy to see us, yes?"

Neither knew that the old native had said, "You should not have come here! You do not belong here with your American and lowland ways! Your lolo deserves to have a proper Igorot burial. He may have loved America and your ways, but he is still Igorot. Who are you to come here and impose your foreign ways on our people?"

59

Bong shone the flashlight on the old man as he walked away, while both stood scratching their heads for a long moment before resuming their search for the C/R. When they found it, Alex insisted on letting Bong go first. The smell was terrible, and reminded Alex of pig farms and sewage plants. A few seconds after Bong shut the rickety door behind him, he said aloud, "Wow, really old-fashion plumbing here. I hope you brought your own paper."

"Oh yeah, I learned my lesson at the airport," Alex replied, as he reached in his pocket for the wad of paper towel that he always kept with him now.

Bong handed Alex the flashlight, and told him he would meet him back at the house. "Don't you need the flashlight?" Alex asked.

"No, I'll just walk extra slow. Besides, my eyes have adjusted to the dark."

Alex opened the door and immediately heard grunting noises. He pointed the flashlight down the hole cut in the middle of the wood, and was astonished to see several large pigs jostling in a pit ten feet below the toilet. Alex immediately thought of leaving to use the indoor toilet, but necessity forced him to stay.

After stepping out of the C/R, Alex began walking quickly toward the lighted house, sweeping the flashlight beam before him. Suddenly, a strong breeze swept over him, and once again he felt the presence of someone nearby. He pointed the flashlight in all directions, but saw nobody, just tendrils of fog creeping in to surround him. What the hell was haunting him, and why? The feeling faded, and he quickened his pace.

Then he thought he heard someone calling out his name; and seconds later, he knew he did. At first it sounded like the voice was coming from his left, but then he heard his name being called from the opposite direction and then from behind him. The misty fog that had suddenly settled into the area made it difficult to see beyond ten feet or so. He stopped and pointed the flashlight in all directions. This time he saw someone through a break in the fog—a figure wearing a red hooded coat, standing and facing him. He twisted the head of the small flashlight, trying to focus the beam to get a better look. It seemed to be the same person who had appeared in his dreams and on the passing bus. Alex called out, "It's you from the bus. Who are you, and what do you want?"

He tried adjusting the beam again, but before he could get a better look, the person turned and disappeared into the mist. He was too scared to stray away from the trail to follow the mysterious person, so he hurried back to the house. When he got to the porch, Bong came up to him with a puzzled look on his face. "Are you okay? You look like you just saw a ghost. What were you looking for out there?"

"Did you see that man in red?" asked Alex, handing him the flashlight.

"What man? I just saw the flashlight beam moving around like you were looking for something."

"Did you at least hear someone calling my name?"

"No, but the winds up here tend to sound like people or animals. I remember stories about 'talking winds' in the mountains when I was a child. It's probably just that," Bong replied helpfully.

Not wanting to seem like he was imagining things or losing his mind, Alex just agreed with Bong and followed him back into the house. As he entered, one of his aunties noticed the look on his face and said something to Pael that caused his uncle and those around him to laugh. Pael called to Alex, "I forgot to tell you about our efficient plumbing system outside." Alex laughed along with them, pretending to be shocked at seeing pigs beneath a toilet.

On his way to the bedroom, Alex detoured to the casket to get one last look at his lolo. There were several people crowded around the coffin, so he sidled past to catch a glimpse of the old man...who seemed to be smiling again. Just after passing the casket, he caught a whiff of a floral scent carried on a light breeze that chilled him more than it should have. He looked around to see if anyone else had noticed it, but no one seemed to.

He was really beginning to wonder if he was losing his mind, or if he was just so damned tired that he was imagining things. It had been a helluva long day.

Upon entering their bedroom, Alex found a small twig the length of his hand, studded with small white flowers, lying on his pillow. He picked it up and sniffed; as he suspected, the flowers smelled just like the breeze that had wafted through the *sala* as he passed Lolo Santo's casket. "Did you put this on my pillow?" Alex asked Bong.

"No, but maybe your auntie did."

"I don't think so. She left the room before us, and I remember tossing the pillow on the sheets just before leaving the room,"

Bong picked it up, took a deep, appreciative sniff, and said, "I didn't know *samaguitas* grew up here. Maybe someone else from Manila is here too."

Alex thought about telling Bong about the fragrant breeze downstairs, but decided to keep it to himself. Instead, he asked him if it were possible that the flower grew in the mountains, but Bong didn't know for sure, and told him to ask one of his aunties the next day. Bong handed him the twig and went to bed. Alex did the same, but made no attempt to sleep. Instead, he lay on his back, examining the twig with his eyes and nose.

It didn't take long for Bong to fall asleep; his buzzing snore filled the room minutes after he said good night to Alex. As hard as Alex tried, though, he couldn't sleep. At first the snoring kept him awake, but then thoughts of his most recent encounter with his red-hooded friend preoccupied him. He knew he had to wake up early to get ready for Lolo's funeral, but just lay there with eyes wide, wondering what was going on. *Who was that person? Why does he keep appearing? Did Lolo really grin at me? Is there a ghost following me? How did the flower get on my pillow?*

Finally, after about two hours of wondering, his eyes closed and he fell into a much-needed sleep.

For once, no ghosts haunted his dreams. He awoke to the sounds of roosters crowing in the pre-dawn twilight, feeling he'd just gone to sleep moments before. He wanted to sleep longer, but knew he needed to get moving. He checked to see if Bong was awake, and saw that he was no longer in bed. He smelled food cooking and heard people talking downstairs, so he went to the bathroom to splash cold water on his face.

When he went downstairs, he found a few people still there from the night before, as well as others he didn't recognize. He glanced at the casket, and saw that it had been closed, and that people had stacked bouquets of flowers on top of it. One of his aunts saw him and called him over to the kitchen to eat breakfast, where he joined Bong and his relatives at the table. As he ate and listened to their conversation, he began wondering if he would ever meet the person who was suppose to give him his inheritance. So far, nobody had approached him as his lolo said they would in his last letter.

After breakfast, curiosity got the better of him, and he approached Pael, who was outside by himself smoking a cigarette. After some small talk, Alex casually brought up the subject of his lolo's inheritance: "Uncle, did Lolo Santo have a will when he died?"

Pael scratched his head and replied, "Actually, this has been a sore point among some family members. Your lolo left quite a bit of land to certain members of the family, and those who did not receive what they think is their fair share are very upset."

"Land? Is that all he left behind in his will?"

"Actually, no. The second part of his will has disappeared. Nobody knows where it went. Some feel your lolo purposely hid it because he didn't want to spoil anyone."

"I don't understand," replied Alex.

"Well, Father did a lot of travelling after your lola died many years ago, you know? He was a very smart man. In fact, he was one of the first Igorots ever to graduate from college—St. Louis University, with highest honors. He used his engineering and architectural education to make money overseas. Some of your aunties, uncles, and relatives complained about how he made so much money but didn't send enough back here to support them. But your lolo made it very clear that he didn't want us to rely on handouts. He didn't want to feed any laziness or complacency among our people. I'm thankful for this, because if it weren't for this belief, I myself might not have become a colonel. Who knows, I might not even have had the motivation to join the military."

"So you think there's money out there somewhere that lolo hid away?"

Pael smiled and replied, "I doubt it. Knowing him, he probably gave it to charities. He was also a big humanitarian. Big heart for those in desperate need."

With that said, Alex changed the subject so that his uncle wouldn't suspect anything. Later, he went back to his room to get ready for the funeral. While there, he kept thinking about what his uncle had said about hidden money, and how it was most likely the inheritance he was there to claim.

Shortly afterward, he heard the sounds of many voices downstairs. He quickly buttoned up the long white Barong Tagalog shirt his auntie had given him for the funeral. The shirt was white and somewhat see-through. He felt weird wearing white to a funeral, but just went along with it. As he walked out of his room, Bong stood down the hall with a big smile as he looked at Alex in his Barong. "You're supposed to leave it outside your pants," said Bong, as he pointed to Alex's tucked in Barong.

Embarrassed, Alex untucked his shirt. "Thanks," he muttered.

As he began walking down the stairs, he saw several men in blue military uniforms wearing white gloves enter the room. They picked up the casket and carried it outside as the rest of the people who had gathered in the room followed. Many of the women held handkerchiefs to their faces as they wept and lamented their loss.

Alex and Bong followed the crowd out to the dirt road in front of the house and up the road. Alex was surprised that everyone kept walking, and began looking around for a hearse, but saw none in sight. Before he knew it, the road was filled with hundreds of people. He looked ahead to see if there was a cemetery nearby, but saw no indication of one. Just as he was about to ask someone where the burial would take place, the crowd turned toward a nearby house, where the procession ended. He moved forward toward one of his aunties and asked her whose house it was. "This is your lolo's house, darling," she replied, smiling.

He was surprised to discover that his lolo was to be buried right in the backyard of his own home. His auntie took him by his hand and guided him closer to the casket. There was already another headstone there, marked with the name of his lola. Pael leaned over to Alex and said, "This is where your Lola Dolores is buried. Your lolo will be buried right next to her, as he requested."

The funeral lasted several hours, as each auntie, uncle, and close relative took turns giving some sort of speech of farewell to his lolo. Toward the end of the ceremony, the priest asked everyone to bow their heads as he began the closing prayers. In the middle of his prayers, Alex raised his head slightly and looked around at everyone praying. As he was about to lower his head again, he caught a flash of red beyond the trees. It was the annoying person in the red coat again! He quickly looked around to see if anyone else had seen him, but they still had their heads bowed. When he looked back toward the trees, he couldn't see the mysterious person anywhere.

After the funeral, everyone began walking back to Wawak's house for the reception. Alex stayed behind, pretending to pray some more; but instead of praying, he scanned the area with his eyes, looking for the figure in the red hooded coat. *Maybe he's the one who has my inheritance,* Alex reasoned. But after five minutes or so, he gave up his search and joined the last of the crowd on their way back to Wawak's. A moment later, a figure sidled up to Alex and introduced himself. "Hey man, how you doing? I'm one of your cousins, Gene. Your auntie Mona's oldest."

Alex turned and saw a young fellow in his late twenties, with long hair that hung down just below his shoulders. He had a much lighter complexion than the rest of Alex's relatives, and walked with a rhythmic sway, as if he were listening to music only he heard. His accent was unique, but sounded slightly familiar.

Alex shook his hand and replied, "Nice to meet you."

"So, how do you like the Philippines so far?"

"It's very different, but overall, I love it."

"Would you like to see some nice places tomorrow? I told Uncle Pael that I could show you around, since he has to be somewhere."

"Yeah, sure. What's there to see or do around here?"

"There's a very nice place in Sagada that I'm sure you'll like. I think your lolo would want you to visit—if you know what I mean."

Alex stopped in his tracks and said, "Oh—okay. I know exactly what you mean."

Gene smiled and immediately began walking away. As he did, he turned back and said, "I'll pick you up in the morning, okay?"

"See you then." *Finally*, he thought. He felt a thrill of excitement as he turned to walk back to the house. Thoughts of paying off his debts with the inheritance danced in his mind, and he even began entertaining thoughts of rehiring the people he'd laid off, then expanding and diversifying API. He'd wanted to do so for a long time, but couldn't because of the recent economic downturn.

By the time he'd returned to the house, Alex's newfound energy had worn off. One of his aunties noticed how tired he seemed, and suggested he take a nap while everyone prepared for that evening's feast. He gladly agreed and proceeded to his room. Once inside he lay down, closed his eyes, and continued thinking about what to do with the inheritance. The babble of voices grew louder as more people began filtering into the house. Even with the door shut, the noise was too loud for him. He turned to his side and clamped a pillow over his ear. That worked, muffling the noise to a bearable level. Slowly, his eyelids became heavier, and he found himself drifting into a deep sleep.

Midway into his sleep, he heard a muffled voice calling out to him: "Alex, Alex."

It sounded like someone had entered the room and was trying to wake him. He felt the presence of someone nearby, an eerie sensation that made him reluctant to open his eyes. Slowly, he lifted the pillow from his head, and turned to see who it was...but saw nobody around. This was starting to annoy him, but still he felt goose bumps as he surveyed the empty room. The door was still shut tight, and the windows were closed.

Even as the shivers went up his spine and the hairs on his arms stood at attention, Alex managed to convince himself that the sounds came from the people downstairs, and tried going back to sleep. But shortly after placing the pillow back over his ear, he heard the voice calling his name again. This time he flung the pillow off his head and immediately looked around, but still, nobody was there.

But what if they were under his bed?

By now, his apprehension had evolved into a frightened curiosity. As much as he was scared to look below, he couldn't stop himself from inching his body closer to the edge of the bed to investigate. Once at the edge, he slowly lowered his head to see if anyone was there. Sure enough, as soon as his visual field broke the plane of the mattress below, he saw someone in a red coat lying on their back, arms folded over each other, hands resting on their chest in the classic death pose.

Alex immediately sprang up, threw himself back against the wall, and snatched one of the wooden axes from its holder. "Who the hell are you, and how did you get in here!" Alex shouted as he brandished the axe. "Show yourself! What do you want, and why do you keep bothering me?"

The person responded by repeating his name : "Alex, Alex, Alex." Then they crawled out from under the bed and slowly stood, facing the direct sun coming in through a window, back toward Alex. His fear escalated, his heart pounding deafeningly in his ears. The person turned around, but the sunlight from behind and the long hood still made it impossible to see a face. Alex peered harder, but only saw darkness...but then a pair of yellow glowing eyes appeared in the darkness under the hood. The person reached out his arms and began walking straight toward Alex, like a Hollywood zombie preparing to choke him. Alex raised the axe, but before he knew it, a pair of hands was grabbing both shoulders, lightly shaking him.

"Alex, Alex, wake up. You're dreaming, man. Wake up," said a voice.

Alex opened his eyes and saw Bong's concerned face. He realized with a shock that, once again, he'd only dreamed of the person in red.

"You okay, Alex?" asked Bong. "I heard you yelling from the hallway, and came in to see what was going on."

"I was dreaming...right?"

"Yes, I guess you were. You've been sleeping for almost five hours. Come on now, join us outside. They made plenty of food, and all your relatives are waiting for you to join them in their *cañao*."

"What's a *cañao*?" he asked.

"I just learned the word myself," Bong replied proudly. "It's a party, a feast. Your uncle told me they are celebrating your lolo's life, and your homecoming after so many years away."

There's that word "home" again, Alex thought.

He stood up and followed Bong downstairs to join everyone else. The sounds of many voices, laughter, guitar playing, and singing filled the air. As he walked out the back door, people began clapping and cheering. Alex smiled, surprised, as Auntie Toring sat him down at one of the tables with several of his uncles and cousins. Pael picked up a large round earthen jar. On top of it were four loopholes connected to rope handles. The lid was made of hand woven reeds. Everyone smiled as it was set it on the table.

Pael dipped a small ladle into it and pulled out a scoop full of reddish dripping liquid. As he poured it into a glass, small grains of red rice accompanied it. He handed it to Alex with a big grin on his face. "This is *tapey*," said Pael. "It's better than beer."

"Try it," said Bong. "It's even better than the *lambanog* coconut wine we drink in Manila."

Everyone at the table already had cups filled with *tapey*, and raised them in a toast. Alex raised his cup, and waited for someone to say something. Wawak stood with his cup held high, and paused for a moment. "To Lolo Santo's life and Alex's return home!" he said aloud as he raised his cup higher.

The rest replied, "To Lolo and Alex," and then drank the *tapey*. This was the third time Alex had heard the Philippines referred to as his home, but this was the first time he actually felt like it was. He smiled and drank the homemade liquor. It was somewhat sweet, with a *sake*-like taste to it. He lifted his cup again, and drank the rest in several quick gulps. "That's good stuff," he said aloud. "Kinda tastes like Japanese *sake*, but better."

Wawak reached over to pick up Alex's cup for a refill. Alex smiled and thanked him by nodding his head. A lady then placed a large plate of food in front of him. He looked at the food with delight, and immediately began eating.

Both Bong and Alex were soon enjoying themselves a great deal. The smiles and laughter of Alex's relatives were so contagious that both found themselves having the time of their lives. At one point, Bong became very impressed with the closeness of Alex's family, and stood up to toast his appreciation for being allowed to share it with them. "Thank you for your hospitality," he said. "Here's to everyone here, and all the Igorots in this land!"

After they drank to the toast, Bong remained standing. Everyone could tell that he was already experiencing the effects of the *tapey,* and began giggling and laughing at him. He rolled his eyes into the back of his head trying to find something else to toast. Then he heard some of Alex's relatives shouting suggestions in Kankanaey and said loudly, "Here's to the most linguistic people I have ever met." Everyone laughed and drank from their cups. After gulping down his *tapey,* Bong sat back down.

Alex leaned over to him and asked, "What do you mean linguistic?"

Bong wrapped his arm around Alex's shoulder and explained how impressed he was to learn that most of Alex's relatives spoke four or five languages, among them Bontoc, Kankanaey, Ilocano, Tagalog, and English. Some even spoke other neighboring dialects. One of the men at the table listened to what Bong was telling Alex, and laughingly interjected, "You know, he even thought everyone living here in the mountains was Ifugao!"

Everyone laughed, including Bong. "I got another one for you," he said. "When I was a kid living in Manila, my parents told us stories of how Igorots were dangerous primitives who came into the city to kidnap kids. Every time Igorots came to dance in the streets for money, our folks came out to tell us to run inside the house, and we did."

The men weren't laughing anymore. They just smiled and listened to Bong's story. Immediately after Bong finished telling his story, Pael smiled, shook his head, looked up to the sky and said, "Lord, forgive the lowlanders, for they know not what they do," and then laughed out loud. Everyone followed suit.

After about an hour of eating and drinking, several of the men stood and picked up several flat, round metal instruments. Alex thought they looked like frying pans without the long handles attached. Their sizes varied from about a foot to a foot and a half in diameter, and they were all about two inches deep. They were bronze in color, and each featured a small, palm-size wooden handle attached by a long string.

With an instrument in his hand, Wawak leaned over to Alex and told him they were called *gangsas*. The men grabbed the handles in one hand and spun the *gangsas* so that they didn't dangle too loosely in their hands. Then they began hitting them with sticks to create a unique clanging sound. They formed a small circle facing each other as they continued hitting the little gongs. Within seconds, they had developed a uniform rhythm, and then started lifting their feet and bobbing their bodies to the beat of their music. They formed a line, and began proceeding in circles while playing their instruments and moving their bodies to the beat.

The sound had a somewhat primitive sound to it, but Alex found himself enjoying its melody. Soon, several of the women began dancing around the men, waving their hands in the air as if in surrender. Some had their fists closed with thumbs sticking out, as if they were making a "thumbs up" sign. Unexpectedly, several young ladies took him by the hands and pulled him up from his chair to join the group dance.

At first he was reluctant, because this was all too new for him, but as more people began clapping and cheering him on, he gave in and joined the rest in their circle. One of his aunties gave him a *gangsa*, and he began hitting it with a stick. At first, he found it difficult to stay in beat with the others, but soon he was playing in rhythm.

Alex lost himself in the fun of playing the instrument and following the rest in their dance steps. Then one of the men draped a red native cloth over Alex's shoulders. He didn't know what to do and looked over at his Uncle Pael, who also had a cloth draped over his shoulders, and imitated his moves. He raised his arms in the air while holding the cloth as if it were his wings, and danced. Then one of the pretty ladies approached Alex with her hands in the air. Again, he didn't know what to do, and looked over at Pael. The dance turned into a sort of courtship dance in which Alex was supposed to be a rooster, preening, strutting, and fluttering off the ground in attempts to gain the hen's interest.

Alex was all smiles by now. After noticing how much he was perspiring from all the fun, he gave the cloth to another man and sat back down to cool off and have a drink. Bong congratulated Alex on his dancing, patted him on the back, and handed him another glass of *tapey*. "This is the Igorot way of celebrating!" one of the men at the table said as he raised his glasses for another toast.

"To Igorot dancing!" said Alex.

After several more rounds of *tapey*, Alex picked up two *gangsas*, handed one to Bong, and both joined those still dancing. Many people took turns dancing with them, and every now and then, he stopped to pose for pictures. It was the most fun he'd ever had, and he didn't want it to end; but as the *cañao* approached the early morning hours, people began leaving to go back to their own homes.

By three o'clock in the morning, Alex was very drunk and barely able to stand on his own. Bong was already passed out at the table, along with several others. Alex stood up and began stumbling back to his room, but his Uncle Wawak saw him and caught up to him before he was able to leave. "Not yet, *ading.* First you have to get your *watwat,*" said Wawak, as he placed his arm around Alex's shoulder and turned him around.

"My what?" asked Alex.

"Your *watwat.*"

"That's what I mean. What's my what what?"

Wawak just laughed and walked him to one of the elders, who was sitting on his haunches cutting pieces of fatty pig meat from a carcass and handing it out to people who were leaving. Alex leaned against Wawak to keep himself from falling and watched the process. The recipients took the meat they were given and either stuffed it into their leather coat pockets or in their cowboy hats.

When it was Alex's turn, he drunkenly smiled and said, "To go, please."

The old man saw it was Alex and dropped the piece of cooked meat he was holding, reaching out to grab the last pig, which wasn't cooked yet. Wawak carefully sat Alex down onto a chair and helped the old man cut into the belly of the pig. It was Alex's first time to see an animal slaughtered. As the blood-drenched intestines spilled out, he felt a rush of vomit racing its way up his throat, but managed to hold it in. The old man reached into the bloody pig and cut off a piece of organ. He shook it several times to remove the excess blood before holding it up in the air toward Alex. "Special *watwat* for you," Wawak told Alex.

"Awesome!" he said, with a big uncertain smile on his face. Alex reached out, grabbed the raw meat, and held it up, saying, "My *watwat!*" Then he did as the others before him had done, and stuffed it into his shirt pocket.

Wawak laughed and helped him back up to his feet. "Time to sleep it off now," he said to Alex.

"Okay, uncle, but you got to tell me what the hell a *watwat* is and what I'm supposed to do with this piece of meat."

"Let's just say it's the equivalent of an American thank-you gift for attending, and yours was the most special. Come on now; let's get you to your room."

When Alex finally made it back to his room, he collapsed onto the bed and fell into a drunken sleep.

CHAPTER 6

Alex woke to glaring sunlight in his face. His head was pounding, and he felt very dehydrated. On any other day he would have stayed in bed, but he knew that Gene was on his way to pick him up. No hangover was going to stop him from getting his inheritance, so he rolled out of bed and went to take a quick bath.

When he stepped into the bathtub, he immediately noticed that there was no showerhead. An empty bucket underneath the faucet quickly reminded him of how he used to bathe as a child. He turned on the faucet and waited for the bucket to fill, then squatted and used a plastic cup to splash water over his head and body.

Once he was completely wet, he picked up a small bottle of bath soap and squirted some into the palm of his hand. He looked around for something to scrub his body, but only saw a small, smooth river rock. Again, flashbacks of bathing as a child entered his mind, and he picked up the stone and began scrubbing his body with it.

After bathing and changing into new clothes, he went downstairs to see if Gene had arrived yet. It was early, but there were several women already eating breakfast in the kitchen, his Auntie Toring among them. Upon seeing him, she invited him to join them. Apparently all the other men, including Bong, were still sleeping off their drunkenness. As he ate, Alex kept looking at the clock, wondering when Gene would arrive.

"Don't worry, Gene will be here soon," Auntie Toring said to Alex.

"Good. I was going to ask him last night what time we'd be leaving today, but he didn't come to the party."

"That's probably because he had to drive some of your cousins back to Baguio after the funeral."

Alex shuddered. "Ah. Now that's an exciting drive." As he watched Toring dunking her bread into her coffee, he asked, "So, how is Gene related to me again?"

She took a bite of her coffee-soaked bread and replied, "He is your first cousin. His mother, your Auntie Mona, is your father's youngest sister. He was one of your lolo's favorite grandsons, because he was always teased and picked on by other boys because of his light complexion. Your lolo took pity on him. Boys at his school used to tease him by telling him that he was not really an Igorot, and that his true father was some American that his mother had an affair with—which isn't true. His dad, your Uncle Badol, is FBI."

"FBI?" interrupted Alex, certain that it couldn't mean what he thought it did.

"Full-Blooded Igorot," replied Toring, as the other ladies smiled. "Gene was always getting into fights over it. Things got worse when he left the Mountain Province to go to school in the city. There, many kids made fun of him because he was an Igorot. They mocked his bowl-shaped haircut, his funny accent, and his inability to speak good Tagalog like the rest of the kids. They teased him the way we Igorots are always teased by telling him he had a tail, that he was stupid, backwards, and such.

"One day a boy made the mistake of cornering him and shouting to the kids crowded around them that his real dad was a drunken American who had a one-night stand with his mother. Like your *manong* Brian, this infuriated Gene so much that he pulled out a knife and threatened the boy. Fortunately, nobody got hurt that time—but needless to say, Gene never had another altercation with any of the lowland kids at that school."

Just then, Gene himself entered the house. His hair was a mess, and he wore dark sunglasses. Alex grinned, relieved; Gene smiled back, and swayed into the kitchen to join them. "Have you been up all night again?" Toring asked Gene.

Gene removed his sunglasses, kissed Toring on the cheek, and said, "Good morning to you, too, Auntie. I got back close to midnight, and then had a few drinks with friends. I would have stopped by for the big *cañao,* but I was tired from all that driving."

"You'd better eat, then, so you have energy for the day," said Toring.

Gene sat down as Toring brought him a plate and cup; meanwhile, he reached into his pocket for a rubber band and pulled his hair back into a ponytail. Toring looked at Alex and rolled her eyes while mimicking Gene. Alex and the ladies at the table smiled and chuckled at her poking fun at him. Gene just smiled, turned to Alex, and asked, "How was your big bash last night?"

Alex swallowed a mouthful of chocolate meat and replied, "Awesome!"

"Yah mon," said Gene. "It's like you're the long-lost celebrity who's come home after so many years. Righteous, mon."

Alex was intrigued with Gene's mannerisms. He began to wonder where Gene had picked up his strange accent, which sounded like some mixture of the local argot with a slight reggae influence. He also noticed that Gene wore up-to-date, trendy jeans. "You okay to drive?" he asked.

With a big smile, Gene replied, "Yah, don't worry, I got my three hours of sleep."

Unsure whether to take him seriously or not, Alex just said, "Good to know."

Gene noted that Alex was finished eating, and gulped down the rest of his coffee. He stood up and told Alex that they should leave before it got too late; both thanked Toring and the rest of the ladies, and left in Gene's topless jeep.

The bumpy road played havoc on Alex's head as Gene drove them to the neighboring village of Sagada. On their way, they picked up two of Gene's friends, who had been up all night drinking with Gene. Unlike Gene, they showed clear signs of being hungover...especially the one who vomited over the side just after boarding the jeep.

Gene introduced them as Rodney and Sammy, brothers who had grown up with him. Like him, he explained, they'd also been teased a lot as children—not because of their skin color, but because they were smaller and skinnier than the rest of the kids. It didn't help that they were also dyslexic and did poorly in school. They'd hung around with Gene because none of the other kids wanted to play with them, and the resulting bond they'd formed had kept them together ever since.

They immediately began engaging Alex in conversation about life in America—American women in particular. Alex was glad to provide answers. "Is it true most of the women have booby jobs?" Rodney asked.

"Booby jobs?"

"You know, fake boobies like the Baywatch girls," interjected Sammy.

"Oh, yeah . . . yeah, I guess a lot do have implants," laughed Alex, "but I wouldn't say most."

After almost a half hour of such questions, the brother's hangovers got the best of them and they closed their eyes and leaned their heads back to sleep. Alex sat in the back of the jeep, enjoying the fresh air blowing around him while looking out onto the splendor of the surrounding mountains. The weather was perfect for travelling, infinitely more pleasant than that of Manila. The temperature, humidity and air quality were all much better, and Alex found himself liking the Cordillera much more than any other place he had ever been. "We're almost there mon," Gene said presently. "Only about fifteen more minutes."

"Great, but what exactly are we seeing in Sagada?"

"Bomod-ok waterfalls, and the famous historic caves."

The sound of cascading water became audible as they approached their destination. Soon Gene parked the jeep, jumped out, and handed Rodney and Sammy their backpacks. Alex grabbed his own small shoulder bag, which contained his camera and camcorder, and followed the three down a beaten path through a small patch of banana trees. Midway through the trees, Sammy stopped and cut down a four-foot length of banana stalk with his pocket knife.

They came to a narrow stream lined with boulders and followed it a short distance, until they reached the waterfall. Alex stopped momentarily to marvel at his surroundings. The water cascaded from about two hundred feet above, and made a contrasting white silhouette in front of the green, rocky face of the fall. They proceeded forward and climbed a large, partially moss-faced boulder where they sat for lunch.

Gene opened his backpack and took out containers of food that his mother had prepared for them that day. Sammy pulled out his knife and cut the banana stalk into four equal pieces. Rodney took a piece and began placing rice, meat and vegetables on it. After handing it to Alex, Gene watched as Alex began eating with his hands. "Dude, you don't need a spoon or fork? Do you eat like this at home?" asked Gene.

"No, this is only my fourth day eating with my hands. How am I doing?"

"Righteous, mon. You learn quickly. Very good," chuckled Gene.

An occasional spray of mist blew over them from the falls twenty feet away, but it didn't bother Alex. As he ate, he stared at the waterfall, and soon closed his eyes to listen to the roar that filled the air. He felt at peace sitting there, as his hangover seemed to dissipate into thin air. Gene began telling Alex stories about how Bomod-ok was their lolo's favorite place to visit. Every time Gene, Sammy, or Rodney saw Lolo Santo approaching their houses, they became very excited, because they knew he would be taking them there for lunch, fun, and relaxation. This used to happen at least once a month, before his lolo became too old to walk up the hill and climb the rocks.

After finishing lunch, Gene started talking to Rodney and Sammy in Kankanaey. Alex had no idea what they were saying, so he just continued taking in his surroundings. Shortly into their conversation, Alex noticed Rodney and Sammy turning their heads toward him as they talked. He realized they were talking about him, and started paying attention to their vocal inflections and body movements while pretending to take no interest in what they were saying.

Each time the word *"insan"* came up, Rodney and Sammy looked at him. Then it began sounding like Gene was giving Rodney and Sammy some sort of instructions, given the way they were listening intently and nodding. Alex thought it sounded like they were planning something, and didn't want him to know about it. Alex began to suspect that they were talking about his lolo's inheritance. Suddenly, he wasn't sure if the three had good intentions after all—or whether Gene was actually the person his lolo had referred to in his letter. Worried thoughts began to run through his mind. *What if they're here to steal my inheritance? Should I trust them?* Cousin or not, Alex knew how money could make people do stupid things. His imagination ran wild as he entertained the possibility that they had plans to rob him later.

After conversing amongst themselves, they re-packed their backpacks and began heading back to the jeep. This time Alex kept his guard up and let the three walk ahead of him, just in case he needed to get away for some reason. He picked up a sharp piece of stone and put it in his camera bag just in case he needed to protect himself. As they walked back to the jeep, Rodney and Sammy periodically turned around to see if Alex was still there. Alex felt deeply suspicious about their behavior ,and kept his distance.

They drove a short distance and soon arrived at the caves. As Alex cautiously followed them toward the entrance, he studied the unusual appearance of the mountain. Its green sides had sharp grayish stones peeking above the vegetation; they almost looked like spider webs at a distance. As they approached it, Gene stopped and turned to wait for Alex to catch up while the other two kept walking.

Alex put his hand into his bag and clutched the sharp stone as he continued walking toward Gene. When he had nearly reached him, Gene turned, continued walking, and began describing to Alex how people there used to hang the caskets of their dead in the air, and how there were many caskets stacked inside the caves even today. Then he began talking about the intricacies of the coffins and how they were made of tree logs. "Mon," said Gene, "Sometimes the hollow spaces in the logs were so narrow that people had to break the bones of the body to make it fit."

By now, Alex was becoming concerned about his safety. *Why is he telling me all this?* he wondered. *Does this burial ground have something to do with me? There are three of them and only me. What should I do?* He kept his face expressionless, not showing any signs of his incipient panic; instead, he pretended to be amazed at the scenery, and slowed down to give himself a little more distance in case he needed to run.

When they arrived at an opening of a large cave, the three Filipinos took off their backpacks and set them down. Still keeping his distance, Alex called out, "Now what?" Gene smiled and approached Alex, carrying something in his hand. Alex slowly reached into his camera bag again, clutching the sharp stone. As he approached Alex, Gene opened the leather pouch he was holding and pulled out a folded piece of paper.

Alex let out a silent sigh of relief as he watched Gene unfold it. "Actually, Alex, I didn't bring you here just to sightsee," said Gene. "I promised Lolo Santo something."

Still clutching the stone, Alex responded, "What was that?"

"I promised him that I would bring you here and give you this map. You see, he left you something, and this map will take you to it."

"Why here, and why the secrecy?"

Gene looked into Alex's eyes and said, "This is where he hid something years ago. When we were kids, we helped him hide it, and swore not to tell anyone. It's a box, but I don't know what's in it. There were times I wanted to find out...and in fact, we tried to find it about ten years ago, but couldn't remember where it was. It's like a labyrinth in there. You need a map, or you can get lost for days. I eventually told Lolo about our attempt, and he forgave us. We never tried again. I guess he knew we could keep a secret after that, and he was right, because for all these years we never told anyone...until now."

Alex's fear subsided, his gut feeling telling him that Gene could be trusted. He unfolded the aged paper and began trying to decipher the map. Gene told him that recent rains had flooded certain areas of the caves, and that they would need to accompany him three-fourths of the way or so to make sure he didn't get lost. He also told Alex he needed to leave his bag behind and strip down to his underwear, because they'd have do some swimming. Alex was reluctant to disrobe, but did when they did. Gene sealed the map in a plastic bag, replaced it in the leather pouch, and tied it around his wrist.

The four made their way into the large opening, which sloped downward at a sharp angle. About twenty feet in, Alex stopped and looked up at the brightly lit entrance above, then proceeded to follow Gene. The walls of the cave were made of a type of stone that reminded him of the stalagmite- and stalactite-laden caves he'd visited in Tennessee as a child. Small waterfalls cascaded down the walls and into the little knee-deep stream they were splashing through. Surprisingly, enough natural light made its way in through various crevices and cracks to see almost everything around them.

Alex was soon wading through waist-deep water as they passed slippery narrow passages, vaulted chambers, mineral-rich waterfalls, and spectacular rock formations. They came to an apparent dead end and stopped momentarily. Gene checked the map, frowning. "Yeah, we're still on course," he said. "The water has risen here, so we'll need to swim through a short passage to get to the other side of this wall."

After packing away the map, Gene took a deep breath and went first; Rodney and Sammy followed. Alex looked around for another way, but saw no other openings, so he took a deep breath and submerged. The water was amazingly clear, and he could see the way ahead with no problem. Seconds later, he surfaced and stood up in chin-deep water.

As they moved forward, the water level eventually went back down to their waists. They came to a second dead end before long, and Gene was certain they needed to swim under again to reach the other side; so without looking at the map, he dove and began swimming. The three followed, with Alex again trailing.

This time the water was darker, because there wasn't as much natural light as before. Alex felt himself struggling to hold his breath, and started worrying about how much longer they needed to swim. For a split second he thought about turning around, but kept swimming with a greater sense of urgency. Just when he thought he couldn't hold his breath anymore, his hands rubbed the bottom and he looked up to see weak sunlight. He broke the surface gasping for air; the other three were treading water, trying to catch their breaths as well. "Wow, that was a little longer than I expected," said Gene.

Rodney and Sammy laughed and splashed water at him, then swam toward the far wall until they were able to touch the ground with their feet, and walk up a gradual incline. The visibility quickly worsened, so they proceeded deeper into the cave at a much slower pace. "It's all uphill from here," said Gene, as they climbed slowly upward.

They reached the top of the incline and wriggled through a very narrow opening; it was so narrow that they had to inch sideways to get through. After about thirty feet of that, the passage opened up to a large cavity lit by a lot more daylight from apertures a hundred feet above. There were five small openings in the wall, which all led to different passages. "This is where we'll wait for you, cuz," Gene said.

"So how far is the box from here?" asked Alex.

"You're maybe ten or fifteen minutes away. Just follow the turns shown on the map, and you won't get lost."

Alex entered the passageway indicated on the map, and began following the directions indicated. The map wasn't to scale, so the distances between turns were longer than he expected. After almost a half hour of following the trail, Alex began to wonder if he'd taken a wrong turn at some point. Rather than turn around, though, he proceeded until he reached the fork in the passageway marked with an "X" on the map.

He looked around, but didn't see any anything resembling a box. He walked about twenty feet down both passageways, but still didn't see it. Now certain he'd taken a wrong turn somewhere, he'd just turned around to make his way back to Gene and his friends when he noticed a small niche in the wall above.

It was several feet too high for him to look inside, and there wasn't anything around that he could use to stand or climb on. He made several attempts by jumping as high as he could, but still came a foot or two short. Then he remembered climbing the unusually narrow hallways of his house in the Philippines as a kid, by the simple expedient of leaning his back against one side of the hall while using his feet and legs on the other side to push his body up. Would that work here...?

It was much harder than he remembered, but he eventually managed to scoot his way up the walls of the narrow passageway. When he reached the niche, he turned his head around as much as possible until he saw, from the corner of his eye, the silhouette of a small rectangular object. Aha! With his legs and back firmly anchored, Alex carefully stretched both arms behind his head, grabbed the box, and slowly shimmied his way back down to the floor of the passage, excitement thrumming through him.

The box was made of very hard wood, and weighed less than ten pounds. Alex's initial hopes of a box filled with gold were crushed when he realized it was far too light to be filled with any coins or metals of any kind. His hopes rekindled as his mind began entertaining thoughts of paper currency, stock certificates, or other light objects of great value. Eager to see its contents, he placed his fingers inside the horizontal creases and slowly pried the tight lid off.

Lying inside was some sort of a cloth blanket. His anticipation mounted; he knew it must have been there to keep the contents dry and safe. But the bright light of hope in his eyes darkened when he pulled it out and saw nothing underneath. *It must be inside the cloth,* he thought, as his eyes lit up again. Realizing that the contents could be very old and fragile, Alex unfolded the cloth with great care. His eyes filled with disappointment when he opened the last fold to reveal nothing but the cloth itself.

"What the hell!" he shouted. "This can't be *it.* I came all the way to the Philippines for a stupid old blanket?!"

He threw the cloth aside and sat down on his haunches with his hands clasped above his head, thumbs resting on the crown of his skull. The anger swelled up inside him as he thought of his financial problems back home. He looked at the cloth again, and began wondering if it might be some sort of ancient relic worth a fortune. He quickly picked it up and began examining it.

By then, his eyes had adapted to the dimness, and he was able to see that the cloth appeared to be very old, and was definitely hand-woven. It was still too dark for him to be sure of its colors, but he knew by the shading that there were at least three different ones. As he examined it, he also discerned peculiar embroidered images along the edges. Most were unrecognizable. The only ones that seemed familiar were the images of what he thought looked like a snake and person. After examining its entirety, he held it out in front of him. It was a little longer than him, and about three feet wide. Not much of a treasure. "These must be some sort of ancient symbols. This has to be worth something," he muttered. "Otherwise, lolo wouldn't have gone through all that trouble."

Just then, a cold breeze swept through the tunnel. Goose bumps sprang up on his arms, and he found himself shivering from a dramatic drop in temperature. Still somewhat wet, he instinctively wrapped the cloth around his shoulders to help keep him warm. As soon as the cloth covered him, he felt an unusual warmth emanating from it. He looked down, and saw that the images along the edges seemed to be glowing in the dark. Within seconds, he was sure of it; the glow brightened into a fire-like blaze—and the symbols began moving, as if they were alive. Alex closed his eyes and blinked several times, because he couldn't believe what he was seeing.

Another blast of wind filled the tunnel; it kept coming, increasing in speed. Before he knew it, a funnel of wind surrounded him, like a tightly-contained tornado, swirling around him so hard that the blanket was whisked off his shoulders. But instead of disappearing into the vortex, the blanket began slowly circling him in the opposite direction. The bright symbols grew larger with each passage, until they finally leapt off the blanket and hung in the air around him while the blanket and winds kept spinning.

The symbols transformed into clear, burning images twice his size. Around him floated a lizard, a snake, an eye, a shield, a spear, a star, and a human figure. The eye grew larger, while the other figures remained the same size. His pulse quickened in his ears as the eye slowly floated toward him. Unable to move his legs, Alex leaned backward and closed his eyes as it approached. He could feel the heat radiating from the eye, but was too afraid to look at it directly. Soon, however, the fear vanished; the only thing that remained was his curiosity. Alex slowly opened his eyes and found himself staring straight into the glowing eye, which hung inches from his face. Filled with awe and curiosity, he slowly raised his hand to touch it.

His hand passed right through the eye. Alex cringed as a loud explosion crashed in his head; a burst of air, accompanied with an intense bright light, shot out of the eye, seeming to light up the entire mountain from within. Except for the eye, the symbols disappeared into the vortex as the loud rumbling sound of rushing water filled the air. The temperature in the cave plunged twenty more degrees, and the clean smell of fresh water filled his nostrils.

With the eye still floating next to him, Alex slowly walked toward the rumbling, as if in a dream; he wasn't surprised when a wall of water surged around the bend in the narrow passage and slammed him against the side of the corridor, knocking the wind out of him. A half-second later the tunnel was filled to the top with water, leaving him no air to breathe. He turned desperately in all directions, looking for any openings or signs of air. Unable to see any, he scrambled towards the ceiling and began clawing at the stone in search of something to breathe, but to no avail. He knew he couldn't hold his breath much longer, and helplessly looked at the glowing eye.

Then the bubbles of his last breath floated past his eyes, as everything went dark and a feeling of weightlessness came over him.

The darkness gave way to light suddenly, and he found himself floating within the mountain. He looked down and saw the tunnel he'd just been in, and realized the water had receded. He stared at his lifeless body laying unconscious on the ground, the blanket next to him. Gene, Rodney, and Sammy suddenly appeared, flashlights bobbing in the dimness before their beams converged on his body. Gene ran to his side, fell to his knees, and rolled Alex onto his back, then bent over as if to hear whether he was breathing. He shook his head, and Rodney immediately began pushing down on Alex's chest and counting. "Hey, it's me!" Alex shouted from above. "Can't you hear me?" They continued as if he weren't there at all; clearly, they *didn't* hear him.

Alex wanted to drift down and touch them, but felt himself suddenly yanked away. Within a split second he had floated through the wall and outside the mountain, and found himself speeding away into the sky, at lightning-like speed. When he turned around, Alex found himself in a dark place. There was no sense of speed, until a bright light appeared in the distance and he found himself moving rapidly toward it. He'd never seen or felt anything like it before. The transparent white light was surrounded by buttery yellow rays of the brightest and purest color he'd ever experienced. Surprisingly, despite the brightness, it didn't bother his eyes a bit. An awesome feeling of love and compassion radiated from the white light; and as he approached, images and silhouettes of people began appearing all around him. They all seemed to know him, but he was unable to recognize any of them, because he was moving along so fast.

Just when he thought he was about to enter the light, he took a sharp turn into a blinding vortex, where he suddenly regained his sense of gravity as he spun, moving so fast that he became dizzy and lost his breath. His spot-filled eyes stung as he sped through the windy tunnel of light. Loud, breathy voices echoed in his ears. They kept asking him, "Who are you? Do you know who you are? Why are you here?"

A sudden blast of air filled his lungs, and all the light and voices disappeared. He opened his eyes and found himself standing on bare dirt. His head involuntarily turned to the side, and he discovered he was standing in a clearing surrounded by trees and lush undergrowth. Still feeling dizzy and disoriented, Alex tried moving, but couldn't.

For a long moment, the total loss of feeling and inability to move made him think he'd somehow become paralyzed.

Then his right hand moved on its own, appearing in front of his face. As it began, embarrassingly, to pick his nose, he was shocked to see how small and dark his arm and hand were. His hand dropped and his body began walking on its own, eyes focused on a break in the trees ahead. Sensation came roaring back as he walked, to his enormous relief, but he was still unable to control his movements.

When his head glanced down to check the trail, he saw that his body was that of a teenage boy—a practically naked one. Apparently, the only clothing he wore was a small loincloth that covered his genitals . He wanted to pinch himself to see if he was dreaming, but his body wouldn't answer his mind's demands. Struggling to make sense of what was happening, Alex finally reached the realization that he was mentally himself, but physically someone else. Somehow. *Obviously, I'm dreaming again,* he thought. *Wake up now, Alex. Wake up!*

His body just kept walking.

Is this really happening? he wandered. It certainly felt real when the boy stepped on something sharp and grumbled as he hopped away, then stopped to dig a thorn out of the sole of his foot. Maybe he could communicate...? *Hello!* he shouted mentally.

His body stopped in its tracks and peered upward. While the boy's eyes watched several chicken-like birds flap by overhead, Alex immediately noticed a large patch of white light in the sky above him. It looked like the same light he'd headed toward before he found himself in the vortex that brought him to where he was now. The boy paid no attention to it, though it was readily visible; his eyes were focused on the birds.

Something clicked as his senses suddenly connected with the those of the boy he occupied, and he realized the kid didn't even see the white light. *What the hell?*

A woman's voice caught both the boy's and Alex's attention. "*Fanusan, Fanusan, ay innungnong mo nan kokolang?*" she called out, and her voice sounded so much like his dead mother's that Alex's thought, for one heartbreaking moment, that it might be hers.

Alex didn't understand a word she said, but the boy turned around immediately, and Alex saw a woman standing outside a strange-looking house built of stone and wood, with a baby tied to her back with a woven blanket. She wasn't his mother, but she *was* the boy's. She repeated the same words to him; he heard the words emerge from her mouth in the same language, but his mind automatically translated them into English: "Fanusan, did you check the trap yet?"

The boy replied, "*Inungnong ko et edwani.*" Alex couldn't believe he'd just spoken another language—but he had. He'd told her in a respectful tone that he would go check the trap now. She told him to hurry, so he turned and began running into the woods.

If this isn't a dream, then what the hell is going on? Alex wondered. *The kid is obviously named Fanusan, and their language sounds like Kankanaey. Are these my distant ancestors?*

Fanusan slowed as he entered the narrow path that led into the forest. About ten feet down the path was some sort of wooden, square-framed contraption that stood a couple of feet high; in the middle of the square was a wild chicken-like bird that looked just like the ones that had flown over moments ago. The bird struggled to escape, but the cinch around its neck was too tight. Without hesitation, Fanusan grabbed the bird by its neck and removed the snare. Then he picked it up by its feet and walked back to the clearing as the bird fluttered its wings and squawked, trying to escape. Instead of bringing it to the woman, he took it instead to a man waiting for him next to a small open fire.

Without a word, he handed the chicken to the man—his father?—and watched the man put one of its wings on a flat piece of wood lying on the ground. He picked up a stick and began beating it from the inside tip of the wing back toward the bird's body, while his other hand held the head and other wing to keep it from escaping. Fanusan just stood and watched, though Alex found the action needlessly cruel. He wanted to tell the man to stop; but all he could do was watch.

 Once Fanusan's father had beaten the bird's wing from the tip to its side, he did the same to the other. Finally, he laid the animal's neck sideways on the block and handed the stick to Fanusan. Again, Alex wished he had control over the boy, but he remained a helpless passenger. Fanusan accepted the stick and began using quick blows to beat the bird from end to end as its squawking began to die down. After a while, the chicken showed very little signs of struggle. That's when the man took over, holding the chicken's feet and wings in one hand while killing it with one blow to the back of its head with the wooden handle of an axe.

The man put down the axe, picked up a knife, and removed the beak, tongue and crest of the chicken. He handed the bird to Fanusan, who then held it over the fire and began singeing all the feathers off. After they'd crisped and fallen away, he brought the smelly charred bird to the woman and handed it to her. In her native language, she said, "Thank you, Fanusan. You are getting better at preparing the *pinikpikan*." Again, Alex was amazed that he understood everything she said.

Fanusan smiled and replied in his language, "Thanks. I'll get the *etag*." As he said this, Alex learned that *etag* was the smoked flesh of a pig. He ran to fetch the plate of salted smoked pork his parents had prepared earlier.

CHAPTER 7

Though Alex had absolutely no control over his new body, he soon realized that he could tap the boy's knowledge and memory if he concentrated. As Fanusan went about taking care of his daily chores, he learned that he was a sixteen-year-old Igorot boy living in the village of Bontoc, located high up the Cordillera Mountains of northern Luzon in the Philippines. A few years back, a strangely pale missionary had told him that it was the Year of Our Lord 1781, though precisely what a lord was and why he had years named after him, especially so many, made little sense to Fanusan.

He'd also learned from the missionary that the first explorer had planted the Spanish flag on Philippine soil in 1571, and since that time the Spaniards had conquered the lowlands a piece at a time. Alex, who had a good grasp of history, realized that they'd done it much the same way Cortés had conquered Mexico: with swift attacks, using steel arms and armor against the natives' primitive stone, bone, and wood. During their conquest, military outposts had been established throughout the lowlands, and Christian missions were built for Augustinian and Dominican clergy.

The Spanish clergy had already converted most of the lowland Filipinos, but were eager to convert the Igorots as well. No doubt they honestly believed the Igorots would be better off in a progressive Christian world than wandering naked through the mountains, with neither king nor master to look after them. The Spaniards were also very interested in the gold mines located in the mountains—as just compensation for civilizing the Igorots, of course, while supporting their church and state.

By this time, the Spaniards already had Christian missions along the lowlands that bordered the Igorot lands. Attempts to establish missions within Igorot territories had failed, none lasting more than ten years because the Igorots just didn't want them. Needless to say, the social interactions between the Spaniards, lowlanders, and Igorots were marked with constant tension and ambivalence.

Things were tense in part because of the Spaniards' desire to control all trading and commerce between the three groups. Worse, some Spaniards were taking lowland Filipinos and Igorots as slaves, and Spaniards favored their Filipino-Spanish subjects who were loyal to Spain, "protecting" them from those who were not. So although trading did take place between the Igorots, Spaniards, and their subjects, fighting was also common. The Igorots of Benguet, for example, had recently fought off the Spaniards who were trying to seize their gold mines.

Matters were made even more complicated by the fact that some lowlanders allied with the Spaniards against the Igorots, while others allied with Igorots against the Spaniards. While all this was taking place, the people of Fanusan's village went about their normal lives, mostly unaffected by what was going on below.

Once the chicken had finished cooking, Fanusan's mother called out to him, urging him to come inside to eat. As he began walking toward her, Alex considered the house that stood behind her. Its high rectangular grass roof stood approximately twenty feet above the ground;

its top dimension was a seven by seven foot square that flared down and widened to a fifteen by twelve foot bottom. Below the roof were seven-foot walls. The back wall was made of stone, the others of wooden boards. Surrounding the house was a low bamboo fence with an assortment of pig, carabao, and dog skulls hanging on it. Apparently a carabao was something like a water buffalo, or at least that's the image that came to Alex's mind when he saw the skulls.

As he approached the entrance, he noticed that bare, hard-packed ground served as the floor. The entrance was an unobstructed aisle that led to the various compartments of the house. The first room on his left was used to thresh rice. Next to that was a small kitchen. A little further down was a ladder leading to the second and third floors, which were used for storage.

The absence of windows made the room very dark; the only light came from a smoke hole high in the ceiling. At first he couldn't see anything except the ambers of a banked fire. Eventually, his eyes adapted, and he saw how devoid of furnishings the place seemed. Along one side was an assortment of pots, jars and wooden plates. Along another was a collection of woven blankets—blankets very like his lolo's legacy.

He crouched on the floor next to the woman, and tickled the baby tied to her back. Next to her sat the man who had butchered the chicken, and a girl of about ten. He didn't know any of their names—for some reason those were blocked to him—but knew they were Fanusan's family. Like him, his father wore only a loincloth covering his genitals; his mother and sister wore narrow woven skirts, leaving everything else exposed.

As they sat around the fire on their haunches, Alex peered at the food and immediately began wondering how so little of it could feed everyone. There was a small pot that contained the chicken and soup, a small bowl of rice, and another bowl of cooked *camote* leaves. It seemed like a meal for two at most, not four. A part of him was so hungry he wanted to grab the rice and meat and eat it all before the rest got to it, but he could do nothing, because Fanusan was content to eat his equal share.

Midway into his meal, Alex realized that the last time he'd sat down at a family meal was probably when he was Fanusan's age. As simple as it seemed to him, eating with Fanusan's family felt good, because it brought back fond childhood memories of gathering around the kitchen table. As busy as Alex's father was with his work, they always made it a point to eat at least one meal each day with everyone at the table. The discussions, laughter, and arguments that occurred through the years were a source of comfort that Alex hadn't experienced for far too long. He hadn't realized, until now, how much he had missed it all.

By the time they finished their meal, darkness was falling, so Fanusan and his sister left the house and began walking to separate places to sleep. Alex didn't understand why the children slept in separate buildings. Fanusan went to the *fawi,* where the young unmarried boys slept. His sister joined the rest of the village's unmarried girls at the *olag.*

The *fawi* was a small structure about eight by twelve feet in size, with low stone walls and a grass roof. It was used as a dormitory for unmarried males during the evening and as a community hall where meetings and celebrations took place during the day. When Fanusan entered, Alex was shocked to see a basket of human skulls hanging in one corner. He wanted to believe they were fake, but knew they were real. Unfortunately for Alex, Fanusan lay down directly underneath it. As he lay on his back, Fanusan stared up at the ceiling, forcing Alex to see the grinning skulls whether he wanted to or not. Alex wanted to roll on his side or close his eyes, but Fanusan remained on his back with his eyes wide open for quite some time.

Finally, to Alex's relief, Fanusan's eyes began to close.

The following day began early, as Fanusan woke up well before dawn. Yawning, he went outside and sat on the ground, waiting for the sun to rise. As he sat, he saw his father busy feeding the pigs and preparing their breakfast. Upon seeing that a fire was not yet lit, Fanusan ran towards the firepit. Making fire was something his father had recently taught him, and he took every opportunity he could to practice.

His father saw him approaching, and gestured for him to proceed with making the fire. Grinning, Fanusan picked up two pieces of dry bamboo. One of the pieces had notches cut into the sides, and the other was shaped like a chisel. He laid the notched piece onto the ground and held the chisel-like piece in both hands. Slowly, he began rubbing the chisel-shaped piece on the stationary piece. After about a dozen strokes, a smoky tang filled the air from the friction. After a hundred more stokes, a tiny friction- fired particle fell onto the tiny cone of charred dust already created by the friction of his efforts. As soon as he saw the bright little spark, Fanusan picked up some dry grass and touched it to the cone of fire dust until the grass caught. He smiled proudly, and proceeded to add small pieces of wood to his little cooking fire.

Several hours later, his sister returned from the *olag* with a hungry look on her face. His mother also appeared, with his baby brother strapped to her chest in a traditional carrying blanket. As she moved around, the infant suckled milk from her breast. They eventually gathered around several wooden plates that were placed on the bare ground near the fire. On the plates were the hot rice, *camote* roots, and salted pork that his father had prepared that morning. They sat on their haunches and began eating with their hands.

After breakfast, Fanusan's mother strapped the baby on her daughter's back, and both headed for the rice fields to work. Alex found it interesting to see other young girls and boys walking around with their little brothers or sisters strapped to their backs. He couldn't imagine this taking place in America. Fanusan and a few other boys followed the women and girls to the rice fields with their seven-foot-long *kalibs,* or bird brooms.

When they arrived there were no birds in sight, so Fanusan and the rest of the boys just sat on their haunches and waited patiently. As they sat, Alex watched the rice farming activities taking place nearby. There were several groups working the fields; two groups were turning the soil, while another transplanted young rice seedlings. Fanusan's mother was working with the group standing in ankle-deep muddy water turning the soil. The women only wore loose skirts, while most of the boys and girls were naked. Some of the girls, including Fanusan's sister, wore clumps of *camote* leaves to cover their genitals.

The women struck the earth with their long thick sticks and then trampled the mud with their feet as the young children played nearby, pretending to also work the fields, or building miniature stone walls that imitated the real ones that were used to hold water in the fields. As the women worked side by side in unison, they sang the words, "Turning soil is very hard work, but eating the rice is very rewarding!"

After approximately fifteen minutes of watching, a flock of small birds swept low over the fields, and the boys sprang up and swatted at the air with their *kalibs*. They knocked a few birds to the water, then grabbed them up before they could recover, made sure they were dead, and tossed them in a basket to be eaten with dinner. As they waited for another flock, Fanusan caught sight of a young boy no older than five playing near his mother, who was busy transplanting. The naked little boy saw a duck wandering nearby and began walking toward it. As he approached it, the duck moved away. Fanusan found it amusing, and just watched the boy's repeated attempts to get near the duck.

Finally, the boy took a handful of young rice seedlings and camote leaves, stretched his arm out to entice it, and inched toward the wild duck. The duck slowly made its way to him, and began eating the plants that fell from his hand. Suddenly, the little boy aimed his penis at the duck to urinate on it—but when the duck saw this, it darted its head forward and bit the kid's penis.

The boy jumped back, screaming, and then ran to his mother, crying while squirting urine all over himself. When he reached her, he cried even louder as he told her what had happened. She checked to see if he was bleeding, but saw that he was not and laughed. Fanusan laughed too, and if Alex could have, he would have been rolling on the ground with mirth.

Later that morning, Fanusan and his friends walked back to the village with the few birds they'd caught. When they reached the village, they set the birds aside and went to the pig pen where other older boys and men were already gathering manure into clay pots. The wretched stench didn't bother them at all, but Alex found it repulsive.

Fanusan began scooping manure into two large clay jars with a large wooden spoon. Alex felt like vomiting, but it was all in his head, as Fanusan continued handling the pig poop without any thoughts to all the germs and filth. When his two jars were three quarters full, he slid a wood pole under the handles of both jars and used it as a yoke to lift them in the air. With jars dangling on both sides of him, he followed the others toward the rice fields where the women were working. The jars were very heavy for Fanusan, but he did not complain.

To get to the fields, they had to cross a wide, shallow river. When they arrived at the riverbank, some of the men put down their harnessed jars and removed their loincloths. Those whose cloths were soiled with pig manure quickly rinsed them in the river before draping them over their wooden yokes. Fanusan did not remove his, for some reason, but immediately began wading across the waist-high water.

Alex felt very awkward. It was one thing to be among naked men in a public locker room at the gym, but it felt very strange to be working alongside them. As they approached the area where all the women were working, none of the men bothered to put their loincloths back on. When they reached the women at the rice fields, they emptied the jars directly in the water, where the women turning the soil began stomping it in the mud. Alex was amazed to note that none of the women or girls looked at any of the naked men any differently than if they'd been clothed. This absence of sexual interest amazed him; he couldn't imagine it back home.

Later that afternoon, Fanusan was idling in the village when he saw some boys walking toward the river. There were about ten at first, but others began joining them as they started shouting the word, "*Fûg-fûg-to'!*" Alex understood it as some sort of game for boys. Fanusan and his friends quickly joined the others, running toward the narrow end of the river, where the water ran shallower and swifter. When Fanusan arrived, he saw that there were just as many boys from a neighboring *ato* (village) waiting for them on the other side. He saw several play shields made of woven basket material lying on the riverbank, and picked one up.

The boys walked toward the river. The water was cool, and especially shallow along the edges. The shoreline and bottom were covered with smooth river rocks of various sizes. The boy next to him picked up several stones—and just then, he felt something hit his shield. The next thing he knew, the boy next to him was throwing the stones at the boys across the river. Not paying attention, Fanusan was hit squarely on the forehead by a flying stone.

"What are you doing!?" shouted the boy next to him. "Attack! Attack!"

Fanusan came to his senses quickly, picked up a stone, and hurled it at the other side without aiming. Their side began advancing into the river, but they were soon retreating as the other side quickened their pace and threw an overwhelming amount of stones. One of the older boys on his side shouted and urged the rest to throw faster, and began moving forward. Fanusan and the rest followed. After hitting one boy in the genitals with a rock, Fanusan began laughing uncontrollably. Alex was shocked at how dangerous their game was, and couldn't believe how much fun Fanusan and the rest were having.

After several minutes of battling each other, Fanusan's side began hitting more boys with greater accuracy. Within minutes, they found themselves in the middle of the river, standing waist deep. Soon after, they reached the other shore, and the opposing boys retreated back to their *ato* as Fanusan and his friends shouted words of victory.

When he returned to the village, a few of his friends joined him in a game that involved the throwing of pretend spears. They weren't allowed to play with the real thing yet, so they made their own out of dry reeds. One boy rolled a fruit across the ground while the others threw their pretend spears, trying to hit it while it was moving. At first, none of the boys hit their targets; on the second attempt, only Fanusan hit the fruit. He was clearly the most skilled spear thrower in the group, hitting the fruit twelve of the twenty times it was rolled, while the next best boy only hit it five times.

Later that evening, one of the village elders stopped by the open stone-walled court that adjoined the *fawi*. The boys knew him as The Storyteller, and enjoyed listening to his stories. He was very old but much respected because of the number of heads he'd taken in his younger years. The boys always looked forward to seeing the tattoos he proudly displayed on his chest, arms and face, recounting his fame for all to see.

Upon seeing The Storyteller enter the court area, Alex couldn't help but notice how much he looked like his Lolo Santo. As he stared at him, he got the feeling that he was somehow related to the old man, or at least to Fanusan and the people in the village. Soon, the other boys began filtering in the court to listen to his stories.

Since it was brought to the old man's attention that a snake had almost been killed several days ago by one of the younger boys, he decided to tell them the story of O-wûg. He sat down with his cup of *basi* liquor and waited for the rest of the boys to join them from inside the *fawi*. While waiting, he reached up and removed the small woven basket cap from the back of his head that contained his pipe and tobacco, and leisurely smoked his pipe.

Once everyone arrived, he proudly told the story. The boys listened intently as he said, "Long ago, shortly after the Great Flood, there once was a strange man from Mount Pulog who came into our village and married one of our women. They both lived here for many moons. When he died, his friends came to the funeral and a snake, Owug, also came to attend the funeral. When the people wept, Owug also wept. When they put the dead man in the grave, Owug came to the grave and looked upon the man, then went away. Later, when his friends observed the death ceremony, Owug also attended. From then on, Owug was a friend and companion of our people. Sometime later, it was somehow discovered that Owug was once a man of our people. I think he was one of our ancestors who survived the Great Flood. This is why we never kill Owug. If he crosses our path on a journey, we stop and talk. If he crosses our path more than three times, we turn around, because he knows a bad *anito* lurks ahead, waiting to kill us."

One of the boys in the group, who had heard the story of Owug plenty of times, respectfully asked the old man to tell them the story of the white men whom some of the elders had seen wandering the mountains. The old man gave them a brief troubled look, and pursed his lips as if he didn't want to talk about them. Fanusan could tell that he was uncomfortable, but hoped he would still tell the story, since he hadn't been around to hear it last time it had been told. He wanted to know more about the missionary's people.

The old man drank the last of his *basi* and said, "Many moons ago, more moons than the fathers of my father could count, came great houses that floated over the endless waters of the lowlands. Our creator, Lumawig, threatened them with savage waves and strong winds and rain, but he took pity on them when he heard them praying for mercy. They were not praying to him, though, and this made him curious. Instead of turning them away, he calmed the storm and had the winds show them the way to our beautiful land. When the houses arrived at our shores, strange beings called *castillanos* made their way to our beaches. These beings were half-beast and half-man. They grew hair all over their bodies like animals and tried to hide it by covering their bodies with strange metal and cloth. They were very clever beasts, and tricked Lumawig into believing they were friends by offering the lowlanders strange gifts and foods from their lands. Soon, they tricked the people into joining them in their villages, where they were treated badly and often killed. Lumawig told our people to avoid them, for they were controlled by evil *anitos*. Lumawig reminded us to battle them as he had taught us to do with our enemies. He tells us that these beasts will eventually raid our villages, searching for heads for many moons to come. We must take their heads before they can take ours. This is why you must grow to become great warriors like your fathers and their fathers before them."

Alex was troubled by what he was hearing, and wanted to tell the boys not to listen to this man's ignorance. He wanted to tell them that the

Spaniards were there to help them progress, so that they could eventually become successful people. He wanted to tell them that the white man could help them modernize, so they wouldn't become the poor country that he knew they *would* become. "If only you knew how prosperous you could be in the future..." Alex wanted to tell them, but to no avail. "Don't you want to be like Japan and other the great countries in Asia?"

Though Fanusan had no problem sleeping that night, Alex couldn't stop thinking about how primitive these people were. The story about the *castillanos* got him thinking about how similar it must have been for the Native Americans when the *Mayflower* first landed in America. The thoughts of how American Indian culture had been practically destroyed led him to start thinking about whether or not the colonization of these lands by whites would, in fact, be in their best interest. *That's it!* Alex thought. *That must be why I'm here—to prevent the murder and assimilation of these people, who are probably my ancestors. But how am I going to do that if I can't even control the body I'm in?*

He wished he knew more about his ancestry, so he could make sense of what was happening. He began to blame his parents for not teaching him more about his heritage—but then recalled the times his father had taken him to meetings of the local Igorot organization, *BIBBAK.* He remembered a gathering when his father had danced and played the *gangsa* with other men. The memory of seeing his father wearing only a g-string with black socks and dress shoes made him laugh inside. *I can't blame Mom or Dad,* he admitted. *They tried teaching me through their stories, but I just didn't want to learn.*

Alex knew his lack of interest was rooted in the fact that he'd grown up a minority in a mostly white society. He didn't want to learn how different he was because he didn't *like* being different. Being different was the source of most of the teasing he'd suffered from kids at his school. His heritage was the last thing on his mind as a kid. But his interest in learning about his heritage had taken a 180-degree turn since inhabiting Fanusan. Something about the boy and his people intrigued him. He wanted to know more about them, since it was clear he was somehow related to them.

The following day, Fanusan and his friend, Falikao, joined their fathers and other men in a hunt for food. Fanusan was very excited, because this was his first hunt! Unlike the pretend reed spears that he was accustomed to playing with, his father handed him a real spear with a metal spearhead. He called it a *sinalawitan* because the spearhead had four barbs at the bottom of both sides. "You must never go outside our village without the *sinalawitan*," his father instructed him sternly. "You must protect yourself from bad *anitos*. They are found everywhere. They will flee upon the sight of this spear, but are not afraid of spears that do not have two or more barbs."

"I will always keep this with me," affirmed Fanusan, as he was handed the spear.

He took the spear and balanced it in his hands. He felt powerful holding it, and looked at his friend, who also held one in his hand. Falikao wanted to show off and threw his spear at a tree fifteen yards away, but missed completely. Fanusan aimed at the same tree and hurled the spear with such accuracy that it landed right in the middle of the trunk. Fanusan smiled at his friend before they both ran to fetch their spears.

The group spread apart as they slowly walked through the never-ending forest of pine trees with their spears at the ready position. After walking for nearly an hour, they slowed down and came to an eventual halt. He saw his father, who was ten yards ahead, gesturing at him to move very slowly to his left. Fanusan turned and did as his father instructed, taking a step only every few seconds.

After moving several yards over, he saw several deer feeding about twenty yards away. This was a very special thing to see, because deer were not as plentiful as wild hogs and other game. The deer were protected from the rest of the group by a tight grouping of trees, but they were in striking range of Fanusan, who was the only one with a clear throw. He slowly raised his spear, but in doing so cracked a twig under his foot, causing the deer to raise their heads. When Fanusan made another step toward them, they suddenly began running. As they ran, Fanusan focused his aim on the last deer and sent his spear soaring between the trees. It struck the deer in its left hind leg, sending it tumbling to the ground. Falikao, who was closest to it, ran toward it as the rest followed.

They all stood around it and waited for Fanusan to arrive. When he did, his father handed him another spear and instructed him to pierce its heart. Alex looked at the deer's eye, which stared at him as Fanusan raised both hands without a trace of hesitation and plunged the spear into its heart, killing it instantly.

Fanusan was ecstatic that his first kill was a deer! Usually, a boy's first kill was a pig; it had been many years since a boy had taken a deer on his first hunt.

On their way back to the village, the two boys followed the adults, feeling very proud for taking part in a successful hunt. In addition to the deer, the group also killed two wild boars. But then, no more than a thousand steps from the village, they came upon a few men from their village talking among each other. When Fanusan reached the adults, he saw something disturbing.

The men they had encountered were carrying a dead man and woman back to the village. Their arms and feet were bound, and they were tied to long branches, like the dead animals the hunters carried back with them. Both were naked and bloody from fatal gashes to their abdomens and chests. One of the men held a blood-covered battleaxe; another hefted a spear, its spearhead dripping blood onto the ground. It didn't seem to faze Fanusan, who just stood there waiting to continue on to the village, but Alex was beside himself with shock and horror. He recognized the woman from the rice fields the day before, and couldn't believe those men had murdered someone from their own *ato*.

After several moments of talking, the hunters went ahead with their catches. When they arrived at the village, Fanusan's mother was just returning from working in the fields. She'd been busy all day with the other women, planting the new crop, and was covered with mud. Fanusan ran to her and immediately began telling her about his deer kill.

She listened with a smile, and said she was very happy that their hunt had been a success. More meat was always welcome.

Shortly after telling her of his adventures, he overheard his father telling his mother that one of the married men of the village had been caught with a woman not his wife in the woods, and both had been killed for committing adultery. Apparently, the wife of the man suspected his infidelity and told her parents, who arranged a trap to catch them in the act. They knew the location of their rendezvous point and sent men there to hide. When the man and woman arrived and began having sex, the men hiding behind the trees sprang out and killed them instantly.

Alex was surprised to see little emotional reaction from Fanusan's mother upon hearing the news. She was only a bit surprised, because the last time an incident of adultery had taken place had been years before Fanusan's birth. The villagers blamed evil *anitos* called *futatus* for inhabiting their bodies and causing them to commit adultery. It surprised Alex that they held the *anitos* responsible instead of the man or woman. The way he understood it, neither were to blame for their adulterous actions. It was totally the fault of the *futatus.* That hadn't saved the adulterous couple's lives, however.

Then, out of nowhere, thoughts not his own entered Alex's mind for the first time. Fanusan was reviewing what his parents had taught him about *Lumawig.* Alex learned that their god had established strict rules for Igorots to follow. *Lumawig* had instructed them not to lie, because good men do not care to associate with liars. He instructed them not to steal, and insisted that all people should try to live good, honest lives. A man was allowed only one wife, and if he disobeyed this dictum, his life would be demanded of him. A home was to be kept pure; an adulterer should not violate it. Most importantly, all should live as brothers and sisters. Alex considered his world, and how his society constantly violated his God's stern instructions. The Igorot lifeways made an intuitive kind of sense to him. *Maybe they're not as primitive as they seem,* he decided.

The following day, Fanusan and Falikao brought a group of girls several baskets filled with fresh camote for them to pare. One of the girls whispered something funny into the ear of another and the group began giggling. Then, one of them snuck behind Fanusan and pulled off his *suk'-lang* cap from the back of his head and ran off. Fanusan looked at the giggling group of girls and then his friend.

"Go now, you need to marry," insisted Falikao. "She might be the one. Go, go!"

Fanusan wasted no more time, chasing the girl toward the *olag*. As he approached the *building,* he noticed two girls leaving with wide smiles on their faces. Once inside the olag, he saw the girl dangling his fez-like *suklang* in front of her in a teasing manner. Alex knew where this was going and became excited. He began congratulating Fanusan for what was about to take place. Alex thought, "If you're anything like me, you're about to get lucky!"

Her name was Lang'-sa. She was sixteen years old, and the only daughter of one of the most respected warriors in the village. She was considered by many of the boys to be one of the prettiest girls in the village. Fanusan found her almond-shaped eyes and joyful smile very attractive, while Alex admired her perky breasts and the curves of her well-proportioned body.

Alex quickly learned that this was not his first time in the *olag* with her, as they both immediately removed what little clothing they had on and embraced each other. After caressing each other for several moments, they lay down together and covered themselves with a woven blanket while rubbing up against each other. "This is our fifth time together," Fanusan whispered into Langsa's ear. "Do you show signs yet?"

"Yes, my mother told me that I show signs of a baby. She is happy," replied Langsa as her breathing became heavy from the physical contact.

Fanusan smiled with joy, rolled on top of her and said, "Then you will be my bride. We are compatible, and are meant for each other."

For some reason, Alex was unable to feel the physical pleasure that Fanusan was experiencing. A bit disappointed, he began thinking about their relationship as they engaged in the heat of passion. Having sex before marriage was nothing new to him, but this seemed very different.

This was no simple case of two teenagers having sex for pleasure's sake alone. First, there seemed to be no sense of wrongness in what they were doing. There was no sneaking around. All the girls who saw them enter the *olag* probably knew what they were doing, and they made no attempt hide their actions and be quiet. The fact that Langsa's mother was happy about her pregnancy led him to believe that they had no moral standards against premarital sex.

This intrigued Alex, and he immediately began reading Fanusan's mind. He learned that Fanusan had entered into the relationship with one thing on his mind, and it wasn't sex. This came as a shock to Alex. Instead, Fanusan was hoping to find out if Langsa was the one he would marry. It was a trial relationship, to see if both were emotionally and physically compatible with each other. They already loved being around each other, but the news about her pregnancy was the determining factor that resolved the issue of their compatibility.

The trial aspect of their relationship was nothing new to Alex. People did it all the time in his world, but everyone he knew got involved in the trial concept for pleasure's sake, or to see how long the relationship would last. Few did it with marriage as the ultimate goal. In fact, he couldn't think of any of his friends who had marriage on their minds upon starting a relationship with a woman. The concept seemed to continually deteriorate in his world. Given all the broken families, failed marriages, and fear of commitment, many people believed marriage would soon be a thing of the past.

Then it dawned on him. *Purpose,* he thought. It was the one thing that clearly differentiated Fanusan's trial relationship from his world's idea of trial relationships. Both had purpose in their actions, but those purposes were clearly different. Fanusan's world put marriage first as the purpose of their relationships, whereas his people focused on selfishness and personal pleasure.

As Fanusan rolled off her and lay next to her, smiling, Alex reflected that his own life had little purpose. It basically evolved around the accumulation of wealth, notoriety and acceptance. Suddenly the simple, mundane things he had been observing through Fanusan began taking on new meaning. Things such as making and sharing meals, hunting, farming, storytelling, and even games all had a purpose to them. Even though he didn't agree with all of those purposes, it didn't change the fact that everything had a purpose—even the execution of the adulterers. What impressed him even more was how each purpose was centered on other people. It was painfully evident that not only did his life lack purpose, but the little purpose it *did* have had revolved around him alone.

For the first time in his life, Alex wasn't proud of who and what he had become.

As Fanusan tried to sleep later that evening, Alex remained alert, still struggling with his purpose in life. He no longer felt as successful as he'd once believed. He began to believe that Fanusan and the others were better off *not* being colonized by the Spaniards. Despite their primitive ways, they seemed happier than he had ever been in his civilized world. These people didn't need material toys to make them happy. Alex wanted the same feeling in his life—but he didn't know how to go about finding it.

Fanusan's eyelids finally closed and they fell asleep—only to be jolted awake by a woman's scream nearby. Fanusan sat up immediately and heard more women screaming. The last time he'd heard that kind of screaming was when he was five years old, and his village was attacked by another *ato*. Within seconds, one of the old men in the *fawi* came up from behind and placed his hand over his mouth to insure he didn't make any sound. "Shhhh," he whispered into his ear. "The enemy is here. Come now, we must hurry."

Once the man removed his hand, Fanusan turned to see the younger boys being led outside by the older boys and men. He saw two six-year-olds still standing there, frightened and confused, so he grabbed their hands and led them out the *fawi*. On his way out, he took a spear with two barbs, remembering what his father had told him about the evil *anitos,* and led the two boys into the nearby forest. He instructed them to lie on their stomachs behind some bushes, and covered them with piles of dry needles and branches. Fanusan saw that one of the boys was very frightened, so he lay down next to him to make sure he kept quiet. Then he felt something wet on his arm, and realized the boy was so scared that he was peeing. He placed his arm over the boy's back, pulled him closer to him, and whispered to him to stop crying, or the evil *anitos* might hear him.

The boy froze in silence as the voices of strange men filled the air. The voices kept getting closer and closer, and Fanusan clamped a hand over the boy's mouth moments before one of the strange men stopped inches from their heads. Fortunately, the men did not notice them, and moved farther into the woods.

It was too dark to see anything, so Fanusan closed his eyes and kept as still as possible; but sudden war cries yanked his eyes open. He recognized his father's voice and became very concerned. He was still unable to see anything, but could tell by the sounds that they were fighting each other. Suddenly, the clouds shifted enough to allow moonlight to illuminate the village. When he lifted his head, he saw men with spears and axes in their hands running back into the woods in retreat. He didn't recognize any of them, and assumed they were from another *ato.* Then he saw his father and two other men chasing the enemy into the woods, and smiled with relief that his father was alive.

Out of nowhere, two strange men came running toward Fanusan and the boys. A spear suddenly pierced the neck of one of them from behind, sending him tumbling forward right in Fanusan's direction. The man's head fell inches away from Fanusan's eyes, causing him to start and leap to his feet in fear. As soon as he stood, the other man turned and saw him. Both stared at each other for a moment. Fanusan saw that the man was holding an axe in one hand, and someone's severed head in the other hand. He didn't want to attract attention to the little boys, so he ran the other direction, hoping that the man would not see the children. He thought for a split second about grabbing the spear he'd left on the ground next to the boys, but decided to keep running, knowing that the spear would keep the evil *anitos* away from the children.

The man was about to pursue him when several villagers came running toward him with spears in their hands. Upon seeing them, he ran in the opposite direction, toward the dark forest, in retreat. Fanusan did not see him retreat, though, and thought he was still being pursued by the stranger, so he kept running for his life.

Fanusan knew that the moonlight made him very visible, and he grew increasingly frightened. Then the bright patch of light appeared low in the sky—and Fanusan was running toward it. "What's he doing?" Alex thought. "Doesn't he know the enemy will see him more clearly?" But then Alex read Fanusan's mind, and realized that the white light wasn't visible to him at all. Indeed, the closer he got, the darker it became. Alex was amazed how the light above made everything darker instead of brighter.

It was so dark, in fact, that Fanusan tripped over a large tree root and sprawled full-length on the ground. While on the ground, he dimly saw several old tree trunks lying on top of each other, forming a little shelter perfect to hide in. He scurried under the trunks, tucked his head between his knees, and balled up. He tried to control his breathing, but found it too hard. His heart pounded so loud in his ears that he was sure the enemy would hear it. After a few minutes, he slowly raised his head to see if he could see the strange man, but couldn't see anything because of the clouds that hid the moon again.

Fanusan became worried that the moon might re-emerge, so he reached around him and gathered clumps of pine needles to camouflage himself. Sure enough, the clouds parted again and the moon made everything visible, including him. Alex noticed that the bright patch of light had disappeared. Unwilling to move from his spot, Fanusan held the pine needles in front of him and looked out into the night.

Before long, his stomach began making gaseous sounds, and he quickly felt the need to empty his bowels of his last meal. He tried to hold it in, so as not to be seen or heard moving, but pinching his buttocks shut wasn't enough to stop nature. Rather than soil his loincloth, Fanusan slowly moved to an area shaded from the moonlight, pulled the loincloth to one side, and squatted.

As he finished relieving himself, Fanusan reached for a few large leaves to wipe himself clean...but when he grabbed a handful, he also touched something cold and slippery. Immediately after touching it, the sound of rustling leaves from his other side caught his attention. He jerked his fingers back from the slippery object and peered into the area where the rustling sounds had come from.

The moon disappeared behind the clouds again, making it hard for him to see. He heard something else moving in the direction where he'd touched the slippery thing, and turned his head to investigate, but saw nothing. The sound moved from one side of him to the other, and he kept turning his head, trying to find the source.

After a long moment of uncertainty, the moon came out from behind the clouds to illuminate the world. Fanusan's eyes widened as he stared directly at a twelve-foot *ulupong* cobra before him, with its head standing three feet off the ground, hood flared wide. Alex wanted to get out of there immediately, but Fanusan just remained there, squatting in awe. "Owug," he said to the snake. *Kid, that ain't no friendly snake,* thought Alex urgently. *How 'bout we get the hell out of here?*

The snake remained erect for several more moments, until Fanusan stretched out his right arm. It sensed his movement and began slithering toward him. "Owug," Fanusan said again. "I know you are one of us. I know you are friendly. and I am not afraid of you anymore."

The snake stopped right in front of them, and raised its flared head until it was inches from Fanusan's face. Alex realized suddenly that it looked exactly like the snake image that had come to life in the Sagada Caves. Fanusan smiled; the snake leaned forward and began wrapping around his shoulders, and continued wrapping itself around him, like a boa constrictor. Alex was in a state of panic, but Fanusan remained calm, as if he thought the snake were playing with him. Maybe it was.

Once the snake had totally wrapped itself around him, it began to glow brightly, just like the images had in Sagada. Within seconds, it was brighter than fire, the lambent glow flickering throughout its entire body.

Before Alex could make sense of anything, a blast of blinding light surrounded him, and he felt himself floating and gasping for oxygen again.

CHAPTER 8

A burst of fresh air filled his lungs as Alex opened his eyes, to discover that he had somehow been transported back to the village...or so he thought. But as his body looked around, again through no volition of his own, he realized that this wasn't the village he was familiar with. Nor was he a sixteen-year-old any longer; his much-larger arms and hands gave him the impression that he was in the body of a man in his 20s or 30s. And from the height he stood off the ground, that man was more or less the same height Alex himself was, five foot seven.

He soon learned that his body was broad, with muscular shoulders proportionate to the rest of his body. The only thing covering his dark, sun-baked skin was a loincloth, like before. His coarse jet-black hair reached just below his shoulder blades, and his bangs were cut short above his eyebrows. His feet were somewhat deformed, he realized, because the big toes were spread away from the other toes at nearly a 45-degree angle. A large bunion on the basal joint of each big toe added to its deformity.

The hut he stood in front of was marked with a square wooden sign with the number "20" painted on it in white. That was odd; Fanusan's people didn't use writing. The rising sun, morning dew, and the absence of people outside led him to believe it was still very early in the morning. He reached up to scratch an itch on the top of his head, and discovered that he was wearing the same kind of basket-like woven cap that some of the men from Fanusan's *ato* wore.

When his head turned upward to stretch his neck from side to side, Alex again noticed the bright patch of light in the sky above him. The mysterious light continued to baffle him, though his current body didn't seem to notice it. *Maybe it's some kind of passageway back to reality,* he thought. *Or maybe it's God looking down at the world...or maybe it's just a kind of beacon showing me the way out of here.*

The sudden sound of hammering caught his new body's attention, and he proceeded to walk towards it. After passing several huts, he encountered two white men pounding a wooden sign into the ground. A young Filipino man joined him, and watched for a moment. Then he began speaking to him in Ibontoc; and just as before, it took a few seconds before the language entered his ears in English: "...do you think it says, Bolee?"

Alex's new body turned his head toward the man, but remained silent. *So, my name is Bolee this time,* Alex thought. He wondered what had happened to Fanusan, and whether the boy had escaped the snake safely. As the men pounded in the sign, he continued to explore the area with his eyes until his companion said, "Hey, wake up. Did you hear what I said?"

Bolee snapped out of his state of wonder and looked at the man. "What do you think that's for?" the man asked Bolee a second time.

Bolee glanced at the white men, then shrugged as if to say he had no clue. Alex, on the other hand, could easily read the sign the men were installing: "Voting station. Roosevelt or Parker. One bean one vote."

After the sign was securely in the ground, the men nailed pictures of Theodore Roosevelt and Alton Parker above the white-painted words.

Then they pulled out two *gangsas* from a bag, along with a handful of beans, and placed them under the sign. The two white men noticed Bolee and the other man staring at them, but just smiled. After they'd finished laying everything out, one of the men held a bean in the air and placed it in one of the *gangsas* in a demonstrative manner.

"One bean, one vote, now," he said loudly—in English, which Bolee and his friend didn't understand. The other white man smiled at Bolee and said, "How ya'll doin this mornin'? Ya got what ya'll asked for. This is gonna be a good day fa ya'll."

The man next to Bolee smiled and replied in Ibontoc, "You look funny. Why do you hide your hairy animal bodies with all those clothes? You are very ugly!"

"Yessir, whatever you say," one of the white men smilingly replied.

"You don't really understand 'em, do you?" asked the other as they left.

"Hell no. I'm just doin what the boss says, bein' nice ta the monkey folks."

A light breeze brought the smell of cooking food to Bolee's nose, and he looked around to see more people moving about throughout their little village. His stomach rumbled, and he began walking toward one of the huts. A woman from the hut he was walking towards saw him, and gestured for him to go inside and eat.

Bolee stepped into the hut and saw meat, vegetables, and rice waiting for him. A young boy and an older girl joined him and began eating. While eating, Alex read Bolee's thoughts and learned they were his close relatives. The lady's name was Zag-tag'-an. Her daughter, Udao', was fifteen years old, and her son, Sĭt-li'-nĭn, was nine years old.

Zagtagan was Bolee's aunt. Her first husband had died from the foreign disease called smallpox, which came to Bontoc with a Spanish soldier eleven years ago, and killed almost three dozen Igorots. Her second husband, who also happened to be the older brother of the newly appointed village leader, Nathaniel, had recently died while fighting the Americans, shortly before the end of the Philippine-American war. It was then that Alex realized why there were white men wandering freely in their village: according to Bolee's memories, they were living in America now, in a sort of human exhibit.

It angered him—as it did Bolee—to realize they were basically zoo animals.

Nathaniel had brought Zagtagan to America with him because he feared that she would be vulnerable to the American soldiers roaming in and out of Bontoc. It was Igorot custom to wait at least a year before remarrying, so she would be alone for a while with no one to protect her, and reports of rape by American soldiers made him concerned for her safety. As scary as it was for Zagtagan to go to the land of their enemy, she trusted Nathaniel and felt safe with him.

"You are up very early today, Bolee," said Zagtagan as they finished their meal. "Did you sleep well?"

"I did not," Bolee replied. "I had a strange dream last night."

"What did you dream?" asked Udao.

"I dreamed that a snake of fire attacked me."

"Did you kill it?" asked Sitlinin eagerly.

Bolee looked at the young boy. "We do not kill snakes," he said sternly. "I watched it dance circles in the sky, and then it stopped and came down right at me. I wanted to run, but I couldn't move. It just kept coming right at me. Then I woke up."

Sitlinin stared at Bolee with a scared look on his face. "Is it going to come after us?" he asked his sister.

"Don't listen to Bolee," Udao scolded. "He's just trying to scare you. *Lumawig* will protect us, silly. He is the most almighty, even greater than the white man's god."

Later that afternoon, as he wandered through the village, Bolee came across a group of teenage boys practicing their bow-and-arrow skills. One of the boys saw him and handed him one of the bows. "Show us how to do it right!" he urged Bolee. Smiling, Bolee nocked an arrow, drew back the bowstring, and aimed at one of the straw-bundle targets. When he released the arrow, it cut smoothly through the air and hit the target dead center. Alex was amazed, but Bolee just picked up another arrow and repeated the feat as if it were second nature. He was clearly the best marksman of the group, and hit the center of the target in all of his twenty attempts.

After archery practice, Bolee led the boys to the other side of the village. When they arrived, he immediately noticed the large crowd of white people seated behind the bamboo fence perimeter. Most of the men wore suits, and the women were dressed in long skirts and dresses. Many waved fans to keep their faces cool.

Smiling, Bolee picked up one of the *gangsas* that was neatly stacked in the middle of a well-stomped dancing area. As he picked it up, Alex realized that the handle was actually a jawbone of some sort, with human-like teeth in it. He hoped it was from a monkey. *"Ballangbang,"* Bolee said aloud as he began softly striking the *gangsa* with his stick. The other young Igorots followed, trying to create the desired melody. Once the melody was achieved, Bolee and one other Igorot began creating the *elwas* sound: the distinct contrasting beat in perfect rhythm with the rest of the *gangsas*. Soon, the *gangsas* reverberated in harmony, and Bolee began leading the *Ballangbang* dance. Hunched forward in the *menyuko* position, the rest of the Igorots carefully followed Bolee in a singlefile line as he began moving in a circle. Each time Bolee's right foot performed the *sikwat* motion of kicking up, so did theirs. Each time his body did a *menposipos* rotation, so did theirs. Alex felt great energy and emotion from the dance they were performing, and soon realized it was a victory dance. *How ironic,* he thought, considering that they were the ones being displayed like animals.

Although Bolee's eyes looked straight ahead and at the ground, Alex watched the white people from the corners of his eyes as he kept dancing in circles. Some of the men had their arms folded, hands cupped under their chins or stroking their beards. Others laughed and pointed at Bolee and his companions, laughing at the "monkey folks."

Anger began building within Alex. He resented that Bolee and the rest were there just to amuse or entertain the white onlookers. As Bolee continued dancing, Alex wondered again about the fate of Fanusan and his village. He had hoped to stay there longer, to find out whether they would be colonized by the Spaniards. Maybe this was their fate. Maybe they'd become slaves, only to be displayed in the white man's human zoos. Alex couldn't get over the fact that his people were apparently looked upon by the Americans as animals. Nor did he recall anything in his American history classes about such an event. He thought Americans and Filipinos had always been friends.

The crowd grew louder and more excited as Bolee and another man put down their *gangsas* and picked up spears and shields from another stack. The melody changed, and some of the Igorot women joined the dance. Bolee held his spear in the air outside the circle while the other man danced inside the circle, holding up his own spear. As Bolee entered the circle to battle the other man, the white men in the crowd began shouting with excitement. The two pretended to battle by lunging at each other and striking each other's shields. Each time they did this, the crowd let out cheers and laughter. Finally, Bolee made a final lunge and pretended to kill his opponent while the *gangsa* players and women surrounded them and danced.

After almost an hour of dancing, Bolee and his friends put the props back in the middle of the dancing area, let out a few warrior-like cries in unison, and strode toward the opposite perimeter. There they squatted on their haunches and carried on conversations amongst themselves. Bolee reached up and removed his woven basket cap, taking out the pouch of tobacco and pipe that he stored inside. His friends did the same as Bolee walked to a nearby open fire to light a small dry branch. After lighting his pipe, he brought the stick to the rest so they could light their own pipes and hand-rolled cigars.

Bolee turned to look at the observers, and saw that many appeared to be amused by the way the Igorots used their woven caps to store things. Some of the white men were also having fun trying to imitate the Igorot way of sitting. They would squat and try to lower their rear ends to within inches from the ground like the Igorots, but couldn't even get within a foot without falling over. Bolee saw several men fall, and laughed to himself.

After they had smoked and rested for several minutes, another group of men arrived to take their turns dancing for the onlookers. Most of the people in the crowd stayed to watch them, and newcomers arrived in a steady trickle. Once the new dancers began their performance, Bolee walked back toward the main part of the village, where he saw smoke rising from cooking fires. On his way he came upon a group of Igorot children listening to a white man talk to them. He joined them to see what was going on.

The white man stood behind a black box that was mounted on a tripod, and was moving his arms into the air and pointing up a nearby tree. He was trying to convince the boys to climb the tree, but they didn't understand what he was saying. Then, the man pulled out a small piece of candy and gave it to one of the boys. That boy happened to be Sitlinin. Bolee called out to Sitlinin after he accepted the candy. The boy turned to Bolee, and asked him if the white man wanted him to climb the tree. Bolee said he didn't know.

"Just tell them to climb a few feet in the air. That's all," the man hollered to Bolee. Bolee didn't understand a word he said, of course. Alex wanted to tell Bolee's cousin that that was indeed what the man wanted, but as with Fanusan, he had no control over what Bolee said or did. Then Sitlinin shrugged, placed both hands on the trunk of the tree, and began climbing. The white man with the box nodded and clapped his hands. As soon as Sitlinin reached six feet up the tree, the man began doing something with the black box.

Suddenly, it created a small explosion, and a flash of light and smoke filled the air. Bolee's cousin showed no signs of fear, and continued ascending up the tree. Alex heard the man say triumphantly, "Now I got proof that you savages got tails like monkeys!" When Bolee looked up at his cousin, Alex noticed how the dangling portion of Sitlinin's G-string resembled a long, thin tail as it trailed down the middle of his buttocks.

Then he remembered the Filipina lady at the airport, and how she'd thought that Igorots had tails. *How stupid can people be?* he wondered.

Later, Bolee returned to the village, where a big commotion had begun growing amongst his fellow Igorots. He found the village leader, Nathaniel, surrounded by villagers as he stood next to another white man. This one towered above Nathaniel, and had a big belly that sagged over his pants. Unlike most of the white men Bolee had seen, he lacked a mustache or beard, and did not wear a suit, bowtie, and hat. Instead, he wore the newest fashion of the traditional Filipino Barong Tagalog shirt, which displayed rainbow-colored stripes that draped over his big belly and reached well below his waist. His darkly tanned skin displayed the wrinkling and cracking of a man often in the sun.

Nathaniel introduced him to everyone as Mr. John. The large man smiled, revealing a large wad of tobacco in his mouth. As Nathaniel told the group about Mr. John's recent travels to the lowlands of the Philippines, Mr. John spit out a large glob of dark saliva. This reminded Bolee of the Igorots who lived several days from his hometown village, who chewed betel nuts and spat out globs of red saliva. The recollection made him smile.

Mr. John spat again and began saying in his unusual accent as Nathaniel translated, "I love y'all's country, though I neva been up in them there mountains y'all are from. I'm glad y'all are now part of this great country we call America. This heeya is the greatest World's Fair in the history of ouwa fair nation, and y'all's the biggest attraction heeya. More people are comin' ta see ya'll than anythang else. Y'all's drawin a bigga crowd than them Olympics goin' on yonder. It ain't fair that theys only providin' y'all with a few dogs a week. I know how it feels not ta have ya favorite meat. Trust me, I just bout died from missin' a fat ole steak wid taters when I was in y'all's country. Like I always said, ever dog's got its day and every man's got their meat. Yall deserve better, so I'm giving y'all 200 well-fed Missouri dogs. Y'all ain't gonna find healthia dogs than what we got heeya."

After Nathaniel translated this, everyone started cheering and thanking Mr. John.

Two other white men then entered, each pulling five medium-sized dogs behind them on ropes. After Mr. John said, "Bon appétit," Nathaniel instructed someone from each hut to claim a dog for that evening's feast. Bolee immediately stepped forward and picked one of the dogs, a big red one, and grabbed the rope that wrapped around its neck. He pulled the muzzled dog toward their hut while some of the other young men followed.

Once they were halfway to the hut, one of his companions ran ahead and returned with a spear. The dog growled under the canvas muzzle and tried to escape, but a boy struck its head with the side of his axe head, rendering it unconscious. The other young man placed the spear between its legs while two others tied the front and rear paws together. He and Bolee then picked each end of the spear and lifted the dog in the air as it hung upside down. When they arrived at an area used for butchering animals, they laid the dog on a flat piece of wood. Mr. John followed to observe the slaughter.

After removing the ropes, Bolee picked up a large bolo machete, then swung the blade downward across the dog's neck. The blood spurted into his face and eyes, but he just wiped it off with his forearm and continued, while Alex felt sick and disgusted as he watched himself butcher the dog. As hard as Alex tried, he couldn't control Bolee. He couldn't even close his eyes; he was forced to watch everything Bolee saw and did.

Midway into the slaughter, screams caught Bolee's attention. He looked up to see a small group of white women standing on an ivory-colored concrete balcony above, holding a banner while screaming, "Savages!" at them. Alex saw that the banner read "St. Louis Women's Humane Society."

Mr. John looked up at the ladies and responded laconically, "Howdy, ladies. I'd like ta invite y'all to my establishment in town for sum fine dinin'. My menu includes such delicacies as dogberries and cream, dogfish, and kennel cakes."

The women glared at him in anger and disgust. One lady said, "You're just as bad as the rest of them savages!"

Another shouted, "Haven't you read *The White Man's Burden*? We're supposed to be civilizing those savages, not encouraging them in their animalistic ways!"

Two white men who had been watching the butchering with keen interest looked at each other and then at Mr. John, their faces bright with amusement. After hearing the woman's comment about "The White Man's Burden," one turned to another and said, "Y'know, Vince, I ate at Mr. John's restaurant yesterday, and everything tasted great!"

"What did you have, Tom?" asked Vince.

Tom smiled and said, "I tried some of that dogfish, and that sausage-like thing in the middle of a small loaf of bread."

"You mean that Dachshund sausage sandwich?" responded Vince.

"That's what they call it in New York, but here they use that hot Polish kielbasa. What we have here is a..." Thomas paused momentarily, "...a hotdog! Yeah, a hotdog!"

Mr. John heard this and shouted, "Hotdog? Boys, I like how that sounds. I think y'all just invented a better name fer them sandwiches. From now on, this Fair will be known as the birthplace of hotdogs! C'mon out later and I'll give ya some free ones."

Tom and Vince shook hands and congratulated each other for coming up with such a catchy name. The ladies became so upset that they turned their noses up in the air and walked away, calling Tom and Vince savages and beasts. The two looked at Mr. John, winked, and walked away shouting, "Hotdogs, hotdogs, get your hotdogs here!"

Later that afternoon, Bolee and the rest began their feast of dog, rice, and vegetables. There were still many whites along the bamboo perimeter fences, watching them. The Igorots were used to their constant presence, and it didn't bother them much anymore—except for Bolee. Bolee harbored negative feelings for the white man. To Bolee, the Americans were no better than the Spaniards who had tried and fail to conquer their people after 300 years, though they had taken the rest of Philippines. Alex was glad to learn this, because he knew that Fanusan and his village had probably survived and preserved their way of life.

The Americans, though: this new white evil had recently fought a war against the Spanish and the Filipinos, and won. Bolee's village had never been attacked by the Americans, but he well remembered being on constant guard in case they did come under attack. Some of his uncles had been killed fighting the Americans, while rendering aid to Igorot villages more easily reached from the lowlands.

Bolee's dislike for the Americans grew when he was practically kidnapped and hustled onto the ship that had brought him to America. The Igorots on the ship were accompanied by other Filipinos from various islands. Nathaniel and a few of the other educated Igorots understood some of their languages, and one day they heard several Tagalog-speaking lowlanders talking about the atrocities their people had experienced at the hands of American soldiers.

Later that day, Nathaniel told Bolee and the rest about what he'd heard: stories of how innocent Filipinos were being slaughtered, tortured, and raped by Americans. One of the lowlanders even showed him an old piece of paper that he'd taken from a dead American soldier two years ago and kept ever since. It served as a reminder of how cruel the Americans were. The paper displayed a disturbing cartoon that had been ripped out of what Alex realized, upon thinking about it, was the editorial page of an *American Evening Journal* publication. It depicted American soldiers lined up in a firing squad formation, aiming their rifles at four blindfolded Filipino children whose hands were tied behind their backs. An American officer stood next to them with his sword drawn, ready to give the order to fire their weapons. The caption, in large script, read, "Kill everyone over ten." Beneath the caption was the name "Gen. Jacob H. Smith." The bottom caption read, "Criminals Because They Were Born Ten Years Before We Took The Philippines."

Bolee had learned a lot about the Americans, as well as the other Filipinos who were also on the ship, through Nathaniel and the other educated men. To Alex's surprise, some of the Igorots and many of the lowlanders weren't on the ship voluntarily; they had been physically forced into the ship. Others were tricked into going by being blatantly lied to, told they were going to help harvest food at a nearby island for several weeks. Alex also learned that the only reason Bolee pretended to like the white men was so that no harm would fall upon his auntie and cousins. He did this by following Nathaniel's plan, pretending he was actually his auntie's husband.

It made him uneasy to do this, but it was the only way Nathaniel knew he could keep them safe.

Midway into their feast, Bolee stood, walked over to the open fire next to his hut, and sat down next to Nathaniel and his family. Nathaniel and his wife were eating with their two sons as Bolee joined them. Nathaniel could see that Bolee had something on his mind as he approached. Nathaniel wasn't his real name, of course; it had been given to him by the Americans who brought them there. His true name was Pĭt-ta'-pĭt. He was in his late thirties and had learned English while attending classes taught by European missionaries. Since he was a child, he had been interested in learning more about the white people and their ways. As he grew and learned from missionaries and traders, other Igorots began to share his interests.

After the Philippines had lost their war with the Americans, Pittapit had been approached by an American military officer, who asked him if he was interested in visiting America for eight or nine months. He was never told that they would be exhibited like animals at the World's Fair; he was told only that it was an opportunity for Igorots to learn about the riches of America, and that the American government would reward those who went with silver. Without hesitation, Pittapit agreed, and helped the Americans gather hundreds of other Igorots from his home village, Bontoc, and two other Igorot villages. He was so instrumental to the Americans that they appointed him the Igorot "chief", which was a term foreign to them. Alex smiled when he realized that Pittapit was from Fanusan's village. He might even be one of the boy's descendants; who knew?

Despite Pittapit's desire to learn white ways, he was still very much in touch with his Igorot heritage. He had refused to cut his hair when asked to do so by missionaries in the past. He did not like to wear shirts and trousers, because they were uncomfortable, and felt that Igorots who wore them were no longer real Igorots. His chest proudly displayed the large *chaklag* tattoo that the American soldiers liked because of its resemblance to a ram's horn. All these features, coupled with his ability to speak English, made it a very easy decision for the Americans to appoint him as the leader of the Igorots going to America.

"Pittapit, how much longer do we have to eat dog every day?" Bolee asked Nathaniel plaintively.

Nathaniel finished swallowing a mouthful of meat and responded, "Until the Americans give us something else. Why, are you getting tired of eating dog?"

"Yes," Bolee replied. "I love dog, but not every day. They gave us pig before to make *etag,* and they also provided chickens for our *pinikpikan.* This is what we are used to eating on a daily basis. Why can't we have more?"

"I asked them this already, and they told me it was hard to find pigs," replied Nathaniel. "but I know they're lying by the look in their eyes. I think we're eating dogs because this is what the white man wants to see. Do you see how it amuses and offends so many of them? Mr. John speaks the truth when he says we are the most popular thing the white man likes to see at this 'Fair' of theirs. Don't worry, though, because Mr. John has promised to eventually bring us chicken and pigs."

"How much longer are we to stay here?" asked Bolee. "Without our crops, I cannot keep track of time anymore, but it feels like we have been here too long."

Nathaniel didn't know how to reply, and just reached out for his spear to look at the notched lines he had been making since their departure from home. "Let's see," he said as he examined the notches. "We left in the middle of our first season, *In-na-na*. I think we have the equivalent of two more *Inana* seasons left before we go back home. For now, we will continue to show our strength and intelligence."

"Will I have to go to their school, like Udao?" Bolee asked.

"I don't think so," responded Nathaniel. "You are too old."

"Good, because Udao told me that she shares the school here with the lowlanders who came with us. Some are Datu, Christians, and I forgot the other names she told me."

"That is correct. I spoke to the teacher of that school, and she told me that it surprises her that we Igorots are the most intelligent of all the Filipinos that she is teaching. You see, Bolee, they look at us and think we are stupid because we live simply and expose our bodies to the elements instead of following their ways. To be honest, the more I learn about them, the less impressed I am. I am in awe at their weapons, of course, but feel pity for their ways. I think they can learn much from us."

"Really? What do you mean?" Bolee replied, puzzled.

Nathaniel stood up and gestured to Bolee to wait momentarily as he went inside his hut to retrieve a jar of *tapey*. He returned and scooped out a measure of *tapey* for both of them. As they drank it, Nathaniel's wife joined several other women nearby in weaving their traditional Igorot fabrics with their hands and feet.

Nathaniel finished his coconut cup of tapey, set it down, and continued, "I have learned from the white missionaries back home that our families impress them. They have often commented on how much better we take care of each other than their own people do. It was pleasing for them to see how we men are able to stay faithful to one woman. Apparently, it is common for the white man to take on multiple wives, one after the other, and sometimes even more than one at once. I saw much evidence of this from the Spaniards before, and now the American soldiers back home. They like to take our women and those from the lowlands to satisfy their pleasures, even when they already have their own wives abroad—or even with them. We are not like them, Bolee.

We are not only stronger warriors, as you know, but we please *Lumawig* by not abandoning our families and taking on other women just to please ourselves."

"But adultery happens once in a while," Bolee interrupted.

"And what do we do when this happens?" Nathaniel asked.

Bolee cleared his throat and replied, "We kill them and send their bad *futatu* spirits to the neighboring mountains or pigs."

"Indeed we do, but the white men do not punish the offenders," replied Nathaniel. "They do their god shame, but it is as if it is an accepted behavior for them."

"I don't like how they look at our women," said Bolee. "More and more of them are beginning to cover their breasts and shoulders like the white women, because they do not like how the white man's eyes look at them."

"Yes. It is shameful."

Just then, they were interrupted by Nathaniel's wife, who urged Nathaniel to follow her. Bolee stood up and followed them to the other end of the village, where they heard shouting. When they arrived, Bolee saw Udao and asked her what was going on. She pointed to two men, and told him they had been accused of stealing. Bolee stood on the tips of his toes to raise himself so he could see the men she was pointing to. They were being restrained by a group of men. One man was short and stout, the other taller and skinny. Both had bloody mouths, and one had a bleeding gash on his forearm.

Nathaniel listened as a woman accused the young men of stealing her rice and one of her chickens. Both denied the crime, pointing fingers at each other. The slender man insisted that the stout man was the thief, since he was fat and always liked to eat. The stout man accused the slender man of wanting to have bigger muscles, which drove him to steal other people's food. Nathaniel reminded them of how serious a matter it was to steal another villager's property, and urged them again to tell the truth; but both strongly denied their involvement.

Nathaniel asked the crowd for some uncooked rice; within seconds, the lady whose rice and chicken had been stolen handed him a cup filled with rice. He instructed each of the accused to chew a small amount. After almost a minute of chewing, he had both spit out the rice onto the piece of wood he was holding. Nathaniel examined it and found that the wetness of both mouthfuls was the same. Unable to determine who was lying, he summoned two of the older men in the village.

The two men in their late forties came forward with two live chickens in their hands. They told everyone including Nathaniel to move away as they questioned the suspects separately. After approximately fifteen minutes of interrogation, the two men pointed to the slender man and identified him as the thief. To prove their conclusion, they killed the chickens, cut them open, and laid one in front of each suspect. They pointed out that since the gall of the chicken that lay before the slender man was found to be almost entirely exposed, he had clearly lied. The slender man looked at the all-knowing gall and nodded his acceptance of the verdict. Alex read Bolee's mind and learned that if the gall had been hidden by the upper lobe of the liver, like that of the chicken in front of the stout man, then innocence would have been the verdict for the slender man.

Nathaniel told the guilty man that he would have to give the lady he stole from ten days' worth of rice and five dogs. The man agreed and walked away in shame. Then Nathaniel asked the crowd to be quiet so that he could address them. The crowd fell silent as he began speaking: "My people, this is our first trial since our arrival. Let this be a reminder of who we are and who we are not," he said. "Look around us, at the white people who watch us even after the sun has fallen. We are not like them. Stealing is not what *Lumawig* wants us to do. These are the ways of the Spaniards, Americans, and other white men. They take for themselves. They accumulate for themselves at the expense of others. They seek to please only themselves. We are not like them in that way.

"What we do is for our families, for our people, for *Lumawig*, and *not* for ourselves. If we do otherwise, this does not please *Lumawig*, and it will eventually lead to evil falling upon us and our people. The white missionaries tried to teach me that a man is supposed to be a good servant to his god. In a way, I believe they are correct. Even *Lumawig* teaches that our *tako* or soul, as the white man calls it, is a faithful servant of men. We must remember this, otherwise it becomes the bad *futatu* spirit that we see plaguing the white man. Unlike the white men, we must practice what we preach."

Even though Nathaniel was talking about white men specifically, Alex felt like the chief was talking about him specifically. He began reflecting again on how his life had always been about achieving society's definition of success. He had always put his career and himself as Priority #1 in his life. The more he thought about it, the more self centered his life seemed.

It bothered him to realize how so little of it revolved around other people and the development of real relationships. His thoughts shifted to all the women and girlfriends he'd had, and how each relationship had been about satisfying his lust. Many of his relationships had lasted just one night, while none had lasted longer than six months. His relationship with Heather was headed down the same road. He'd always vaguely felt that premarital sexual relationships were wrong, because he'd been raised Catholic by his parents, but it wasn't until now that he truly felt the wrongness in his actions. Like the thief who'd stolen the rice, he'd stolen innocence from the women he'd manipulated.

He came to the painful realization that his life was exactly the kind of life Nathaniel was describing so negatively.

After the crowd dispersed and went on with their evening, Bolee walked back toward his hut with Udao. As they walked, she told him that several of the women from the two other Igorot tribes had told her how good a leader Nathaniel was becoming. This intrigued him, as leadership was a new concept for his people, so they began discussing it. They decided it must have been introduced by the Spaniards, since it sought to give power to one person over the rest.

Alex read his mind, listened to their conversation, and learned that the Bontoc Igorots differed from the other Igorots there because they had no concept of leader or "chief," as the Americans called Nathaniel. Instead, they had a sort of council of old men called the *intugtukan*. The only thing a man needed to become a member was age. It didn't matter how much intelligence or influence one had, all were considered equals in the *intugtukan*. These were the men who heard, reviewed and judged individual disputes. They also made peace treaties, and declared, accepted and rejected invitations of war. Even when the *intugtukan* could not make decisions, the village would act as a unit.

Alex found it easy to see why Bolee and Udao found the concept of leadership by one man strange. He also related to their rejection of it, because they believed it would eventually lead to the appearance of the bad *anitos* known as *futatus*. This got him thinking about all the corruption in political and corporate America. *Maybe it's best these people aren't modernized,* he mused. *After all, it's probably this whole concept of being #1 that has led people to become so selfish and self-centered—like me.*

When Bolee and his cousin passed by Nathaniel's hut, Alex looked at Nathaniel and saw him not as a man who viewed himself as a leader, but as a man who considered himself the voice of the village. He watched as Nathaniel sat behind his wife next to the fire and held her in his embrace. That reminded him of his parents, and how his father would come up behind his Mom while she was cooking and embrace her.

How did I fall so far from the tree? he wondered.

Alex envied Nathaniel, because he had not yet experienced true love. All his relationships with women, whether overnight or for months at a time, had been designed to achieve his own pleasure or to boost his ego. He paid no real attention to the woman's needs or desires. None of his relationships bore the makings of a lasting relationship. This realization made him sick to his stomach, and the pride he'd once felt from having all those women in his life soured to utter self-disappointment and disgrace.

For the first time in his life, he experienced a sadness that was so sharp it physically hurt. So much regret, shame, and personal disappointment filled his heart that it not only affected him, but it somehow physically affected Bolee as well. Suddenly, his host stopped walking and fell to ground in pain. Udao heard him hit the ground moaning, and turned around to see him balled up in pain.

She rushed to his side and examined him, to see if he had been stricken by some kind of weapon. "What happened? Are you all right?" she asked frantically.

"I don't know," Bolee moaned. "It hurts. It hurts all over."

The world suddenly grew dark as Bolee's eyes closed on the sight of Nathaniel hurrying over to where he lay, and Alex felt a flare of fear as Bolee slipped into unconsciousness. He himself remained alert. He was even able to see things, although Bolee's eyes were closed; and it took him a moment to realize that, while he remained trapped in Bolee's body, his vision and consciousness had shifted to Udao. He strained as hard as he could, but could make no connection with her as he had with Bolee and Fanusan.

Alex watched Nathaniel grab Bolee's arm and wrap it around his shoulders while Udao did the same with the other. Both gently stood up, lifted him upright, and half walked, half dragged him to Nathaniel's hut.

Zagtagan was several huts away, weaving with other ladies, when she saw Nathaniel and Udao dragging Bolee toward the hut. She stopped what she was doing and ran to them. When she arrived, she felt Bolee's forehead and became concerned, because it was burning from fever. She yelled at Udao to get cool water, and Udao ran out and returned with a brimming jar. Zagtagan soaked a cloth in the water, and placed it over Bolee's forehead while attempting to bring him back to consciousness. She spoke loudly and even slapped his face a few times, but Bolee just lay there limp and insensate as his auntie held his head on her thighs and rocked him back and forth like a baby.

Within minutes, many people had gathered around the hut to see what was happening. After several failed attempts to bring Bolee back to consciousness, Nathaniel asked Udao to tell him exactly what happened. Udao told Nathaniel that Bolee had been healthy and strong one second, and then suddenly fell ill without explanation. "This must be the work of a bad *anito* that wants to kill Bolee," said Nathaniel's wife. She knew they needed the village exorcist, and said to Udao, "Quick, go get the *insupak* while there's time." Udao quickly broke through the observing crowd to find the old man. Several minutes later, she returned with the old *insupak*.

The crowd parted, allowing him to enter the hut. The *insupak* was the oldest Igorot on the reservation, nearly seventy years old and half-blind from severe cataracts. He wore a red long coat woven by the village women and walked surprisingly quick for his age; in fact, his feet left a small cloud of dust behind him as he quickly shuffled across the dry ground toward Bolee. Everyone fell quiet, looking respectfully at his wrinkled old face as he walked past them.

When he saw Bolee laying there on his auntie's thighs, he instructed everyone, including her, to leave the hut and wait outside. At this point, Alex's vision moved to the old man; though it was blurred and obscured, it was better than not seeing at all. After a few moments of examining Bolee, he lifted Bolee's head and rested it on his thighs as he sat there with his feet crossed. he began rubbing Bolee's forehead gently with one hand as he bent forward, saying, "*Anito* who makes this person very sick, go away." He repeated this over and over, mumbling low, and frequently exhaling his breath to assist the *anito's* departure. This went on for almost an hour, but Bolee's fever seemed to get worse.

As a last-ditch effort attempt, the old man called for the performance of a *wachaowad* ceremony to drive away the evil spirit from him. He suspected that the *anito* came from the man who had stolen from the woman earlier, so he instructed Nathaniel to return to where the man had been found guilty with certain items for the ceremony. After the old man taught him what to say when performing the ceremony, Nathaniel went back as instructed, carrying a live chicken in a basket, a small amount of *tapey*, some rice, and a stick. Alex's consciousness and vision immediately left Udao and shifted into Nathaniel, even as he still felt Bolee's body burning with the fever.

When he reached the location, Nathaniel walked towards the perimeter fence that separated their village from a small patch of trees. He ignored the American observers on the other side and proceeded with the ritual. After setting the chicken, *tapey,* and rice on the ground next to the fence, he picked up the stick and waved it towards the trees and repeated the words, *"A-li-ka' ab a-fi'-ik Bolee en-ta-ko' is a'-fong sang'-fu."*

One of the Americans looked to his friend and asked, "What's he doing?"

"Dunno, this is the first time I've seen this," the other replied.

Nathaniel heard their whispering and suddenly remembered a story of how a white man's *anito* had once killed many people in a neighboring *ato*. He repeated the words several more times, but a nervous glance toward the hut and the *insupak* who stood in its doorway revealed that Bolee showed no signs of improvement.

Again, he thought about the white man's murderous *anito*, and decided to say the ceremonial words in English. "Come, soul of Bolee. Come with us to the house to feast," said Nathaniel. He repeated the words in English several more times, but after no signs of improvement, resumed in Ibontoc. Still nothing happened, and he become very worried, because he knew Bolee would die if he could not entice the *anito* to leave.

As Nathaniel desperately repeated the words, Alex felt himself drifting out of Bolee towards the trees. As he floated away from Bolee and Nathaniel, the words coming from Nathaniel's mouth started to sound like garble. For some reason, he was no longer able to understand Ibontoc.

The feeling of weightlessness increased, until Alex felt like a feather ascending towards the sky. He looked down once more, and saw that he was already several hundred feet above the ground. The entire Igorot reservation, and the World's Fair itself, shrank as he continued to ascend.

The bright patch of light suddenly appeared, directly above him. *Finally,* he thought. *This is it for me. Please have pity on me.*

Alex was ready to give up and die when he looked towards the clouds and suddenly saw the *insupak* hovering above him. The old man wore a red native cloth over his head, making it seem as if he were wearing a hood. Was the old man the mysterious person in the red-hooded jacket who had been haunting him over the last few days? He wanted to get a closer look at his face, but the old man stayed far enough away so that his face remained unseen. But it had to be the *insupak,* didn't it?

The red-hooded man pointed downward in the direction of Bolee's limp body, then disappeared into thin air. As soon as he vanished, Alex felt himself falling rapidly toward the ground, headed straight towards Bolee. The closer he got, the more he experienced the feeling of disappointment and regret that had led to Bolee's collapse.

As Alex re-entered Bolee, the native man briefly opened his eyes and saw a pair of wrinkled hands rubbing his forehead, just before he passed out again. Zagtagan and Udao were the first to see his eyes open. They turned toward the crowd and told them what they had seen, and suddenly everyone began believing that Bolee would recover.

The old man confirmed their belief, and asked everyone to return to their huts so he could finish treating Bolee. Within minutes, everyone was gone, including Zagtagan and Udao. Alex desperately wanted to see the face of the old man, but he was looking out of those damaged eyes again, and Bolee remained too weak to open his own eyes.

Deep into the night, well after everyone else was sound asleep, the old man continued rubbing Bolee's forehead and mumbling the same words over and over. Alex tried opening Bolee's eyes, but couldn't. Finally, the old man looked around to make sure nobody was watching. The coast was clear, so he leaned forward and spoke to Bolee in English: "Alex, your journey is not over. You have a long way to go yet. I realize you are scared to find out more about your true self, but there is nothing to fear, for you have yet to discover the treasure that awaits you. When I slap this man's face, you will regain consciousness and face your destiny."

The old man slapped Bolee , and Bolee immediately opened his eyes. Everything was blurry, even more so than the *insupak*'s vision; neither Bolee nor Alex, whose vision was inhabiting Bolee again, could see clearly. Bolee rubbed his eyes, attempting to clear his vision. Alex was very anxious to see the mysterious man; but as soon as Bolee's vision cleared, Alex found himself staring at the fire-like glow of an Igorot shield.

It was hard to tell, but it looked like the red-hooded man was crouched behind the shield, holding it in front of Alex's face. Then the shield was suddenly pulled away, and the next thing he saw was the fire-like glow of a spear being held by the blurry image of the red-hooded man. Everything was blurry except for the shield and spear. Like the cobra, both items were identical to the images he'd encountered on the blanket and in the air at the Sagada Caves. Again, he tried focusing on the man, but Bolee's vision remained blurred. The spear suddenly cocked backward, giving Alex the impression that it was about to be thrown at him. *No, no, please no!* Alex thought.

Bolee was still too weak to try to stop the spear, and before Alex could sputter out another thought, the spear was flying towards Bolee's chest.

CHAPTER 9

As a blast of fresh air entered his lungs, Alex opened his eyes to find himself lying back against several sacks of rice. He immediately smelled a terrible, sour stink. He was inside some type of building, but the lighting was so poor that it was hard to see anything. Sunbeams of light streaked through the small openings in the wall, casting bits and pieces of morning light here and there. He heard a chewing noise and turned his head to his right, only to be startled by the huge head of a carabao right next to him, chewing some sort of cud while exhaling its nasty, sour breath on the person Alex inhabited.

As he jumped back, startled, he bumped up against a rifle leaning against the rice sacks. His body grabbed the rifle as it fell, stood, and held it in the small beam of light that lit up the carabao's head to examine it. The sunbeam also revealed the sun-browned but relatively pale skin of his wrist. His wrist remained in the light as the body examined the gun, and Alex looked harder to make sure he was really a white man.

Just then, the door of the barn swung open to let in a blinding blanket of light. Alex's body raised his hands in front of his eyes to block as much of the direct light as possible, to keep it from blinding him, as moans and groans filled the air. He looked around the barn and saw at least a dozen white men lying on their sides and backs, with their hands also raised in front of their eyes.

"Reveille!" shouted the backlit silhouette of the man standing in the middle of the opened door. "Up and at 'em, ladies! Time to put those Nips into the ground! Muster at 0700 outside the officer's quarters, which, for those of you who don't remember, is where the villagers fed us last night!"

"Hey, Sarge," moaned a man sitting up next to Alex. The person Alex was in looked down at the man speaking to him and nodded his head in acknowledgement, while wiping the sleep from his eyes with one hand. The man pointed to the rife in Alex's hand and said, "I think that's my rifle."

Alex's body handed it to the man and turned his attention back to the silhouetted man, who hollered, "Sergeant Tebow!"

"Yessir!" Alex's body replied briskly.

"We're moving lighter than light today. Weapons and rounds only. If it jingles or jangles, lose it. The Nips listen to that classical shit they call music and their ears are trained to pick up crickets pissing a hundred yards away. I want to be up their diapers pulling the trigger on their balls before they have any hint of what's about to go down. If we're going to rescue our friends from that shitty camp, we have to be silent and deadly!"

"Silent and deadly! Understood sir!" Tebow replied confidently.

Alex could not believe that he'd just spoken perfect English; he'd become accustomed to hearing himself speak Ibontoc. As he was trying to get his bearings, his new body walked out of the barn and into the sunlight. Once outside, Alex glimpsed the bright patch of light in the sky again. This time it was farther away than normal.

It was only a bit after 0600, and the temperature was already in the mid-eighties. He saw some Filipino men splashing water on their faces at a little creek ten yards away and decided to join them. As he approached, one them turned and looked at him as if he were a stranger. He seemed surprised that Sgt. Tebow was about to join them.

When Tebow greeted the four Filipinos next to him, Alex still couldn't believe he was speaking English. Moreover, he still couldn't believe he was *white*. One of the four men turned toward the others and said something in Tagalog. Hearing them speak bewildered Alex even more, because unlike before, he no longer understood a word they said. Their language sounded much different than the Ibontoc and Kankanaey that his ears were accustomed to hearing, and began to wonder if being a white man had something to do with why he didn't understand them.

Alex tried to read the mind of Tebow. His first attempt worked. A bit surprised, Alex quickly learned that the Filipinos next to him were part of a 200-man guerrilla force led by a Filipino officer named Captain Ongtengco. These men were referred to as Scouts. They wore normal U.S. Army uniforms with specially made leather boots to accommodate their unusually large, wide feet. Most of them spoke good English because they'd attended high school, which was taught in English. For Tebow, fighting alongside these men was normal; but it was something Alex still needed to adjust to.

One of the Scouts handed Tebow a small wooden bowl filled with a half-dozen large, cooked eggs and gestured to him to eat one with them. He was hungry and gladly picked the largest one, held it in his hands, and looked at it curiously. It was larger than any egg he had ever seen, which led him to think that it wasn't what he'd initially thought it was. He looked at the Scouts and asked, "Um...is this a chicken egg?"

Unfortunately, *these* Scouts didn't speak English, and just looked at him with confusion. "Chicken," he said. "Is this chicken? You know, buck buck buck," he said as he imitated the movements of a chicken with his head and arms.

The men instantly knew what he meant and began shaking their heads, grinning. One held up an egg and said, "*Balut.*" The others repeated, "*Balut,*" and began quacking like ducks. When Tebow learned it was a duck egg, he smiled and displayed a "been there, done that" look on his face. He was about to peel the egg when one of the Scouts grabbed his hand and gestured at him to follow his example.

Tebow agreed, and watched the Scout's instructions. First, the Scout held the egg upright and punched a small hole in the top with his knife. Tebow reached for his own knife, and did exactly what the Scout did. Then the Scout turned the egg upside down and drank the juices that dribbled out of the hole.

"Mmmm," said Tebow, as he drank the liquids. "A bit sweet and pleasant."

The other Scouts smiled, each with an impressed look in his eyes, and encouraged him to continue. Tebow didn't know what the big deal was, so he just awaited for the next instruction. The Scout then began slowly removing the shell patch by patch, starting at the hole. As Tebow did the same, he quickly learned that this was no normal egg.

Staring at him in all its ghastly splendor was something that reminded him of a science experiment gone horribly wrong. The blood drained from his face as he stared at a small duck fetus, surrounded by its own albumen with sprawling red blood vessels all over it. A tiny beak jutted out from the skull, while pin feathers poked out here and there. Tucked in another area was an unidentifiable yellowish organ that looked vital in some way. The yolk?

A slimy membrane covered everything, shimmering in the sunlight. The Scout gestured that he should empty the egg into his mouth, but the thought of just having swallowed the thing's amniotic fluid made Tebow feel like vomiting. The Scout then slurped the fetus into his mouth, and chewed loudly. Alex was just as grossed out as Tebow as he heard what he thought was the crunching of tiny bones...but he wasn't sure if that was real, or just Tebow's imagination. After slowly chewing and swallowing the contents of his egg, the Scout intentionally let out a big belch, smiled from ear to ear, and looked at Tebow as if to challenge his manhood.

The other Scouts couldn't help but laugh hysterically at the sight of Tebow's ghostly face and frozen body. They began holding their arms out while thrusting their hips, as if they were suggesting that the *balut* would make him a stronger lover.

To Alex's horror, Tebow said, "What the hell," as he closed his eyes and slurped the fetus into his mouth. The Scouts began cheering as they continued to laugh. Unlike the Scout, Tebow chewed as fast as he could before swallowing the duck fetus in its entirety. To his surprise, it actually tasted pretty good. Alex thought so too.

The demonstrating Scout rubbed his stomach and asked Tebow, "*Masarap?*"

Tebow replied, "If that means delicious, then yes, delicious. Tastes kinda like...kinda like...quack quack quack," he said.

The Scout patted Tebow on the back, and said "*Aswang Puti,*" which (as Alex later learned) was a white version of a vampire-like creature of Filipino folklore. Tebow had no idea what it meant; he jovially raised his hands in the air, as if he'd just knocked out a boxer. The Scouts returned to their unit and continued smiling while referring to him as "*Aswang Puti, Aswang Puti.*"

After they left, Tebow knelt and bent forward to splash water on his face. While doing so, Alex looked at his reflection in the creek's surface. Through the ripples he made out that Tebow's hair was light brown, his nose long and pointed, and his eyes blue. Alex had a flashback to his childhood years, recalling how he'd often looked in the mirror, wishing that he looked more like his white friends. He particularly remembered how he was always pinching his nose, wishing it weren't so flat, and crumpling up his hair, wishing it weren't so straight. *I guess I finally got my wish,* he thought.

As he stood, a number of other Scouts came to greet Tebow. They must have just spoken to the other Scouts, because they addressed him as "Sergeant *Aswang Puti.*" Amused, Tebow bowed graciously, accepting the fact that he had a new name amongst the Scouts. These men spoke English, unlike his earlier friends, and had just returned from a reconnaissance of the POW camp. After a few humorous exchanges about his recent breakfast, Tebow engaged the Scouts in a short conversation about the camp.

According to the scouts, they had found it impossible to enter without being detected. They also told him matter-of-factly that they had observed the cold-blooded execution of several American prisoners, which was performed in broad daylight in front of all the other prisoners. The soldiers were dragged blindfolded before the audience, forced to their knees, and each shot in the chest. Immediately after being shot, and before their bodies fell to the ground, Japanese officers had beheaded them with their swords.

The thought of the brutal execution caused Tebow's gorge to rise, and sent shivers up the man's spine. Alex felt the same horror, and began wondering why he was there, and what any of this had to do with him. Then Tebow caught sight of the officer who'd woken him up. He leaned down and took one last gulp of the fresh artesian water from the creek, said goodbye to the Scouts, and began jogging toward the officer.

"Sir!" Tebow called out.

The officer heard him and stopped, looked around to see if anyone else was nearby, and replied, "What's up, cuz?" The officer was Lieutenant Dave Daly, Tebow's older maternal cousin. They'd both grown up in Springfield, Massachusetts, and were very close. Daly was a year older, having graduated from Notre Dame University and become an Army officer at the Officer Candidate School located at Fort Benning, Georgia. Tebow had graduated from the University of Florida and was half way into OCS when the war's escalation made him want to head for the front lines sooner than later. He left Fort Benning and entered the Army as an enlisted soldier. As fate would have it, he found himself serving in the same battalion with Daly: the Army's new Ranger Battalion.

Daly was a tall, skinny man whose gaunt face always made him look like he hadn't eaten for weeks. Tebow, on the other hand, was somewhat shorter and fifty pounds heavier, with a very muscular build and a face that looked like he *always* had plenty to eat, even when he didn't. Physically, they were so different that nobody would have guessed they were first cousins. They both served in F Company's second platoon; however, they didn't spend much time together, since it was considered unacceptable for enlisted soldiers to socialize with officers. From the very beginning of their assignment to the Rangers, they had agreed to keep their kinship to themselves, to prevent any accusations of favoritism. Tebow always saluted his cousin and followed his orders to the letter, as any good sergeant would.

Neither man had seen much action since arriving in the Philippines. They were part of the invasion of Leyte, which was expected to be very dangerous; but when they landed on the island, the Japanese had already evacuated. On the afternoon of January 27, their commander, Lieutenant Colonel Neu, had returned from the Army headquarters with orders for the men of Company C. His packet had also included a special order for F Company's second platoon: They were to partake in a raid-and-rescue mission to free American POWs from the Japanese concentration camp in Baguio.

Colonel Neu told the men that the raid would be extraordinarily dangerous, and assured them that unlike Leyte, the intelligence for *this* mission was correct. He advised them that they would have to hike thirty miles into the mountains through heavily occupied areas, and that some, possibly many, of them would not make it back alive. Never had their unit been tested under such circumstances, and this made the cousins excited—yet very nervous.

"Gonna be another hot one," Tebow said to Daly as he approached him.

"Cut the bullshit, Amos. It's been hotter than hell ever since we landed on this Jap-infested island. What's really on your mind?"

"You know me too well, L-T." Tebow looked him in the eyes and said, "Dave, the intel I'm hearing from these Scouts is that the Baguio POW camp is huge, much bigger than we expected, and surrounded by nothing but flat land. They say it's impossible to approach it undetected, even at night."

Daly nodded. "Don't worry about what they say—just follow me and we'll be fine. I've got something up my sleeve." He wiggled his arm to illustrate.

"You mean besides that bony arm?" Tebow grinned and saluted him, then said softly, "Don't worry; I got your back. I promised Aunt Cathy I'd bring you home alive, and I damn sure don't want another strapping from her. She's got a strong arm."

"Ha! I promised Aunt Pam the same about you. Except she said she'd take a shotgun to me if you came home in a coffin. Loaded with rock salt, of course."

***

They spent a long, grueling day going over their plans for the raid, adjusting them to fit the new information acquired from the Scouts. With less than three hours before sunset, Daly and his platoon of thirty Rangers began their trek toward the Baguio camp. The plan was to have F Company flank the camp and attack it from the rear. While the Japanese focused their attention there, C Company would attack from the front and the Scouts would keep reinforcements from crossing a nearby bridge to reach the camp.

"I hate this fuckin' tall grass, Sarge," one of the Rangers said to Tebow as they pushed through the six-foot congon grass that grew everywhere.

"Yeah, me too, Jones," replied Tebow. "It makes me itch like crazy."

An hour and a half into their trek, Tebow caught up to his cousin to see how much farther they had to go. Daly raised his clenched fist in the air, signaling a stop, then pulled out his map and compass to review their progress with Tebow. After perusing it for a minute or two, he reported, "We're about two klicks from the POWs. Straight ahead."

Tebow stood on his toes and raised his head toward the direction they were going, but was unable to see much because of the congon grass. As he looked, though, Alex caught sight of the patch of light in the sky, approximately a mile ahead of them. He did the conversion and realized that two klicks was just over a mile. Something told him they were on the right path.

As the sun set and the tropical daylight began fading quickly into night, Daly led his men into a deep, weedy ravine that snaked along one side of the camp towards the rear, where they were to breach the wire fence and attack. Tebow saw the look of concern in his cousin's eyes as he looked ahead. He crawled up next to Daly, and saw that the ravine only concealed them for another hundred yards or so. After that, they had to cross sixty yards of grass that was cut no higher than three inches from the ground: a killing field. The Japanese soldiers in the lookout towers would easily see them, and mow them down from above with their machine guns. Their rescue mission suddenly looked like a suicide mission.

Afraid that some of the men would sense his cousin's sudden worry, Tebow donned a look of confidence, turned to the men behind him, and loudly whispered, "As soon as night falls, those Nips aren't going to know what hit them."

The Rangers closest to him quickly passed down his message, and it traveled all the way back to the last man in the ravine. The nervous tension that filled the ravine was quickly replaced by a new sense of confidence as a result of Tebow's words. Daly sensed it immediately, and shot his younger cousin a look of gratitude.

As night set in, they approached the end of the ravine. Unfortunately, the full moon had already risen, lighting up the killing field almost as well as stadium lights. This deepened Daly's concerns, because it seemed impossible that they'd be able to cross the open area without being seen. He hand-signaled the men to stay put as he and Tebow crawled fifteen yards ahead for a closer look. After distancing themselves from the rest of the Rangers, they considered the well-lit remaining sixty yards. They were near two lookout towers and at least three heavily re-enforced pillboxes, all of which were manned with heavy machine guns itching to use Rangers for target practice. The moonlight made the Japanese soldiers so visible that the insignia on their uniforms were easily visible. Tebow whispered, "How the hell are we supposed to cross that undetected?"

"Good question. Maybe we wait and hope for clouds to come our way."

Tebow snorted. "You gonna pull that surprise out of your sleeve anytime soon?"

"I hope so," Daly sighed. "No guarantee that it'll happen, or even that it'll work, though." Both looked up at the sky and saw nothing but stars and a bright full moon.

Alex didn't see the bright patch of light, and wondered why it wasn't there anymore.

"I don't see any clouds, and we're already behind schedule," whispered Daly after a long moment. "The attack won't commence until we fire the first shots, and I just know Charlie Company is wondering what the hell's going on. We got to do something fast, or this whole mission is blown. I think we're just going to have to charge the fence with rifles blaring."

"That's suicide," Tebow replied flatly. "There's gotta be a better way."

Daly looked at the ground and said, "I don't know, cuz. Thought there was, but you know, things don't always go the way I plan them. I planned on becoming an officer with a comfy admin MOS, but look where that plan got me—in this shithole."

Tebow continued peering forward and said, "There you go again, beating yourself up for nothing. Just because things don't go the way you plan them doesn't mean your real plan in life has changed."

"What the hell do you know about my plan in life?"

"I don't, but God does. He said in the Bible, 'For I know the plans that I have for you, plans to prosper you and not to harm you, plans to give you hope and a future'."

"Man, Aunt Pam and Uncle Bob sure drove that deep into you. You really believe all that stuff?"

"You bet your ass, Dave. If we die today, it's all part of a bigger plan."

"Okay, Amos, but I'd prefer to get through this alive. What do we do now?"

Tebow paused. The only thing he could think of was the one thing he'd been doing all his life: "We listen. We just listen for what comes next."

That's when a deep, subliminal drone that they hadn't been paying attention to suddenly grew into a huge roar, and the shadow of an airplane swept over the ravine and into the camp. Both looked up in the air, but couldn't see what had passed over—though Alex saw that the incredibly bright white light had reappeared. It was clear to him again that only he could see it, for Daly made no mention of it and Tebow turned away without noticing it. But as soon it appeared, the moonlight disappeared as a dense cloud rolled in overhead, and everything turned pitch black. Daly whispered excitedly, "There she is! A little late, but right in the nick of time!"

The plane roared over them again. It didn't sound like anything Tebow had ever heard before, but in the darkness, he caught the gleam of his cousin's teeth. He was grinning. "What the hell was that? It doesn't sound like a Zero *or* one of ours."

"Don't worry. It's the cavalry, coming over the hill."

The Japanese became very alarmed as they scurried frantically under shelter, shouting at each other. All their faces were turned toward the sky, scanning it to identify what had just flown over. As the plane came back around, it passed low, buzzing the length of the camp.

"Hell yeah," said Daly. "Midnight Madonna is here! It's one of those new planes they named Black Widows, but I've heard them called Midnight Madonnas."

"If it starts firing at the Nips, we're up shit creek," said Tebow, knowing that heavy Japanese reinforcements were nearby, and that any weapons fire would surely trigger their attention before the Scouts were ready. But all it did was draw their attention, making pass after pass without firing a single shot from its cannons.

"It's got their attention," Daly whispered. "Time to go."

Tebow passed the word down the line with hand signals and harsh whispers, and soon Second Platoon of F Company moved swiftly toward the fence while the Japanese fixed their terrified eyes on the sky. The Americans made it completely undetected, and the men equipped with wire snips cut several openings through the fence. Each man then took aim at a Japanese soldier, and waited for Daly's first shot to signal the barrage. A few moments after the Black Widow made its final pass, the moonlight began to reappear, just enough for the Rangers to clearly see the silhouettes of the enemy soldiers. Daly aimed his rifle at the head of a sentry located in one of the watchtowers, took a deep breath, held it for a split second, and gently squeezed the trigger.

The rifle cracked, the sentry fell, and suddenly the air around Tebow was filled with the crackle of gunfire as he and the other Rangers took out their chosen targets, mowing down the Japanese closest to the perimeter. The volley hit the enemy so fast and hard that they had no time to react before they died of terminal lead poisoning. One of the Japanese in a pillbox was shot so many times in the neck that his head flew off his body and landed a few feet away, eyelids twitching and mouth wide. Alex stared with horrified fascination until Tebow looked away, directing his attention towards the buildings he was advancing toward, firing at every Japanese soldier he saw.

The weapons fire and screams of the surprised guards magnified suddenly as the men of Charlie Company broke through the main gate and joined the melee. Everything was happening amazingly fast, and the battle was taking shape as a very uneven fight in favor of the Americans. Before long, the entire camp was filled with Rangers, and the Japanese were desperately trying to escape the massacre.

Tebow broke open the door of the first building he reached and saw a dozen men trying to hide. Some were in the corners balled up, while others just stood in the open with their eyes closed, as if hoping to make themselves invisible. He grabbed the nearest prisoner by the arm, but he resisted and crawled desperately away.

"We're Americans!" shouted Tebow. "We're here to set you free. Don't be afraid!"

"Don't listen to him!" yelled one of the prisoners in the dark. "They're Nips pretending to be Americans! They're just playing their sick games with us again! They want us to run so they can use us for target practice!"

"No. No. *No*, goddammit!" shouted Tebow. "I really *am* an American. We're Army Rangers, come to rescue you!"

"What the hell is a Ranger?" ask one prisoner.

"If'n you's American, prove it!" shouted another.

"Shit, we don't have time for this!" retorted Tebow. "There's Nips crawling all over the place out there. We gotta go!"

"Nobody move!" shouted the first prisoner.

Tebow quickly grew agitated with the stubbornness of the prisoners and shouted, "I'm Sergeant Amos Tebow, U.S. Army Rangers. It's a new outfit, specifically intended for missions like this one! I went to the University of Florida. We Gators haven't had a winning season since 1934, and last year we didn't even have enough players to make a roster because of this godforsaken war! My cousin, on the other hand, went to Notre Dame, and can't stop bragging about Knute Rockne and the Four Fucking Horsemen. He's very excited about their coach, that Leahy guy, and takes his Irish blood way too seriously. Is that American enough for you?"

"Ho-lee shit!" shouted a parched voice. "I cain't believe this Tennessee boy would ever be glad to see a Gator!" With that said, the officer from Tennessee stood up, walked to Tebow, and embraced him with all his might. Tears flowed from the man's eyes as he turned toward the dark room and told everyone to follow him out. One after the other, the men complied, some reluctantly.

Both Tebow and Alex were beside themselves; they couldn't believe the condition of the prisoners. The men were barely clothed, their bones prominent beneath their skins, and some were covered with sores. A few were barely able to walk, so the Rangers draped their twig-like arms around their shoulders and helped them out of the building.

Once out in the open air, Tebow discovered that the other Rangers were having an equally hard time getting the other prisoners to leave their barracks. He saw one Ranger strong-arm one of the prisoners to the door and then kick him from behind to get him out with the others. The shouting and questioning in one barrack was so loud that the Rangers fired their rifles into the air to scare the prisoners into leaving. They must have been used to the sound of weapons, though, because they still refused to leave. At that point, the Rangers exited the building and tossed in smoke grenades. Finally, the prisoners stumbled out, their arms raised, and the Rangers gathered them up.

Many had no idea where they were going. Most had apparently never been outside the prisoner's fenced-in area in the middle of the camp. When the Rangers yelled at them to head for the main gate, many went the opposite way, because the main gate to the prisoner's yard lay in the opposite direction of the camp's main gate. It was truly havoc, and the Rangers grew increasingly nervous that the evacuation was taking too long and that the Japanese reinforcements might show up at any time.

Tebow saw a few prisoners thirty yards away running the wrong direction, and dashed off toward them to turn them around. When he drew closer, he began yelling instructions at them to turn and go the other way. Five prisoners heard him, stopped, and turned around as Tebow pointed them into the right direction. The other four just kept running the wrong way. Tebow shook his head in frustration and began pursuing them. When he was about fifteen yards away from the men, he realized that they were running much too fast to be frail, malnourished prisoners. Then he noticed one of them wearing those funny-looking Japanese split-toed boots. Just as he realized they were actually Japanese soldiers dressed as escaping prisoners, all four stopped in their tracks, turned, pulled out pistols, and opened fire on him.

Tebow immediately hit the dirt and rolled to his left behind a dead Japanese officer. Bullets whizzed by his ears as he squirmed his way into the meager cover. Cursing, he aimed his rifle and squeezed the trigger, but nothing happened; the fucking useless thing had jammed! Again! The

Japanese soldiers saw this, and continued firing their pistols as they advanced toward him. Tebow grabbed the dead soldier and pulled him on top of himself as a shield.

Seconds later, he moved his head to see how close they were. A feeling of helplessness overwhelmed him when he saw they were only a few feet away, swords drawn. Unwilling to die lying down, he threw the dead soldier off him and began to rise. The moment he did, the nearest Japanese soldier began to swing his sword towards Tebow—an instant before his head exploded from a bullet shot from behind. The man's lifeless body staggered forward, its momentum carrying it into Tebow, knocking him to the ground and landing on top of him. More shots rang out from behind the Japanese, causing their bodies to jerk with multiple bullet strikes, taking all three down in seconds. Tebow shoved the dead man off him and saw his cousin standing fifteen yards behind the four dead Japanese soldiers, his M-1 carbine smoking. "Who's got who's back *now*?" yelled Lt. Daly, grinning before running off to assist the other Rangers.

It took a while, but the prisoners were finally rousted out, gathered in, and herded toward the river. Many were in much worse condition than the Rangers had expected; after their adrenaline got them out of the main gate, they began to collapse from sheer weakness and shock. Rangers found themselves making stretchers by tying uniform coats to two rifles and carrying those who were unable to walk. Alex was aghast; it was one thing to watch movies about the war, something totally different to see its atrocities up close and in person. All the killing and violence was becoming too real for him.

A Filipino scout from Ongtengco's outfit suddenly appeared before Daly to inform him that they had been unsuccessful in destroying the entire bridge, and that they needed to hurry and take protective measures just in case they were overrun by the enemy. Daly and the rest of the Rangers could hear the fierce fighting in the distance, but had no idea who had the advantage. They became very nervous; if the Scouts lost, it wouldn't take long for the Japanese reinforcements to catch up to them.

Finally they reached the river and crossed it. Waiting on the other side were a dozen or so carabao-driven carts that local farmers had gathered to help with their escape. Though they now had transportation for the weaker prisoners, they still weren't sure if the Scouts had succeeded in their mission, because they could still hear fighting at a distance. They loaded the carts with prisoners and kept pushing on. After about an hour, the battle sounds suddenly stopped. The Rangers hustled to the rear of the column, leaving Colonel Neu's detachment in charge of the POWs—just in case Ongtengco had failed and they ended up having to hold off the Japanese soldiers.

Still pressing forward, the Rangers followed in the rear, constantly looking over their shoulders to see if the Japanese were coming. Long minutes went by, and then the Rangers felt a rumbling in the ground. Their first thoughts were that Japanese tanks were approaching; but before their imaginations could get the best of them, the pounding of horses' hooves filled the air as two Filipino Rangers came riding toward them. The Scouts caught up to Daly and informed him of their success in completely destroying the bridge. Relieved to hear the good news, Daly ran to the front and informed Colonel Neu in turn.

The rest of the trip took longer than expected—much longer than it had taken them to get to the camp. This wasn't surprising, in retrospect, given the condition of the POWs. It gave Alex plenty of time to reflect on what had just happened...but he *still* couldn't figure out how it possibly had anything to do with him. Could it be that he was related to one of the Scouts? No—they weren't even Igorot. As hard as he tried, he couldn't come up with anything to connect him to the recent events. All he could do was go along with events, as he'd been doing since he left the Sagada Caves.

Midway through their return trip, Tebow struck up a conversation with one of the former prisoners, one of the fortunate few strong enough to walk. The man turned out to be an allied Australian soldier, Private Jonathan Hurlow. He told Tebow horrific stories of how he and thousands of Australian, British, American, and Filipino prisoners had been first marched to an old Filipino military camp before being relocated to Baguio.

In his strong Australian brogue, Hurlow recalled how they were forced into a camp that was built to accommodate perhaps one-fifth the number of prisoners brought there. When they arrived, the Japanese commander made it clear that they were captives and not prisoners, and would be treated as such. They also made it clear that the rules of the Geneva Convention did not apply to them. There was no running water, very little food, and their sanitary conditions were limited to slit trenches. To compound matters, the heat was intolerable. The flies that fed on their shit and flew out of the maggot-infested trenches swarmed over the place, spreading all sort of diseases. Hurlow broke down crying when he recalled how malaria, dysentery, and other diseases had began killing literally hundreds of men each day. Within a week, all the 70+ other survivors in his unit died in that hellhole. He was the only one who had survived to be relocated to Baguio.

Tebow became ill and upset at what he was hearing. Even Alex, who had several Japanese-American friends, became enraged. For both, their dislike for the Japanese soldiers they had encountered rapidly scaled up to pure hatred. "Was it any better at Baguio?" Tebow asked quietly.

"If you call a place to piss and shite and food every other day or so better, then yeah, I guess you can say that it was," replied the soldier. "But those Nips were a wicked bunch of blokes." Hurlow went on to tell him of the terrible games the Japanese played to trick prisoners into trying to escape, just so they could shoot them. He spoke of the inventive tortures that took place, and how beheadings were a common occurrence. When he mentioned how the Japanese sometimes left the dead body of an executed prisoner out in the open with his genitals stuffed in his mouth, Tebow felt like vomitting.

As they kept walking, Alex looked at all the prisoners lying in the carts. Tebow couldn't keep his eyes off them. Even with the stories he'd heard from the Australian, he still couldn't fathom all they had been through. A newfound sense of appreciation for their service settled in along with the profound sense of hatred toward the Japanese.

Fortunately, the Japanese never caught up, and they encountered no other enemy units during their trip back. When they arrived at their headquarters, they were greeted by the commanding General himself, Walt Krueger, who congratulated them for their bravery and success. The prisoners received medical treatment immediately, and Tebow joined the rest of his fellow soldiers in their reward of several rounds of whiskey.

CHAPTER 10

Shortly after the rescue at Baguio, Sergeant Amos Tebow, U.S. Army Rangers, received a meritorious battlefield promotion to Second Lieutenant. The promotion came partly because of his exemplary leadership and desire to become an officer, but mostly because the Army was desperate for more officers, due to the fact that reinforcements had never arrived at Bataan as promised. By then, the American forces in the Philippines were on the verge of defeat.

The prewar plans known collectively as War Plan Orange-3, designed to defend Corregidor and Bataan for six months until U.S. reinforcements could arrive, weren't going according to plan. Most of the U.S. Pacific Fleet had been destroyed at Pearl Harbor in the act that thrust the States into the war, and until it could be reconstituted, reinforcements would be slow in coming. With the American troops seriously short of supplies and the Imperial Japanese Army's continual overwhelming attacks, the end result was likely to be an American surrender.

Tebow had seen what had happened to those who surrendeɪ the Japanese, and vowed to go down fighting. Alex didn't blame him.

Shortly after his promotion, Lt. Tebow was handed his first order as a commissioned officer. He'd been attached to the 15th Infantry unit of the 2nd Battalion, which was trying to help restore the main line of resistance broken by the 20th Japanese Infantry Regiment. The high command was very concerned about the Japanese units that had broken through the American's main line of defense, to form isolated pockets of resistance. Everyone knew that anyone sent to any of the pockets was sure to see plenty of combat.

As he was driven down the main trail to his new unit, Tebow asked his driver, a lanky Negro, to slow down at the sight of Filipino Scouts carrying the bodies of their comrades and those of their enemies past on stretchers. He watched as they organized the bodies alongside of the road. The driver told him that a battle had just taken place nearby. "This here checkpoint was taken over by the Nips not too long ago," he said in a low voice. "A whole platoon of our fellas was wiped out by them slant-eyed bastards. These Filipino Scouts just walked right in there and took it back. The area's secure now."

As Tebow watched, both he and Alex thought of what likely awaited him at his new assignment. The bodies scattered along the road were a stark reminder that Alex was very likely to see more killing in the days to come. *I've seen enough,* he thought. *I'm ready to go home.* He focused all his energy on imagining he was back in his body at the caves, hoping that it might transport him back to the reality he knew—but nothing happened. Then he thought that if he admitted his mistakes, he would return; so he concentrated and thought, *Okay, I know I've been a selfish bastard. I've learned my lesson.* Nothing happened; he was still trapped inside of Tebow. *What else am I suppose to learn from all this?* he wondered. *I've had it. I don't want to see any more killing!*

No dice.

When Tebow arrived at his new assignment, he reported to a Major Dachille. Dachille was glad to see him, because he'd recently lost two of his lieutenants in battle and was desperately shorthanded. After a brief introduction, Dachille invited Tebow into his tent for a drink.

When they entered his tent, Dachille reached into one of his cargo pockets and pulled out a small flask containing brandy. He sat down on an empty ammunition crate and asked Tebow to sit as well. Then he unscrewed the flask and poured brandy into two canteen cups. Tebow gladly accepted it and took a swig while Dachille read his file. After skimming it, Dachille poured them another round. He sipped thoughtfully, closed the file, and nodded in approval of Tebow's credentials. "It was a great thing you Rangers did for our men in Baguio," Dachille said.

"Thank you, sir," Tebow replied soberly. "I'm glad we were able to get our guys out of that hellhole."

The two men spent the next half hour talking about where Tebow was from, and how he and his cousin had managed to end up in the same unit. Dachille seemed to take an immediate liking towards Tebow—partly because of his participation at Baguio, but also because he was the first battlefield commissioned officer to serve under him. To Dachille, it was an advantage for his new lieutenant to have come from the enlisted ranks, because the Filipinos in his command needed a leader who had fought in the trenches.

After their conversation, Tebow asked Dachille for more details about his new assignment. Rather than replying verbally, Dachille stood up and asked the lieutenant to follow him outside. As they strode through the dense bamboo surrounding the camp, he
heard the sounds of a few men talking nearby in a half-familiar Filipino language. They sounded very close, but because the bamboo was so thick, he was only able to see a few yards ahead. After walking only fifteen yards or so, they came to a clearing.

Gathered in the clearing were several dozen Filipinos, sitting in deep squats with their rear ends nearly touching the ground. They wore small loincloths that covered their genitals, and all were barefoot. Most also wore the coat portion of a U.S. Army uniform, unbuttoned and without any shirt underneath. Some wore red embroidered headbands, while others wore basket-like caps on the crowns of their heads. Each had an odd-looking axe close at hand, as well as an M1 Garand rifle.

Tebow had never seen Filipinos who looked like these, and began to wonder if they even *were* Filipino. These men didn't have the fair skin, long noses, and height typical of the Scouts, most of whom had some Spanish heritage. For Tebow, it was easy to mistake a Scout for someone of Latin origins; but these men were truly indigenous.

As Tebow looked on with bewilderment, Alex was happy to see such a familiar sight. *Igorots,* he thought. *Maybe now I'll start getting some answers.* He looked as closely at them as he could, trying to see if any resembled the Igorots he knew, but everybody looked new to him. He couldn't help but notice that some of the men had the same kind of chest tattoos he remembered on the Igorots before. *Maybe they're from the same villages.*

"Sir, are these Scouts?" Tebow asked Dachille.

"Scouts?" Dachille replied facetiously. "No, son, these are Igorots."

"What's that? Are they Filipino?"

"To the untutored eye, yes. But I wouldn't call them that to their faces, because that would imply that their people were conquered by the Spaniards, and they don't like that," cautioned Dachille.

"Weren't they? I thought they were part of Spain for centuries."

"Not these people," Dachille said. "They're from a place way up in the mountains called Bontoc. Whatever you heard or read about the Spaniards conquering the Philippines, it's not all true. From what I understand, the Spaniards were never able to conquer these people, so to imply that they're "Filipino" is to also imply that they were conquered by King Philip of Spain. That's where they got the name "the Philippines" from, did you know that? At least that's what the Chaplain told me."

"Hmm. What else do you know about them?" asked the newly minted lieutenant.

"Well," drawled Dachille as he took another swig of brandy from the cup he carried with him, "From what I've seen at their village and from what the experts tell me, they're pretty much a peace-loving and industrious people. In fact, you won't believe the engineering feats they've accomplished in making all those intricate rice terraces along their mountains. I myself am an engineer by degree, and I was very impressed to see their terraces. It's no wonder that magazines like *National Geographic* call them the Eighth Wonder of the World. Don't let their peaceful nature fool you, though, because they fight with a ferocity that makes the Scouts look tame."

Tebow blinked. He didn't know of any group that fought more fiercely than the Filipino Scouts. "How and why is that, sir?" he asked.

Dachille smiled and replied, "How? Well, you'll just have to see for yourself. All I know is that at the moment, they're really pissed off at the Nips for raping the women of one of their villages. And just last week, we came upon a massacre of women and children in the middle of the woods. It looked like the Nips lined them up front to back and shot them dead. I've never seen angrier men. You wouldn't know it to look at them, though. They're going to serve their revenge cold."

"It pisses me off just hearing about it," replied Tebow.

"Yeah, well, you've heard the expression an eye for an eye, right?"

"Sure," answered Tebow.

"For these men it's a head for an eye," said Dachille, as he drew a thumb across his neck.

"You mean...?"

Dachille took another drink and replied, "These people have been cutting heads off their enemies since the beginning of time. They're goddamn headhunters, and they're good at it. And frankly, the Nips deserve worse." His lips narrowed to a thin, hard line.

Tebow looked at Dachille with a confused expression, wondering if the Major was making it up. Dachille saw the doubt in his eyes and said, "Look at some of the older men. See anything unusual about any of them?"

"You mean those big tattoos on their chests?" said Tebow.

"Yeah," answered Dachille. "Those big tattoos are awarded only to a man who's taken a head from one of his enemies. The Scouts are afraid of anyone who wears that tattoo. Hell, even I keep my distance from the tattooed men. I don't even talk to them or look them in the eyes. I just let their sergeant deal with them on my behalf."

With that said, Dachille called out to one of the Igorot men: "Sergeant Sutton!"

The man looked at Dachille, responded by nodding his head, and began walking toward them. When he arrived, Dachille introduced the sergeant to Tebow, and told the lieutenant that the sergeant would be his right hand man from then on. Sgt. Sutton just looked at the Lieutenant with a stoic look and saluted him.

Sutton looked very much like the other men in the unit, except that his legs were noticeably stockier than the rest. To Tebow, he appeared to be in his early to mid thirties, but Alex knew that he must have been somewhere in his early fifties. His uniform shirt displayed a set of worn sergeant stripes on each sleeve, without a rocker, and was unbuttoned. Tebow noticed that there were no tattoos on his chest, and was very interested in finding out why.

"So, Sgt. Sutton," Tebow said politely, "Is it true that the men out there with tattoos on their chests have beheaded an enemy?"

In very good English, Sgt. Sutton replied, "That is correct, sir."

"And you seem to be their same age, yet you have no tattoo," Tebow commented. "Why is that?"

"Many of us are now Christian, sir," replied the Sergeant. "We no longer practice the old ways. Because of your American missionaries and priests, some of those men with tattoos are now also Christians, and they no longer partake in such traditions; but there are many who still do."

Tebow glanced at Dachille, concerned. Dachille said quickly, "They are fully aware that the Army forbids such activities, isn't that correct, Sergeant?"

"Yes sir, that's correct," replied the Sergeant, who then turned to address Tebow. "Sir, we were just about to eat. Would you like some food?"

Normally, officers didn't share meals with enlisted men, but Tebow still felt like an enlisted man at heart. Furthermore, he wanted to get to know this strange looking bunch; but before he accepted the offer, he asked Dachille, "Sir, would it be acceptable if I put aside our regulation forbidding the fraternization of officers with enlisted men for the purpose of getting to know more about my command?"

"Spoken like a true field-promoted officer," replied Dachille proudly. "This isn't the regular Army, son. Here you need to adapt to your surroundings. You're not leading a passel of boys from Hicksville USA. These Igorots are seasoned warriors accustomed to sharing their meals with other warriors. They respect us not because of our commissions, but because we share enemies and battlefields with them. They don't recognize our leadership traditions. They recognize only bravery, and if you prove your bravery to them as a warrior, they'll respect you for that. I'm not even sure if they really understand our concept of leadership, to be honest—but they damn sure understand bravery, and what it takes to be a great warrior. Hell, from what the Sergeant told me, they don't even have village chiefs in Bontoc."

With that said, Sgt. Sutton asked one of the Igorots to bring some food to the two officers. One man quickly cut two small pieces of a wide banana stalk and placed some rice, cooked camote leaves, and meat on them. Both officers and the sergeant sat together on crates of ammunition while waiting for their meal.

"As you know, Lieutenant," said Dachille, "our supplies have practically run out. Fortunately, the Nips' eyesight is so bad that their pilots dropped a bunch of crates filled with rations near American camps instead of theirs. If it weren't for that, we might be starving by now. You're lucky, though, because these men were able to find some real meat this morning."

The Igorot handed the officers their food and went back to sit with the rest of his brothers-in-arms. Tebow glanced at the food, then looked to the sergeant for utensils, but saw Dachille eating with his hands. Half of Tebow's first handful of rice made it to his mouth, the other half landing on his lap. Not wanting to waste more food, he raised the stalk to his mouth and used his fingers to sweep the rice and vegetables into his mouth. Then he picked up a chunk of meat that resembled a sausage cut into two-inch pieces and ate it. "Finally, some real meat," he said, savoring the fatty juices that flooded his mouth.

Dachille looked at him, smiled, and continued eating. Tebow was so hungry that he finished his ration much sooner than the others. As he wiped his mouth, he noticed both men looking at him with a smile. "Haven't you ever seen a hungry man before?" Tebow said, smiling.

"Do you know what haggis is?" asked Dachille.

"Sure, it's that sausage the Scottish stuff into intestines. Is that what this is?"

Dachille looked at the sergeant and gestured for him to answer. Sutton wiped his mouth with his sleeve and paused before replying, "The Major calls it kennel haggis, sir. We call it *asu*, but you can just call it dog."

The lieutenant's eyes immediately opened wide, his cheeks ballooning as he placed his hands over his mouth to keep from vomiting. The Igorots began laughing, and appeared to be placing bets on whether he would throw up or not. Tebow's eyes crossed as he felt the food making its way up. "Oh shit!" laughed Dachille. "Hold that food in, Lieutenant! That's an order! That there is the food of warriors!"

Finally, Tebow regained his self-control, and did manage to keep his food down. The same Igorot who had brought them their food earlier returned with more. At first, Tebow waved his hands, gesturing that he'd had enough, but the Igorot gave him an angry look. Not wanting to offend him, he accepted the second serving. The man flashed him a big smile and walked away. "So the rumor about the natives eating dogs is true," said Tebow, around a mouthful of *asu*.

"Between dog and monkey, which the Scouts like, I'll take dog any day," replied Dachille. "I recently tried monkey stew, but when I saw a hand in the bowl, I felt like I was eating a baby."

Thinking of his experience with the balut, Tebow turned to Sutton and asked, "How about you? Do you like monkeys?"

The sergeant shook his head. "We don't eat monkey, because many of us still believe that, like the eagle and snake, monkeys were once men."

"Is dog a favorite of your people?" asked Tebow.

The Sergeant snorted. "The papers in America say it is, but they tell half-truths and mostly lies. Our favorite meat is chicken. Then there is pig and fish. Sometimes we eat our carabao, but dog is at the bottom of our preference. However, our distant neighbors, the Benguet, prefer dog over pig and fish; and there are some in the mountains who do not eat dog at all, because they use dogs for hunting and guarding. When I was a child, the Americans liked to watch us eat dog because it was amusing to them."

"Imagine that," said Dachille.

After finishing their meal, Dachille called for a meeting with Tebow, Sutton, and another sergeant to discuss the next day's mission. Inside his tent, Dachille spread a map over several crates stacked as a table. The map showed the 11th Division's main defensive line. A circle labeled "Small Pocket" was displayed just inside the east side of the main line. Northwest of that was a larger circular area labeled "Big Pocket." The west end had a finger-like protrusion labeled "Upper Pocket" shown breaching the main line.

Dachille pointed at the Upper Pocket, then leaned forward and said, "All right, men. Now that the Small and Big pockets are secured, General MacArthur wants this salient attacked tomorrow. He wants the Nips pushed out so that our main line of defense is restored. While the 92nd and 45th Infantry will be attacking here, we'll attack from the east. As with the other pockets, we don't know the exact number of troops the enemy has hunkered down there. What we do know is that they're probably well dug in, with tunnels to move from point to point—so expect the unexpected. "

Dachille paused for a moment to allow them to grasp what he'd just said. Then he looked at Tebow to gauge his reaction. "Any questions?"

"What kind of artillery support can we expect, sir?" Tebow asked.

"None," Dachille replied heavily. "The bamboo and trees are so dense that high trajectory shells will only result in overshoots, shorts, and tree impacts that could cost the lives of our own troops. Also, our 75-mm machine guns are useless here. Like the Small and Big Pockets, this is going to be another battle of rifles, bayonets, and axes."

After the meeting adjourned, Tebow approached Dachille in private. "I remember how nervous I was when I first led men into battle. It's natural," said Dachille, before he could even open his mouth.

Tebow looked at the ground and responded, "Sir, it's not so much that I'm nervous about leading the men." He raised his head and continued, "It's just that I'm concerned about how thick the jungle is here. I wasn't trained for this kind of combat, and quite frankly, I'm not sure I'm qualified to lead the men tomorrow."

Dachille looked at him with understanding and said, "Son, most of us haven't been trained in this kind of terrain. This was all new to me when I first got here, too, but I know you're more than qualified for this mission. You have the heart for it, but if you're gonna succeed tomorrow or any other day with these Igorots, you'll need to drop that notion of trying to be their leader. They're not looking for a leader. They're looking for a fellow warrior. They have a keen instinct about people. If they know you're a warrior, they'll stay by your side. Trust their instincts out there. They know their way around better than anyone I've ever known. You'll be fine, Lieutenant."

"Thank you for your vote of confidence, sir," Tebow replied, straightening. "You're absolutely right. I won't promise zero casualties or even a victory, but I will promise you this: You'll never see any soldier on this island fight as hard as I will. You'll never see any man push himself as hard as I'll push myself and this platoon. You can count on me, sir."

Dachille clapped him on the shoulder. "I know I can, Lieutenant."

That night, Alex found himself becoming anxious to take on the Japanese. He no longer wished to leave Tebow, the fear that he'd felt earlier had almost entirely disappeared. Thoughts of what the Japanese had done to the American, Filipino and Allied prisoners infuriated him, fueling a sense of vengeance that he'd never experienced before. He knew what Tebow was capable of, and he wanted to unleash serious payback on his newfound enemy.

The next morning, Tebow led his 30 men into the bamboo thicket toward the Upper Pocket. The visibility was no better than 10 yards in any direction and, in many areas, less than half that. The men were spread approximately 10 yards apart, their eyes constantly scanning their surroundings. Every now and then the wind would blow, stirring up an unsettling clacking of the bamboo stalks high above. This rattled Tebow somewhat, but he remembered what Dachille had told him, and relied on the keen senses of the Igorot Scouts.

Like Alex, Tebow was a bundle of nerves; and without realizing it, his nervousness was slowing down the platoon's rate of advance. Sutton did notice this, however, and moved up closer to his commanding officer, so that he was only five yards to the right. He kept pace with Tebow for about 10 yards, then began advancing ahead of him. Tebow picked up his pace to keep up with the sergeant.

A sudden burst of rifle fire echoed in the distance, and everyone immediately stopped, crouched, and raised their own rifles, aiming at nothing but bamboo, vines, and trees. After a long moment of silence, another volley sounded. Tebow wasn't able to determine the distance or direction it was coming from, so he gave the hand signal to keep advancing, this time at a slower pace.

They soon came across a small clearing no bigger than 20 yards wide by 15 deep. Sutton and the adjoining Igorots began moving towards the sides of the clearing to walk around it, but Tebow failed to notice their detour and entered the clearing. The Igorots to his left, taking their cue from Tebow, joined him in the clearing. Sutton caught sight of them from the corner of his eye, and immediately stopped—just as the ground five feet in front of him slowly rose a few inches. Without hesitation he fired a burst from his Garand into the crack between hidden trapdoor and true ground, drilling a neat trio of holes in the Japanese soldier's temple before he had a chance to open fire on the unsuspecting lieutenant. Suddenly enemy soldiers began popping out of the ground from all directions to fire at the platoon. Forewarned by Sutton's quick action, Tebow and his men hit the ground and engaged the enemy as they appeared.

Most of Tebow's shots were blocked by or ricocheted off the ubiquitous bamboo, but he managed to hit a few of his enemy. Feeling vulnerable, he crawled as fast as he could towards the hole where Sutton had shot the first Japanese soldier. It was the perfect cover. When he reached the hole, he dragged the dead man out and jumped in. In normal circumstances, he couldn't have been able to yank a full-grown man out of a four-foot hole in the ground, but his blood was pumped full of adrenaline.

Once inside, he methodically shot as many Japanese as he could see, carefully choosing his shots and taking them down like clockwork, one after the other.

The Igorots quickly became separated into three groups. One chased the enemy into the forest at one end of the clearing, another did the same at the other end, and Tebow, Sutton and the rest scrambled to find shelter against the overwhelming number of Japanese who had them pinned down near the clearing. From what he could see, Tebow sensed that the enemy was beginning to flank them to their advantage. He spotted a nearby group of dead fallen trees and bamboo, leaped out of his hole, and sprinted toward them. The trees provided protection on three sides. Sutton and nine other Igorots eventually made their way to Tebow, as they continued taking heavy fire from ahead and to either side. According to Sutton, there were at least 30 Japanese soldiers firing at them.

The gunfire soon slackened, as both sides realized that their rounds were being deflected or stopped by the thicket of bamboo and trees. They held their positions for fifteen minutes, selectively shooting at their enemies, conserving their ammunition. Tebow knew he and his men were sitting ducks, and would eventually be either flanked or overrun; they had to do something before that happened. So he ordered Sutton to hold that position, while he took several of the Igorots with him on a flanking maneuver. But to his dismay, the sergeant misunderstood him—or did he?—and proceeded to jump out of the shelter, followed by seven other men. Three followed Sutton; the other four went in another direction, each with a battle axe in one hand and a rifle in the other. Tebow and the remaining two Igorots immediately began laying down covering fire.

The enemy had just begun to return fire when the bloodcurdling yells of Igorots pealed through the jungle. Tebow caught sight of the group of three Igorots running from hidey-hole to hidey-hole, slaying the Japanese with their axes before they react. One would flip up the trapdoor with the barrel of his gun, while another knocked aside the enemy soldier's gun with his axe and the third finished him off with his axe. It was a horribly efficient process. As soon as the Igorot strategy became apparent to the Japanese, they began leaving their holes so as not to be sitting ducks for the Igorots' bloodstained axes—making them easier targets for Tebow and his group. The three Igorots eventually disappeared into the bamboo, continuing their reign of terror.

Sutton's battle cries immediately diverted Tebow's attention to the other side of their position, where the sergeant and the other three Igorots had headed. Sutton and two of the others were running toward holes that held Japanese soldiers; the fourth Igorot was held up fighting two Japanese soldiers, who had appeared from behind a dead tree trunk. The Igorot quickly planted his axe in the chest of one enemy while, with his other hand, he shot the second man in the head with his rifle. Before he was able to pull the axe out, two more Japanese came up from behind.

One pierced the Igorot's abdomen from behind with his bayonet, while the other shot him in the arm, causing him to drop his rifle.

Within seconds, there were three Japanese soldiers surrounding the wounded Igorot. One shot the Igorot in the shoulder, then plunged his bayonet into his abdomen, sending him to his knees. Though on his knees, the Igorot continued to clutch his axe, but was barely able to move his arm. Rather than surrender, he let out one last bloodcurdling cry, glared at his enemies, and managed to swing his axe once more. After missing badly, he refused to stop fighting, and managed to drag his axe on the ground to prepare for one more swing—but then a Japanese officer drew his sword, and with one swift move, sent the Igorot's head rolling into the blanket of bamboo leaves. The man's body remained upright for a moment, and Tebow couldn't believe what he saw next: the headless body of the Igorot made one final attempt to swing the axe before it toppled over.

At the sight of this, the two Igorots jumped out of the shelter and ran screaming toward their slain friend. Tebow's adrenaline was really pumping now, but he remained behind the trees, unable to move. Alex was infuriated and wanted to avenge the fallen Igorot himself, but remained a helpless observer.

As he watched the shocking images, Alex remained transfixed by a flashback that entered Tebow's frozen mind. Tebow was a child, sitting inside a car, looking out through the back window at his father struggling with a masked man. The man had just stolen a lady's purse; and when his dad caught sight of it, he stopped the car and ran out to stop him. All little Amos could do was watch as the masked man pulled out a knife and stabbed his father in the abdomen again and again, until he fell on his knees before toppling over to die, much like the slain Igorot. The flashbacks not only left Tebow frozen, but also affected Alex. For some reason, he felt the same pain Tebow was experiencing; he felt as if his own father had just been stabbed.

What the hell's going on with me? he wondered.

Then Tebow phased back to the real world and saw the Igorots running toward the Japanese pouring out of their hidey-holes. Alex shook off the pain from the flashbacks and began thinking of ways to help them. His empathy for Tebow and his strong desires to help the Igorots sent a surge of energy into Tebow that caused him to stand up. If Alex had possessed eyes at that point, they would have widened. *What just happened? Did I do that? Am I able to control his actions?* For the first time, Alex felt he had some influence, if not control, over the man's body. Tebow sprinted as fast as he could toward the two Igorots, who were already engaging the three Nips who had just killed their friend.

Ten yards away, he pointed his rifle at one of the enemy, the man who was fighting with the first Igorot, and shot him in the head. A split second later, he pointed the .45 caliber pistol in his left hand at another man, who had just sent the second Igorot soldier spinning to the ground with a vicious karate kick, and shot him multiple times in the chest. As both enemies fell, Tebow tried to shoot the third Japanese, but discovered he was out of bullets. Without hesitation, he dropped his weapons, pulled out his field knife, and charged at the third enemy—the officer with the sword. With a smirk, the man raised his blade and swung at Tebow, who parried the sword with his left arm without thinking. Luckily, he mostly caught the flat of the blade, and the tough fabric of his blouse bunted some of the force, so all he ended up with was a shallow slash along the back of his forearm—as he discovered much later.

In the here and now, the force of his unexpected parry caused the officer to spin far enough around that Tebow was able to sink his knife into the man's left kidney. As he gave it a vicious twist, the officer screamed and fell to the ground, taking Tebow with him. When they hit, the Japanese planted his knee in Tebow's solar plexus, though whether it was by accident or design Tebow never determined.

Paralyzed and unable to breathe, Tebow rolled off the officer and onto his back. With the knife still lodged in his own back, the Japanese man slowly rose to his knees, panting. He saw that his sword was too far away to reach, and went for his holstered pistol instead. Tebow was helpless to do anything but watch as the enemy unsnapped the holster and pulled out the pistol to shoot him.

Just as the enemy was about to pull the trigger, Sergeant Sutton suddenly appeared and plunged his knife into the back of the Nip's skull. The man jerked aside, enough that the bullet plowed into the ground next to Tebow's ear. With one quick blow and a hoarse cry, Sutton decapitated the dying man with the axe in his other hand.

The sergeant stood by Tebow with the officer's gory head in his hand as Tebow regained control of himself, picked up the enemy's pistol, and began firing on approaching enemy soldiers. *One man, one shot*, he thought, putting his bullets between the eyes of each man. He didn't have that Expert Marksman medal for nothing, no sir.

When the pistol clicked dry, Sutton hurled the officer's head into the clearing for the other Japanese to see, let out a ferocious battle cry, and plunged into the fray. This disoriented the Nips long enough for Tebow to roll behind a tree, grab his M-1 carbine, jam in a new clip, and reload the Colt. He left his knife in the Jap bastard's back; he'd get it later.

Thus rearmed, the lieutenant sprinted into the sea of bamboo, seeing things with such clarity now that every Japanese soldier within ten yards of him seemed five times larger than normal—and therefore five times easier to hit. Sutton and the others followed right behind him. Now that the enemy was easily visible, each round had its designated target in the head or chest of a Japanese soldier, and each went just where he wanted it.

Finally, they regrouped with the Igorots who had flanked the other side of the clearing. There was no longer anything to shoot at, which was good since Tebow's pistol was empty and the rifle nearly so. He stopped to take a breath and look around, and he and Alex were startled to see nothing but dead Japanese soldiers scattered through the forest behind them. His heart was thundering in his ears, his eyes wide and nearly bulging out of their sockets. The Igorots stared at him in awe. Sutton noticed Tebow's neck bleeding, so he respectfully approached his lieutenant and picked several long slivers of bamboo from his skin. They must have splintered off nearby stalks that took bullets intended for him.

As they stood there catching their breaths, the crackling of rifle fire in the near distance caught their attention. Sutton immediately climbed the skinny trunk of a nearby tree to reconnoiter. There were no lateral branches for the first twenty feet of the trunk, so he used the sheer strength of his hands and stocky legs to pull himself up the trunk. When he was nearly 40 feet above ground, one of the Igorots called to him quietly. "Sitlinin!" the man said, then began exchanging words with the Sergeant in their native Ibontoc.

Alex was shocked by what he'd just heard, as Tebow asked the Igorot standing next to him, "What did he call Sgt. Sutton?"

The Igorot replied with a heavy accent, "Sitlinin. That is sergeant's real name. It is too hard for American GI tongue, so they call him Sutton."

Suddenly, the image of Sutton climbing the tree triggered something strange in Tebow's brain. Déjà vu images of a young Igorot boy climbing a tree flashed through his mind. He felt like he knew that boy from somewhere, but couldn't pinpoint when or where. Once again, Alex couldn't believe what had just happened. *How did Tebow see those things when he was never there?* I *was there with Sitlinin, not him.* Unless somehow Tebow had seen the photo of Sitlinin climbing the tree at the old World's Fair at some point, his thoughts had connected with Alex's when Alex realized that Sutton was actually the little boy from the World's Fair village.

Maybe these physical bodies I'm in are starting to connect with me, he thought. *Or maybe they* are *me.* Alex had never believed in reincarnation, primarily because he'd been raised Catholic and taught that it wasn't possible...but now he was beginning to wonder. *Maybe I'm a reincarnation of Tebow and the others I've connected with.*

Sutton climbed back down from the tree to see Tebow struggling with his déjà vu experience, and he snapped the lieutenant out of his puzzled state by slapping his back. Tebow shook his head and headed in the direction the sergeant was pointing.

They finally caught up with the other Igorots who had split off earlier. Together, they moved along the eastern side of the salient and systematically defeated in detail all Japanese resistance they encountered. By the evening of the next day, the salient had been reduced to half its size, and the Japanese Army by several hundred soldiers. Remarkably, the Igorots only sustained three casualties during the intense fighting.

When they returned to their camp, the Igorots gathered and began opening the tin cans of sardines and pickled vegetables that they'd taken from the dead Japanese. Meanwhile, Dachille brought out an unlabelled bottle and handed it to Sutton. The sergeant thanked Dachille, immediately poured some into a canteen cup, and handed it to Tebow. Tebow noted a look in the sergeant's eyes, one that made him feel recognized and accepted as a warrior—and that made him feel very good indeed. Tebow raised the cup, gesturing a toast, and drank it as the sergeant walked away.

"Wow, what the hell was that?" Tebow sputtered with wide, tearful eyes.

"I think they've accepted you as a warrior," Dachille replied jovially.

"No sir, the drink. What is that, sir?" replied Tebow, as the hooch burned its way into his gullet.

"Ah, that. They call it *basi*," Dachille answered. "I call it sugarcane moonshine. I brought a few bottles back from my last trip up the mountains."

A moment later, as Tebow was trying a second cautious sip, one of the older Igorots with a chest tattoo picked up an empty sardine can, removed a round from his rifle, and began tapping the can with it. The others picked up other empty tins and did the same. Soon they were making music and playing in rhythm. Tebow and Dachille watched in amusement as the men began their ceremonial war dance. The men tapped their tins in a four-count rhythmic beat with an emphasis on the third tap. Then they made a single-file line and began following each other in a counterclockwise circular pattern. They swayed and shuffled their feet to the tempo of their improvised music. "Do they do this often, sir?" Tebow quietly asked Dachille.

"As often as they can. They seem to do a lot of dancing and banging on things where they're from. Sounds primitive to me, but I kinda like it. Normally they use these little bronze gongs, but I wouldn't allow them to bring them on this campaign because they're so loud. They know how to improvise, though. Like I said, they're very industrious and smart." With that, Dachille handed Tebow the bottle of *basi* and returned to his tent. Tebow stayed to watch the Igorot dance in circles.

Each time they made one complete revolution, the circle became smaller as their spacing tightened. Every now and then they coiled together toward the center of the circle and then uncoiled in a spiral motion. At one point they stopped, faced the center, and chanted some words in Ibontoc. After their second time of doing this, Tebow walked to Sutton, who was observing along with the others who weren't dancing.

"What are they saying?" he asked the sergeant.

Sutton—Sitlinin—replied, "*Cha-kay'-yo fo'-so-mi ma-pay-ĭng'-an. Cha-kay'-mi ĭn-kĕd-se'-ka-mi nan ka-nĭn'-mi to-kom-ke'-ka.* In English, it means something like 'You enemies, we will always kill you; we are strong,' and so on." Tebow nodded in acknowledgement, and continued watching until one of the Igorots approached them to tell them that Dachille wanted to meet with them in his tent immediately.

Tebow knew it was about the orders that the Major had just received from headquarters. When they approached Dachille's tent, a colonel whom Tebow didn't recognize was just leaving. Tebow and Sutton saluted him and watched his jeep drive off. Then they entered the tent, and Major Dachille immediately told them that they would be going back into battle the following day. When asked what their mission was, he told Tebow that they would accompany the 192nd Tank Division into the Japanese salient.

"Tanks?" asked Tebow in disbelief. "I thought it was common knowledge that tanks are useless up here, sir. We've lost too many tanks as it is, haven't we?"

Dachille shook his head. "I tried telling that to the high command, but they seem to think there are openings they can enter through." He spread open a map and pointed to several arrows indicating the avenues of approach. Tebow looked closely at the maps, considered things carefully, and began to think that it might *just* be possible. "If this map is correct, maybe they can at that, sir," commented Tebow. "I hope the high brass know what they're doing." He looked to Sutton and asked, "What do you think?"

Sutton was apparently thinking of something else, and was caught off guard. He quickly focused his attention on Tebow, but it was clear he hadn't been paying attention to what his superior officers had been discussing before being asked his opinion. Tebow could see that he was distracted and didn't want to embarrass him, so he immediately began speaking for him: "I think you would agree that unless these paths are cleared and unobstructed, the tanks they want to take into the jungles will be helpless. Am I right?"

"That is a correct assessment," Sutton replied.

"These are our orders, gentlemen," Dachille said sharply. "Like it or not, we're going to carry them out tomorrow—or die trying."

Both Tebow and the sergeant came to their attention and saluted Dachille, saying, "Yes sir!" in unison.

When they left the tent, Tebow asked Sutton, "What were you thinking of in there that distracted you so much?"

Sutton said calmly, "Something I have been thinking of since I took the head of that Japanese officer. Something that I have to do before tomorrow."

Before Tebow could ask more, the sergeant turned and started walking back toward the rest of his men, apparently intent on getting whatever it was over with right away. Tebow watched him walk away, frowning, then began walking back to his tent—before changing his mind, to Alex's relief, and following after Sutton. When he reached the Igorots, the lieutenant hung back behind some trees and looked into the clearing where his Scouts were bivouacked. He saw the sergeant lying on the ground with his bare chest exposed. One of the Igorots with a chest tattoo approached him, holding a leather satchel, and kneeled down next to him.

Another man brought a small bowl of hot water—Tebow could see the steam rising off it—and the tattooed man placed a burned spruce branch into it, then rubbed the black soot from the needles into the water until the water was pure black. As he did this, the other man rubbed the soot from the needles of other seared branches, collecting it in another bowl. This he dumped periodically into the bowl of hot water. Soon there was so much soot mixed into the water that it became a thick black paste.

The tattooed man then dipped a sharpened stick into the bowl of soot and began tracing lines on Sgt. Sutton's chest, outlining the same design that the other tattooed men had on their chests. The design started on the arm where the bicep and shoulder met, then swooped up and down the chest, where it ended between his nipples.

Then he reached for a curved piece of animal horn that looked like it had come from a bull or carabao. From one side of the horn protruded several metal needles. He lined up the needles on the outlined design and started tapping them into the sergeant's skin repeatedly with a piece of wood. Sutton didn't move or give any indication of pain as the man tapped at the rate of one to two taps per second.

Soon, Sutton's entire chest was covered with blood.

Much later, when the tattooer had finished with the needles, he poured hot water over Sutton's chest and washed the blood off several times. Then he took the remaining bowl of inky soot and rubbed it across Sutton's chest. Tebow could see the man's chest already welting all over from the needle pricks. After his entire chest was covered in soot, two men wrapped his chest with thin white gauze from their first aid kits. The gauze quickly turned black and red. Once they finished, everyone, including Sutton, began dancing, beating on their little tin cans.

Early the following morning, as dawn peeked over the mountains, Tebow led the men down the path toward the rendezvous point. Sutton walked beside him, and Tebow could see that the severely welted chest beneath the man's unbuttoned uniform coat still had soot rubbed all over it. He was concerned about infection and wanted to say something, but a little voice inside told him to just keep quiet and move on.

When they reached the rendezvous point, they met up with the tank unit waiting for them. Tebow and his men spread out and entered the jungle first, with the tanks clattering along behind. So far the map was correct, though some of the trails were barely wide enough for the tanks to pass. After half an hour of creeping through the jungle, the small paths began narrowing rapidly, and the Igorots found themselves chopping down bamboo with their axes and long bolo machetes to make way for the armor.

Suddenly the paths simply ended. Tebow peered at the map again to see if they had gone astray, but couldn't tell for sure. Sutton also looked at the map, and he was certain that they had followed it correctly. "This map is not correct," Sutton told Tebow.

"Damn HQ! I *knew* they'd fuck this up. Bad maps, bad intel, always lying about reinforcements and supplies arriving. Those guys up there have no friggin' clue!"

Tebow turned around and made his way back to the tanks. As he approached, the operators exited their vehicles and began talking amongst themselves. When he reached them, he saw that many were shaking their heads, while others were just looking at the ground in frustration. "There's no goddamn way we're gonna be able to navigate through all this," said a Warrant Officer of the 192nd with JACKSON stamped on his helmet, as he pointed at the foliage, vines, and creepers that blocked 90 percent of their visibility.

"It's even worse up ahead," replied Tebow. "Do you have the same map as I do?"

Both compared maps, and saw that they were identical. The WO cursed. "I'm getting tired of all these wrong goddamn maps. This is the fourth time since we landed."

One of the sergeant's of the 192nd interrupted with, "Sir, if we try going farther into this jungle, the Nips'll eat us alive. We'd be sitting ducks waiting to be plucked, one by one. There's no room to maneuver."

"No shit, Sherlock." Jackson stalked over to his radio man and contacted his superior officer. He explained the situation, but the officer on the other end insisted that they move forward and informed them that they were no more than a few hundred yards from the enemy. Just as Jackson signed off in disgust, a crackle of rifle fire in the distance caught everyone's attention. They fell silent; after a long moment with no further shooting, Tebow and the Warrant Officer continued discussing the situation. A few moments later, Sutton came running up the trail and interrupted them with a salute.

"Sirs, a few of my men just came back from recon. They stumbled upon some Japanese in their holes about two hundred yards away. They shot them, moved forward, and discovered at least several hundred enemy troops digging in and moving around. They're definitely there."

"Are they heavily armed?" asked Major Dachille, who had just joined them from the rear to see what was holding up the advance.

Sutton saluted Dachille and replied, "Sir, my men were not able to tell because of the poor visibility—but they were able to find new paths through the jungle. I think the map is correct after all. It must be old, though, because the clear paths shown have been overgrown by vines and bamboo in many places. The regrowth is so thick that my men almost didn't find their way back to us."

"Well, fuck," said Dachille, which pretty much summed up their situation.

Jackson and Dachille walked back to the radio man together, and after some initial difficulty, spoke to someone in charge at headquarters. They confirmed that the enemy had been sighted, and re-explained how impossible it was to attack with the tanks. To their dismay, they were ordered to attack *without* tank support. Both officers returned to Tebow and the rest of the men gathered in front of the tanks to relay their orders. "With all due respect, sir," said one of the higher-ranking tank operators, "if they're heavily dug in and there are that many Nips out there, we don't stand a chance on foot. It's suicide."

"Then a suicide mission it is, soldier," Major Dachille snapped. "We have our orders, and by God we're gonna follow them or die trying! Is that understood?"

The soldier stood at attention and replied, "Sir, yes sir!"

"That's what I like to hear," said Dachille as he turned to Tebow. "Lieutenant, go with Sutton and prepare your men for an all-out assault on those slant-eyed bastards."

"Yes sir," replied Tebow.

As Dachille was turning to walk back to the rear, Tebow caught a look of concern in his eyes that told him that even Dachille knew they had little chance of survival. This same feeling transposed itself on Tebow's face as he turned to see Sutton, who looked concerned at what he saw in his eyes. Before he could say anything more, Sutton turned and sprinted towards his men.

Tebow began slowly walking toward his men as the thought of possibly having to surrender entered his mind. Rumors of how the Japanese were overwhelming the unreinforced American troops and the likelihood of MacArthur surrendering had already made their way into the lower ranks of officers. Tebow was beginning to think that surrendering might be the honorable thing to do, if it were done in such a way that he could save the lives of his men and those of the 192nd. He didn't want to, given what he'd seen at the Baguio camp and heard from the prisoners, but he might have no choice.

Then he realized that he didn't have anything white to use for a flag. *Maybe I could rip a white shirt off a dead Nip,* he thought sardonically.

Halfway back to where he'd left the Igorots, Sutton appeared, jogging toward him. Behind him were the rest of the Igorots. Sutton called out,

"Please tell the soldiers to get in their tanks, sir! We will get them through."

They must have found a way, Tebow thought, immediately turning around to sprint toward the tanks. When he reached them, he told Jackson that his men had found a way in, and that they would lead them through the jungle. Immediately, the tankmen returned back to their vehicles and lowered themselves inside. Sutton reached Tebow first as Tebow demanded, "You found a way in?"

"Nossir, but we spotted several enemy squads advancing toward us. They're only a hundred yards away. We need to attack right now!"

Still unclear about the plan of attack, and mindful about what Dachille had told him about trusting the instincts of the Igorots, Tebow just watched as Sutton and the other Igorot sergeant, who the American soldiers called Joe, began hoisting Igorots onto the tanks one by one. On each vehicle, one Igorot positioned himself above the main 75mm turret while others clung to the armor above the tracks on either side of the tank, one hand hooked into the small window opening and the other clutching his bolo or axe. Two other Igorots stood on top of the hull above the 75mm gun, next to the American operating the smaller 37mm turret mounted on top of the hull.

The Igorots on top of the tanks yelled instructions to the Americans, while the Igorots below them began hitting the sides of the hull with the backsides of their weapons. The tank operators quickly picked up on the tapping against the hull as their navigational guide. In a matter of minutes, the tanks began moving forward, guided by the Igorots.

Tebow and the remaining Igorots moved ahead of the tanks and began cutting away as much of the understory vines and creepers as possible, so as to leave evidence of a trail to follow. They encountered the Japanese no more than 75 yards into the jungle. They dove for cover and took aim at the advancing enemy. At first their numbers seemed overwhelming—until the American M3 tanks appeared.

Tebow paused for a moment to watch in total awe as the first two tanks entered the battlefield, with the Igorots mounted on them tapping the hull and firing their pistols at the Japanese nearby. The 75 mm and 37 mm turrets immediately opened up on the enemy. The image of the tanks ridden by the fierce Igorots, screaming out their bloodcurdling war cries and firing their pistols with surprising accuracy, coupled with the spectacle of the tank rounds bellowing from the turrets in massive flashes of fire and flame, was a sight never before seen by either side. It was such a frightful sight, in fact, that the Japanese offered very little resistance. Most turned tail and ran for their lives.

Before the fighting began, Tebow had accepted the fact that they would probably sustain heavy casualties, given the obstacles the jungle created and the number of Japanese thought to be waiting in ambush. The level of initial resistance from the Japanese only supported his fears at the beginning of the fight; but now, with the tanks and Igorots on the scene, he believed they had a very good chance of winning the battle. Although the jungle was at its thickest at their location, the Igorots still navigated through the maze at an impressive pace. Fortunately for them and the tanks, the surrounding bamboo protected them from the thousands of rounds fired at them by the Japanese.

The deeper they moved into the salient, the more Japanese they encountered. The enemy knew they were no match for a head-to-head confrontation with the Igorot-ridden tanks, so they attempted a pincer maneuver so they could attack from both sides of the column. The maneuver would have worked if it hadn't been for the quickness of the Igorots on foot. Immediately after recognizing their strategy, Tebow and his men surged forward with all their might, decimating the Nips before they could flank the tank units.

As the fighting progressed, the Japanese continuously repeated the flanking attempt, since they had no chance of defeating the tanks head on. Realizing this, Tebow had his Igorots spread out to cover more ground, so that none of the Japanese could slip through in the dense bamboo. Wondering how the tank unit was holding up, Tebow paused for a moment to look behind him. As soon as he saw that they were still doing well, he turned to see a Japanese soldier standing just fifteen feet away, pointing a rifle right at him. The soldier squeezed the trigger..and Providence saved Tebow's life, because the firing pin clicked on an empty chamber. Snarling in frustration, the Japanese soldier dropped his rifle, drew his sword, and charged. Tebow raised his own rifle and squeezed the trigger—but *his* rifle jammed. If it hadn't been so fucking serious, he would have laughed. He desperately reached for his pistol, but knew it would be too late, as the soldier was only steps from sinking his sword into him. Raising his rifle in both hands, he just hoped he could use it to block, and possibly break, the Nip's sword.

Then, out of nowhere, something flew by his ear and impaled the Japanese soldier in front of him. It was a spear. Someone behind him had thrown a *spear* right into the soldier's neck. The spear hit the man so hard that it put him straight down on his back, sending his legs flying into the air. Tebow stood over the soldier and watched the blood spurting out of the entry wound, then turned around and saw a tattooed Igorot almost thirty yards away, watching him with a blank expression.

Tebow was amazed by the man's accuracy, given the distance; there must have been more than fifty sizeable bamboo poles that the spear had to needle through before hitting its target. The lieutenant saluted the Igorot, then removed the spear from the Jap's neck and sank it into the ground for the man to retrieve before moving on.

The fighting continued with such fury that by late afternoon it became one-sided, with the Japanese on the verge of annihilation. After the fighting was over, Major Dachille and several senior ranking officers from HQ walked through what had once been a strongly defended Japanese salient only to find themselves in awe of the destruction they saw. Thanks to the bravery of the Igorots, the Battle of the Pockets had ended in a victory for the Allies, with the Japanese 20th Infantry's utter destruction. As a reward for their achievements, Dachille's entire unit was given two full days of R&R.

Three days later, Tebow drove Sutton to a nearby Mobile Army Surgical Hospital to have his chest treated for minor infections from the tattooing. While they were there, he took the opportunity to check on three of his Igorot soldiers, who were recovering from minor gunshot wounds sustained during battle. He was particularly interested in seeing the man with the tattoo who had saved his life with his spear. As they entered the large tent full of patients, one of the patients from the 192nd tank unit recognized them and called out, "Hey L-T! Over here!"

As Sutton walked toward one of the doctors to have his chest looked at, Tebow saw a man with a bandaged face beckoning. He headed over to him, wondering who was behind the bandage. When they reached him, the soldier told Tebow who he was, picked up a folded newspaper, and handed it to him. "Thought you might want to read what Dugout Doug had to say about that day," said the soldier.

Tebow opened up the newspaper to see an article titled *Igorots Astride Tanks in Bataan Wipe Out a Japanese Regiment.* "Go to the paragraph I circled," said the soldier.

The Lieutenant's eyes scanned to the circled paragraph and read, "Recounting the story of this exploit to a group of his officers, General MacArthur is quoted as having said that although he was cognizant of many acts of heroism on battlefields all over the world, 'for sheer, breathtaking and heart-stopping desperation, I have never known the equal of those Igorots riding the tanks'."

Tebow folded the newspaper, handed it back to the soldier, and told him, "You did an outstanding job too, soldier. We couldn't have done it without you."

"Thanks, L-T. That means a lot."

Seven cots down were the Igorots. Tebow walked down to them and thanked them sincerely for their bravery in battle, then stood next to the older man's cot and saluted him. The man nodded in acknowledgement, then motioned to him to reach below his cot. Tebow bent over and picked up the red cloth headband that the Igorot normally wore and handed it to him. The Igorot shook his head, said, "Sïk'-a," and gestured for Tebow to keep it for himself. With a look of sincere appreciation, Tebow accepted it, rolled his eyes back trying to remember how to say thank you, and finally said, "*Siya achi sa.*"

Just then Sgt. Sutton joined them, wearing clean white gauze bandages on his chest. He saw what Tebow had received as a gift, smiled, and saluted him. After exchanging goodbyes with the other Igorots, Tebow and Sutton left and boarded their jeep.

Just before they drove off, Sutton engaged the parking brake and hopped out of the jeep, telling him he'd forgot his penicillin inside the tent. As soon as the sergeant entered the patient's tent, a young Filipino boy ran in front of the jeep and towards the nearby forest. Tebow watched him go, curious. The boy stopped just outside the forest and turned to look at Tebow, jumping up and down and pointing into the trees. With his other hand, the boy beckoned for someone to come see. Tebow looked in the other direction to see who the boy was waving to, but saw nobody around. It finally dawned on him that the boy was beckoning to *him.* Why he had no idea, but it seemed important.

Tebow jumped out of the jeep and jogged toward the excited boy. When he reached him, he looked in the direction the boy had pointed, and saw something moving behind a tree. The boy began to nudge him from behind, urging him to go into the forest and investigate. Tebow gently pushed the boy away as he stood looking at the tree. The boy continued nudging him, but Tebow refused to move. Finally, the boy let out an unexpectedly deep growl and pushed Tebow so hard that he was sent flying 10 yards into the forest. He hit the tree he was looking at and fell to the ground.

"Holy shit!" said Tebow, rubbing his forehead. "What the hell was that? That couldn't have been him!" Knowing the boy was too small to have thrown him that far, Tebow turned back to see if somebody else was with the boy; but by then, the kid had vanished. Then he heard something moving behind an adjacent tree, and slowly got up and walked around it to see what it was.

It turned out to be a giant lizard of some sort clinging to the side of the tree. To his amazement, it was almost five feet long, with a huge head and pitch-black eyes that stared at him as it flickered its tongue in the air.

Tebow didn't know whether it was dangerous or not, so he slowly shuffled backward to create more distance between him and the lizard. The lizard saw him move, descended to the ground, and crept toward him. As it approached, its dark leathery skin began to glow. Tebow rubbed his eyes when he realized it was also growing rapidly in size as it advanced.

Within seconds, the lizard had doubled in size and burned bright white—just like the snake, shield, and spear from the blanket in the Sagada Caves. Alex realized that the lizard had been back at Sagada, too, and knew now what was to come. As Tebow fumbled his hands across the ground, feeling for a rock or stick to throw at it, Alex thought, *Oh no, not* again.

As the light became too intense to look at, Tebow raised his hands in front of his eyes, trying to block as much as possible while keeping his eyes on the apparition. He was more than a little shocked when the lizard said in a deep, echoing voice, "It's time to go, Alex."

"Holy *shit*!" shouted Tebow. "What *are* you, and who the fuck is Alex?"

The lizard shook its head vigorously and leaped straight for Tebow, slamming against his chest. As they flew backward, Alex found himself spiraling again into the familiar blinding tunnel of light, gasping for air.

CHAPTER 11

Alex woke up gasping for breath. Once his lungs filled with oxygen, he found that he was lying snug in bed. *Oh God, it was all a dream.*

Then, he heard a woman shouting "*Gising na! Gumising ka na!*" and knew he was wrong, because she was shouting in what sounded like Tagalog. As the body he was in cut its eyes toward the door, he realized, *Shit! This isn't my bedroom!*

His new body felt so tired that he didn't want to move. Instead, it tried ignoring the loud voice coming from the hallway. After a minute of silence, he heard the wood floor in his room bend and creak from someone's footsteps as they entered and pulled the window drapes wide open. Daylight flooded the room, and the person Alex was inside rolled over to cover his head with a pillow.

The pillow was ripped away by the same woman he'd heard yelling. With one eye open, his body looked up at the woman. Alex saw a pretty Filipina in her early forties talking to him, but for a moment nothing she said made any sense to him. When his other eye opened, the Tagalog words slowly changed to English.

"*Gising na.* Wake up already! You sleep too much, Brian!" she said. "You had better wake up now or else. Your school called me yesterday and told me you have been late almost every day since school started. The school is less than a kilometer away! What have you been doing these past two weeks?"

Brian? Alex thought. *Could it be...?*

His body didn't want to deal with the woman, and pulled the cover over his head. As it looked down at his feet, Alex saw the body of a skinny young brown boy about Fanusan's age. The lady quickly pulled the blanket off his head and pinched his nose, causing him to finally get out of bed, groaning and protesting.

"Today I don't have to be at work early," she said. "I will drive you to school, so that I know you are getting there on time! Now hurry up, you have less than an hour."

Something about getting a ride to school made Brian smile. After the lady left the room, he walked into the bathroom to brush his teeth. When he looked into the mirror, Alex found himself looking at a very young version of his *manong* Brian. *Oh boy, now what?* But something seemed off, and it took a moment for him to realize that this Brian lacked the nasty scar that he remembered seeing on his *manong's* cheek.

After getting ready for school, he walked into the kitchen and joined the Filipina at the table. On his plate was a serving of rice, *longanisa* sausage, and a fried egg. He greeted her and began eating. First he mashed his egg into his rice, and mixed it together so the yolk was equally distributed throughout the rice. Then he cut the *longanisa* into small bits with his spoon. Once everything was well mixed, he splashed soy sauce on it.

As he ate, Alex noted how flexible and limber the woman was; she sat on her chair with one knee raised to her shoulder, her foot resting on the chair. He found it amusing to see a woman sit this way at the kitchen table. It also amused him to see how she ate her *pan de sal,* salt-bread, by dipping it into her cup of coffee before taking a bite.

Her name was Estrellita, but she preferred to be called Lita. She was a very beautiful Ilocano who had graduated from nursing school in Baguio City before marrying his uncle Joseph. She was fluent in Ilocano,

Tagalog, and English, but did not speak Ibontoc, Kankanaey, or any of the other Igorot languages. Her complexion was very light. Like many of the other Filipinas in the city, she hated having dark skin. Whenever possible, she avoided direct sunlight and she constantly bought the latest skin-whitening lotions and creams that hit the stores.

To Brian, this idea of striving for the lightest complexion possible was still new. He'd never heard anything like it until he left his hometown in the mountains and began intermingling with lowlanders; no one back home worried about getting dark skin. In fact, all the kids loved to spend hours playing along the Chico River, and none of their parents were ever concerned about their skin getting dark. It seemed to him that the lowlanders associated beauty with features normally seen in people with Spanish or Caucasian blood. "Auntie Lita..." Brian said in Ilocano.

"Tagalog, Brian, Tagalog," she corrected. "You need to practice your Tagalog here. What, darling?"

"Why do I have to keep going to school here?" he said in the other language. "Can't I go back home and finish my schooling there?"

"How many times do we have to tell you, darling?" she replied. "You won't get the proper education up there! Your parents want what is best for you. Look at your Lolo Santo. He was valedictorian in high school, one of the first Igorots to ever graduate college." *With highest honors at St. Louis University*, both Alex and Brian thought simultaneously, one in Ilocano, the other in English. Lita went on, "Now he is very successful and travels all around the world doing very important jobs. You don't want to be a farmer or miner all your life like your parents, do you?"

"Why not?" replied Brian.

"Because they don't want you to be," she firmly replied. "They want you to be like your lolo, your uncle Joseph, and the other successful Igorots on your father's side of the family. You should be proud that you have a high-ranking military officer, a college president, lawyers, doctors, important politicians, and successful businessmen for uncles. You should strive to be like them. This is why your parents asked your uncle and me to take care of you while you finish your schooling here."

Brian said nothing, keeping his disappointment to himself. *Doesn't anyone care about what* I *want? What's wrong with my parents? My father is content as a miner, and my mother loves farming rice. They're happy. Why must I be like my uncles and lolo?*

After listening to Lita and feeling Brian's disappointment, Alex thought about his own career, and why he'd chosen it. Like Brian, Alex had wanted to be like his father; but unlike Brian, he wanted to be like his father because of the money and prestige, not for the sake of being happy. Alex had always equated happiness to materialistic and superficial things, not inner satisfaction. *I'm good at what I do,* Alex thought defensively, *And I've made good money doing it.*

Normally, these self-affirmations made Alex feel good about himself, but the memories of his father telling him that he was "too creative" to work in the investments arena bothered him. *Maybe he was trying to tell me something all those years ago,* Alex thought. *He was right about my creativity. I love the arts, music, and writing. So why have I been doing something I* like *instead of something I* love*? Because I'm good at it? Because of the money?* Instead of feeling good about himself, the same void that had always haunted him filled his heart again.

Brian felt relieved to be driven to school, but at the same time reluctant, because he still had to *go* to school. On their way, Brian looked out the car window, dreading another day of hell. A few blocks away, he saw the same group of boys who regularly bullied and teased him hiding around the corner, waiting for him. He smiled with relief as they passed them unnoticed. When they arrived at the school, he stepped out of the car and looked around to make sure it was safe.

Lita immediately rolled down the window and shouted in Tagalog, "You better walk on the shady side of the street when you come home. You're getting too dark!"

Brian shook his head in embarrassment and ran to the schoolhouse doors. For the first time, he was one of the first to take a seat in the classroom. As his classmates began making their way into the classroom, a girl stuck her tongue out at him in a mocking fashion as she walked past him. Brian just dropped his head and stared at his desk.

Why did she do that? Alex wondered.

Then someone from behind slapped him on the back of his head. "You got lucky today," whispered a boy in Tagalog. "You can't hide from us forever."

The boy to his left leaned over and whispered, "Where's your tail, monkeyboy?"

Alex felt bad for Brian. The things Brian's classmates were saying to him rang an all-too-familiar bell: they reminded him of his grammar school years in America during the 1970s. Except for him and one other Filipino boy, his school was all white; so naturally, he was the subject of frequent racial teasing. Many of the kids, particularly the older kids, called him nip, pinhead, chink, zero, ahso, gook and zipperhead. At first, Alex didn't know what those words meant, but later he learned they referenced Japanese, Chinese, Korean, and Vietnamese people.

After his first class ended, Brian made sure he remained in his seat until almost all the kids left. He also made sure the teacher was right behind him as he left the classroom. The kids were waiting to tease him in the hallway, but when they saw the teacher, they just gave him mean looks and left. Brian stayed close to the teacher and followed her down the hallway until he made it to his next class unscathed.

He spent the rest of the day going from class to class that way, dodging and hiding from the school bullies. He was successful at avoiding them all day, but was worried about his walk home. It was Friday, and the only thing on his mind was getting home without having to deal with his mean classmates.

The walk home was worse than the walk to school because the boys, and sometimes girls too, threw mud-balls and sticks at him, stretched his underwear out of his pants, ripped pages out of his books, and sometimes even threw dirt down his shirt. They couldn't do this in the morning for fear the school principal would see what they were doing to him. This had been going on for two weeks, ever since he'd arrived at the school.

The dreaded school bell rang, and all the kids were excited to leave—except for Brian. Instead of rushing out the doors like the rest, he bought time by volunteering to help the teacher clean the chalk boards in his classroom. After all the boards were cleaned, his teacher thanked him and began turning the lights off.

Brian knew he had to leave, so he slowly entered the hallway and walked towards the main door. When he arrived, he carefully peeked out its small window. Twenty feet beyond the door stood the bullies. He knew they were waiting for him. He was surprised to see them there; normally they were farther away from school, but this time they wanted to make sure he didn't slip away like he had that morning. He immediately turned around and headed for the side door. When he opened it he saw that the coast was clear and began running, constantly looking over his shoulder. When made his first turn around the building, he stopped instantly at the sight of the bullies. He turned around to run, but found more kids behind him. Trapped, with nowhere to go, he just stood there and stared at the ground.

"What are you looking for, your tail?" demanded one of the boys in Tagalog, as they all closed in on him.

"Show us your tail!" shouted another boy in English.

"What are you doing here, anyway? You don't belong here. Go back to the mountains!" another shouted in Tagalog.

"Come on, guys," a girl's voice said. "You might make him cry, and then his parents will come and kidnap us and take us to their mountain hideouts."

All the kids laughed. Brian looked up and saw that it was the same girl who had stuck her tongue out at him earlier. Her boyfriend placed his arm around her as if to congratulate her for telling the joke. She saw Brian looking at her, and stuck her tongue out again. What had he done to deserve that?

One of the bigger boys grabbed his books out of his hands, held up the history book, and said, "What are you doing with this? This is about

Filipino history. You're mentioned nowhere in this book, because you're not Filipino!"

"Please," Brian begged in his broken Tagalog. "I don't want any trouble. I haven't done anything to you guys. I just want to go home."

"Listen, he can't even speak Filipino," the boy holding his book said. "Blah blah blab la. Quit trying to talk like us. You sound like a monkey!"

Then a boy from behind grabbed Brian's pants by the waist and began pulling them down, shouting, "Let's see how long his tail is!"

Brian tried pulling the boy's hands away, but another boy grabbed him from behind in a bear hug. He started to cry as he tried squirming out of the boy's arms. Two others joined in, each picking up one of his legs and pulling at the bottom of his pants. Meanwhile the girls in the crowd started kicking at him with their patent-leather shoes. Out of desperation, Brian cocked his head back, striking the nose of the boy holding him in place. The boy cried out, immediately let go of Brian, and cupped his hands over his bleeding nose. "Tail! Tail! Tail!" the kids began chanting.

When Brian hit the ground, he reached into his pocket and pulled out a small folding pocketknife, which he flipped open and began swinging at the kids who were about to grab him again. They backed off as he swung violently. One of the girls who had tried kicking him let out a loud scream upon seeing the knife. Finally, he was able to free his ankles from the grasps of the other boys who were trying to pull his pants off.

He stood up, still holding out the knife while pivoting in all directions to ward off the kids. Then he started shouting words of hate at them in Kankanaey. One of the boys lunged at him from the side and knocked the knife out of his hands. Brian leaped after it, but another boy got to it first and swung it at him, just missing his face.

The commotion was immediately broken up by the whistle and shouting of several teachers running toward them. The boy dropped the knife, and everyone began running away. Brian quickly grabbed the knife and chased after his tormentors, screaming hateful words in Kankanaey.

Finally, he was tackled by a teacher and reprimanded. All the other kids, however, managed to escape. Naturally.

One of the male teachers held Brian in a headlock while another held his hands firmly behind him to keep him from swinging at them. Brian continued shouting hateful words in his native language, while tears streamed down his face. After a long while, he managed to calm down and was escorted to the Principal's office.

While he was sitting in the Principal's office alone, Brian saw his uncle and auntie arguing in Tagalog in the hallway. The principal just stood next to them and listened. They spoke so fast that it was difficult for him to understand, but it seemed they were trying to blame each other for his actions.

On their way home, neither said a word to each other or to him.

Later that evening, Brian sat on his bed, listening to his aunt and uncle arguing again behind closed doors. This time he was able to understand them better. It sounded like his uncle was defending his actions, dismissing it as self defense. His aunt didn't want to hear it, of course: the only thing that concerned her was Brian's expulsion from school because of what had happened. She said that it was Brian's fault, and that he should never have pulled the knife.

Brian didn't want to hear any more of their arguing, so he laid his head on the bed and pressed the pillow over his ears. It only muffled their noise, so he went inside his bathroom, shut the door, and turned the sink faucet on to drown out their shouting. A half hour later, his uncle knocked on the door. "You okay in there?" he asked in Tagalog.

Brian turned the water off, opened the door, and saw his uncle standing just outside, leaning against the doorframe. Alex couldn't help but notice how much Joseph looked like his late father. In fact, for a split-second Joseph *was* his father.

Joseph was the fourth youngest of his twelve aunts and uncles. Brian didn't know him very well, because he lived so far away in the city of Manila, and rarely made it back home except for Christmas and New Year's. Many people back home spoke of him with high regard, because he was a successful lawyer and had a beautiful home in the city; but there were an equal number who pitied him for putting his career before almost everything else except his wife. These people often frowned on the fact that he was in his mid-30s without children, and had stopped going to Mass.

"Yes," replied Brian in Ilocano. "I was just washing my face with a towel."

"Please, Brian," Joseph replied in Tagalog. "At least try speaking Tagalog. Sooner or later, you will need to."

Brian replied in Kankanaey, "My parents don't speak Tagalog at home, so why must I?"

"Very well," Joseph replied in Kankanaey. "We can talk about that later. I just want to make sure you're okay. I know what it's like to be teased by lowlanders."

"Uncle, they tried to pull off my pants in front of everybody. They keep saying I'm hiding a tail. Even the girls made fun of me, and some even tried to kick me when I was down. I didn't want to use my knife, but I was so scared!"

His uncle nodded thoughtfully, and Brian, fighting off tears, expected another round of "Just ignore them" and "Don't stoop to their level," pieces of advice that wouldn't do him any good at this stage. But when Joseph spoke, he said, "You need to understand the complexity of the discrimination Igorots endure from lowlanders. You were lucky this time, Brian, but next time someone could get hurt—or even killed." He peered at the boy for a long moment, then said, "Stay right here," and left the room.

Moments later, he returned with several books, and asked Brian to sit down on the bed. Brian sat on the corner while Joseph pulled a chair from the hallway and sat across from him. "The thing with the pants—I didn't know that's what had happened," said Joseph. "I probably would have done the same if I were in your shoes."

"But Auntie Lita said it was my fault," Brian said, as he fought back tears.

Joseph replied, "Don't be upset with her. She just doesn't understand sometimes, but she still loves you. You know, Brian, when I was younger, I had no idea why the lowlanders treated us so differently. So one day, when I was in college, I began doing a lot of research into our history and the history of the Philippines. To make a long story short, the lowlanders just don't know much about us. For more than three hundred years, they were under Spanish rule. That means most of their original lifeways changed. They learned the ways and religion of the Spaniards, but never really knew about us as a people , because we refused to surrender our culture to the Spaniards'. You can't expect more than three hundred years of ignorance to change overnight. It will take some time."

"Is that why they say we're not even Filipino?" asked Brian.

"Good question," replied Joseph, as he placed the books he was holding onto the bed next to Brian.

"What are these, uncle?" asked Brian as he looked at one of the books, which was titled, *Political and Cultural History of the Philippines.*

"These are the first books I read to learn more about the discrimination between us Igorots and the lowlanders. One of my first theses I wrote for college was about the origins of the word 'Filipino'."

Joseph pulled out a thin folder from inside one of the books, which held his college paper. He flipped through several pages until he found what he was looking for. Joseph was about to ask Brian to read it, but he saw Brian's facial expression and realized that all the English words already overwhelmed him, so he went ahead and read it aloud in Kankanaey, adding some of his own words to help him understand better. Brian listened attentively. "The word Filipino comes from the word Filipinas, of which Philippines is the English translation. Filipinas was the name given our islands by the Spanish explorer Ruy de Villalobos in 1543, in honor of the Spanish crown prince, Philip—or Felipe, as he was called in Spain. He later became King Philip II. He was king of Spain from 1556 to 1598.

"When the Spaniards arrived, they named the land Filipinas, but they did not call the natives Filipinos. Instead, they were referred to as Indios.

This was the same term used by Columbus for the indigenous people of the New World. The Spaniards were so obsessed with the question of race that they went through unrelenting efforts to differentiate and categorize the people of the Filipinas. Those full-blooded Spaniards born in Spain were called "Españoles-peninsulares" or "Peninsulares." Full-blooded Spaniards born in the Filipinas were called "Insulares." In Spain, the term "Insulares," along with "Criollo" or "Americano," had a negative connotation, because these people were associated with the primitive Indios. Also, many Spaniards considered the new colonies of the Filipinas and New World to be dumping grounds for the misfits and criminals of Spain. These places harbored Spain's rebels, thieves, gamblers, prostitutes and so forth.

"A racially based caste-like system was established in the Filipinas to establish a hierarchy of superiority and inferiority. Any Spaniard with Indio blood, known as "Mestizos," bowed to the Insulares. The Insulares bowed to the Peninsulares, and the Indio bowed to everyone.

"Eventually, the Indios became educated and began accepting the ways of the Spaniards as part of their culture. This made them socially acceptable to the Insulares and Peninsulares, especially since progress had given all three groups a common economic base to protect. Later, the term Filipino, which had begun as a racial concept, evolved to delineate a group characterized by education, wealth, and Spanish culture. This eventually became the national identity for everyone, including the Indios."

As hard as Brian listened, apparently Joseph still noticed a bit of confusion in his eyes, because he stopped and asked, "Did you understand what that meant, Brian?"

"I think so," Brian answered. "It sounds like Filipinos were really anyone who became part of the Spanish culture."

"Close enough," said Joseph. "So you see, because our people were never conquered by the Spaniards and we refused to become subjects of Spain and its culture, we remain who we are today: Igorots."

"So it's true," said Brian. "We really aren't Filipinos."

Joseph paused, apparently not wanting Brian to come to that conclusion, because he replied, "On a historical level; yes, but on a geographical and national level, no. Our people have always shared the same island as the lowlanders; so we are also Filipino. I guess it's like the American Indians. They are Indian by culture, but called American because they share the same land as the Americans who immigrated to their land."

"Only they were conquered by the white people!" Brian said with a big smile.

Joseph chuckled and continued, "It amazes me today how many of the lowlanders don't even know their own history. I think one person must have heard this explanation long ago, and repeated only the part about not being Filipino to others, and since then half-truths and stereotypes about us have spread like wildfire. For too many lowlanders and westerners, we're still primitive people with tails who take heads and eat dogs."

Brian was becoming very interested in the conversation; he wanted to learn more about his people and the misconceptions that prevailed outside his hometown. His knowledge even of Igorots was limited to what he knew about his Kankanaey and Bontoc relatives, because his parents rarely took him and his siblings to places outside the Mountain Province. Brian said, "Uncle Pael told me that some of his friends from another tribe who went to school with him hated being called "dog eaters," because their people never ate dogs. They valued their dogs too much as protectors and hunters to ever eat them. I also remember him telling me that other Igorot friends didn't like us, because our people used to attack their tribe, because they were timid and didn't like to go to war."

"Let me tell you a story," Joseph responded. "There were once three Igorots from different tribes who got lost during a heavy rainstorm one night. They found a public place to eat and went inside. The Ibaloi man was overcome by his timid and shy nature when he saw many people in the room, and immediately left. The Kankanaey immediately made himself at home and went straight into the kitchen, served himself, and then went to lounge in the owner's favorite chair with a hot cup of coffee in his hand. The Kalinga left shortly after the Ibaloi because nobody offered him any water when they entered. You see, Brian, like the many different tribes of American Indians, we Igorots have our own differences. Everyone is different in a way, and this is why we should try our hardest not to let these differences turn us into bad people. God does not want us to become bad people."

"Do you mean Jesus, or Lumawig?" asked Brian.

"I mean God, the Christian God," he replied.

Brian's eyes lit up and he asked anxiously, "Can you tell me about Lumawig?"

"Why?" Joseph replied with a surprised look. "You're a baptized Christian. You don't need to know such things."

Brian felt very disappointed, and stared at the floor. For years, he had wondered about the Igorot god. Each time he asked his parents or one of his uncles or aunties to teach him about Lumawig, they just told him to go and play. Joseph saw how let down he was and said, "Okay, but just this once, and don't tell your parents I told you this, okay?"

Brian happily answered, "Yes," in Kankanaey, but immediately changed it to Tagalog to please Joseph.

"Let's see...it's been a while, so bear with me while I recall the story... Okay, I've got it now. Lumawig is the personified god of the Bontoc Igorots. At the beginning of time, the lower lands of Bontoc were flooded with water. Lumawig came down to help the people of Bontoc. The first two people he saw were women. He took one of the women as his wife; her name was Fukan. After marrying her, he stayed with the people of Bontoc and taught them how to farm, build houses, hunt, and everything else they needed to know to live happily. There are even many stories of miracles he performed while living in Bontoc. One day, Lumawig had an argument with Fukan; and because he was very ill and couldn't think straight, he sent her away in a floating log down the river with several of their children, while keeping five children with him. She eventually re-married and sent her children back to Lumawig, but before they could

194

reach their father, they were killed by the Kanyu. Later, Lumawig learned of her re-marriage and killed her.

"After his work in Bontoc was finished, he and three of his sons went to the top of Mount Pokis, and he and one son flew into the sky, way above the clouds, and disappeared. He left the other two behind, but nobody knows what happened to them. I heard a story from an old man once that one of them died, and the other moves through time by leaping from body to body of people throughout history."

Upon hearing that part of the story, Alex briefly entertained the possibility that he might be the long lost son of Lumawig, because it was the only thing that made sense to him so far. Then he went on to think that if he *was* the son, what was the purpose of this moving through time? Was he looking to re-unite with his father?

Meanwhile, Brian asked Joseph to tell him some more stories. They spent the next hour talking about the different Igorot tribes. Brian had plenty of questions, and Joseph tried to answer them to the best of his ability. Of the many topics discussed, two really captivated Brian's interest. The first was the topic of headhunting. Brian learned that not all Igorots took heads. According to Joseph, most of the headhunting was done by the Kalinga, and his ancestors, the Bontoc and Kankanaey. It disturbed him to learn that their god, Lumawig, supposedly taught his ancestors to go to war and take heads.

The other topic that fascinated him was how his uncle connected characteristic traits of modern-day Igorots to their ancestral roles as agriculturalists or hunters. Those whose ancestors who had been predominantly gatherers and farmers tended to stay in the mountains, while people like his ancestors, who had been mostly hunters, eventually left the mountains to find better opportunities elsewhere. Brian understood now why his lolo and several of his uncles had left the mountains for jobs overseas and in other parts of the Philippines; and it made sense to Alex as well.

To prevent Brian from forming narrow-minded stereotypes, Joseph was quick to point out that there were exceptions to all the common

Igorot stereotypes . He gave the example of an Ibaloi who was the loudest and most self-confident person in his circle of friends at college. After several more examples, Joseph noticed how late it was, and wrapped up his storytelling. He stood up, patted Brian on the back, and said, "Tomorrow I will go to another school to enroll you, so that you can start there on Monday."

Brian immediately felt sick to his stomach. He'd been hoping his uncle would be more sympathetic to his desires and let him just go back to his hometown, and was so disappointed that a sharp pain wracked his stomach for the rest of the evening. He couldn't sleep, as the thought of having to face more ignorant lowlanders filled his head.

He spent most of the following day outside in the backyard, caring for his uncle's badly neglected vegetable garden. Lita watched him from the window as he pulled weeds and tilled soil, listing to the sounds of other kids playing in the neighborhood—kids who would never play with a "monkeyboy" like him. She seemed to feel bad for him, and went outside to convince him to go play with the other kids, but he refused, telling her he was having a good time doing what he was doing.

Upset at his stubbornness, Lita stormed back inside, and left the house to go shopping shortly thereafter. She seemed to go shopping a lot.

Brian wasn't lying when he told her he was having a good time. Working with his hands in the soil was something he was accustomed to back home. It was a normal, routine chore there...but didn't feel like a chore to him anymore. It was the only thing that made him feel at peace. His connection to the land was a connection to his heritage.

Late that afternoon, as he was putting away the gardening tools and preparing to wash up for dinner, a few of the bullies from school spotted him through the chain link fence. They snuck into the neighboring yard and hid behind some trees. When Brian turned his back toward them to put the tools in the shed, one of the boys threw a rock and hit him in the leg. Brian felt the sudden pain, and turned to see who'd done it.

The boy showed his face, yelled, "Monkeyboy!" and threw another stone. Brian tried ducking, but it hit him in the shoulder. The other boys started throwing stones at him, and Brian quickly dropped everything and ran inside the house—but only so he wouldn't be tempted to take a shovel or hoe to one of them. "That's right! Run, you chicken!" yelled the boys.

Brian stormed to his room, shut the door, and crawled under his blanket in tears, frustrated and angry. Soon, Joseph knocked on the door. Brian ignored him. "Brian," his uncle called out as he continued to knock.

"I'm changing clothes," Brian replied in Kankanaey.

"Okay," replied Joseph in Tagalog. "I just want you to know that there's food in the refrigerator when you get hungry. I have an important meeting to go to, and your auntie is still out shopping. She will be back in two hours and then she will take you to see the new school to meet the principal. Okay?"

Again in Kankanaey, Brian answered, "Okay, but I'm not hungry now. I'll wait for auntie so we can eat together."

After Brian heard the front door shut, he rushed to the window and watched his uncle drive off. He began to panic, knowing that he was about to go to the new school and would probably get questioned like a criminal about the fight at his last school. This could not end well. Determined not to go back to school here in the lowlands, he began packing a bag with clothes and his few valuables. Afterward, he went into his uncle's bedroom and opened a box that he knew contained money. He took enough to cover the cost of a bus ticket back home, wrote a small note that said, "I will pay you back soon," and left it on top of the box.

It was growing dark as Brian left the house. Fortunately, he knew how to get to the bus station; it was only a kilometer past his old school on the same street. Trying to beat the darkness, he began jogging down the street. To his dismay, less than a block away he caught site of some of the bullies, who spotted him as well. They started running toward him, and Brian immediately turned down a different street and ran as fast as he could. He looked over his shoulder, saw the boys catching up to him, and turned another corner. As soon as he turned, he saw some people leaving a church, and quickly ran toward the open doors. When he reached the doors, he looked over his shoulder again and didn't see the boys. Inside the hallway entrance was the men's C/R, and upon seeing it, Brian entered and locked the door behind him.

Brian stood in front of the mirror and looked at himself. For a moment he began imagining what he would look like with a different haircut, wearing clothes like the city kids'. Then he sat on the toilet with his pants on and listened. He soon heard the scampering of feet and the sound of a boy saying in Tagalog, "He's not in here. Quick, he probably went down the other street. Hurry, let's get him." Bastard.

Brian listened to them running off and remained sitting on the toilet for a while. After a few moments, someone tried opening the door and knocked. Brian could see by the shadow under the door that the person was an adult. He flushed the toilet and left the C/R. Still worried that the boys were nearby, Brian walked into the church. The lights were dimmed, but a handful of people still knelt in the pews, praying. Brian walked to one of the far corners, entered a pew himself, and slid his bag underneath. He kneeled and pretended to pray, so the others wouldn't suspect anything.

As Brian knelt, Alex realized it had been almost fifteen years since he was last inside a church. He'd attended a Catholic grade school, where he frequented church and attended Mass every Sunday with his parents. After grade school, his parents had to struggle just to pay the bills, so they enrolled him in a public high school. The absence of God at school was something very new to him; he knew vaguely about the separation of church and state that the American Founding Fathers had enshrined as law, but until then it had had little personal meaning to him. Many of the kids in public school made fun of the Catholic school kids and their religion. Before long, he allowed the influence of his peers to change his view of religion itself. By the time he was able to drive, he pretended to go to Mass on his own, but never did more than pop by the church to pick up a church bulletin for his parents to see.

As Brian remained kneeling, the forgotten feelings of peace and calm that Alex had once experienced at church caught up to him. He realized suddenly just how much he missed it. It felt so good that it put him in a state of reflection about his spiritual life. For years, he had thought that he didn't need religion to make him happy. He subscribed to the idea that he was in control of his own destiny, and that only he could determine his own happiness. It was a good idea, and sounded reasonable...but something had always been missing. Even with everything he owned, all his accolades and all the beautiful women he had access to, he still had a void that he couldn't fill.

It didn't take him long to realize he'd been away from his faith too long. His lack of a spiritual life looked him straight in the eyes of his heart. Everything that had happened since he'd left his body behind in Sagada Caves had proved to him that he had very little or no control over anything in the universe. In a way, lacking that control was like having a heavy burden lifted off his shoulders; if his fate was in someone else's hands, then he could rest, and stop taking responsibility for the weight of the world and his place in it. But he knew, deep down, that he would have to take the wheel again at some point; and when he did, he decided, his spiritual life would be a top priority.

Alex's thoughts were interrupted by Brian's thoughts of returning to his uncle, so that he could give school in the city a second chance. Brian began thinking about what his uncle had said, about needing to conform to city life so that he could become well-educated and successful like his uncles. Rather than praying, he tried annunciating several Tagalog words correctly under his breath. He found it difficult to pronounce the words without his Igorot accent. After several failed attempts, he said to himself, "Come on, you can do it! You can be just like the rest of them."

As Brian continued practicing his Tagalog, he began thinking about his hair and clothes. He wanted a normal haircut, like the rest of the boys, and he knew he needed to buy new clothes in the fashion of the day. Perhaps he could start avoiding the sun, too. His head bent in an attitude of prayer, he began thinking of as many ways as possible to hide his Igorot heritage; and in a way, Alex supposed he *was* praying.

As all this passed through Brian's mind, Alex couldn't help but notice how much Brian reminded him of himself as a child. Rather than stand up to the ridicule and teasing he'd received, he had allowed what others thought of him to dictate his life. His desire to be socially accepted was so strong it led him to abandon his heritage, his cultural values, his faith. Like millions of others, he'd assimilated into the Great American Melting Pot.

It was painfully clear to him that his weakness as a child had contributed to his current narcissistic way of life. He felt a deep pang of disappointment as he thought about Fanusan and Bolee, and how their simple belief in spirits and their pagan god had awaked his appreciation for the spiritual side of life. Their pagan belief system was real. They never had to go to school to learn it. It was not forced upon them. It was just part of their everyday life. In many ways, they were spiritually more authentic than most of the so-called "religious" people he knew back home. This authenticity was something that he lacked growing up as a Catholic, and it was something he had come to deeply appreciate.

He realized that the spiritually deprived society he lived in could actually learn a lot from the spirituality of his Igorot ancestors. Was that why he'd been forced onto this journey of discovery? Or was there more to it? *Who* had put his feet on this path—Lolo Santo? Lumawig? God Himself? Or something either more or less divine?

Abruptly, Alex recalled the scar on the face of his *manong*, and the story that Auntie Virgie told him about how Brian had sustained the nasty wound. The young Brian kneeling there had no such scar yet. Alex was convinced that if Brian returned to his uncle, he would eventually get into the fight that would result in the injury, and knew he had to do something to prevent Brian from making a serious mistake. He not only wanted to prevent the incident, he didn't want Brian to make the same mistake he'd made in allowing other people's ideas to influence who he was.

For the second time, Alex's empathy and sincere compassion for the body he was in overcame the natural boundary between his consciousness and his host's. A renewed energy surged into Brian; the boy could hear Alex's voice from within, telling him to be strong and proud of who he was. He thought it was God speaking through his conscience, telling him that he belonged with his parents, with his roots. He looked up at the crucifix and said, "*Igorotak.* I am Igorot. Thank you, Lord, for making me this way. Please forgive those kids, because they do not know any better."

After making the sign of the cross, Brian picked up his bag, genuflected outside the pew, and left the church. It was very dark outside, but there was just enough moonlight for him to see the surrounding streets. Alex could also see the bright white patch of light low in the sky. It was less than a kilometer away now, and Brian happened to be walking straight towards it...though of course it wasn't visible to the boy.

When he reached the bus stop, he could see that hardly anyone was inside the terminal. Then a car pulled up near the door and a young man in his early twenties stepped out, walked toward the glass doors, turned, and waved goodbye to the driver. He then proceeded to the ticket counter. Brian walked to the door, but kept to the side, so the man at the ticket counter didn't see him standing there. A few minutes later, Brian heard the engine of a car start, and waited as it moved slowly toward the exit. On its way out, it passed the front entrance. Brian immediately stepped up to the door, pausing just long enough to wave toward the car and say loudly, "Bye, uncle. Thanks for the ride!" He went to the ticket counter, where he had no problem purchasing a ticket back to Bontoc.

The bus didn't depart for another hour and a half, so Brian sat down on a chair across from the young man in his twenties. He looked at the floor as he swung his legs back and forth under the chair. He knew the man was looking at him, but kept looking down until the man said "Sssssst," catching his attention.

Brian looked up at the man questioningly.

"Where are your parents?" asked the man in Tagalog.

Fearing the man would detect his accent and question him further, Brian just looked back down at the floor. The man shrugged. "Okay with me."

Just as Brian was about to pick up his bag and move to the other side of the room, he was distracted by the entrance of a blue-uniformed man wearing a badge: a Philippine National Police officer. Brian watched surreptitiously as the officer went to the man at the ticket counter. As soon as the officer passed him, Brian picked up his bag and began walking to the C/R. Before he was able to make it, though, the man who was sitting behind him stood up and pointed at Brian. "There's your runaway!" he shouted.

The officer and Brian locked eyes, and then Brian began running toward the door. But the officer was too fast, grabbing him by his shirt. Brian tried wriggling out of his grasp, but the officer was too strong and quick. Finally, he stopped trying to get away as the officer's hand clamped down on his shoulder muscle like a vise, sending a sharp pain through his entire upper body. "Is your name Brian?" the officer sternly asked in Tagalog.

Wincing in pain, Brian replied, "Yes."

"Your uncle and auntie are worried sick!" scolded the officer. "Let's go, we're taking you home. Don't you know it's dangerous to be traveling alone at night?"

"I don't want to go back!" Brian shouted in Kankanaey. "I hate it here!"

Unable to understand what Brian said, the officer grabbed him by the arm and began leading him to his squad car. Brian reacted by trying to break free, but that only led to more pain as the officer twisted his arm into a painful arm bar. Once at the car, he tossed Brian's bag into the back seat and forced him to follow. The officer remained outside, slamming the door shut. There were no handles on the insides of the doors. As the car slowly drove away, Brian became suspicious of the look on the PNP officer's face.

It was too dark to see who was in the front seat driving, but thanks to a few scattered streetlights, Brian could see the back silhouettes of two people. Whether they were male or female he couldn't tell, just that they were adults. Before he could say a word, the person on the passenger side turned and pointed a big flashlight directly at Brian before tossing something onto his lap. With spot-filled eyes, Brian looked down and saw the box from the Sagada Caves. To him it was just a wooden box, but it sent a thrill of fear through Alex. As they passed the headlights of an oncoming truck, Brian/Alex looked up and saw the red-hooded person behind the wheel of the squad car.

Then the box opened on its own, and everything around him suddenly exploded with blinding light.

CHAPTER 12

Alex felt better prepared this time. The familiar disorientation and lack of air didn't bother him as much, because he knew they were temporary. As he felt himself slipping into a different realm, he braced himself for what lay ahead.

He opened his eyes, only to see the passage of blue skies and clouds as he felt his body flying and the force of gravity yanking him downward. The sudden impact with the ground jarred his senses and knocked the wind out of his lungs. His body lay motionless on its side for a split second, until someone's foot kicked out and pinned his shoulder to the ground.

Alex looked straight into the sun and saw the silhouette of the man who was standing on him, but the glare made it impossible to see his face. Fear and helplessness overcame him when he saw the sun's rays bounce off the shiny blade of a sword that looked to be on its way to his chest.

Before Alex realized what was happening, his body snatched up a spear that happened to be lying next to him and thrust it towards the upper half of the dark figure. Blood sputtered onto his face as he heard the gargling sounds of a man choking to death on his own bodily fluids. With the spear lodged in his throat, the man fell forward and onto Alex's body. Alex quickly regained his breath and pushed the dead assailant off him before standing up to face another attacker.

While desperately trying to regain his bearings, he instinctively unsheathed the sword at his side, raising it as if it were a baseball bat, squatting slightly into a fighting stance. The assailant appeared to be Japanese, but not like the ones he remembered from his encounters as Tebow. This man's hair was pulled back and tied into a chonmage topknot; he wore a dark brown, ragged kimono that draped over loose pants. The leggings below his knees made his pants balloon, giving them the appearance of something an old-fashioned Spaniard might wear. The only thing that resembled the Japanese soldiers Amos Tebow had known were his *Jikatabi* split-toe boots.

The two men slowly circled each other, stalking carefully sidewise while closely observing each other's movements. Then, without any warning, Alex's body made one swift maneuver with his sword that sent his opponent falling to the ground, clutching at a spurting vein in his neck. Alex heard a third man approaching from behind; with his eyes still facing forward, he dropped to one knee, raising his sword above his head to block his cowardly assailant's blow. Then he spun around and nearly cut the man in half with one precision swing to his abdomen.

Alex was simultaneously aghast and impressed. This body's fighting instinct was so much sharper than Tebow's had been, and moved so swiftly that it amazed him. Never would he have imagined that he would ever possess such fighting skills with what was obviously a samurai sword.

Katana, something in his mind whispered, then: *Who am I, and how did I learn such skills?* and *Who were these men, and why did they attack me?*

He wiped his sword blade on the clothing of the dead man lying before him. It was not a contemptuous act, just something that had to be done to protect the blade from degradation. When his body looked closely at his blade, inspecting it for damage, he was shocked to see the reflection of a Japanese man with a similar type of *chonmage* and clothing as his assailants, except that his were much nicer, cleaner, and intact. A wave of nausea washed over him, and Alex couldn't tell whether it was his own or came with the body he inhabited. One thing was certain; he didn't like the idea of being inside the body of one of his recent enemies. *This is a sick joke. Not so long ago I was killing them, and now I've* become *one of them. Why Japanese? Anything but Japanese!*

Instantly, a massive amount of information and memories belonging to his body surged into his mind, and everything about his new identity became crystal clear in that instant. He inhabited Shiro Nakamura, and the people he had just killed were bandits who had tried to rob him. Apparently they thought he was a wealthy samurai because of his neat appearance and valuable swords. The joke was on them.

What they couldn't know was that Shiro *had* been a high-ranking samurai under Lord Tokugawa, once the reigning Shogun. After Tokugawa surrendered his power to the Imperial Court during the recent civil war, Shiro and the rest of Tokugawa's samurai chose to take different paths. Many gave up their titles as samurai and accepted positions in the Imperial military, while others chose to die honorably by killing themselves in accordance to the *Bushidō* code they lived by. Shiro and several others became *ronin,* free samurai who wondered the land searching for a new master to serve, often selling their skills as mercenaries to make a living. Shiro and the other *ronin* often found themselves subjugated to humiliation or satire because they were no longer considered nobles, and were unemployed, without stipends.

After cleaning his sword, Shiro mounted his horse, which had hidden itself in a nearby copse of trees, and continued down the dusty path. Several hours later, he reached a small farming village. There looked to be fewer than thirty meager houses scattered about. It seemed almost deserted, as most of the people he saw were in the nearby vegetable fields working.

He stopped for a moment to watch the farmers, then continued into the village, hoping to find some food and drink to buy with the little money he had. Two young boys caught sight of him, dropped the stones they were playing with, and ran inside their house, slamming the door behind them. This continued in domino fashion, the sound of doors slamming filling the air as Shiro continued onward. Eyes peeked out of the windows and openings of some of the homes, but he saw no other people out-of-doors.

He stopped in front of a store decorated with a small sign that claimed it sold rice, vegetables, and miscellaneous goods. Like most buildings he passed, its door also slammed shut at the sight of him. An old man's face appeared at the front window for a moment, and then disappeared. Scowling, Shiro dismounted the horse, walked to the door, and knocked. There was no reply; only silence.

"Why do you close your door to me?" Shiro asked sternly. The sound of his borrowed body speaking Japanese left a bad taste in Alex's metaphysical mouth. *Could things get any worse?* he wondered. Shiro continued, "I come in peace. I only want to buy some food and something to drink."

With that, the door slowly opened and a wizened face peered out. He took a good look at Shiro and opened the door wide. Shiro bowed, introduced himself, and entered. The man returned the bow and said, "Shiro-san, I am Oda. I beg you, pardon our fear. Since the end of the war, we have had our share of bandits coming into our village to steal and harass us for food and sometimes our women."

Shiro replied, "Indeed? I can assure you I am not one of those men. In fact, I was attacked by a small gang of them a few hours ride away. They were no ordinary bandits, though. Those men were samurai—fallen hard, but samurai."

"Yes," replied Oda. "I suspect they once served Lord Nakane, but he is dead now, and his estate has been seized by the Emperor."

"Well, all I want is to buy some food, and I'll be on my way," said Shiro. "I do not have much money left, so if you can spare any extra, I would be greatly appreciative."

Somehow, Alex could sense that Oda knew there was something special about Shiro. He knew Shiro was a samurai by his hair and demeanor, but he also knew Shiro was nothing like the gang of samurai who harassed them. Something about Shiro led him to believe that he was, in fact, an honorable man. Oda felt a sense of compassion for him, and decided to offer him a free hot meal before he left their village.

Shiro was surprised at his offer, but accepted it graciously and sat at a small table near the tiny kitchen. "Your accent, Shiro-san is not from here," commented Oda as he prepared the food. "May I ask where you are from?"

"Kagoshima," replied Shiro. "Many days from here. More than two weeks' ride away."

As Oda continued preparing the meal, he noticed the three small crests on the sheath of Shiro's two swords. He became very curious and purposely brought him chopsticks and a glass of *sake* so he could get a closer look. When he got closer, he immediately recognized the three gold leaves in the circle as the crest belonging to the family of the former Tokugawa Shogun. Shiro noticed him studying his sword, but remained silent.

"Shiro-san," said Oda as he brought over a bowl of vegetables, fish, and rice. "What brings you to our village?"

"With all due respect, Oda-san, you see my sword. You know the Shogun is no more; therefore, you perceive that I am *ronin*. Do we really need to play word games?"

"So sorry, Shiro-san. I mean no disrespect, and *ronin* or no *ronin*, you're the first Tokugawa samurai to ever visit our village. I am honored. May I sit and join you?"

Shiro nodded and said, "Thank you, Oda-san, for your honesty. I too must apologize for my abruptness in the face of your generosity. It has been difficult travelling as a *ronin*, because of the many jokes and humiliation I have been subjected to. Please sit. It has been quite some time since I shared a meal with an honest man."

Halfway into the meal, and after answering many of Oda's questions about himself, Shiro asked him about the bandits. Oda told him that the gang consisted of at least twenty samurai who sought to seize control of the local villages, including this one, by instilling fear into the hearts of their people. They were successful, because the Imperial government had no interest in the area, and never came to see the wrongs that were taking place. He told Shiro that they were helpless, because those currently living in the village were farmers who possessed no martial skills to protect themselves. The bandits had recently come into neighboring villages and demanded 50% of their harvest, threatening to kill ten people and rape their women if they did not meet their demands.

Shiro also learned that one village in the lower valley had been decimated by unusually heavy rains that had affected their harvest; and when they could not provide the harvest demanded by the samurai, 12 villagers and a child had been killed. When Shiro heard about the child's death, he became enraged. In his mind, these men were no longer samurai, because true samurai would not do such a thing. It went against the seven tenets that he lived his life by, which included rectitude, benevolence and respect. "When is your next harvest?" he asked.

"We are harvesting as we speak," replied Oda. "But with such little rain this season, we are worried that we will not have enough for ourselves after the samurai take their share. This was why everyone looked so scared when you rode in. They must have thought, like I, that you were one of the samurai coming to see how much we have harvested so far."

Shiro saw the look of despair in Oda's eyes, and knew Oda was thinking of a way to ask him to help their village. *Don't get involved,* Shiro told himself. *Just get some supplies and move on.*

Just then, a young farmer barged in. "Father," said the farmer as he looked right at Oda, ignoring the samurai. "Come quickly! Mr. Kurisu from the next village is badly wounded and needs help!"

Oda hurried outside to find a man barely hanging onto his horse. Shiro slowly stood, walked to the window, and watched from indoors as Oda and his son gently helped the man down. His face and chest were badly bruised and bleeding, and he was unable to stand or sit up. Oda and his son put the man's arms around their shoulders and carried him inside.

Then two women and three men came rushing in with bowls of water and clean rags. They began washing Kurisu's wounds, causing him to wince from the pain.

Oda knelt next to Kurisu and asked, "What happened to you, Kurisu-san?"

Barely able to speak, Kurisu whispered, "The bandits were just at our village to collect their share of the harvest; but when I told them that we weren't finished yet, they killed two men and beat me and my three sons. They told me to come here and tell you that you have one more week to finish your harvest—or else." Kurisu began coughing up blood, but kept trying to talk. Oda placed his hand over his mouth and told him to rest. When the others finished dressing his wounds, they made a stretcher from cloth and bamboo and carried him to Oda's house.

After everyone left with the injured farmer, Shiro sat back at the table and resumed eating his meal. The things he just heard about the bandits disgusted him. Upon feeling Shiro's disgust, Alex began having a change of heart toward Shiro, realizing that he was in fact a good person, at least by the mores of his culture. He could feel Shiro's sincere compassion for the beaten man, and hoped that Shiro would help these villagers. Several minutes later, Oda returned with a very concerned look on his face. He was silent and in deep thought, almost forgetting Shiro was still there. Then he saw Shiro lifting his bowl to his mouth to finish the remaining soup.

He picked up the bottle of *sake* and turned to Shiro. "Shiro-san," he began, "we have very little to offer you, but would you—"

Before Oda could say another word, Shiro interrupted: "Oda-san, if you can afford to provide me with food and shelter, I will stay and help your village as best I can against these dishonorable and shameful men."

In great joy and apparent disbelief, Oda let out a breath of surprise, smiled from ear to ear, and bowed repeatedly. Still keeping a calm and almost emotionless demeanor about him, Shiro politely asked for his empty cup to be refilled with *sake*. Without hesitation, Oda reached out for his cup and refilled it as he continued bowing in gratitude. "Is there anyone here who can fight?" asked Shiro. "Anyone at all?"

Oda's gleeful expression quickly turned to one of concern as he replied, "We are all farmers, Shiro-san. None of us has ever learned to fight...but we are willing to learn."

"Nobody?" replied Shiro.

"Nobody," Oda confirmed. "But we can learn. We can learn."

"This is not good," Shiro replied, shaking his head. "I was hoping for at least a handful of men to help me, and there is no time for learning. Let me think about this more tonight."

"I understand," conceded Oda. "But remember, we are eager to learn."

The sun was already beginning to set, and Oda excused himself so that he could prepare a room for Shiro to stay in. Shiro remained alone in the store, drinking the last of the *sake*. Part of him wanted to leave at first light, because he knew the odds were overwhelming; but another part of him knew he had to stay.

Alex wondered which part would win.

Oda returned and asked Shiro to follow him to his newly prepared room. As they walked through the village, people lined up to express their exuberance by bowing at Shiro as he passed. At one point, two men pretending to know karate addressed him as "Shiro-sensei." *Oda must have already spread the word,* Shiro thought.

They entered a house, and Oda explained that it had been owned by an old farmer, who become very ill and passed away almost two years before. The house was very small, with only one room for sleeping and eating, a room for bathing, and a small kitchen. Shiro was impressed by how clean it was, despite having been empty for nearly two years.

After a quick tour of the house, Oda asked Shiro, "Do you have any family?"

Shiro immediately sensed that Oda wanted to stay and talk for a while, and let out several big yawns. Oda got the hint, said good night, and left the house. Shiro closed the door behind him, and turned around to look up at the ceiling with a smile. "Finally, a roof to sleep under," he said aloud.

Wasting no time, he went to the hot bath someone had already prepared, removed his clothes, and entered the small, square wooden tub. Hundreds of *ri* worth of fatigue and humiliation instantly dissolved into the water. He might have stayed there all night if it hadn't been for the water cooling down, and his feet and hands becoming like prunes.

After drying off, he carried a lantern into the main room, where he opened the sliding door of the closet-like space that held the blankets and mattress. He unfolded the mattress, prepared his bed on the tatami-matted floor, and lay down with his sword by his side. He blew out the lantern and settled in.

Several minutes later, he heard the creaking of wood from footsteps near the entrance.

He grasped the handle of his sword, pretending to sleep. The front door opened slowly, and his keen sense of hearing detected the soft footsteps of a woman. With slitted eyes, Shiro watched the amber light of the lantern she held move across the paper-paneled door that separated his room from the narrow hallway entrance. Then the lantern was placed on the floor, and two slender hands slowly slid the door open.

Shiro saw a woman kneeling at the doorway and sat up. She bowed and smiled at him in a timid yet teasing manner. When she placed the lantern in front of her inside the room, Shiro's eyes doubled in size. In front of him was a very beautiful young woman in her mid twenties. Her hair was beautifully arranged in a geisha-like manner. The elaborately layered kimono and natural beauty of her face would have seduced any man, especially one who had been without a woman for quite some time. "Good evening," she said in a soft, sweet voice. "My name is Satsuki."

Clearing his throat, he replied, "Satsuki. I am Shiro Nakamura. Why are you here?"

Satsuki picked up her lantern and scooted a few feet closer to Shiro, still on her knees. As she folded her hands onto her lap, he noticed that they were quivering slightly. He sat up completely, and watched her slowly loosen the fancy *obi* sash that wrapped around the slender waist of her kimono, enough so that the upper portion of her kimono opened ever so slightly, revealing a hint of cleavage. "Oda-san tells me you wish to stay in our village for a short while," she said, as she slowly moved her shoulder, allowing layers of her kimono to fall away, exposing more of her chest.

"What else has Oda-san told you?" asked Shiro, his eyes remaining in direct contact with hers.

Alex, on the other hand, couldn't help but gaze upon her exposed shoulder from the corner of Shiro's eye. He was captivated by her natural beauty and timidly sensual demeanor. He knew he wanted to change his outlook toward women, but her beauty reminded him how difficult a task it would be. Still, he snapped himself out of the trance and focused on her eyes as Shiro did...but even her eyes were too beautiful. *Oh man, this is not going to be easy,* he thought.

Satsuki looked at Shiro and replied, "Nothing else, Shiro-san. I just came to introduce myself to you, and keep you company tonight."

It had been too long since Shiro had been with a woman, and he was becoming very aroused. Alex knew where this was leading, as he himself was spellbound by her beauty and shyness. Shiro knew that Oda must have sent her there so that he wouldn't change his mind about staying to help...but something inside him was telling him to control his lust.

Alex was very impressed by his host's conscious attempt to control himself. *You're a much stronger-willed man than I'll ever be, Shiro,* he thought.

Satsuki, realizing that Shiro was resisting her advances, seemed to become worried. "Am I not to your liking?" she asked in a small voice.

"Come closer," he replied.

As she scooted forward, her kimono dropped even lower, exposing her entire cleavage and almost all of one breast. When she came within a foot from him, she said something that surprised both Shiro and Alex: leaning forward slightly, she murmured, "I can keep you company, Shiro-san. I know how to keep samurai happy. I have been with the samurais of Lord Nakane, and I can be with you too."

When Alex heard this, he sensed something in her voice and eyes that told him she really didn't want to be here. Behind her seductive actions was a young woman who knew her actions were wrong and shameful, but who nonetheless felt compelled to seduce him. Instead of seeing another beautiful woman before him, ready to satisfy his carnal pleasures, he was beginning to see someone who deserved to be treated with kindness and respect.

Strangely enough, Alex discovered that Shiro was having the same thoughts. He realized that her perception of a samurai was tainted by what she had experienced at the hands of those dishonorable dogs of Lord Nakane. This bothered him greatly, because he did not want to be associated with pillagers, rapists, and the murderers of innocents in anyone's mind. He knew he was different than they; he knew better than to ignore the Enlightened Path he believed in, that he lived for.

Alex quickly read Shiro's thoughts, and learned that the "Enlightened Path" was something that Shiro's father, a famous samurai, had taught him as a child. It was a unique interpretation of the *Bushidō* code that focused on its tenets as virtues to be applied to one's everyday life. To his father, the virtues of rectitude, courage, benevolence, respect, honesty, honor, and loyalty had to be at the core of a samurai's very being. They had to dictate everything in his life.

He learned that Shiro's father rejected the traditional stance that once someone gained truthful knowledge, he had to put that knowledge into action. He rejected it for two main reasons: First, this would mean that one can possess knowledge prior to or without corresponding action. Secondly, it would also mean that one can know what the proper action is, but still fail to act upon it. This implied that knowledge and action are two separate things, something they rejected. Instead, they taught that there was no way to use knowledge after gaining it because knowledge and action were unified as one, and for any knowledge to be true, it must be unified with action; otherwise it constituted delusion. Only through simultaneous knowledge and action could one gain truth. Truth was not relegated to any select number of tenets, but to all of them.

Unfortunately, not all samurai were like his father. Shiro had grown up knowing many samurai who selected which tenets to build their lives around. Many focused on courage, honor, and loyalty, while ignoring the rest. Many displayed scholarly knowledge of all the tenets, but did not unify that knowledge with their actions.

As these realizations flashed through Shiro's mind and heart, Alex became very intrigued at what he'd just learned. At first, he'd thought that his own hesitation to sleep with Satsuki had influenced Shiro's, but now he realized that he'd had nothing to do with Shiro's decision. Shiro's training and upbringing were the real reason he was able to resist her seduction. Either way, he was glad to know that Shiro would do the right thing.

"Please, Satsuki-san," said Shiro in a compassionate voice. "You are very beautiful to see, but I also see much beauty inside. Let it grow. The energy that flows through you has been dirtied, and I do not wish to darken it further because I am samurai. So please, cover yourself."

Satsuki looked very surprised, and relieved at the same time. At first, she apparently thought he might be drunk or joking; upon realizing his sincerity, she pulled her kimono over her shoulder and covered her chest in an embarrassed manner. "I feel ashamed, Shiro-san," she said, looking the other way.

"Do not be," answered Shiro. "I am curious, though: how long have you been carrying around your darkness?"

Satsuki, still appearing embarrassed, began telling him how she was forced to entertain the late Lord Nakane at the age of sixteen. It started with performing traditional dances with other girls from the local village. Nakane quickly took a keen liking of her beauty, and began having her perform private dances for him. One day, he forced himself upon her. Within a week, he was sharing her with all his high-ranking samurai. Shortly thereafter, the samurai began physically abusing her. She endured their cruel treatment for nearly two months until one day, she was nearly beaten to death. She couldn't withstand it any longer and wanted to take her own life, but something within her convinced her to run away instead. The following day she ran away to this village, where she lived with her aunt since then..

As she was telling Shiro her story, the merit of Shiro's refusal to sleep with her became clearer to Alex. Alex couldn't help but reflect on his own life again, because this was the very first time he'd ever seen beyond the physical beauty of a woman. Then Heather came into mind. After months of being with her, he still knew very little about who she really was. He was just having fun, and knew that within a few months, if things went as they usually did, he would soon be looking for another woman to be with. *Is this who I really am?* he asked himself.

The thought bothered him. Compared to Shiro, he was pathetic. *How did I let myself get this way?* he wondered. *Here's a man who just turned away someone beautiful and sexy because something within told him it was the right thing to do...yet I know I would have been too weak to resist her temptations. He doesn't even have to stay and help these people. The odds are suicidal—yet he probably* will *stay, because that's who he is.*

Alex realized that he was neither as strong nor as noble as Shiro.

He listened as Shiro began telling her how he, also, had almost killed himself after they lost the last battle that forced his master, the Tokugawa Shogun, to surrender to the Emperor. Although the Emperor offered clemency and positions in the Imperial military to those loyal to the Shogun, Shiro never entertained the idea of serving the new Imperial government, because they were trying to create a "modern nation" by eliminating the entire class of samurai. Instead, he was torn between killing himself by committing *seppuku* and wandering the country looking for employment as a *ronin*. Many people criticized him and other *ronin* for not choosing *seppuku,* and some considered him a man without honor. He, on the other hand, justified his choice by pointing out to her that the Enlightened Path was not limited to a samurai's life while serving a lord or master. It applied to his entire life, regardless of his employment status. Then he went on to say things that continued to catch Alex's attention, piercing him to the core.

"I may not have a lord and master to serve anymore," said Shiro. "But I am still samurai and I will use the virtues to serve others to the best of my ability."

"You are a very lucky man," replied Satsuki. "Most men go about their daily lives without a noble purpose."

Shiro heaved a sigh of relief, as if he were glad to find someone who understood his point of view. Alex realized that Shiro really enjoyed talking with Satsuki, because she was the first person in a while to truly understand him. For months, he had travelled the countryside, misunderstood as a shameful sword for hire. He never allowed it to bother him, because he knew who he was; but it made things difficult for him to find food, favor, and decent work in the villages he travelled through. In response to Satsuki, Shiro said something that struck another nerve in Alex:

"Thank you," Shiro said, as he bowed. "So few see it that way. A samurai not walking the Enlightened Path is only samurai by name. The same is true for a *ronin*. I feel sorry for people who go through life without a purpose, but I have even more pity on those whose purposes bear no loyalty and do not contribute to the greater good."

That sounds like me, Alex thought. *He's talking about me. I'm the person he pities. All these years I've studied hard to get the right degrees, worked my ass off and accomplished a lot more than most people my age...but I still feel empty at times. That's got to be it. I have no real purpose except to make money, boast about my accolades, and satisfy my ego through material things and women. What have I contributed to this greater good he's talking about?*

Shiro and Satsuki talked well into the night about themselves. As they found out more about each other, a different kind of attraction grew between them. For Alex, it was foreign, for it was an attraction of mind and heart. Several hours later, Shiro caught Satsuki looking at him with great infatuation. It surprised him, because it was the first time she had looked at him that way. She quickly picked up on his surprise and snapped out of her unintentional gaze before excusing herself because it was already late in the evening. With a noticeable blush on her face, they bowed to each other and said goodnight.

As Shiro lay in bed with his sword still at his side, Alex continued to reflect on his life. He thought about all the charity functions he'd attended and the contributions he'd made...but he only did those things for tax relief purposes and media exposure, didn't he? It saddened him to realize that all he had accomplished had been done to satisfy his own ego and physical needs. Then he began wondering why the American school system had never taught him anything about using his skills and talents for noble causes, or for any purpose greater than himself. *Am I just a product of my materialistic world? If a samurai, a man skilled in the art of killing, can apply his skills for the greater good, I should be able to apply my true talents to something more meaningful! Am I even capable of that?*

Alex struggled with such thoughts for the rest of the night, even as Shiro slept. The next morning, Shiro dressed and left his humble dwelling to find Oda. The village looked just as empty as it had when he'd first arrived the previous day; the door to Oda's store was closed, and so he thought that everyone must still be sleeping. Then he heard a distant babble of speech somewhere at the other end of the village. He followed the sound and came upon a large group of people gathered around Oda and several other men. As he approached, the villagers turned and bowed to him; he returned their bow. Oda looked at him and gestured for him to come to the front of the crowd.

"Shiro-sama," Oda called, now using the highest honorific for addressing one of higher rank. "Good morning."

"Good morning," replied Shiro. "What is this about, Oda-san?"

Oda looked up at him and said, "We have spoken of your willingness to help us with our problem with those bandits, and we all want to help anyway we can. I know you are disappointed that we are just farmers, but surely, there must be *something* we can do. None of us want you to leave. The bandits will arrive any day now, and—"

Shiro interrupted: "Oda-san, I am going nowhere. I told you I would help, and I will honor my word as a samurai. I thought of a plan last night, but I will need as many strong men as possible to help me dig large pits. I have heard a rumor that nobody can dig a pit better and faster than a farmer...?"

When the villagers heard this, they all volunteered, boisterous with excitement. Before Shiro knew it, he had fifty men and boys willing and able to do the work. Shiro smiled and continued, "I will also need plenty of freshly cut bamboo."

The villagers knew exactly where to get that, too. A sense of hope began permeating the air. As it peaked, Shiro drew his sword into the air and shouted, "We will show them that this village will not stand for their shameful acts anymore!"

The crowd cheered as their new savior pumped his sword into the air several times. Concerned about the daunting task that lay ahead of them and the limited time they had, Shiro quickly calmed them down and explained his plan. They were going to create several pits throughout the village, with pointed bamboo spears at the bottom. These pits would be used as traps for the bandits to fall into. The villagers loved the idea and knew it could work, because they had used pit traps to capture wild boars and other animals in the past. The plan elevated everyone's hope— except for one man's. This man walked straight up to Shiro and stood directly in front of him. "Shiro-sama," the soft-spoken man said, "How will we get the men into the traps?"

At first, the crowd jeered at his question; but it was so sensible that, as the implications sank in, they all began entertaining the same thought. A murmur washed through the crowd. Shiro looked the man in the eye and nodded once. Then he looked at the crowd and told them plainly, "This is a good question. To trap animals, you need bait. To trap animals like *these*, we will need to lure them in with beautiful women."

A dead silence fell over the crowd. They knew that it would be very dangerous to use women as bait; some of their women had already experienced horrific things at the hands of these samurai. They all knew this, and many of the women lowered their heads, as if to indicate that they weren't going to volunteer for such a thing.

Then a voice spoke out from the crowd: "Shiro-sama is right!" shouted Satsuki. "Those animals only know what is best for their penises. I will help!"

Other young women were inspired, and they also began volunteering. Soon there were a dozen young women willing to lure the bandits into the traps. One of the old ladies stood up and also volunteered, saying, "How about me?" The crowd laughed, their hopes restored; but their laughter gave way to the immediate sense of urgency, and everyone began splitting up into groups and organizing themselves.

Satsuki approached Shiro and said, "Come now, we have prepared your breakfast."

Shiro bowed to her and said earnestly, "You were very brave to volunteer. It made the plan easier for us all to believe in."

"But I am very scared," she whispered.

He murmured back, "Do not worry. I will protect you with my life."

Satsuki smiled timidly, bowed, and replied, "I know you will, Shiro-sama. I have faith in you."

After a quick but hearty breakfast, Shiro began marking out the locations for the pits. Each was strategically located between homes separated by narrow passages, so the passage would funnel the bandits together before they fell into a pit. He instructed each group to make the pits at least eight feet deep and long, and almost as wide as the passage, but to leave just enough room for the women to run past them along the sides.

Just in case the bandits came earlier than expected, two men were sent out on horseback to keep a lookout from the top of a small hill approximately one *ri* away. The hill provided a vantage point that would enable them to spot the bandits with their telescope more than two *ri* from the hill (as near as Alex could tell, a *ri* was about three miles). This would allow them ample time to ride back to the village to sound the alarm.

Groups of teenagers and their mothers ventured into the nearby bamboo forest and began cutting bamboo. Each dragged long, thin culms to the village, where they were cut into arm-long pieces, the ends sharpened to nearly razor sharpness. The women used palm rope to tie the sharp pieces together, creating self standing panels of deadly spears.

Everyone worked very hard until sunset, because nobody knew how much more time they really had before the bandits arrived. A day had already passed since they had received the warning from Kurisu, and everyone knew the bandits could come any day now, despite their promise to wait a week. By the end of the day, four pits had been dug to Shiro's specifications, and all the bamboo spear panels were complete.

That evening, while Shiro ate his dinner with Oda and other villagers, Satsuki secretly prepared a hot bath for Shiro. After preparing the bath, she went outside to the small *Hachiman* shrine to pray for his safety even though he was a trained samurai, for she knew he would be greatly outnumbered. Alex witnessed this, as if from Satsuki's eyes, and wished he knew how to communicate it to Shiro.

As for Shiro, he woke at the crack of dawn and walked toward the nearby creek where the villagers obtained their water. He found a flat grassy surface, sat down cross-legged, straightened his back, and looked briefly at the water rippling over the creek bed before closing his eyes. Alex was wondering what he was doing even as Shiro's thoughts slowly disappeared; somehow, Shiro was able to clear his mind of everything. Soon Alex found himself in a state eerily void of any thoughts except his own. The only thing he could sense was the sound of Shiro's breathing. After being privy to his hosts' thoughts and memories for so long, Alex found this sense of isolation almost disturbing. He had no idea what was going on, but he felt very calm and serene. Rather than question it, he also began focusing his attention on Shiro's breathing; and soon the clutter in his own mind subsided. There were no longer any questions about the past or worries about what might happen later. There was just the present moment and Shiro's breathing.

It was a sense of freedom that he had never felt before.

Alex totally lost track of time as he sat there within Shiro, breathing in every present moment as if it were the only one that mattered. When Shiro finally opened his eyes, normal thoughts returned and re-filled the void as if they had never been gone. His other senses came back online, and Alex heard the sounds of people talking and moving around, and the pounding of wood. *How long has Shiro been out?* he wondered. *How was he able to block out all this noise?*

Shiro had no answer for him, but when the samurai stood up, Alex immediately felt a renewed sense of strength and clarity. There was such a sense of calm in every step Shiro took that Alex couldn't sense the least trace of apprehension or fear, despite the fact that the bandits were likely to show up at any moment. No, Shiro just went about his way, focused on what needed to be done right then. The future would come when it came.

As Shiro walked past the villagers, they bowed, greeting him with proud smiles and good mornings. All the adults and most of the teenagers and children were busy working on the pit traps. Oda caught sight of him, and motioned for Shiro to join him at breakfast. Shiro nodded, and they ate outside on the porch. As they did, Shiro watched the people around him working. He felt a quiet sense of pride. There was a group of women weaving reed covers to place over the pits to one side of him, and another group inspecting the bamboo spear panels. He saw men carefully lowering other men into the pits with ropes, to position the bamboo spears that others lowered down to them. "This is very good," he commented.

"The food?" asked Oda, lifting an eyebrow.

Shiro smiled wryly and replied, "Yes, but also the cooperation that is taking place here. I feel more confident with each moment."

After finishing his breakfast, Shiro stopped at the first pit and was eagerly greeted by the men there. They weren't sure how to position the spear panels, so Shiro directed them from above. Once the men knew what to do, Shiro moved on to the other pits and gave similar directions.

After all the spears were properly positioned in the pits, the villagers proceeded to lay the large reed covers over the pits. The covers were supported by several long bamboo poles that stretched across the pit; each pole was notched in such a way that it would easily break when weight was applied to it.

By afternoon, they were ready for the final touches. Thin woven blankets were spread atop the reed covers and securely tied to the corners of the cover to keep it in place. Once that was completed, the villagers began carefully spreading dry dirt over the blankets. They paid meticulous attention to how the dirt was spread, to ensure that it looked like it had always been there.

They were halfway finished with the second pit when the sound of horses caught everyone's attention. It was the scouts returning from the hill; and judging by their speed, Shiro knew the bandits couldn't be far behind. Shiro calmly told the men working at the nearest pit to hurry, and then instructed the women to take the children into the designated areas of the nearby forest to hide.

Alex was impressed by Shiro 's calmness. The other two pits traps he had planned weren't finished, women were frantically running around gathering the children, and many of the men showed signs of panic; yet Shiro remained as cool as if this were any normal day. Alex felt absolutely no trace of anxiety in him. At first, Alex himself was a ball of nerves; but Shiro's calm enabled him to focus on the present moment with clarity.

Then a brief concern dashed through Shiro's mind, and Alex was quick to pick up on it. *Aha, so he's human after all.* Alex was surprised, though; it wasn't any type of fear or anxiety. Instead, Shiro was wondering whether or not he would be reborn into the samurai class if he should die; if, indeed, the samurai would continue as a social class. Perhaps they would give way to the Emperor's "modern world." And indeed they would, though Alex himself would have died before he allowed Shiro to know that.

It was clear that Shiro had accepted the possibility of his own death, and Alex realized that this was partly why he was so calm. Whether he lived or died, Shiro knew that good had been done, and saw no need to worry about anything but this moment. *This must be how he's able to kill with such fearlessness and without flaw*, Alex thought.

Then he thought about himself. Would he die if his host died? He had no idea. He did know that he didn't believe in karma or reincarnation...but until it happened, he'd never dreamed he might occupy another person's body and live life through them. *So: rebirth or Heaven? I'll leave that to the theologians. All I know is that good will come out of this if we succeed, and if we don't, at least we'll die trying. That's good enough for me.*

For a split second, Alex was astounded that he'd just thought that. But it gave him a great feeling of peace nonetheless.

The women continued to gather all the children into one group, while the men finished covering the second pit with dirt. The other two pits were still uncovered and exposed, so Shiro told Oda to gather several men and place barrels, bales of straw, and other things in front of them to hide the pits from plain sight.

The two sentinels rode into the village and found Shiro waiting for them. Both looked very scared and nervous. They rode up to Shiro and frantically told him that they had seen sixteen samurais and an empty wagon approaching on the main road. They looked to be well-armed with swords, spears, and a few rifles.

"How much longer before they arrive?" Shiro asked calmly.

"Less than an hour," said one.

"How is that possible?" asked Shiro.

Both men stared at the ground for a long moment; then, taking his courage in hand, one looked up and told him that they had accidentally fallen asleep, and didn't see the invaders until they were less than a *ri* from their post. Alex was outraged; if he had been in charge of Shiro's body, he would have beheaded the men on the spot.

Shiro just dismissed them from consideration as if they were beneath his notice, which they were to him now, and looked around at everyone else. He could see their panic, and knew he had to get them focused on the task at hand. With a commanding but calm voice, he shouted, "Listen!" Everyone instantly stopped in their tracks.

"The raiders will arrive sooner than expected," he continued. "We need to focus. Women, go now with the children into the forest, and stay there until someone comes for you. Men, I want two groups hiding near each pit with anything you can find to use as weapons. If nothing else, use leftover bamboo spears. If any of the bandits get past the pits, you must attack them. You are stronger as groups, so attack them as a group. Do not attempt to fight them individually.

"You teenagers: disguise yourself as adults and go out into the fields. Pretend to work so they suspect nothing out of the ordinary. If they charge at you, run back here. Do not run further away from the village—and avoid the forest at all costs.

"Satsuki-san, you and the other ladies must position yourselves in the open between the pits. Try to be as convincing as possible. We only have the two pits ready, so split up and lead them only to those pits. If you go anywhere else, we might not be able to help you in time. Oda-san, you will be with Satsuki-san's group, since you will be the one to greet the bandits. Remember, beg them to spare lives, but offer the women in exchange."

"*Hai,* Shiro-sama!"

Everyone began taking their places while Shiro and five men hid in the house nearest to Satsuki's group. The men with him were armed with spears that they had carved from tree branches and hardened in a fire, as well as the long machete-type knives they used to cut tall grasses and reeds. All were very nervous, for this was their first time to engage in any kind of fighting. One was so nervous that his spear was tapping on the floor as his arms trembled. Shiro placed his hand on the man's shoulder and gave him a look of encouragement; the farmer nodded, and quickly gained control of himself.

Twenty minutes passed, and there was no sign of the bandits. It was the longest twenty minutes of their lives. As they continued crouching on the floor, Shiro peeked out through the reed shades that covered the window. He watched Satsuki and the women squatting and paring vegetables, chatting amicably, as if they had nothing in the world to fear. Then he noticed that the women had loosened their tops and slit their lower garments to expose more of their legs. Suddenly, Satsuki turned and looked at the window, knowing that Shiro was there watching over them. She smiled as if to signal that she was not afraid. Shiro smiled back, even though she couldn't see his face.

Then he heard the drumming of hoofbeats, and the first of the bandits rode into the village center. The women screamed theatrically and dropped their vegetables, then ran and stood behind Oda, who had walked out to meet the riders. As the bandits approached, a plume of dust from the horses drifted over Oda and the women, causing them to place their arms over their noses and faces.

Shiro saw that one of the bandits was dressed differently that the others. Once the dust had passed, he saw the man's face and immediately recognized him. He was a fellow samurai who served the Shogun alongside Shiro during the civil war against the Emperor. It angered him to discover that his former comrade was part of this criminal group, but he just kept still and waited to see what happened next.

Oda bowed to the men, but they did not return the courtesy. The leader just sat on his horse with his hand on his sword hilt, glaring at Oda. Then his glare moved to Satsuki. As soon as she saw him staring at her exposed cleavage, she closed her blouse by crossing her arms in front of her chest, and looked at the ground, pretending to be scared.

"Do you have our share of harvest?" demanded the bandit leader.

Oda bowed in a pleading manner and replied, "Please—it has been too dry this season to produce the amount of grain you are asking for. We only have one-fourth of that, but please take it all. We do not want any more trouble from you, sir."

"You pathetic peasant!" scolded the leader. "Trouble you will have! You insult me in front of my men by offering a fourth of what is required. Spare me your excuses about the rain. I have heard them all!"

"But sir—" Oda pleaded.

"Silence!" the leader said, then shouted to the men behind him, "Go and bring me fifteen men and boys. We will teach them not to insult us again."

Before the men dismounted, Oda got down on his knees and pleaded, "Please do not kill any more of our people, great lord! Have your way with our women instead, but please, no more killing!"

The women pretended to be surprised and shocked at Oda's plea. The leader was also surprised, and turned his attention to the women. They looked at the bandit and gave him a sad look of submission before turning their eyes to the ground in shame. One of them pretended to weep on Satsuki's shoulder, saying that she did not want any of them to touch her. Instead of comforting her, Satsuki grabbed her by both shoulders and shook her. "Control yourself!" she said. "If it means our men's lives are spared, then we must do as Oda-san says. Besides, these pigs wouldn't know what to do with a real woman anyway!"

Then she turned to the bandit leader, and snarled as she loosened her top to expose more of herself to him. "You're the little bitch that ran away from Lord Nakane, aren't you?" replied the leader, smiling evilly. "I remember you."

Satsuki spat at him and yelled, "You may force yourself upon me again, but you will have to catch me first, you pig!"

The samurai looked at her in great anger and shouted to his men, "Get that bitch! Save her for me. I'll show her what a real man is!"

Four men dismounted, and Satsuki began running toward one of the pits. Half the women followed her, while the other half dashed toward the other pit. The four men laughed perversely and chased Satsuki's group, shouting crude insults at them.

"Save some for us!" the leader shouted to the four.

Already things weren't going as Shiro had planned. There were still twelve men on horseback, with Oda still on his knees, helpless. The men next to Shiro were so frightened that they dropped their weapons and crawled to the corner of the house to hide. Shiro remained calm and continued watching.

Meanwhile, the four bandits began gaining ground on Satsuki and the other women. Just before they reached the pit, Satsuki and two women split to the left of the pit, while the others ran to the right side. The bandits saw this and immediately stopped in their tracks, knowing that there was some sort of trap ahead. When Satsuki and the others met each other on the other size and saw the men running alongside the pit, instead of crashing into it, some of them began screaming.

The men on horseback heard their screams and began laughing.

Alex saw this through Satsuki's eyes; Shiro had no idea what had happened, because he could see neither pit from where he was. The screams told him something had gone wrong, but his instincts told him to stay put. Meanwhile, the women turned and ran for their lives toward the low ridge that separated their village from the vegetable fields. Satsuki was the first to reach it, and jumped down into the fields. The others followed immediately, but one was tackled by one of the bandits before she could jump. The other bandits shouted their perverse taunts as they jumped off the ridge. Their taunts immediately changed to gasping moans of pain as they looked down to see sharp bamboo spears sunk into their abdomens by the village men crouching below.

The fourth bandit heard the dying sounds of his friends, thrust the half-naked woman away, and drew his sword. "It's a trap!" he shouted.

Before he could say anything else, two village men shoved their bamboo spears into his abdomen. The bandit fell to his knees and, moaning, turned his head to see a group of men standing over him with garden forks, thick pieces of wood, and rocks in their hands. With his dying breath, he let out an agonized scream and swung his sword at the villagers, only to be pummeled to death in seconds.

Upon hearing the warning and scream, the rest of the bandits immediately dismounted and drew their weapons. Shiro shook his head upon seeing that; they had given up their greatest advantage. Truly, these men had no concept of strategy and tactics. Had some stayed on horseback, they could have ridden some of the villagers down while the others dug the rest out of their hiding places,

The leader told four of them to follow in the direction of the scream, while he and the others went toward where the other group of women had disappeared. As the four dashed off, the leader drew his sword and approached Oda, raising his sword to decapitate the old man. With surprisingly calm presence of mind, Oda threw two handfuls of dirt into his assailant's eyes, causing him to hesitate; this was enough to give Oda the opportunity to run toward the other pit, with seven remaining bandits in pursuit.

The samurai looked confused, as if he couldn't understand how the old man could possibly have defied him instead of just kneeling there, meekly waiting to be beheaded. Most peasants would have.

Meanwhile, Alex "saw" the first other four bandits reach the narrow passageway containing the second pit, where they found a small group of men standing over the dead bandit. Infuriated, they charged with their swords held high. The first man to reach the pit stepped on the notched bamboo and plunged to his death. The next two saw him fall, but it was too late; they too fell forward to be pierced by the bamboo, dying too quickly to scream. The fourth man stopped just in time, with one foot in the air and the other on the edge of the pit. He regained his balance and looked up, sneering...but more villagers appeared behind him with rocks. They launched all they had at the bandit, sending him to the bottom of the pit. This one had time enough to scream piteously before dying.

The other seven men continued to chase Oda, while their leader stayed behind wiping the dirt from his eyes. Once Shiro saw the leader by himself, he ran out of the house with his sword drawn and attacked him. Still unable to see clearly, the leader swung at Shiro, only to have his sword simultaneously blocked and removed from his hand. Then he was staring in disbelief at the wide slice in his abdomen made by his own sword, wielded left-handed by Shiro. He fell to his knees, then face-down in the dust.

Shiro stepped forward to make sure the bandit was dead, as Alex's consciousness flashed to a view of the seven chasing Oda. Leading them was the samurai whom Shiro recognized. He saw Oda stop suddenly, then turn to look back at them; noticing something strange about how the old man had stopped, the samurai stretched out an arm and stopped the others from pursuing. "He *wants* us to catch up to him," the samurai said. "It is another trap. Let him run. Come, we need to check on the others."

They ran back toward their horses and found their leader lying in the dust, headless, with his own sword standing in the ground next to him. They looked around to see if the assailant was nearby, but saw no one. Then the former Tokugawa samurai turned to the rest and warned them, "This is not the work of any farmer or peasant. There are others here, helping these people."

"Indeed." Shiro appeared from behind one of the houses, and began approaching them with his sword still in its sheath. "Looking for me?" he asked simply.

Three men surrounded him, their swords already drawn. None of them said a word as they slowly circled Shiro. Then Shiro closed his eyes and tilted his head toward the ground. Two men simultaneously lunged at him, their swords aimed at his head and back. With his eyes closed, Shiro's other senses were heightened greatly; he could hear the sound of their movements and feel the pressure of the air as they pushed through it, and of course they stank. At the last second Shiro drew his *katana* and, with one fluent move, cut a gaping wound in the abdomen of one and nearly severed the head of the other. The third man charged then, but Shiro stopped him dead in his tracks by throwing his *kodachi*, his short sword, into the bandit's neck.

With four bandits left, thirty village men appeared with their assorted makeshift weapons. Some of them even held the swords of dead bandits in their hands. Shiro slid his *katana* back into its sheath, silently apologizing to it for not yet removing the bandit blood that tainted it; then he pulled his *kodachi* from the one dead bandit's neck.

"You can either take the dead away with you on your wagon, or stay here and die," Shiro said loudly to the remaining four bandits.

The bandit that Shiro knew slid his sword back into his sheath and said, "Shiro-san. Do you remember me?"

"Yes," replied Shiro. "I remember you, Toshi." He deliberately left off the honorific. "You have lost your way, and have become a disgrace. You are supposed to be a samurai! You *all* are supposed to be samurai! What has happened to you?"

Toshi laughed bitterly and replied, "Where have you been, Shiro-san? Don't you know that the day of the samurai is over? When our Shogun surrendered to the Emperor, the Imperial court decided to abolish our social class. Our lands and stipends were taken away, we can no longer wear our swords in public, and even our *chonmage* topknot is banned. There *are* no more samurai! I am only doing what I must to survive."

A villager holding one of the dead bandits' swords pointed at one of the four bandits whom he recognized and shouted, "Enough talking! This is not about survival! This man raped my wife, and then killed her for no reason. They are animals!"

The bandit smiled, stepped forward and mockingly said, "Oh, she was your wife? She was so good. In fact, she wanted me so much that she pleaded for me to take her as my mistress. I had to kill her because I didn't want her following me around all the time."

"Bastard!" shouted the villager as he charged the bandit with the sword. The bandit sidestepped his advance and tripped the man, laughing uproariously. The farmer scrambled to his feet, but one of the other bandits drove his sword into the man's shoulder, causing him to drop the sword. Then he kicked the villager to the ground.

All four bandits drew their swords and taunted the villagers, saying things like, "Who do you filthy peasants think you are? We will kill all of you, then take your wives and daughters to do with as we wish!"

Upon seeing their friend on the ground bleeding and hearing the taunts, the village men let out bloodcurdling cries and simultaneously charged the four remaining samurai. Toshi was able to escape from being surrounded, but the other three found themselves quickly outnumbered. They managed to fend off a few villagers and even seriously wounded three, but there were just too many for them to deal with. Within seconds, the three were killed by bamboo spears, swords, and pitchforks.

Toshi looked wildly at Shiro, who said quietly, "Karma. This is the depth to which you have fallen, old friend. Will you drown?" He stepped forward to confront the failed samurai, if only to protect him from the wrath of the villagers, who had decided the other three were sufficiently dead and were ready to charge Toshi. The mob halted, forming a large circle around the two as they began to stalk each other in a circle, *katanas* in hand. Shiro said to Toshi, "In memory of what you were, I will allow you to leave this village in peace, if you break off now and never return. This will be your only warning."

In reply, Toshi swung his sword laterally toward Shiro's neck, but Shiro's blade met his midway. He immediately went from parry to attack, and quickly tried two other maneuvers in succession, but they were blocked. Then Shiro found himself defending himself from two quick strikes, one aimed at his neck and the second at his abdomen.

After the initial flurry of blows, they paused and moved slowly apart, their guards still up. "Not bad, old man," said Toshi. "You haven't lost your touch."

"You still have some minor skill yourself," Shiro admitted.

Then Toshi attacked with several lightning maneuvers, but Shiro successfully blocked each and countered the last blow by forcing Toshi to turn his back for a split second as his momentum, and Shiro's blow, twisted him around; Shiro immediately struck downward at Toshi's neck, but Toshi was too quick, blocking his stroke while still facing the other way. Toshi spun turned around and made another attempt at Shiro, who blocked it and leaned in to strike Toshi hard on the temple with the butt end of his sword. The blow stunned him long enough to allow Shiro to apply a series of arm bars that disarmed him while simultaneously dislocating his shoulder.

Toshi fell to his knees and looked up at Shiro in defeat.

In a humbled tone, Toshi said, "Shiro-san, you are correct about me losing my way. I have lived in shame these past several months. I turned away from our code to follow these men and allowed them to determine my destiny." As he spoke, Alex thought for sure that Shiro would spare his life. Toshi was now admitting to his wrongdoings, and Alex was convinced that Shiro would show compassion. After all, they had fought honorably on the same side during the war.

Then Toshi said, "Please, Shiro-san, at least let me go with honor."

"*Hai, Toshi-san.*" Shiro bowed and stepped back a foot. Alex thought he was stepping back to allow Toshi to leave...but instead, Toshi unsheathed his *tantō*, a long dagger, pointed it toward his abdomen, and plunged it into his stomach. After the blade entered him, Toshi painfully yanked it right to left across his entire abdomen, leaving a steaming wound with bloody intestines spilling out.

With one swift movement, Shiro slashed with his *katana* and sent Toshi's head tumbling to the ground. A stream of blood erupted from Toshi's neck and spurted onto Shiro's face as the body collapsed on its chest, to bleed the remainder of Toshi's life onto the dry dirt.

Alex was horrified at what Shiro had just done; though he realized, from Shiro's thoughts, that he believed he had done an honorable thing in helping Toshi compensate for his crimes and move on to his next life. As the blood pooled on the dirt, the chirping of nearby birds coupled with the brisk sound of Shiro's sword returning to its sheath created a surreal moment that Alex knew he would never forget as long as he lived.

The village men cheered, waving their weapons in the air and shouting words of victory. Satsuki, who was now hiding in the woods with the other women, was the first to return; without hesitation, she ran back to the village as fast as she could, with the rest of the women and children following, awed and jubilant.

Back at the village, Shiro snuck away from the celebrations and toward a stone basin holding water. A few splashes of cold water onto his face turned the water blood red. Exhausted from the fighting, he sat on a small barrel and watched the villagers celebrate. They deserved it. The look of victory in the men's eyes, the happy smiles of relief expressed on the women's faces, and the children running around happily made Shiro feel good inside. Despite Alex's disapproval of Toshi's suicidal ritual, and Shiro's hand in it, he admired Shiro for what he had done and the kind of person he was. In the world Alex came from, it was hard to find someone with such strong character. Shiro represented a world that expressed its values from the inside-out.

Alex wished his world were more like that. Maybe it could be...

The old cliché, "It's not what is on the outside that matters, but what's inside that counts," had taken on a new meaning in Alex' heart. Previous, he'd believed what he was taught: that people were valued based on their achievements, titles, prestige, accolades, degrees, GPAs, fashion, possessions and everything else his world used as measurements of success. All this made him appreciate Shiro and what he stood for even more. He couldn't help but wonder what he would have done differently, had he been taught the importance of purpose and character as a child.

As Shiro sat reflecting on the village's victory, and Alex on his life, Satsuki caught sight of Shiro sitting on the barrel, bent over. She approached him from behind, wondering if he was well. The first thing she saw was the bloody pool of water in the basin, which had a trail of blood leading to him. She covered her mouth with her hand and gasped, thinking he was seriously wounded. "Shiro-sama," she called out as she ran to him, tears in her eyes.

He turned and saw how worried she was. He didn't want her worrying, and smiled to signify his happiness to see her and to let her know he was not hurt. When she reached him, she immediately embraced him and looked into his eyes. "I am not wounded," he said. "Just a little tired."

She quickly checked him for any serious wounds, but found none. When he tried to speak, she placed delicate fingers over his mouth and said, "Shhh." He stopped trying to talk and just looked into her eyes; her steady gaze made him feel something he had never felt before. All the battle scars in his mind and heart, the humiliation of becoming a *ronin*, the disappointments and fears; it all disappeared. Alex was overwhelmed by the feeling of peace Shiro experienced at that moment, because it was totally foreign to him.

Looking at Satsuki, Shiro knew she felt the same way. Her shameful past with the other samurai, her poor sense of self-worth, her weaknesses, the anger she harbored toward men, and everything else that bothered her suddenly vanished, subsumed in their shared emotion. Nothing needed to be said in that moment.

Both knew they were meant for each other.

Their lips met with a gentle intensity that spun the world around them. Nothing mattered then, except that they were together. All the violence that had just taken place was a world away now. For the first time in his life, Alex experienced a kiss that had no taint of lust attached to it; it was a kiss so pure that it made him yearn for that in his own life. Like so many of these new feelings, he had never experienced this before with any of the women he had been with, and wondered if what he was experiencing was true love. He wondered if he might someday share this with Heather...

Sudden screams and shouts broke their romantic trance. Something terrible had frightened the villagers. Shiro and Satsuki ran toward the village center, and saw the men and women frantically gathering their children and running in all directions. A huge cloud of dust drifted into the village, completely blocking the sun, and with it came the drumbeat of horses' hooves. Oda ran their way, a look of fear in his eyes. "They have returned!" he shouted. "They have reinforcements. They must have known our plans!"

Shiro grabbed him by his shoulders, shook him, and said, "Calm down, Oda-san. How many are there?"

"Too many to count," Oda replied frantically.

Shiro let him go, and told him to take Satsuki into the nearest house as he ran toward the village center to see who was coming. But Satsuki refused to go with Oda; instead, she followed Shiro. As he stepped into the open space, where the dust was still gathering and the sounds of dozens of galloping horses thundered down upon them, Satsuki clung to Shiro's arm, begging him not to fight them all.

He looked her in the eye, and told her, "Satsuki-chan. Go inside with Oda-san. I will deal with this." Oda pried her away from him, and both went into the nearest house.

The village center was deserted now, save for Shiro. Everyone was either hiding inside the homes or cowering in the forest. Shiro stood with his arms folded as the dark cloud of men approached. As they did, he could see they were not bandits; they wore full battle armor, and carried flags that read, "New government. High morality." He also noticed that several of the men were armed with Enfield muskets, weapons he had begun training other samurai to use shortly before the end of the war. They were definitely samurai, but Shiro wondered what they were doing here, and why they were armored. The war had been over for quite some time.

When the dust cleared and their faces became visible, Alex's eyes widened. The man in the most ornate armor, their apparent leader, had the same exact face as the Japanese officer Sitlinin had killed in the Philippines! The doppelganger approached Shiro on his horse; Shiro stepped forward to meet him.

What the hell? Alex thought. *It can't be. I saw Sitlinin cut his head off right in front of me.* As Shiro moved closer, Alex was 100% sure that the man on the horse was the same man that his Igorot sergeant had beheaded, only *this* man was not wearing the uniform of a World War II-era Japanese officer.

The doppelganger and his companions looked curiously at the dead samurai scattered about. Then the leader looked at Shiro; their eyes met just before he stopped and dismounted. He took note of the crest on Shiro's *katana*. Realizing that Shiro had been a Shogunate samurai, he bowed; Shiro returned the gesture, though more deeply.

"Greetings," the other man said. "I am Lord Hashimoto. We come here in peace. We are just passing through, and need a place to stay the night. I am hoping your village will allow us to set up camp here, so that we may rest and make use of the stream here."

Shiro bowed again and replied, "I am Shiro Nakamura, a former commander of the late Tokugawa Shogunate and current *ronin*. I too am a visitor here. You will need to speak to the villagers about your request. I am curious, though: where are you headed, and why are you and your men in armor?"

"Have you not heard of the rebellion?" asked Hashimoto.

"Forgive me, but I have not." replied Shiro.

"These one hundred men and I are on our way to join a battalion of two thousand samurai. This battalion will be part of a six-battalion force led by Lord Kawasaki—"

"*What?*" Shiro interrupted vehemently. "But he is the leader of the Imperial army that defeated us! Because of him, the Shogun no longer holds power!"

Hashimoto understood his surprised concern and replied, "Yes, that is true. However, since the Shogun surrendered, Lord Kawasaki has resigned, and is rebelling against the Emperor because of what is happening to us. He is now the emperor's greatest enemy; and because of the Emperor's resolve to permanently erase the samurai from the 'modern Empire' he wants to create, many of us are joining Kawasaki. As a former commander, you would be a great asset to our cause."

Shiro looked to the ground in thought. He found it ironic that the same man who had defeated him now needed his help. He shook his head as he tried wrapping his mind around the thought of helping a former enemy. Hashimoto seemed to know what Shiro was thinking, and said,

"Shiro-san, despite whatever feelings you may have toward Lord Kawasaki, he is the only true leader fighting to keep the Enlightened Path alive."

Shiro's head immediately snapped upward. "What did you just say?"

"You don't remember me, do you, Shiro-san?"

Shiro looked closer at him, but couldn't recall seeing him before.

"I was once under your father's command," continued Hashimoto. "I learned the Enlightened Path from him. You were still a young boy, but I remember how you used to always play with your wooden *katana*. Your father had you a special one made of ..."

"Mahagony," both Shiro and Hashimoto said in unison. They looked long at each other as if to acknowledge the mutual connection between them: the Enlightened Path.

"Your father was a great samurai," said Hashimoto. "It was an honor serving under him, and it is an honor to be here with you this moment."

Shiro bowed and replied, "I am equally honored to be in your presence, Hashimoto-sama. You have my attention. Please tell me more of this rebellion you speak of."

Hashimoto went on to explain how Kawasaki believed that the modernization the Imperial government was trying to achieve would erase all that was good about the Enlightened Path. He told Shiro that the extinction of all samurai would become a reality if something wasn't done to stop it, and that Japan would lose its identity to the Western ways of Europe and America. Then he paused and looked at the beheaded bandit that lay several feet behind Shiro.

"I will consider your invitation tonight, Hashimoto-sama," replied Shiro.

"Wonderful," said Hashimoto, still looking at the dead bandit. "May I ask what happened here?"

Shiro stepped to the side, looked at the dead bandit, and said, "These men were once samurai of the local lord. After the Emperor's forces killed him, they turned to banditry. They have been robbing and pillaging the nearby villages for months. I could not allow them to continue their disgraceful deeds, and this is what resulted."

Hashimoto bowed deeply then, and said, "You are a true samurai, Shiro-san. Most of the samurai with me today do not truly understand the Enlightened Path; they just want revenge for having their privileges and stipends taken away. They are merely angry. Without further training, they could easily take the same disgraceful path as these men, and end up just as dead. This is why we need you. Too many of us are living lives outside our true vocation. Once we restore the samurai to Japanese society, we can teach the Enlightened Path to the younger generation. We can help restore the true identity of the samurai."

The word "vocation" caught Alex's attention. *Could the Japanese meaning for vocation be the same as the English meaning?* he wondered. *Maybe his Japanese isn't being translated correctly in my ears...* Alex was confused, because he thought "vocations" were reserved for religious people like priests and nuns. It sounded strange hearing it used in a secular context, the way Hashimoto had just used it. Indeed, it would be the last word Alex would use to describe the samurai lifestyle; though apparently, his idea of what "samurai" meant did not necessarily match up with reality.

Alex thought, *If a priest's vocation is his purpose in life, then is a samurai's vocation also his purpose?* Rather than compare the differences between the two, he entertained the fact that they both lived purpose-driven lives in the service of others. *If the betterment of oneself for the purpose of helping others is what a vocation is, then I lack a vocation in my life,* Alex realized. *How disappointing; all I have is a career.*

Knowing that Hashimoto believed in the Enlightened Path made Shiro's decision to join them easy...except that his feelings for Satsuki kept getting in the way. He turned and looked into the window of the house where she was hiding, but her face was hidden by the reed window covers.

"I will think about it indeed, Hashimoto-sama," said Shiro. "Meanwhile, you should talk to the villagers about staying here."

"Who should I talk to?" replied Hashimoto.

Shiro turned toward the house again and called out to Oda, who left the house with Satsuki at his back. Shiro looked at Satsuki and gestured at her to stay there, but gave her a smile to indicate that he was still thinking about her. She stood by the door and watched closely.

Shiro introduced Oda to Hashimoto and vouched for his character. Oda welcomed him and his men to the village, and asked them to join them in a feast they were planning. When asked what the occasion was, Oda told Hashimoto that they were celebrating their freedom again. Hashimoto gladly accepted the invitation to partake in their feast, and assured him that they would be gone after a day.

Oda went back to Satsuki and told her to tell the others that these soldiers were friends of Shiro, and that they would be joining the feast. Happy to hear that everything was satisfactory, she ran to the neighboring houses and began telling them to prepare for that evening's celebration. As Hashimoto's samurais dismounted, Oda and other villagers brought them containers of water to quench their thirst. The samurai gladly accepted their water and politely thanked them.

News about Shiro's victory over the bandits travelled back to the neighboring village by way of a messenger. People from that village began showing up at Oda's village with food and spirits, even before Oda and his people had finished cleaning up the dead and backfilling the pits where they'd unceremoniously tossed the bodies. Also joining them were *kyogen* actors who had once entertained Lord Nakane. It had been two long years since they had last performed for an audience, and they were very excited and eager to perform their comical talents in front of an audience that was long overdue for a night filled with laughter and joy.

By late afternoon, almost one hundred people from the surrounding area had arrived, and the celebration was well on its way. Many pigs and chickens were slaughtered for the occasion, and there was more than enough food for everyone. After an hour of eating and mingling, the *kyogen* actors entertained everyone with their impromptu plays.

240

During the *kyogen* performances, Shiro kept looking across the crowd at Satsuki, who occasionally caught his stares and affectionately smiled at him. He pretended to watch the actors, but deep inside he was contemplating whether to join Hashimoto in the rebellion, and how it might affect Satsuki if he did. At the intermission of the performance, Shiro gestured to Satsuki to meet him behind one of the houses.

He waited for her by the stream. He had made up his mind to join the rebellion, but wasn't sure what Satsuki's reaction would be. Normally, a samurai's wife had no say in such a matter, but she was not his wife; so he felt compelled to inform her of his decision, just to see what her reaction would be.

"Shiro-sama . . . Shiro-sama . . . Shiro-sama?" Satsuki loudly whispered in the dark. Shiro looked in the direction of her voice and saw her glowing in the soft moonlight. He called out to her and she came running toward him, but tripped on a rock as she reached him. He caught her just in time. Both looked into each other's eyes as he held her in his arms. She was expecting a kiss; but instead he set her on her feet and moved back a few steps. Sensing something might be wrong, her smile quickly melted to a frowning concern. "What is it?" she asked.

Shiro replied, "I made up my mind about joining Hashimoto and Kawasaki. I will leave with the other samurai when they go tomorrow."

"I understand," she replied, with a very disappointed yet understanding look. "This is something you should do anyway," she said, forcing a smile.

"There is something else," he said.

Still trying to smile, she asked, "What is it, Shiro-sama?"

He turned away from her, looked at the ground, and said, "I am in love with someone, and I am afraid that I might not see her again if I leave for battle."

Satsuki's world dropped from under her feet as she tried to keep a wall of tears in check. Suddenly his refusal to sleep with her that first night made sense. *He is in love with someone else, and he was being loyal to her,* she thought. *How could I have been so blind? Why would he want me anyway? I have done shameful things. I have not one drop of noble blood. I am a farm girl. A peasant. He comes from the higher class of nobles.*

Alex, who was privy to her thoughts for the moment, just grinned mentally and shook his head.

Shiro was waiting for her to say something, but she remained silent. He turned, only to see her back turned to him. Satsuki did not want him to see her watery eyes and fake smile. "Did you hear what I said, Satsuki-chan?" Shiro asked softly.

For a second, she was flattered to hear her name referenced as a term of endearment by hearing *chan* instead of *san*, but she dismissed it as his way of softening the heartbreaking blow that she saw coming. "Yes," she replied, her voice steady, still refusing to look at him. "You are a very loyal man, Shiro-sama, and I admire you for that. Thank you for being honest with me; but why do you tell me this?"

He cleared his throat and answered, "I do not know what I should do. We are not married yet. I want to marry her, but I am not even sure if she would agree to be my wife. Yet if I should die in battle, she will never know my intentions. Or if I am gone for an extended period of time, she may choose another man."

"You should do what you know in your heart is right," she said, lifting her eyes toward the stars.

"What if this woman were you? What would you want me to do then?" Shiro asked her.

Suddenly her eyes opened wide, and her heart swelled with possibility. She didn't want to get her hopes up, however, and turned to him to see if she could read him better. "Shiro-sama," she answered. "You are a great warrior. I have seen how swift and direct your sword can be, but I must respectfully say that your way with words is like our men's way with the sword. What is it you are really asking me?"

He smiled at her witty reply and said, "Ah, you have found my weakness, Satsuki-chan. This is something we samurai do not receive much training in." He moved closer to her as she looked deeper into his eyes. "Satsuki, you are the woman I want as my wife. I would understand if you did not ... "

Satsuki wouldn't allow him to finish his sentence; she placed her fingers over his mouth. With her eyes still locked onto his, she moved her head forward and kissed him. Her world was immediately restored by his kiss, and her heart pounded with joy. When she broke the kiss, she whispered, "I would be honored to give you my life, but are you sure this is what you want? Does my past not bother you?"

He pulled his head back, looked at her again and said, "You are right about my feeble way with words, but interpreting my feelings is something I know better than my sword. As for your past, it is the past. Only the present matters. I have never been more confident about anything than I am about my asking you to be my wife, Satsuki-chan."

She responded by wrapping her arms around him in an intense embrace. Her emotion overwhelmed him so much that it allowed his desiccated heart to absorb the moment as the universe paused to witness their entwined love. After several moments of silence, he continued, "I know it is not spring and my family is not here, but I do not want to wait. I want us to be married here in your village tomorrow. I do not want to go into battle knowing that you are not truly a part of me."

Still embracing him, she looked up and replied, "For someone so traditional, you can be very *un*traditional at times. If an untraditional wedding is what you want, this is what I want as well."

"Excellent," he replied. "We will marry tomorrow at the small shrine at the rear of your village."

Satsuki smiled in agreement and asked, "Does this mean I will need to learn the way of the *naginata* weapon?"

Shiro replied, "If you want, but do not be fooled by the stories you hear about the traditional samurai wife and her *naginata*. When I was a child, it was true that wives were chosen partly for their martial skills. They were expected to fight if need be. But times have changed, and wives have become more like vassals to their husbands." He sighed.

"Vassals?"

"Yes," replied Shiro. "I know of too many samurai who sleep in separate quarters from their wives, only to visit them occasionally when they want to satisfy their lust. The Enlightened Path has not only deteriorated within warriors, but also within husbands." Alex immediately received a surge of new information that taught him that Japanese society at the time didn't consider men having extramarital affairs as anything bad. In fact, it was normal for married samurai to satisfy their sexual needs with courtesans and prostitutes. The Enlightened Path was far ahead of its time, because it discouraged such acts—something Japanese society would also do in its near future. "It sickens me," continued Shiro, "to know that so many samurai live lives contrary to the Path and are now rotting away with mistresses and, more than ever before, with other men and boys. No, my love, I will not subject you to the kind of life that prevails today. I will not be traditional in that way, either."

Alex could see that even then, honorable people who knew what they wanted and the path of duty they would follow, like Shiro, had been the extreme minority. *Some things don't change. I wish I could tell him that the things that prevail in his world will only get worse in the future. Maybe we could change them...*

Shiro and Satsuki heard the *kyogen* actors preparing to resume their performance, and went to look for Oda to announce the news. When they found Oda and informed him, he was so happy that he immediately ran on stage and interrupted the play. "I have an important announcement!" he said loudly, as everyone looked on with curiosity. "Our new friend Shiro-sama has decided that he will join the forces of Lord Kawasaki."

Hashimoto was the first to cheer; everyone else immediately followed. Hashimoto looked at Shiro and gave him a nod of praise. Shiro nodded back, as the rest of the samurai became louder in their cheers. "Also!" continued Oda. "Before he leaves with Hashimoto-sama, he will marry our beloved Satsuki-chan right here in our village!"

More cheering erupted; and many of the village women, who knew Satsuki and what she had gone through in recent years, shed tears of joy for her. Everyone was so happy for both of them that they couldn't stop cheering for a long while. When they did, Shiro jumped on the stage next to Oda, and gestured to Hashimoto to join him. Standing next to the lord, Shiro said, "It is traditional to have family partake in the wedding, but my birth family is far away. Therefore, I would be honored to have Hashimoto-sama partake in the wedding to represent my family of samurai."

Hashimoto bowed in acceptance, and reached out for the two cups of *sake* that one of his men poured for them. He handed Shiro a cup and raised his in the air. *"Kampai!"* he exclaimed.

Everyone in the audience raised their cups of whatever they had and roared, *"Kampai!"* Once the drinks cleared their throats, the cheering resumed.

The evening's festivities continued well past the midnight hour. Some of the neighboring villagers made their way back to their village after the *kyogen* performances, but most decided to stay the night, as they were offered accommodations by the local villagers for that evening. Hashimoto and most of his men returned to their camp by the stream, but many stayed up drinking and making merry with the villagers.

After spending almost the entire time with each other that evening, amongst the villagers and samurai, Shiro and Satsuki finally began saying goodnight to everyone as they made their way back to Satsuki's house. After a long kiss in front of her house, he said good night to her, and began walking back to his own house. He took several steps—then stopped and turned around. She had done the same, and was looking at him with newfound admiration. Alex saw Shiro, through her eyes, as a man with cutting-edge standards that were virtually absent in their society. Neither wanted the evening to end, but both knew it had to.

Satsuki smiled, bowed, and went inside, her face aglow in the light of her lantern.

When Shiro entered his house, Alex realized that his host felt the best he had ever felt in his entire life. Never had things seemed better than they did at that moment. Alex felt happy for Shiro, but he also felt the pain of never having experienced this kind of happiness himself. All that he had experienced since he left Sagada Caves made more sense to him now. The things he had learned about his heritage, about his own life, and what he was missing all started to come together. He began realizing just how much of a gift he had received—and that no amount of money in the world could have bought him the things he had learned.

Shiro walked into the bathroom and found a hot bath waiting for him again. He smiled, knowing that Satsuki had arranged it for him somehow. But as he was about to remove his swords and garments, someone called out his name. He stepped out into the main room and saw Hashimoto standing at the entrance of the house, with a jar of *sake* and two cups in his hands. "Can I share one last drink with you in private, Shiro-san?" Hashimoto asked.

Shiro bowed and replied, "*Hai, Hashimoto-sama, irrasshaimase. Dōzo oagari kudasai.*"

Hashimoto accepted his invitation to come in, and they both sat on the *tatami* floor. As he began pouring the *sake*, Shiro sensed a seriousness in Hashimoto and wondered what was on his mind, but did not say anything; he just accepted the sake handed to him. They both toasted to the evening and drank the *sake* in one gulp. As Shiro lowered the cup from his mouth, he realized that Hashimoto had closed the front entrance behind him. "Hashimoto-sama," said Shiro. "Is there something on your mind?"

"*Hai,*" he replied. "It is about you coming with us to join Lord Kawasaki." He looked deep into Shiro's eyes. "I am afraid you cannot come, Alex."

Alex was shocked. Had Hashimoto truly spoken his name...? *Maybe the* sake *is affecting me too.* Alex thought. *There's no way...*

Then he realized that Shiro's body had frozen like a statue, his hands still holding the cup of *sake* at chest level. Anxious, Alex checked his mind and found no thoughts, no signs of life. *What the hell is going on?* he wondered frantically.

Then he saw that Hashimoto's pupils had suddenly taken on a bright yellow glow.

"Alex," continued Hashimoto, "I am talking to you, not Shiro. Yes, I know who you are in there. I can see you. Both of us can see you."

Can you hear me thinking?

"Yes, Alex. We can hear everything you are thinking."

Still in a state of disbelief, Alex looked around to make sure he was still where he thought he was. He wanted to pinch himself, but couldn't.

How is this possible?

Hashimoto drained his last cup of *sake* and replied, "How is any of this possible? Never mind how it is possible. What is important now is that we make sure you do not join us with Shiro."

Who is this "we" you keep referring to? You and Shiro?

Then someone entered the room. To his utter disbelief, it was the mysterious red-hooded person who had appeared to him repeatedly since his lolo's death. Confused and abashed, Alex watched the man enter the room and stand with his back to them.

You! Who are you, and why do you keep hiding from me?

"I'm not hiding from you," the person replied calmly, in English, as he slowly turned to face Alex. "You just don't want to see me. You're running from yourself, Alex."

And what does that mean? Alex demanded.

The man pulled the hood off, exposing his face. Everything around Alex suddenly began spinning, except for the red-coated man. It was his own face he was looking at: an exact replica of himself, though perhaps more weathered and darker-skinned. The features were identical. The red-coated Alex took off the long coat, and stood in front of Alex wearing only the loin cloth of an Igorot. On his chest was a tattoo of the glowing eye that had appeared to him in the Sagada Caves.

Alex found himself feeling very dizzy and disoriented as he stared at this image of himself as an Igorot from the past. He was so confused and in such a daze that he hardly knew what was real anymore.

"I must be dreaming again. This can't be happening," said Alex.

"It's no dream, Alex. I'm your true self," the Igorot said quietly. "For most of your life, you've been searching for happiness, but you've been going about it the wrong way. The answers you search for don't exist in your career, in material things, in false relationships, or in your physical fitness and well-being. These things only thwart your quest for real happiness. You and too many people of your time are like animals, scrambling after the things that are *supposed* to make you happy."

Feeling offended, Alex snapped mentally, *Animals?*

"Yes, animals," the Igorot replied vehemently. "*Animals* seek only to make themselves happy. When they have a need or drive, they just take to satisfy it. When they're hungry, they take to satisfy their hunger. This makes them feel good. It makes them happy. The human animal does the same. It equates happiness with good health, with having the ability to buy things when it wants, and having the least amount of stress and worry possible." His Igorot self waited for a moment as the Alex trapped in Shiro's body digested what he'd said, then continued: "The answers you seek have always been within you. You just chose to run away from who you are."

Hashimoto reached inside a small bag he'd been carrying, pulling out the magical blanket that Alex had found in the Sagada Caves, and said, "Your grandfather Santo cares for you so much that he gave you this. It contains the secrets of a meaningful and purpose-filled life. Only an enlightened warrior may possess it."

Was Lolo Santo an enlightened warrior? asked Alex, curious now.

"Indeed he was," replied his Igorot self.

Hashimoto held the blanket in both hands, bowed, and stretched out his arms to offer him the blanket. Alex instinctively reached out and took hold of the blanket; upon touching it, he realized his body now extended beyond the framework of Shiro. He brought the blanket close to his chest, and attempted to stand up.

"Finally!" cried Alex, as he looked down at his transparent body, which stood halfway inside Shiro. He stepped outside the samurai, raised one of his transparent hands close to his eyes, and said, "Am I some kind of ghost? I can see right through myself, and what happened to my clothes? I look just like you." He pointed to his Igorot self.

The Igorot smiled and answered, "You have become an enlightened warrior, Alex. You have freed yourself from the physical body of Shiro Nakamura."

"Have I died?" Alex asked.

"No, Alex," replied Hashimoto. "You have the spirit of an enlightened warrior, but you still need to unify it with your physical being, your actions. Once you are ready to accomplish this, you will return to your full physical self."

"And how am I supposed to do that looking like this?"

"You must first find your *dō*," replied his Igorot self.

"Dough? You mean like cookie dough?"

"Ha," Hashimoto laughed. "It sounds the same in your English, but there is an enormous difference."

His Igorot self said, "The Japanese meaning for the word '*dō*' is way or path. They use it at the end of certain words that describe some of their martial and secular arts. Take samurais, for example; they live their lives in accordance with the way of the warrior called *Bushidō*."

Hashimoto nodded and said, "In addition to *Bushidō*, we also have *Kyodō*, the way of the bow; *Aikidō*, the way of the harmonious spirit; *Chadō*, the way of tea; *Shodō*, way of writing; *Kadō*, way of flower arranging; and so on. These are more than just arts. They are a *way of life* for many, especially those who connect to the Enlightened Path."

Alex asked, "Must I learn all of these to find my own *dō*?"

"No, Alex," said his Igorot self. "Your *dō* arises from the way you apply your vocation in life. Each of us is born with a vocation, a purpose. It's different for everyone, but they are all the same in that they are intended to further the greater good."

"This is what separates humans from animals," Hashimoto interjected. "Like animals, humans tend to be takers, always seeking things to make them feel good and thinking only of themselves. Takers find joy from receiving benefits from others, whereas enlightened warriors find joy through living meaningful, purposeful lives. Their joy often comes from giving to others. This is a gift of choice that animals are not blessed with."

"Free will," Alex murmured. He reflected on his life for a long moment before accepting the realization that he was a taker. Even his many donations and involvement with charitable organizations had been intended as little more than tax write-offs and marketing ploys, so he could have more money to spend and grow his business with. Hashimoto and the Igorot did not interrupt his thoughts, giving him enough time to digest the newfound revelations before continuing. "I see why the blanket is so important now," said Alex presently. "It allows me to see beyond myself."

"Correct," replied the Igorot. "You needed to transcend yourself in order to see that *giving of your very being* plays a profound role in the achievement of the happiness that has eluded you for so long."

"Not only is it a vehicle that transcends the self," Hashimoto continued gravely, "It is also one that helps you transcend the present moment."

"That confuses me," replied Alex. "Can you explain what it's supposed to mean?"

Hashimoto bowed and said, "Most certainly, Alex. You see, an enlightened warrior understands that the things that pleasure the self exist only in the here and now. They are like birds that eventually fly away, leaving voids in one's life. This is why the enlightened warrior focuses his life on finding his intended meaning and purpose. By doing this, he is able to connect the past to the present to the future."

"But isn't the present moment the most important thing?"

The Igorot replied, "As long as it involves something bigger than yourself, something for others or for a greater good, then yes. If it centers only on you, then you neglect your past and therefore your future as well. As I alluded earlier, the pursuit of self-happiness actually thwarts the only true happiness that can fill all but one void in life, which can itself only be filled upon reaching one's final destination in the afterlife. This is one reason why the blanket has taken you to the past; to experience things both positive and negative. All these things can bring meaning and purpose into your life. You see, unlike the happiness your society seeks, meaning and purpose are enduring."

"I understand now," said Alex, and indeed, he thought he did. "But how do I go about finding my vocation, my purpose and meaning in life?"

Hashimoto replied, "If you were a child again, what would you do differently?"

"Well, I suppose I would identify what I was good at—what my talents and skills are—and then identify the things I love doing. Then I'd find out if the things I love doing and am good at can actually help people in some way." Alex suddenly realized that he had answered his own question about how to find his vocation in life. He grinned and said, "Wow—I guess all I have to do now is go back in time to identify those things. See my life backwards. This may take awhile."

His Igorot self said with a big smile of his own, "You may have to go back farther than you think; but once you find them, you will find your vocation."

Hashimoto allowed Alex to digest this new discovery for a moment, and proceeded to ask, "Do you remember the great white light in the sky?"

Alex immediately responded, "Yes, it was always nearby."

"Up there," Hashimoto pointed towards the ceiling. "The light is where our true vocation is found. In our world, one's vocation is easy to find, because it is always where the brightest light is. In your world, it is more difficult to find, because the light isn't visible to everyone. It is always there, but it is only visible to those who seek it in the right places."

"Are you saying that we need only to look upward to find our vocations?"

His Igorot self nodded and replied, "Upward, Alex, not down or to the side or behind and ahead. This is something the people of your world fail to understand. The unenlightened go from religion to religion, philosophy to philosophy, place to place, person to person, or thing to thing to find it, when all they need to do is to look up."

Hashimoto and Alex's Igorot self looked up toward the ceiling, arms raised; and magically, the roof dissolved to expose a clear view of the bright white light hovering above them in the sky. Alex looked up and saw a kaleidoscope of images, of people from all backgrounds and walks of life. His Igorot self pointed up and said, "These enlightened warriors currently live in your world. Each of them possesses different skills and talents, but they all fight against the evil in your world by using their talents and gifts to help people for the greater good."

Alex looked closely and saw a wide diversity. Rather than seeing only religious figures, he saw others, such as an Irish rock band that sang songs about love and social justice; an American college football player who used his platform to set a good example for football fans, while helping incarcerated prisoners and poor orphans in the Philippines; a professional female surfer who had lost her arm in a shark attack, and used her experience to encourage and help others; a simple man doing his best to be the best husband and father possible; a fashion designer using her line of clothing to help the unfortunate in Africa; a Japanese master gardener creating inspired gardens that aimed to restore wellness in people; a New York man offering the homeless free haircuts; a mother choosing to have children, knowing that she would be trading in many of society's so-called perks in exchange for mental distress and possibly even depression; a young man developing computer games that promoted good character and values; an artist who used her creativity to help people as an art therapist; a teenager using her summer break volunteering with youth groups; and so on.

Alex's face radiated enlightenment as everything finally became clear to him. "This is what Amos Tebow meant when he told his cousin that there was a plan for him," recalled Alex.

Now that he was convinced that he had a vocation of his own, Alex began reviewing his life so that he could determine what it might be. Hashimoto and his Igorot self placed their hands on Alex's head, and within seconds, his entire past flashed before his mind's eye with supernal clarity.

The first thing that he identified was his father's comments about his creative abilities. It became clear that his father had been trying to help him find his vocation. Then, he identified his desire to write stories and books shortly after his parents and sister died...and saw clearly that his desire to pursue his vocation had been clouded by his desire to become as wealthy as possible.

Pleasant memories of his high school English classes entered the picture. At one point, he'd loved to create those stories, and had received high grades and praise from his teacher. This triggered a flood of other memories that clearly demonstrated his creativity.

Looking back, Alex could see a clear roadmap that was intended to help him identify his purpose in life. He told himself, "If only I had looked upward! If only I hadn't let society and its false ideals lead me astray from the path intended for me..."

Just as he was about to commit to changing his life and pursuing his vocation, Alex was tested by something within himself: his pride. He looked at his accomplishments again, and began justifying them by thinking that he actually *was* helping people all along, through the services and products his business sold. A sense of pride caused him to second-guess everything Hashimoto and his Igorot self had told him so far. His eyes darkened for a moment when he said to the two, "But what's wrong with what I've been doing? I help people by doing what I do."

"Yes," replied his Igorot self. "You help people accumulate wealth, but are you really helping them become better people? Is it for the greater good, or is it only for their or your own good? This is what you should be asking yourself."

Alex realized then that his pride was speaking for him, just as it had for most of his life. "This...isn't going to be easy," he said.

"Certainly not," replied Hashimoto. "Now you see your real enemy. The battles that are hardest fought are those fought against ourselves; but you are now armed with the blanket and the truth, and they will provide you with the weapons you need. Are you ready to take the next step by committing your life to the greater good?"

Alex knelt down and said, "I am, yes."

"Open the blanket, Alex-san," said Hashimoto.

Alex unfolded the blanket and held it draped before him.

Hashimoto continued, "You have experienced violence, war, and evil, so that you may choose the Enlightened Path. The weapons bestowed upon you through your ancestral cloth shall now be a permanent part of you. Each weapon will assist you from this point on."

"First is the eye," said his Igorot self. At that moment the embroidered eye glowed and leaped off the blanket and into his very soul. The energy was so great that it almost knocked Alex down. "The eye is your heritage," his Igorot self continued. "Too many people in your world do not understand the power that their heritages contain. You are Igorot, and your connection to your heritage will keep you grounded. It will enable you to withstand the strongest of storms, which often destroy those without a strong connection to their roots. Since all heritages bring with them both good and bad, the eye will guide you only to the good."

Hashimoto pointed to the embroidered lizard and snake as they glowed. Just as the reptiles leaped into Alex, he said, "The lizard will provide you with the resilience you need to fight off evil influences. The snake provides you with the fortitude to stand your ground for truth and justice. For more than three hundred years, your people have had the fortitude to preserve the goodness of your culture by successfully resisting Spain's attempts to conquer and colonize you, not to mention successfully defeating all others who attempted to conquer your people. Now you have that same kind of ability to stand against the evil forces that lurk in the world."

The shield and spear also leaped into him, this time knocking him to the floor, onto his back. Unable to move, Alex remained on his back as his Igorot self picked up the blanket and held it over Alex as Hashimoto continued. "The shield will provide you with the courage to move forward despite the unknown. The spear will give you the bravery to soar into known situations that would normally send others fleeing."

The only two images that remained were the human figure and the star. As they both glowed, the entire blanket also glowed. Alex fixed his eyes on the glowing blanket as the Igorot draped it over his body. "Now only the strongest of all weapons remain," said Hashimoto.

Just then, the Igorot lay down next to Alex and rolled into him. Both he and the blanket disappeared into Alex, fusing with him. Alex's body reacted by shaking violently for several seconds as an incredible energy surged through his entire being. Hashimoto waited until he settled down before he continued: "Alex. You are now a man armed with purpose, and the star will provide you with the virtues you need to carry out your purpose. You are now ready to live your *dō*—your *Igorotdō*."

Alex looked at his body and saw that he was still wearing the loin cloth, but that he was no longer transparent. His full physical self had been restored. "My *Igorotdō*," he repeated wonderingly, then more confidently: "Yes. My *Igorotdō*."

"Everything from this point on is up to you, Alex," Hashimoto warned him.

Alex nodded. "I understand. How do I find my way back?"

"Just close your eyes. Once you see a glimmer of the white light, focus on it until it surrounds you."

Alex closed his eyes as instructed. After a moment of concentration, a small glimmer of white light appeared and began dancing around in his mind. He focused on it, and the light began to grow. It swelled rapidly, until nothing but white light filled his mind. He opened his eyes, and found himself surrounded by the light. He closed his eyes again, and focused on the thought of returning to his body, and his plans to change his life for the better. He felt his feet leave the ground; eyes still closed, his heart filled with happiness just from knowing that he was going back where he came from.

He couldn't wait to begin his new life.

EPILOGUE

As the bright tunnel of light he was speeding through began to dissipate, he could sense his destination approaching quickly. Within moments, the smell of cooked garlic and Filipino longanisa sausage filled his senses. Suddenly, he found himself lying on a soft mattress, staring at a ceiling.

Alex raised his hands towards his eyes to rub the disorientation away. To his dismay, he saw that they were the hands of child. *Not again...!* Then, to his shock, he heard a familiar voice that he hadn't heard in far too long yell, "Aaahlex! Come and eat now. You're going to be late for school!"

"Mom?" Alex said, his heart jumping into his throat. "This can't be happening!"

He threw the cover off, jumped out of bed, and instinctively rushed to the bathroom. His childhood room was as familiar as if he had never left it. He stood before the mirror and, astonished, stared at his fifth-grade self. He pressed his cheeks and rubbed his hands through his hair to ensure that he was, indeed, looking at young Alex.

Then he stepped back to view as much of himself as possible.

"Alex, are you coming down or not?" his mother called out again.

"Yeah, Mah," Alex called automatically—and was pierced by a feeling of disrespect. "I mean, *wen,* Mom," he corrected himself.

A moment of silence followed, as if his mother were surprised to hear him speak in his native tongue. Curious as to whether she could lead him to speak more of their language, she replied in Kankanaey, telling him to bring down his dirty clothes so she could wash a load of laundry. Alex understood everything she said perfectly, and respectfully responded in Kankanaey, "Yes mother, let me first separate the colors and check that there is nothing in my pockets." The sound of him speaking Kankanaey again made her smile from ear to ear. Also, volunteering to separate colors and check his own pockets, a first, made her chuckle.

He turned his head sideways and peered at his pudgy-flat nose. At this age, he had often pinched and pulled at it, wishing it looked more like all the white noses at school. This time, however, he left it alone, and just smiled with admiration. He was a good-looking boy just as he was.

Then he instinctively walked to his closet to put on his robe, something he usually did to keep the smell of Filipino food off his body and clothes. But rather than reaching for it, Alex looked at it for a moment, then left it alone. He no longer cared what the kids at school might say. "They've got no clue what good food is anyway," he muttered.

As he began picking up his dirty pants and shirts, a crumpled piece of paper fell out of the pocket of his jeans. As he picked it up he saw that it was a notice from school, informing his parents of the upcoming parent-student sports banquet being held next week. Painful recollections of being criticized suddenly came to mind. The last time his parents had accompanied him to a school function was when he'd received his first communion at age eight. That was when his classmates and the older kids had begun teasing him about his parents' thick accent, and began calling him nip, chink, gook, and such. Since then, he had deliberately kept his parents as uninformed about school functions as possible.

No wonder I was going to throw this away, thought Alex. *But not this time.*

He tried removing the creases in the paper by rubbing it up and down along the sharp edge of his dresser. He then neatly folded it, eager to give it to his mother. With the notice in one hand, an armload of laundry in the other, and a big smile on his face, Alex walked down the ever-so-familiar stairs and placed his clothes next to the washing machine in the little room beside the kitchen. The intimate smell of longanisa, eggs, and rice brought great joy to his heart as he sat down at the kitchen table to eat, smiling. He laid the notice next to his mother's place at the table.

His mother noticed the gleam in his eyes and became curious. "Why are you so happy, Alex?" she asked. "It's not the last day of school yet."

Alex's smile grew as he lowered his face inches above the food and took in as much of its scent as possible. Then he made the sign of the cross, folded his hands, and prayed. "Bless us oh Lord and these thy gifts, which we are about to receive from your bounty through Christ our Lord, Amen," he softly said.

It felt good to say the words again, which he had stopped doing once he left home for college. Although now that he thought about it, that life seemed more and more like a dream, and he wasn't sure that it had ever been real.

Then he mixed the egg and rice together with his fork and spoon, before adding soy sauce as seasoning. With his bare hands, he picked up a longanisa and bit off a piece. Still chewing, he pinched a clump of rice and eggs between four of his fingers and placed it in his mouth. After swallowing his food, he looked up and saw his mother looking at him with bewilderment. He realized that was the first time he had prayed before a meal in years without having to be reminded or told. "What is going on? Is there something special about today, Alex?" his mother asked suspiciously.

"Yes, Mom," he replied, smiling broadly. "From this day on, I want to be better."

"Better? What do you mean?"

"I just want to be a better person," he replied.

She lifted a delicate eyebrow. "Is this some kind of school assignment?"

Alex paused for a long moment before replying, "No, Mom. I had a dream that God wants me to be the best person that I can be."

"I see," she replied. "Well, tell me more about this dream of yours."

Alex cringed slightly, and replied, "Well...it's really hard to describe."

"Okay," she replied. "You can tell me later if you want."

He released a sigh of relief and asked, "Can you teach me Kankanaey again? I'm forgetting how to speak it, and I don't want to forget."

Amazed and overwhelmed, she smiled from ear to ear and replied, "Oh, sure. From now on, we'll speak only our native language in this house."

"But what about what the school principal and teachers told us about only speaking English at home so I don't fall behind?"

"Something tells me they're wrong about that. Besides, you will have more than enough opportunity to speak English with your friends."

Young Alex grinned. Suddenly, all was right with the world.

ABOUT THE AUTHOR

Rexcrisanto Delson is an Igorot-American writer who was born in Bauko, Mountain Province, in the Cordillera Mountains of the Philippines. His parents also hail from the Mountain Province: his father from Guinzadan, and his mother from Otucan. During World War II, his grandfather adopted the name "Delson" from an American officer bearing the last name Nelson, thus creating surprising and curious reactions from people who meet the current Mr. Delson for the first time. Although he's lived most of his life in America, Mr. Delson remains connected to his Igorot heritage, and enjoys learning about other cultures.

Mr. Delson's background is a mélange of experiences, which span the financial services arena, Japanese gardening and cuisine, landscape architecture, Japanese Chanoyu, martial arts, the U.S. Marine Corps, coaching basketball, interreligious dialogue, and writing. All have taught him the importance of the need for inspirational things and people. Because of this, he's drawn towards things that inspire people to become the best they can be, especially writing, music, movies, and athletes. Some of his favorites include the book *Blind Courage* by Bill Irwin, the band U2, the movie *Braveheart* starring Mel Gibson, and Heisman Trophy winner Tim Tebow.

When not writing, he enjoys spending time with his family, fishing, sports, bicycling, and increasing his culinary skills, particularly when it comes to sushi. Having grown up in Ernest Hemingway's hometown, Oak Park, Illinois, he now lives in the Chicagoland area with his wife and three children.

***

Rexcrisanto Delson is available for select readings and public appearances. To inquire about a possible appearance, please visit his website.

www.rexcrisanto.com

Printed in the USA
CPSIA information can be obtained
at www.ICGtesting.com
LVHW05091105l224
798314LV00001B/53

* 9 780615 470016 *